Robert G. Barrett was raised in Sydney and now lives mainly as a butcher. After thirty years on the Central Coast of New South Wales. Robert has appeared in a number of films and TV commercials but prefers to concentrate on a career as a writer. He is the author of fifteen books, including *So What Do You Reckon?*, a collection of his columns for *People* magazine, *Mud Crab Boogie*, *Goodoo Goodoo*, *The Wind and the Monkey*, *Leaving Bondi*, and *The Ultimate Aphrodisiac*.

> To find out more about Bob and his books visit these websites:
> www.robertgbarrett.com.au
> or
> www.harpercollins.com.au/robertgbarrett

Also by Robert G. Barrett and published by HarperCollins:

So What Do You Reckon?

Mud Crab Boogie

Goodoo Goodoo

The Wind and the Monkey

Leaving Bondi

The Ultimate Aphrodisiac

MYSTERY BAY
Blues

ROBERT G. BARRETT

HarperCollinsPublishers

HarperCollins*Publishers*

First published in Australia in 2002
by HarperCollins*Publishers* Pty Limited
ABN 36 009 913 517
A member of the HarperCollins*Publishers* (Australia) Pty Limited Group
www.harpercollins.com.au

Copyright © Psycho Possum Productions Pty Ltd 2002

The right of Robert G. Barrett to be identified as the moral rights
author of this work has been asserted by him in accordance with
the *Copyright Amendment (Moral Rights) Act 2000* (Cth).

This book is copyright.
Apart from any fair dealing for the purposes of private study, research,
criticism or review, as permitted under the Copyright Act, no part may be
reproduced by any process without written permission.
Inquiries should be addressed to the publishers.

HarperCollins*Publishers*
25 Ryde Road, Pymble, Sydney, NSW 2073, Australia
31 View Road, Glenfield, Auckland 10, New Zealand
77–85 Fulham Palace Road, London, W6 8JB, United Kingdom
Hazelton Lanes, 55 Avenue Road, Suite 2900, Toronto, Ontario M5R 3L2
and 1995 Markham Road, Scarborough, Ontario M1B 5M8, Canada
10 East 53rd Street, New York NY 10022, USA

National Library of Australia Cataloguing-in-Publication data:

Barrett, Robert G.
    Mystery bay blues.
    ISBN 0 7322 7559 8.
    1. Norton, Les (Fictitious character) – Fiction I. Title.
A823.3

Cover illustration by Mark Vesey
Cover design by Darian Causby, HarperCollins Design Studio
Typeset by HarperCollins in 12/20 Minion
Printed in Australia by Griffin Press Pty Ltd on 80gsm Bulky Book Ivory

5 4 3 2 1   02 03 04 05

DEDICATION

This book is dedicated to Judge Michael Finnane in Sydney.

A percentage of the royalties from this book
is being donated to:

The Wombat Rescue and Research Project
Lot 4, Will-O-Wynn Valley
Murrays Run NSW 2325

and Avoca Surf Club.

AUTHOR'S NOTE

What can I say? I gave Les Norton a year off, now he's back, bigger and better than ever. And nicer. Les might have been a bit of a dropkick in *Leaving Bondi* and a few Christians wrote in castigating me because he porked the girl from Victor Harbor while she was asleep. But if Les hasn't turned out to be a good bloke again in this one, I'll go back on the dole. He just rides off into the sunset at the end: then turns around and rides back again. I think you'll enjoy *Mystery Bay Blues*. I know I enjoyed writing it and had a great time in Narooma doing the research. What a top place. In fact I'm going back for the blues festival again this year and catch up with Neil Mommie and Rhonda. It's the best three days and nights of rock 'n' roll in Australia. They don't call it the friendly festival for nothing. Hey! It was worth writing a book about.

I have to thank all the people that came up to say hello on *The Ultimate Aphrodisiac* book tour. It was fantastic. Look up my website. You might see yourself there. Like the woman that came up to me in Lismore with the top of her dress full of baby possums. And what about Edith? Who drove all the way from Grenfell to Grafton to say hello and get some books signed. She was so nice I was in tears. We've been trying to contact her through the Grafton paper, but we can't. Anyway Edith, if you read this, write to me. There's some presents waiting for you.

The feedback from *The Ultimate Aphrodisiac* was all positive. Some people said it was my best book. Some even said it was the best book they'd ever read. For a grumpy old fart of an awther I was flattered, I can tell you. I've also been doing my best to answer all your letters and I'm catching up. But the other day I found a full box I'd put aside to take down to Narooma with me and forgot all about them. So some replies might be a bit slow coming. But I'm doing my best and I love hearing from you. It makes my day.

Now, all you people wanting Team Norton T-shirts, caps and those red-hot women's tank tops that are causing a sensation: because *The Ultimate Aphrodisiac* was late coming out due to that 9-11 NY event, a lot of people still don't know the book is out there and they don't know the possum lady isn't with me anymore or that I've moved Team Norton up to Terrigal. People are still writing to the old address at Tamarama. So here's what's going on if you want Team Norton gear: to save paperwork, there's no faxes, order forms or Visa. Just write down what you want and your size on a piece of paper and sent it to Psycho Possum Productions, PO Box 382, Terrigal NSW 2260, with a cheque or money order. T-shirts are $35.00. The tank-tops and caps are $36.00. And all the older medium size T-shirts are $25.00, including postage and the good old GST. We'll probably be doing a T-shirt for *Mystery Bay Blues*. And I'm culling a few T-shirts because there's too many titles. There's no more bum-bags, gift packs and other junk. Just T-shirts and caps. But check the website to see what's going on.

There's still plenty of caps and T-shirts available. However, make sure you put a phone number in with order in case there's any drama. The only help I've got at the moment are some blokes sent to me from an employment agency up my way, who told me they were refugees from an orphanage in Rwanda. They don't speak very good English and they've got no arms, so they bundle the parcels up with their feet. One bloke's got both no arms or legs. His name's M'Bunti. But everybody calls him Mat. All he can do is lick stamps. They're all a bit slow and I've got a feeling they're illegal immigrants. But shit! What can I do? They work almost for nothing and it stops people calling me an insensitive racist.

I've been getting a lot of photos from readers wearing Team Norton T-shirts all over the place — from Gallipoli to North Queensland. So I'm going to start putting them up on the website. I spoke to the powers that be at HarperCollins and, to those who send the best photos, we're going to send a couple of good books. I might even get the orphans to 'kick in' a free T-shirt. Also, *The Ultimate Aphrodisiac* will be out in the small size paperback soon. Don't buy one if you've already got the big size. But check out the photo in the back of me and Johnny Johnson and you'll realise why I said Johnny Johnson was so happy to see me. It's a classic. And about those surf things I was going to make, I've decided to give it a miss. They're a good idea. Just too much work involved.

Well, that's about it folks. By the time you read this, the Narooma blues festival will be all over and I'll be having a bit of a holiday down

Avoca, keeping an eye on all the girls keeping an eye on the Les Norton boat crew, while I'm wondering what I'm going to write next. Probably another Les Norton. Though I've got an idea for a book called *Maroubra Girl*. It's about a racehorse. We'll see what happens. Again, thanks for all your letters and your support and I'll catch up with you in the next book. In the meantime, keep checking out my website. You don't know what might turn up on it.

Robert G. Barrett

Yes, thought Norton, as he stepped right from Campbell Parade, Bondi into Hall Street. You might know how to hand it out, but you sure know how to kick a man in the nuts too. Don't you, boss. Les stopped for a moment to look upwards and smile mirthlessly at the sky before continuing steadily towards Cox Avenue and home. It was a pleasant Tuesday afternoon in early spring and Les was in a pair of green cargos, a white T-shirt, cap and an expensive pair of brand new trainers. Despite the day and his new trainers, Les wasn't striding out in the sunshine. He wasn't dragging his feet either. He was just walking along steadily. Very steadily. Thanks again to Eddie Salita. And just when everything was going along absolutely swimmingly.

The harrowing business with the Gull's movie was well and truly behind him now. In all the smell and confusion, the Trough Queen had simply run out of Waverley police station and disappeared never to be seen again. The police searched his unit but so far hadn't found any incriminating evidence. So whether the Trough Queen did the deed could not be proved conclusively. Nevertheless, it did seem more than a little odd, vanishing from a nicely furnished unit and a top rating radio program. Subsequently, police were rather keen to find the Trough Queen so he could help them with their investigations. Not that Les gave a stuff whether the wallopers found him or not. Les was as free as a bird. He'd even had his fifteen minutes of fame. A flicker on TV and a photo in the papers with a few words saying 'Bondi Waiter Cleared On Murder Charges'. Alongside 'Mysterious Disappearance Of Radio Announcer Has Police And Friends Puzzled'.

Now, Les was just another innocent man wronged and his good name almost ruined due to the bunglings of the NSW police. In fact the big Queenslander was so aggrieved and full of self-righteous indignation over what had happened, he was thinking of suing the police for malicious arrest and post-operative, traumatic, something or other. But, balancing that against all the villainy Norton had got away with in the past, he decided to cop it sweet. And speaking of villainy: while all this rattle was going on Les had the money he'd stolen washed quicker than a cup and saucer. He gave it to his accountant who changed it into Euros. She then bought shares over the net in some French IT company, resold the shares and bought into a Belgian IT company. Sold the shares again and cashed them back into Euros, changed the Euros into Hong Kong dollars, then US dollars. Before finally changing them back into Australian dollars. Somehow, amongst all the confusion between the internet, share traders and money changers working out what a Euro was, let alone how much it was worth, when the money got back to Les — all quite legally washed, folded and dried — another two thousand had fallen in, as well as his accountant getting her whack. Les was laughing.

Roxy had done the right thing in Adelaide also. Due to her drugged state and the trauma she'd been through, all she could recollect in her statement to the police was that a tall man named Conrad had saved her, then brought her back to his hotel before driving her home the next day. The police checked the hotel register along with an identikit photo from Roxy, and found no trace of Conrad Ullrich either. However, Roxy was able to identify the ratbags who'd kidnapped her, who were promptly arrested and were now awaiting trial. And Les didn't have to appear in court. Roxy also got her fifteen minutes of fame. She sold her story to a newspaper for thirty thousand dollars; now she was in line for another fifty thousand in reward money. So Roxy was laughing too.

Les flew Roxy to Sydney. She stayed at Chez Norton for a couple of days, then they both flew to Coffs Harbour and booked into the same resort Les had stayed at with Perigrine. Les hired a car and they both had a lovely time swimming, snorkelling and taking in the sights. Porking, drinking expensive cocktails and eating that many lobsters their eyes started poking out on stalks. Then Roxy went back to Victor Harbor and threw in her job to concentrate on her novel. They kept in touch. But between the conspiracy of distance and Roxy immersed in her work they didn't see as much of each other as they would have liked. But Roxy wasn't interested in any men at present and was quite happy seeing Les when she could. Les felt very much the same way about Roxy. One day — he told her, when she was kissing him goodbye at Adelaide airport — you just never know, Roxy. You just never know. Now Roxy was in Perth before heading for Broome to research another part of her book. And Les was in Sydney, back at the Kelly Club and training like a man possessed on his days off. Maybe it was knowing he wasn't going inside that gave Les a new lease on life. Maybe it was Roxy. But Les just had this wonderful feeling of freedom and fitness; along with being unexpectedly cashed up. Then, everything came to a shuddering halt.

After all the drama Eddie had caused him with his exploding cakebox, Les reckoned the little hitman should shout him the other pair of stabilising binoculars. That was okay by Eddie. He even tossed in a spare pair of inversion boots he'd got from the same villain. They were pretty much like the ones Sylvester Stallone used in the Rocky films. A pair of rubber-lined metal tubes, with a hook facing backwards, that you clamped round your shins. Then you swung up onto a bar and hung upside down like a fruit bat doing sit-ups or whatever took your fancy. Les had a chin-up bar in the sunroom which was ideal. He'd only had the inversion boots a week and he loved them — hanging upside down stretching his spine and everything else.

One afternoon Les came home from a run jumping out of his skin and decided to play Batman for a while. He clamped on his inversion boots, swung up on the bar in the sunroom and started swaying back and forth and jigging around. He did a stack of sit-ups then started doing press-ups, pushing and shoving and clapping his hands in between. It was a hoot and Les was loving it. Until Les felt a stab of pain in his lower back. It didn't worry him all that much until he climbed down. Then the stab of pain suddenly turned into searing, gut-wrenching agony and Les could hardly move. The best he could manage was to roll around the floor with what felt like a burning arrow sticking out of his back. It was frightening and Les didn't know what he'd done. But he was almost paralysed, sweating with pain and convinced he'd broken his spine and would never walk again.

Somehow he got to the phone and pulled it onto the floor where the only person he could get was Warren. Going by the urgency in Norton's voice, Warren came straight home from the office. It was definitely no laughing matter. But when Warren found Les all grey-faced and crawling round the floor like a carpet snake with a ruptured hernia, Warren laughed that much he nearly threw his own back out. With Les bent over and barely able to move, Warren got him into his Celica and off to a chiropractor they knew in Rose Bay: Bernie Trelaw. Bernie could hardly see and wore Coke bottle glasses. But he had amazing feeling in his hands and people swore by him. Bernie got Les on the table and after a bit of prodding and pushing told Les he'd slipped a disc. Slipped it almost into another postcode. And if Les thought the pain was bad before, when Bernie started on him Les almost fainted. Bernie cupped one hand under Norton's chin, another round his knees, then Bernie stuck his own knee in Norton's back and bent him backwards like he was a longbow as he worked his disc back in. Les didn't bother about stoically holding everything inside and showing how tough he was. He swore and screamed and cursed Bernie all the way back to Bernie's hometown of Grenfell. After twenty minutes of indescribable misery, Les got off the bench to find his back didn't hurt as much. He still couldn't stand up straight; that would take several more visits, and even then Les was as stiff as a board. But the improvement was remarkable.

Surprisingly, Warren had been a great help, coming home from work to take Les to the chiropractor then the doctor for a further check up and pain killers. Nevertheless, Warren did buy a big cigar, and a pair of horn-rimmed glasses with a false nose and a moustache attached, that he insisted Les wore when he drove the stooped-over Norton around for treatment. Les went along with the Groucho Marx impersonations. But he swore to Warren that as soon as he came good, he was going to buy every Marx Brothers video there was and shove them all up Warren's arse; along with a harp and a rubber horn. Les's back slowly started getting better. But both Bernie and the doctor told him to take it very easy for a while. No running and no strenuous exercise of any kind. A little swimming, breaststroking only. Yoga would be good, and long, steady walks. It was frustrating at first. But Les just took the time off from work and got used to it. Warren often joined Les on his walks and sometimes Warren's latest girlfriend, Clover, would come along too.

Clover was an attractive, well-shaped brunette with long, soft hair and soft, grey eyes that studied you from behind a pair of delicate, steel-rimmed glasses. She worked for a glassware company and lived in Dover Heights, but had moved to Sydney from a small town on the South Coast: Dalmeny. Warren met her at a wine promotion and they'd been an item ever since. Les liked Clover. She was a cheerful, outdoors girl who liked to get out on her boogie board or go snorkelling. She had a cheeky sense of humour, but good country values and always showed Les respect whenever she was in his house. Consequently, Les never had to take a dump in the sink to remind people the dishes needed doing if Clover ever stopped over at Chez Norton.

Through Clover, Les got to meet other people. One in particular was a flamboyant, young man about town, or Bondi at least —

Edwin Everton. Tall and fit with a big, white smile and a square jaw, set beneath a well-groomed head of thick, dark hair, Edwin was handsome and popular, and a good surfer and tennis player. He ran a small import business, mainly T-shirts and clothes from Asia and South America, and once had a few XXL T-shirts over which he let Les have for a bottle of good bourbon. He called round the house now and again and, like most people, Les quite liked the stylish Edwin.

However, if Les got on all right with Edwin, he couldn't cop Edwin's girlfriend Serina. Serina was very good looking and super fit, with orange Astro-punk hair and cool, green eyes, that looked at you as if you were an electrical appliance on special that she was deciding whether to buy or not. Serina was into skydiving, scuba diving, rock climbing and all that thrill-seeking kind of rattle. She taught aerobics and had moved to Sydney from Narooma, a small town on the south coast. Les wished she'd piss off back down there. For some reason Serina had it in for Les, and if they all happened to be out together somewhere, like the Gull's Toriyoshi, Serina had this annoying habit of running her hair back, effecting a supercilious smile then quietly putting Les down by asking him vague questions. Which Les always answered equally as vaguely.

'There's plenty of other jobs around Les, and you own your own home. How come you still work on a door?'

'Dunno. I can't figure it out myself at times.'

'You dress reasonably well, Les. And you can run half-a-dozen words together if the wind's blowing the right way. How come you can't find a lady?'

'Dunno. It's got me buggered.'

'You seem to know a lot of people around Bondi. How come you never get invited to any good parties?'

'Dunno. I haven't got a clue.'

If Serina wasn't doing that, she was always inviting Les to jump out of a plane with her, or abseil down one of the pylons on the harbour bridge. Or go scuba diving someplace with a name like Shark Reef. Les would always politely decline the offer; although underneath he would have loved to have told Serina to go fuck herself with a broken umbrella. But for the sake of good manners Les kept his feelings to himself. Les knew Edwin felt the bad vibe. But Edwin would never tell Serina to lay off. He seemed in awe of Serina to the point of fearing her. If Serina said jump, Edwin would say how high? Les figured that despite all Edwin's machismo and style, he was more than a little pussy whipped. Serina *was* a strikingly good-looking woman, with a lot of nerve.

Although both Clover and Serina came from the same area down the south coast, they weren't close friends. But through Clover, Norton learnt something about Serina that nobody seemed aware of. At least it was never mentioned. Serina got done in WA for conspiracy to import cocaine. She'd been trawled up with a firm who all finished with big sentences. Yet somehow Serina was able to walk. She had vanished overseas for a while, now here she was in Bondi with Edwin in tow, bigger and brighter than ever.

Sadly, it was because of Edwin that Les was out walking in the afternoon. Flamboyant Edwin had unexpectedly committed suicide. There had been a church service, now all Edwin's surfing friends had just held a moving ceremony near the middle of Bondi Beach. Over eighty surfers formed a circle on their surfboards about a hundred metres out from the shore, where they scattered Edwin's ashes over the still, blue water. Les had taken his camera with him and got some nice photos; including a couple through the zoom lens of super-fit Serina in a red bikini, holding the urn.

It was a mystery to everybody why Edwin topped himself because he was a young man who appeared to have everything going for him: good looks, money, a beautiful girlfriend. What also had people talking was the bizarre way Edwin had done it. Evidently, he'd paddled out at South Bondi, wrapped a leg-rope with several lead-weights tied to it around his neck, then just slid off his surfboard. Nobody noticed until his unmistakeable surfboard with the big rainbow on the bottom started 'tombstoning' and a couple of surfers dived down and brought him to the surface. The lifeguards got Edwin to the beach in their rubber ducky where the paramedics tried to revive him. But it was too late.

After their escapade in Port Stephens, Les and Eddie thought they might have smelled a rat. Edwin's parents put on a bit of a turn at the service too, saying their son had fallen into bad company which caused his death. Les and Eddie discussed this on a couple of occasions over a beer at the refurbished North Bondi RSL. But they ended up letting it slide. Oddly enough, Les had been down the beach the day Edwin committed surfboard Hari Kari.

It was a fine Saturday morning and Les was walking round to the bogie hole at Ben Buckler to go snorkelling. He was with a diver–photographer he'd met through Warren, named Ray Bissett.

Ray was a jovial, balding, Bondi boy who was also an accomplished artist and cartoonist. Les liked snorkelling around North Bondi or the bogie hole with a disposable, underwater camera, taking photos of colourful little fish or whatever was around, and one day in the bogie hole a huge, silver salmon swam right up to him. The ocean was clear and Les caught the sun shining through the water behind the fish and fluked several photos that were good enough to appear in *National Geographic*. Les had one blown up poster size and it now took pride of place on the loungeroom wall at Chez Norton. Ray had brought his camera along and this particular Saturday morning he was going to show Les some of the intricacies of underwater photography as Les was thinking of investing in an expensive camera and housing.

The water didn't look all that clear as they walked around the rocks at North Bondi. But it was calm enough. However, when they got round the front of Ben Buckler, the wind was pushing a heavy north-east swell through the bogie hole and past the point that was getting bigger and rougher all the time. After watching it for a while, Ray suggested they brush the bogie hole and just fartarse around in front of the boat sheds. Les agreed. They headed back, only to walk straight into a scene of complete pandemonium when they got to the Big Rock.

A group of scuba divers were standing around the Big Rock; some looked exhausted, others were yelling and pointing. One was screaming for help while he dragged in another scuba diver who was floating on his back. Someone jumped in the water and helped him get the unconscious diver onto the rocks. Then the first diver, an instructor, started screaming and pointing out to sea saying another diver was missing. Not realising the swell was rising, a dive school had gone out and one diver had almost drowned. Another *had* drowned and was still out there floating around on the bottom. Ray snapped off several photos as they watched, then the rubber duckies from the surf club arrived and next thing the place was swarming with paramedics, police, the police rescue squad, and before long a helicopter appeared overhead. There was nothing Ray or Les could do and it was fast turning into a complete shitfight of voyeurs, rescuers and milling scuba divers. Ray took a few more photos and they decided to leave; Les didn't bother taking his underwater camera out of the wrapper. Ray's car was parked up near the bus terminus. Les said he'd walk home; he'd give Ray a ring and they do it again when conditions were better.

Les set off along the beach thinking he'd have a quick swim on the way. By the time he reached Bondi Surf Club another helicopter was circling the point and two police boats had arrived. Then, as he got to the south end, Les was surprised to find another drama being played out on the wet sand.

A crowd had gathered next to a rubber ducky where two paramedics were frantically trying to revive someone. Les didn't stop to rubberneck. But he did have a look as he went past and got a shock to see the person in the black rashy they were trying to revive was Edwin Everton. Les couldn't help but stare for a moment or two, before he continued down to the end of the beach. He left his gear on the sand, then dived in and just floated in the shorebreak, trying to get his head around what he'd just seen; especially poor Everton, blue-faced and belly up on the beach. It was an eventful day and certainly made the evening news. And it was certainly something to talk about that night at the Kelly Club, where Les made a macabre joke about getting two deaths for the price of one.

But, that was then and this was now. Edwin was gone, Les had a sore back and life went on. Les stopped for an apple at the fruit shop next to the butcher's, then proceeded up Hall Street thinking it would be nice to get out of Bondi for a few days. No particular reason. Just a change of scene. Book into a nice resort again somewhere and lie around the pool all day drinking piss and getting his back massaged. Les finished his apple just across the road from the Hakoah Club and stopped. He might have had a rotten, sore back, but that wasn't going to stop the big, red-headed Queenslander from doing his good deed for the day.

A little old lady in a floppy, blue linen hat was trying to cross the road. A shock of white hair stuck out from under the hat and a blue cardigan was buttoned up almost to her chin over a pair of grey slacks and white bowling shoes. She could have been anywhere from ninety to a hundred and fifty, was stooped, and might have reached Norton's armpit if she was lucky. From behind a huge pair of glasses Les could read the worry on her dear old face.

'You having a bit of trouble with the traffic there, sweetheart?' said Les, ambling up alongside her.

The old dear recoiled a bit at first and clutched her handbag tighter. Then she sensed Les meant no harm. 'Yes. I have trouble seeing sometimes,' she replied. 'And the traffic frightens me.'

'Well have no fear. Big Les is here,' smiled Norton. 'Just get on my arm and we'll have you across the road in no time.'

'Oh thank you so much, young man. That would be wonderful.'

'No worries.'

The LOL took Norton's arm and they proceeded across Hall Street. Les could scarcely believe how frail and light she was. It was like a bag of air hanging on his arm. 'Where are you going?' he asked her.

'Into the club. I meet my friend Vera there every Tuesday afternoon for a nice cup of tea. And maybe a little cream cake.'

'Sounds good,' said Les.

'Vera's Polish,' said the old lady. 'She lost her husband during the war.'

'Oh. That's no good. You been friends long?'

'Over forty years.'

'Yeah? Isn't that great.' Les walked the old lady to the steps of the club and gently removed her arm. 'There you go, sweetheart. Now don't go shoving all your money through the poker machines while you're in there.'

'You needn't worry about that,' assured the old lady. 'Though sometimes on pension day, Vera and I might put a few shillings through.'

'Well, I s'pose a few "shillings" won't hurt,' smiled Les. 'Bye bye. And take care now.'

'I will. And thank you very much again, young man,' said the old lady, then entered the club.

Norton waited for the traffic and walked back across the road; he felt that good he almost burst into a run. Having all that strength and being able to help somebody so weak. Then Norton's face clouded over when he reached the footpath and thought of the low excuses for human beings that prey on old ladies like that; bashing them and taking their handbags. Les shook his head moodily. If ever he came across an old lady being mugged and caught the dirtbag doing it, the police would definitely have him up on another charge and no getting out of it. One hundred percent guilty of choking someone to death; then ripping their head off and dumping it in the nearest garbage tin. Les was wondering how many years a bleeding heart would make sure he got for that when he heard a voice to his left.

'How much did you get out of her bag, Les? Enough for a slab of piss and a couple of pies?'

Norton's eyes narrowed menacingly as he turned around to where the voice came from 'What?' he replied slowly.

Standing a couple of metres away was a lean figure, medium height with lank, dark hair falling over a pair of sunglasses perched on a lean face. The figure was wearing jeans, trainers and a black cotton jacket over a black T-shirt with SUN RECORDS on the front.

'The Zap,' Les nodded carefully. 'What are you doing in Bondi? You low life, little piece of shit.'

'Hey. That's not very nice, Les.'

'No. And neither's brassing me for two hundred dollars. You prick of a thing.'

The Zap was Frank Zammit. A part-time musician who surfed and played keyboards in various rock bands around the Eastern Suburbs. When he wasn't doing that, Frank did what a lot of other blokes from Bondi did for money. His best. Frank was about thirty and when he was younger, grew a thick moustache and a line of fuzz under his bottom lip like Frank Zappa. And with his skinny face and black hair Frank uncannily resembled the zany American musician. Naturally he got nicknamed Zappa, which soon got shortened to The Zap. A friend of Warren's once stayed at Chez Norton for a few days and ran up a fair phone bill along with the food and other incidentals. When the time came for him to leave, and in a bit of hurry, he couldn't weigh in. So he gave Warren his surfboard: a near new, DHD, Joel Parkinson signature model. Warren offered it to Les, Les didn't want it, so he sold it to Frank for two hundred dollars. The Zap absconded to Hawaii a week later. The last Les heard of Frank, The Zap had tried to move some dope on the North Shore in the wrong territory and got a ferocious pummelling from the Black Shorts. He was lucky they didn't shoot him. Now here he was, back in Bondi and still in hock to Les for two hundred dollars.

Frank made an open-handed gesture. 'Les. That money I owed you. That was just a matter of bad timing. That's all.'

'Owed?' answered Les. '*Owe* is the word, Frank. Not fuckin owed. And talking about timing. How much time do you think it would take for me to break all your ribs down one side? Say both sides.'

'Not long, Les,' sweated Frank. 'That's for sure. But Les, I'm sorry. I really am.'

Norton shook his head and and started to take off his watch. He was only foxing, but it was fun watching Frank sweat. 'No Frank. You're not sorry. But you soon will be.' Les dropped his watch into his pocket. 'And not so much as a fuckin postcard from Hawaii either. Let alone my two hundred. That's what hurt, Frank.'

Frank took his sunglasses off and put them in his pocket also. If he was going to get some more black eyes there was no use getting his good Ray Bans smashed as well. He made a defensive gesture. 'Now hold on a minute, Les. Before you start. Maybe we can strike a deal here.'

'A deal,' echoed Les. 'I'd deal with the merchant of fuckin Venice before I'd deal with you.' Les cocked his chin. 'Nevertheless Frank. What's your deal?'

'These.' Frank whipped a manilla envelope from his jacket and handed it to Les.

Norton recoiled. 'What's this? Drugs?' His eyes narrowed. 'Frank. If you're offering me dope in a main street in Bondi in the middle of the day, fair dinkum, I'll drag you over to the Hakoah Club, run you through the nearest twenty cent poker machine, and feed you to the Jews. You greasy little turd.'

'It's not bloody dope,' said Frank. 'Read what's on the front of the envelope.'

Gingerly, Les took the envelope and read what was near the left hand corner: Great South Coast Blues Festival. He opened it and took out what looked like three movie tickets. 'Tickets?' said Les.

'Yeah,' nodded Frank, enthusiastically. 'It's a long weekend this weekend and there's a big blues, rock 'n' roll festival at Narooma. Thirty bands. Three days and nights of non-stop rock 'n' roll. Those tickets are worth over a hundred each. You like music, Les. This'd be right up ...'

Frank kept talking away, thinking the more he talked the longer it would take before Norton started raining left hooks and short rights to his scrawny head and body. On the other hand, Les was half interested and he'd forgotten it was a long weekend coming up.

'Hang on, The Zap,' interjected Les. 'Before you start getting too carried away. Are these tickets kosher?'

'One hundred and ten percent,' exclaimed Frank. 'On my delicatessen's life.'

'Yeah?' Les had another look at the tickets.

'Think on it, big Les,' said Frank. 'Pulverising me might be good in the interim. But it's not getting you your two spot back. This is a beautiful way out. And believe me, Les. Being a muso, it breaks my heart letting them go.'

Les studied the tickets for a moment or two more then slipped them into the right side pocket of his cargos. 'All right The Zap,' he said, offering his hand. 'I'll take these and we'll call it square.'

With huge beams of relief shining from every pore on Frank's face, he took Norton's hand in both of his like he was shaking hands with the Pope. He was a split second away from genuflecting. 'You're a good man, Les,' he said. 'Like I just witnessed with that poor old lady a moment ago.'

'Thank you Frank,' replied Les. 'And despite our minor differences, I've always considered you a man of principle also.' Les let go of Frank's hands. 'So what are you doing now, The Zap? Would you like a cup of coffee? I'll shout you one over at the Hakoah. Or a cool one. Name your poison.'

'Les. Your offer is more than generous. But I have to see a bloke about . . . about things you have to see certain blokes about.'

'I understand fully, Frank,' nodded Les. 'Well, if you're going past the Gull's Toriyoshi and I'm there, I'll shout you one.'

'Thanks Les. I look forward to it. I'll see you later.'

Les watched Frank walk off down Hall Street then continued merrily on his way home. Only a few minutes ago he'd been thinking of getting away for a few days; this could be just what the doctor ordered. Plus he owed Warren a favour. He could offer him the spare tickets. Woz might like to go and take Clover with him. She came from somewhere down there. Les arrived home, put his camera away and made a cup of tea. He took it into the lounge with a few biscuits, sat down and opened the envelope again. As well as the tickets, there was a small brochure.

Frank wasn't lying about the bands. There was a heap. Both Australian and international. Little Charlie and The Night Cats, Rusty Zinn, Dave Hole, The Blue Cats, Jeff Lang, amongst others. There were even the two bands he'd seen when he was in Cairns white water rafting. And best of all, Jo Jo Zep and The Falcons. Re-formed especially for festival. With Wilbur Wilde on sax. Shit! Grooving to the old 'Honey Dripper' would be worth the price of admission alone. Les folded the brochure and put it back in the envelope. He was going. Then something dawned on him: where the fuck was Narooma? All Les knew was that it was down the south coast. And where was he going to stay? Being a long weekend in a tourist resort, everything would probably be booked out. It'd be nice driving all that way then having to sleep in his car. That would be real good for his back. Like fuckin hell! Shifty bloody Frank. Maybe this wasn't such a good deal after all. Then the phone rang and the answering service cut in. Les placed his cup on the coffee table. 'Hello. Who the fuck's this?'

'Les. It's Warren. Are you there. Are you there, Les? Les. If you're there, pick up. Les ...'

'Yeah all right. Don't shit yourself.' Les walked over and picked up the phone. 'Yes Warren. What's up?'

'Les? Ohh thank Christ you're there.'

'For you mate, I'm always here. What's your problem?'

'Les. In my room. In the left side drawer next to the computer. See if there's a floppy disc there, will you.'

'A floppy disc. Hang on.'

Norton took the remote into Warren's room, opened the drawer and had a look through the rubber bands, biros, stapling machines, hi-liters and other odds and ends. On a spare mouse pad was a floppy disc. 'Yeah, there's one here,' he said.

'What's it say on it?'

Les had a look. 'On a piece of black it says "Verbatim". Under that "IBM Format". And under that in biro it says "NSW Tourism Promo. 2 August".'

Warren breathed a huge sigh of relief over the phone. 'Ohh thank Christ! I thought I'd lost the fuckin thing.'

'Is it important?' asked Les.

'Reckon,' said Warren. 'There's two months' work in there. It's part of a job we're doing for the NSW Department of Tourism.'

'NSW tourism,' said Les, walking back to the loungeroom and sitting down again. 'There might be a bone there for me, Woz. I've done TV commercials before. And I ain't doing nothing at the moment.'

'Les. You're a fuckin one-eyed Queenslander. Getting you to promote NSW would be like asking a Shi'ite Muslim to sell kosher wine.'

'I dunno,' said Les. 'I can soon be a cockroach if the price is right.'

'Yeah terrific. So what have you been doing today?' asked Warren, changing the subject. 'Shuffling around Bondi, like Marriane Faithfull with an axe-handle stuck up her blurter?'

'No. Not really,' sniffed Les. 'Actually, I've had quite an interesting day.' Les told Warren about the ceremony down the beach then bumping into Frank and getting the tickets for the blues festival. 'And the tickets are right here in front of me, if you're interested, Woz.'

Warren thought for a moment. 'That doesn't sound like a bad idea. Clover might like to take a run down the south coast and see her oldies.'

'Yeah. Where's she come from again?'

'Dalmeny. Just next to Narooma.'

'Right,' nodded Les absently. 'The only blue's finding somewhere to stay down there. You can bet the place'll be booked out on a long weekend.'

'That mightn't be a problem,' said Warren. 'Clover's parents own a house right in the middle of Narooma.'

'They do?' said Les. 'Yeah. But I don't fancy imposing on people.'

'No. They don't live there,' assured Warren. 'They just own it. It's a real old joint. Been in the family for years.'

'Yeah? Maybe they'll rent it out for the weekend. I'll pay the freight.'

'Leave it with me,' said Warren. 'I'll ring Clover and see what's the story.'

'Unreal,' said Les. 'That'd be the grouse if we could get a place to stay.' Les sipped the last of his tea. 'So what's doing? You going out tonight?'

'No. I'll stay home. There's some work I got to catch up on.'

'All right,' said Les. 'I'll knock up something to eat.'

'Okay. See you when I get home.'

'See you then, Woz.'

Les took his mug into the kitchen then had a look in the fridge. There was some chicken and vegetables and things not doing anything. Les started cooking a chicken stew with okra and eggplant and a pot of rice. While that was simmering he put on some music, got his rubber mat out and did some yoga exercises from a book Clover had loaned him. About the only pose he could do properly was a *Cobra*. His back may have been getting better all the time, but it was still sore and if he didn't do as Bernie and his doctor told him, he'd throw the thing out again for sure. Les did what he could then just lay there on his back listening to the stereo. Finally he got up, had a shower and changed into his blue trackies. By the time he sorted out the chicken stew over a couple of cool ones, it was dark and Warren had arrived home. Les heard him go into his bedroom then Warren walked into the kitchen, his Shooter denim shirt hanging out over his designer denim jeans.

'So what's doing, Woz?' said Les. 'Everything okay?'

'Yeah. Good as gold,' said Warren, taking a Carlton long neck from the fridge. 'I'd just forgotten where I put that floppy. That's all.'

'That's all that pot you're smoking,' said Les. 'Your memory's gone. You've got CRAFT syndrome. Can't remember a fuckin thing.'

Warren blinked at Les over his beer. 'Are you talking to me? Hello. Where am I?' He looked at his reflection in the kitchen window. 'Is that me over there? What am I doing here? Whose house is this?'

'Yeah righto,' nodded Les. 'You hungry?'

'Yeah. That smells all right too.' Warren lifted the lid off the pot. 'Chicken?'

'No. It's Alaskan musk rat.' Les sipped some beer. 'So did you ring Clover?'

'Yeah. Everything's sweet. In fact I'll ring her right now and you can talk to her yourself.' Warren went into the lounge then came out a few minutes later and handed the phone to Les.

'Clover,' said Les. 'How are you?'

'Good thanks, Les,' came Clover's cheery voice over the phone. 'Warren told me about the tickets to the blues festival.'

'Yeah. You interested?' asked Les.

'I certainly am,' replied Clover. 'Just because I drop the odd disco biscuit and hit a rave now and again, doesn't mean I don't like good, head-banging, foot-stomping rock 'n' roll, big daddy.'

'You're beautiful, Clover,' smiled Les. 'So what's doing with this house your oldies have got down there?'

'Yes. It's right in the middle of town. About two minutes walk from where they hold the festival.'

'Unreal. Can I rent it over the weekend?' asked Les.

'No. You can't rent it, Les. Sorry.'

'I can't? Ohh shit!'

'No. But you can have it for free. Until the Wednesday after the long weekend.'

Les shook his head. 'Fair dinkum, Clover. You're unreal. When are you going to piss Warren off and get with me?'

'I can't, Les. I'm hopelessly in love with him.'

'Fair enough. So what do I do? Pick the key up from a real estate agent?'

'No. Mum and Dad hardly ever rent it. It's ... it's a kind of family heirloom.'

Les shrugged. 'Okay. So what do I do?'

'You got a piece of paper and a biro?'

Les got a notepad and a biro and Clover gave him instructions. The address was 3 Browning Street. Close by was a Christian Op-Shop. Ask for Edith or Joyce. They'd give him the key. The house was empty at present. Les could move in when he liked. He just had to be out by Wednesday before some people came to steam clean the carpets.

'That sounds fantastic,' said Les, doing a little doodle above the notes and the map he'd drawn, from the instructions Clover had given him over the phone. 'Are you going to stay there too?'

'No,' replied Clover. 'I'll stay with my parents. You and Warren can have it.'

'Okay.'

'But you'll love the house, Les,' said Clover. 'It's got a great view, it's even got a piano. And it's got ... it's got charisma.'

'Sensational,' said Les. 'We can all stand round the piano singing charismasy carols.'

'Les. Give me a break.'

'Sorry Clover.'

'So how's your back?' she asked.

'Getting better. I even managed a bit more yoga this afternoon.'

'Good.'

'All right,' said Les. 'I'll put you back onto Warren. If I don't see you before, I'll see you in Narooma.'

'Okay. Bye Les.'

Les handed the phone to Warren. Warren took it back out to the loungeroom, finished his beer talking to Clover, then walked back into the kitchen.

'So have I got connections? Or have I got connections?' he asked, dropping his empty into the kitchen tidy before getting another beer from the fridge.

'You sure have, old mate,' replied Les. 'The tickets are on the coffee table. Open the envelope and check out the lineup.'

Warren got the envelope, brought it out to the kitchen and studied the brochure. 'Shit!' he said. 'There's everybody here but the Morman Tabernacle Choir.'

'They arrive on Sunday,' said Les. 'Along with the Russian Cossack dancers and Kylie Minogue. All wearing gold hot pants.' Les got another beer also. 'I'll drive down early Thursday morning and beat the traffic. So when you arrive, I'll have the house stocked with plenty of food and piss.'

Warren nodded. 'I'll get away from work as early as I can on Friday. Allowing for the traffic, and picking up Clover, we should be there by about eight or nine o'clock Friday night.'

Les rubbed his hands together with glee. 'That's about when it kicks off.' He winked at Warren. 'I reckon this could be good.'

'So do I,' nodded Warren. 'I can't wait.'

Les served up the chicken which turned out even better than he thought it would. They both stuffed themselves and talked about this and that. Then after they cleaned up, Warren had a shower and locked himself into his computer. Les propped on the lounge in front of the big screen TV he'd shouted himself with the money from Adelaide and watched a video Warren had brought home from work, *Black Hawk Down*. There was heaps of action and bombs going off, which all sounded pretty good coming through the stereo. And Eric Bana wasn't too bad as the laconic, Delta Force, all-American, superhero. But Eric's Kentucky fried, suthin' accent? Les wasn't too sure. By eleven o'clock Norton was on the nod and so was Warren. Les hit the sack looking forward to a long weekend of 'head-banging, foot-stomping' rock 'n' roll.

L es was up before Warren, wearing a blue cotton tracksuit and his new black trainers with the little plastic springs on the bottom. He had some coffee and toast then set out for a walk, leaving a cheap overnight bag with a towel in it at South Bondi. It was another lovely spring day with a light, off-shore breeze, hardly a cloud in the sky, and the morning sun sparkling on the ocean. Les followed the cliffs to Clovelly and back, pleased that his walks were getting brisker all the time. He retrieved his bag then had a swim and a shower at North Bondi, stopping for a while to talk with a couple of blokes he knew from the Cross. When Les returned home with the paper and a road map of NSW, the morning was almost over. He toasted a couple of bacon and tomato sandwiches and washed them down with a mug of tea, then decided he'd clean the car out before he started packing his gear.

Les was jangling the car keys and about to open the driverside door, when he noticed the car was due for registration on Friday. The slip from the RTA had been on his dressing table for a month and he'd forgotten all about it. He'd also forgotten the front tyres were bald and there was a small hole in the muffler. Les shook his head. And I've got the hide to bag Warren about him losing his memory. Bugger it! Without any further to-do, Les locked the house then drove over to Chicka's garage at Bronte.

Chicka was happy to see Les; but he was flat out. He'd order the tyres and a new muffler. Les would have to leave the car and pick it up in the morning; it should be ready by nine, he said. There wasn't much Les could do except nod his head. He told Chicka he'd see him in the morning and caught a taxi home.

It was warmer now and much too good a day to be inside. Les got his banana chair, walked back down to North Bondi and propped on the sand with a book. He went for another swim then caught up with the same blokes he'd been talking to earlier and they had steak, chips and salad at the Rathouse. They followed this with a good, strong coffee at Speedos then Norton went home.

Les spent what was left of the afternoon preparing for the trip. He packed his camera, his snorkelling gear and the binoculars Eddie had given him — along with, what he imagined would be more than enough clothes, a few other odds and ends and his ghetto blaster. He also cleaned his thermos and made some ham and salad sandwiches, figuring on eating something half decent on the way down, rather than a diabetes-burger, fries and Coke. By the time Les had this organised, he'd finished two beers, the sun had gone down and he was eating last night's leftovers while he studied his road map. Narooma wasn't that far away. Four or five hours at the most. Even counting on a trip to the RTA, he should be there in time to pick up the key. He rang Price and left a message on his answering service to say where he was going and when he'd be back. Not that there was any drama at the Kelly Club. Big Danny was filling in admirably and Les could take all the time off he needed to recuperate. Les was checking what was on TV when the phone rang. It was Warren.

'Woz. What's happening old mate?' said Les.

'Not much,' replied Warren. 'I'm at Clover's. We're going to the pictures and I'll stay at her place tonight.'

'Half your luck.'

'Listen. She said if we get down there late, and you've already gone to the festival, there's a welcome mat outside the front door. Leave the key under it so I can get in.'

'Okay mate. No worries,' assured Les. 'Anything else?'

'No. Let's just hope the weather stays like it was today. Did you do anything?' Les told Warren about his day knowing exactly what his reply would be. 'Hah!' chortled Warren. 'And you've got the fuckin hide to bag me about my memory. You wally.'

'Yes. You've got me again, Warren.' Les hadn't told Warren he'd been sneaking a bit of his pot and having a little joint sometimes when he did his yoga with the stereo on. It wasn't a bad buzz. 'I apologise.'

'So you should. All right dude. We'll see you Friday night,' said Warren.

'Okay Woz. See you then.'

There wasn't a great deal on TV. Les watched some rubbish, then *Foreign Correspondent*. After that he climbed into bed with his book, *The Perfect Storm* by Sebastian Junger. All Les could think when he finally turned off the light was there had to be better ways of earning a living than fishing for swordfish off Grand Banks. Before long Les was snoring peacefully.

L es had a sleep-in the next morning. But he'd finished breakfast, changed into a pair of jeans and a T-shirt and was pulling up in a taxi outside Chicka's garage right on nine to find the mechanic putting the last wheel on his car. Les checked the two new tyres, picked up his rego sticker and green slip, paid Chicka and was soon driving out the door heading for the RTA in Bondi Junction. It was a beautiful, sunny day and Les wasn't enjoying the morning crawl along Bronte Road. He found a parking spot near the Cock 'n' Bull and walked round to the Roads and Transport Authority. The queue was surprisingly short and Les was back home attaching the new rego sticker to his windscreen before he knew it. He put his gear in the boot and placed several tapes and an overnight bag next to him. He took a last look at the house and had a quick glance at his watch, then started towards the Princes Highway. Les listened to the radio as far as Sutherland before he slipped on a tape. Seconds later, Barbara Blue was reggaeing the old Janis Joplin song, 'Piece Of My Heart', and Les was heading for the south coast.

The first tape finished and a surfboard sticking out from the roof of a hotel caught Norton's eye as he drove through Berry. He slipped another tape in and The Bellhops started rocking 'Sick and Tired'. After that it was rolling hills full of dairy cattle, with the odd winery on the right and green fields leading towards the ocean on the left. Les cruised through Nowra and Down To The Bone were cruising into 'Bridge Port Boogie' when a green dinosaur with yellow spots attracted his attention approaching the fishing port of Ulladulla. Les kept going, then pulled up before the bridge at Batemans Bay and ate his sandwiches watching the Clyde River pushing out towards the Tollgate Islands. Next came Moruya and Bodalla and Les was thinking the countryside around the south coast looked pretty good. Red Rivers was bopping 'The Girl Likes To Rock It' and it was late afternoon, when the road wound gently down through the surrounding hills and there was the sign: NAROOMA. POPULATION 8000.

Les crossed an iron bridge over a beautiful blue lagoon that spread away to a ridge of green hills on the right. On the left it pushed against a rocky treeline and grassy sandbars before it angled round into a deep channel running towards a narrow breakwater. Over the bridge, a flat stretch of shops and garages on the right faced a long camping area and a tourist centre, then a park at the end. The park was fenced off with hessian and inside were three huge coloured tents amongst a maze of caravans, trucks and trailers swarming with workers. Behind the park was an indoor pool. Les switched the car stereo off as the highway curved to the left and climbed past several shops. The road kept rising, but down on the left a narrow street, protected from the highway by a guard rail, ran past a hotel, a

Chinese restaurant, a cake shop and several other shops. The last shop, next to a vacant lot on a corner, was the op-shop where Les had to pick up the key. Les had missed the side street below and there was no way in except to go back. So he decided to keep going.

Past the vacant lot was a house almost hidden by trees, a dive shop, then the narrow street ended across from a hardware store, near Narooma's one set of lights. Amongst the shops opposite was the newsagency and post office and a large motel overlooking the town. On the left were more shops and an arcade, then an old wooden hotel on a corner. The road levelled off to the right past a camping store and a bit further on Les came to a shopping plaza, with a supermarket and bottle shop. He turned left at the plaza, and drove down past a small lagoon alongside a golf course leading to Narooma Beach. Les did a U-turn at the surf club and took a street to the right that went up to a beautiful, tree-lined golf course overlooking the ocean. Another street full of neat houses and gardens dipped down and up and brought Les back to the wooden hotel on the corner.

Driving back through the lights, the courthouse and police station were up off the main road on the left, then came a modern RSL, a small picture theatre and a garage. Traffic was light and there weren't many people around, and for all the shops doing business, Les noticed plenty with FOR LEASE signs sitting in the window. So this is Narooma, he mused, gazing down towards the lagoon. It sure looks nice. But shit! I reckon it'd get a bit quiet down here. Especially during winter. Les did a U-turn at the garage, then swung past the first hotel into the narrow side street and pulled up outside the op-shop.

It was only small and made of plain, blue fibro, with two windows either side of the front door. On an awning above the door, a sign said: NAROOMA CHRISTIAN OPPORTUNITY SHOP. A table sat in front of each window covered with cups, teapots, salt shakers, and other odds and ends. And another sign tucked in the corner of one window said: DON'T WALK IN FRONT OF ME, I MIGHT NOT FOLLOW. DON'T WALK BEHIND ME, I MIGHT NOT LEAD. WALK BESIDE ME AND BE MY FRIEND. My sentiments exactly, mused Les, and walked inside.

Stacked around the little shop were wicker baskets full of well-worn cutlery, pots, pans, china and other items people had donated, next to racks of clothes and piles of books. Les couldn't see anyone, then he heard voices coming from behind a faded curtain drawn across a small room on the right.

'Hello. Is anybody there?' Les called out.

A few seconds later, an elderly woman, wearing a pair of cheap jeans and a blue hand-knitted top came out from behind the curtain. She had thick, grey hair and peered at Les through a pair of glasses with solid red frames.

'Can I help you, young man?' she smiled.

'Yes. I'm looking for Edith and Joyce,' said Les.

Another elderly woman appeared from behind the curtain wearing smaller glasses, and a white tracksuit. Her hair matched her tracksuit and she wore a hearing-aid in her left ear.

'I'm Edith,' said the first woman. 'And this is Joyce.'

'My name's Norton,' said Les. 'I have to pick up a key for a house in Browning Street. I'm a friend of Clover's.'

'Oh yes,' said Edith. 'The Merrigan house. Miss Merrigan rang us.'

'Yeah, that's her,' said Les. 'Clover Merrigan.'

The two old ladies smiled serenely at Les. 'We've been expecting you,' said Joyce.

Les made an open-handed gesture. 'Well here I am,' he said. 'I just got here.'

'How lovely,' said Edith. 'And how do you like Narooma, Mr Norton?'

Les looked at the woman in the red glasses for a moment. 'Hey, what can I say?' he replied. 'That bridge. They don't make bridges like that anymore.'

'No. They certainly do not,' agreed Edith.

'I'll get the key,' said Joyce.

Edith tilted her face and smiled up at Les. 'Do you know anything about the Merrigan house, Mr Norton?' she asked.

Les shook his head. 'I've got the address in the car. That's all.'

'All right then,' replied Edith. 'Well, it's just up there on the corner,' she pointed. 'Number three. A lovely old house. You can't miss it.'

'Ohh yeah,' nodded Les. 'I think I saw it as I was driving in.'

Joyce returned with a solid brass key tied to a piece of blue cord. 'There you are, Mr Norton,' she said.

Les jiggled the key up and down in his hand. 'They sure don't make keys like this anymore, either.'

'No. They certainly do not,' said Joyce.

Edith studied Les for a moment.' Are you a religious man, Mr Norton?' she asked.

'I sure am,' replied Les. 'Only the other day I was doing a bit of carpentry, and I hit my thumb with a hammer. The first thing I did, was tell Jesus Christ all about it.'

'Oh that's so nice,' beamed Edith.

Joyce studied Les too. 'He looks like a good Christian,' she said.

'Yes he does,' agreed Edith.

Les dangled the key. 'Yeah — well, I suppose I'd better get going,' he said. 'I have to unpack, and everything.'

Edith smiled up at Les. 'Do that, Mr Norton,' she said. 'And enjoy your stay in the Merrigan house. And should you need us, we're always here.'

'And the church is just up the top of the hill,' smiled Joyce.

'I'll keep it in mind,' said Les. 'Goodbye ladies.'

'Goodbye Mr Norton.'

Les turned and walked back out to the car. So that was Edith and Joyce, he mused. Friendly enough for a pair of old bible bashers, I suppose. Are you a religious man, Mr Norton? Les drove to the next corner and stopped.

Browning Street was a short, steep road running down to the water. On the other side was a big, white, weatherboard house with a green roof and a wide verandah overlooking the ocean. The foundations were covered by crisscross, wooden slats; a low, post and rail fence ran beneath the trees surrounding the front yard. There was no gate, just a gap in the fence. Les drove in and pulled up on the grass alongside the front door. He switched off the motor, then got out and had a look around.

The sloping yard was wide and green. Runners and flower beds spread colour around the house and dotted amongst the trees were healthy aloe vera plants and thick ferns. Les walked across to a wooden fence that ran past an overgrown vacant lot, to a barbecue down the side of the house. Pecking around a bush near the barbecue were a couple of magpies. They stopped for a moment to watch Les. Norton gave them a whistle then walked back to the where he'd left the car. Three thick wooden steps led up to the front door. Les worked the heavy brass key into the lock, gave it a twist and stepped inside leaving the door open behind him.

A long, wide hallway, with a bathroom on the left and a kitchen on the right, led past two bedrooms on either side to a large loungeroom with a bedroom on the right. There was a library full of old hardbacks in one corner of the loungeroom, a piano in the other and a sandstone fireplace faced a door leading out onto the verandah. The furnishings were a wooden coffee table and a tan Chesterfield that matched the burgundy carpet. Mirrors and paintings hung on the whitewashed walls along with framed, black and white photos of old Narooma. The ceilings were high and small chandeliers hung from them; a teak rail ran around the walls below the ceiling and all the doors and windowframes were edged with teak panelling. The light switches were the original brass fittings. Les opened the door and stepped out onto the verandah.

The view over the houses and the boats moored along the jetty below was absolutely spectacular. It went up to the trees and the golf links on the right, out to the breakwater, across to the hills behind the bridge and along the coast all the way to Dalmeny. There was a table and chairs in one corner of the verandah and round the other side was a second bathroom. A set of stairs led under the house; Les followed them down. Sitting on the dirt floor were several empty boxes and a stack of splintery timber next to a room with no door.

Inside was a wooden wheelbarrow, some old tools and rusty tins of paint, a small pile of rusty horseshoes and some other junk covered in dust and cobwebs. Les gave everything a quick once over, then went back upstairs to check out the bedrooms.

They were all big and full of antique mahogany furniture and beds. In the back bedroom were a double and two singles; there were also two singles in the nearest bedroom along the hallway and one double in the room across from the kitchen. Les gave the last mattress a push and walked into the kitchen.

As well as an electric stove near the sink, it still had the original wood burner set into one wall. Sitting on the wooden floor in front was a solid table and four highback chairs. There was ample cupboard space, a two door fridge and a large pantry in one corner. A laundry led out to another room at the side with a red cedar table and eight matching chairs. Les walked back to the loungeroom, eased back on the Chesterfield and put his feet up on the coffee table.

The house was like a time capsule left from around the turn of the twentieth century. The only things out of place were the electric stove and the new fridge in the kitchen. So this is the Merrigan house, Les smiled to himself. Apart from being a little gloomy, it's the absolute grouse. And what about that view? Thank you Clover. Les turned to the piano in the corner and couldn't help himself. He went over and lifted the lid then clunked tunelessly up and down on the keys several times before closing the lid again. Whistling cheerfully, Norton went out to the car and brought his gear in.

Les chose the bedroom across from the kitchen; the double bed was comfortable, there were plenty of blankets in the wardrobe and a reading light sat on the dressing table. A door in the corner opened out onto the verandah and there was a window across from the bed. Les opened the window and the curtains swirled gently in the ocean breeze. He tossed his bags on the bed and unpacked.

The bathroom had been modernised a little; shiny green tiles covered the floor and walls and the shower looked new. Les put his shaving tackle in a cabinet above the sink and left a towel on the rack. In the loungeroom, a wooden mantelpiece rested beneath a mirror above the fireplace; the ghetto blaster sat there perfectly above a power point. Les tuned to a local radio station and got Graham Nash wailing 'Military Madness'. He turned the volume down and walked out onto the verandah. The sun was heading for the mountains behind the lagoon and the water in the channel looked like rippling turquoise as it wound its way in from the sea. Les stared at the view for a while then his eyes moved to his watch. He clapped his hands together and minutes later, he was in the Berlina heading for the shopping plaza.

Les hit the supermarket and stocked up on bread, milk, a barbecued chicken, mineral water, and other groceries. At the bottle shop he bought two bottles of Jack Daniels, plenty of mixed beers and a bottle of Bacardi for Clover. On the way back he stopped outside a real estate office across from the older hotel and went to the newsagency. It was quite big and well-stocked; Les got the Sydney paper and a 'What's On' around Narooma. A coffee table book — *Narooma's Glorious Past*, by Jasmine Cunneen — caught Norton's eye and he bought that too. As he placed them in the car he glanced across the road at the arcade. There was a new age clothes store and a food shop at the entrance. Les felt like some corn chips, so he walked over and bought a packet of Dorritos. While he was there he decided to have a look in the arcade.

On the right was a health food store, the other side was taken up by a second-hand shop. Les strolled in munching his Dorritos. The shop was crammed with furniture, office-chairs, electrical appliances, packets of sunglasses, plates, cups, clothes and countless other odds and ends. On the floor was a big box of dolls and sitting on a dressing table next to the box was a kooky-looking bear about the same size as a pineapple. It had a silly smile on its face, sunglasses, and a white tuxedo. Les smiled and absently poked his finger in the little bear's fat tummy. Instantly the little bear went into action, waving its arms around and shaking its head, while from a tiny speaker came Ricky Martin singing two bars of 'Livin' La Vida Loca'. The bear's actions took Les by surprise, then he started laughing at the bear and himself. The bear finished and Les poked it a second time. It didn't take much to set it off and immediately the bear went into action again; arms waving, head rolling, fingers pointing and Ricky Martin belting out 'Livin' La Vida Loca'.

Les was hooked. He finished his corn chips and called out to the owner, a thin faced man in a white shirt, sitting behind a desk near the door.

'Hey mate! How much for the bear?'

The owner knew a mug when he saw one. 'Ten bucks, mate,' he replied. 'It's from Costa Rica.'

'You got me,' said Les, fishing out a ten dollar bill. He picked up the bear and away it went again, waving its arms around, 'Livin' La

Vida Loca'. Les was buggered if he could figure how to turn it off. 'Hey mate,' he pleaded, as the bear kept dancing around in his hands. 'All right if I borrow a chair and break it over this things head? I can't bloody stop it.'

'Hang on a sec,' replied the owner. He fished around under one of the bear's feet and found the switch. The bear stopped immediately. 'There you go.'

'Thanks mate,' smiled Les, feeling a little foolish. He gave the owner the ten dollars and walked back to the car.

Before long, Les had everything put away, eaten some chicken sandwiches and read the paper. The bear was sitting on the piano and Les was standing on the verandah with a cup of tea, watching some people fishing off the jetty. After four hours in the car his back was a little stiff and Les felt he could do with some exercise. There was still an hour of daylight left, and a brisk walk over the bridge to the breakwater and back would be ideal. Les tossed the last of his tea onto the dirt drive separating the Merrigan house from the houses below, got into a pair of shorts, an old T-shirt and cap and his new trainers and set off.

Les came down the hill and passed by the jetty, just in time to see a plump woman pulling in an equally plump bream. The pool was closed, but there was still plenty of movement around the trucks and trailers in the park behind. In the camping area alongside the lagoon, people were sitting outside their mobile homes enjoying an afternoon cool one; several raised their beer holders as Les strode by and he waved back. Past the camping area, the walkway rose alongside the mangroves to a footpath over the bridge. Les peered down into the water at a school of blackfish hanging around an old pier, amazed at how clear it was.

Past the bridge, the footpath curved right, down to a long boardwalk. Les followed it across the shallow end of the lagoon and beneath the tree-studded cliffs above. Apart from one or two others and a few people fishing, Les had the boardwalk to himself, before it ended at a car park and a boat ramp, near a safe beach inside the channel with a shark net across the front. A sandy trail led out to the end of the breakwater, and at Bar Beach a group of surfers were getting some hot lefts running off the granite boulders. Les watched them for a few moments in the fading light then headed for home.

When he reached the jetty Les was feeling good, so he double-timed it up the hill to the house. Yes, he smiled, as he opened the front door, my back is definitely getting better. Another week and it'll be as good as gold. And the first thing I'm going to do is have a paddle and get back on the heavy bag. Maybe have a spar with Billy. After a shower and a shave, Les put on his Levi's shorts, a white T-shirt and his blue And 1s. With a bottle of mineral water in one hand and the tourist magazine in the other, he wandered down to the loungeroom, switched the verandah light on then walked outside and sat down.

It was dark now and cool, but not cold. Les watched the coloured shipping lights blinking on and off at the entrance to the channel; the lights of a boat coming up the lagoon then started flicking absently through the magazine. Amongst the ads for riding schools, joy flights, restaurants and little maps of the Eurobodalla area was a section titled 'This Week In Narooma'. The Blues Festival was the main story. But tonight, they were having the Battle of the Bands and a fireworks display, near the golf course above the ocean. That could be all right, thought Les. And it's close to home. I may as well walk up and put my head in for a while before I hit the sack. Les finished his mineral water and looked at the empty bottle. It was quite refreshing and there was beer in the fridge. But what he really felt like was a nice draught beer — or three. There was a hotel just down the road. Les switched off the light, got some money and headed out the door.

From the house to the hotel via the op-shop was just a quick stroll. The hotel had a red brick front plastered with beer signs and was called McBride's. An entrance next to the bottle shop ran through a gaming room and via a patio on the left was another entrance through two solid glass doors. Well raise my rent, Les smiled to himself, stepping back to check things out. I'm two minutes from the pub. There's another one just up the main drag if this one's no good. Across the road is a bright, shiny 'rissole'. And the Blues Festival is five minutes away along the jetty. What did Jack Nicholson say in that movie? Maybe this is as good as it gets. Les took the side entrance to the hotel.

There was a CD jukebox and a piano on the left as you stepped inside and the bar faced the entrance across several chairs and tables. Around the walls were photos of fishing clubs and football teams and blown-up photos of old Narooma. On one wall was a glass cabinet full of Harley-Davidson memorabilia and above the entrance was a big screen TV. The bar was well-stocked and angled round to the gaming room and the other entrance. Further to the left were more chairs and tables then a bistro surrounded by blackboard menus. Another glass door led from the bistro onto a balcony with a view similar to the one from the house. There were about forty people inside. A few were standing around the bar, some were seated, others were near the bistro eating. Les stepped across to the bar and waited alongside four burly, older men on his left, wearing yellow polo shirts. He wasn't there long before a dark-haired barmaid came over and Les ordered a middy of Carlton Draught.

The four men alongside him were morose, half drunk, and arguing loudly amongst themselves. Les checked out what was written on one bloke's polo shirt: Narooma Big Rock Fishing Club. That'd be right, thought Les. I don't know a fisherman yet that hasn't got the shits about something. Especially when he's on the piss. Les was about to give them a wide berth when the barmaid placed his middy in front of him. Les paid her, then picked it up to take a sip so he wouldn't spill any before he moved. He'd just got the glass to his lips when the fisherman next to him cursed belligerently to the others, waving his arm around to emphasise the point. His arm caught Norton's and knocked most of Les's middy into his face and down the front of his T-shirt.

'Ohh take it easy will you mate,' said Les, flicking beer from his face and half-soaked T-shirt.

The bloke knew he'd done it and half turned his head. 'Get fucked,' he said

'What?' scowled Les.

'You heard. I said get fucked.' The fisherman then ignored Les and continued arguing with his mates.

Les tapped him on the shoulder. 'Hey mate. You just knocked my beer all over me. I think you could at least say you're sorry. Not tell me to get fucked.'

The fisherman turned around and pushed a miserable, fleshy face, stinking of beer and cigarettes in front of Norton's. 'Well, I'm telling you again. Get fucked. And don't poke your fingers in me, you cunt. Or I'll take your beer and shove it up your fuckin arse.'

One of the bloke's mates put his head in. 'What's up, Mick?' he said.

'Ahh this whingeing big prick reckons I spilt his beer.'

'Tell him to get fucked.'

'I just did.'

Norton's face started to turn purple. He couldn't believe it. Isn't this lovely, he fumed. I've got a bad back. I'm in town just to have a good time. And I need a fight like I need an enlarged prostate. But I'm fucked if I'm gonna cop that. With a friendly smile on his face, Les turned and tapped the bloke on the shoulder again. The fisherman turned around and scowled.

'What the fuck do you want now?' he snarled.

'Hey Mick,' said Les. 'You like fishing do you mate?'

'What?'

'I said, you like fishing, mate?' repeated Les. 'Well, hook into this.'

Les thumped his head onto the bloke's nose, smashing it across his face like a soft-boiled egg. The fisherman screwed his eyes up with pain and blood started running down his chin as Les slammed his knee into the bloke's groin then dropped an elbow into his jaw. The burly fisherman fell to the floor out cold, splitting his head open against the bar on the way down. The other three looked at Mick lying on the floor for a second, then came at Les swinging. Les blocked their punches then stepped in and nailed the one on his left with a straight left, breaking the bloke's nose. Les hooked off the straight left into the next bloke's face, splitting his cheekbone open like a ripe plum. Then Les set himself and slammed a murderous, short right into the last bloke's face, pulverising his mouth and knocking out his front teeth. The bloke's legs folded like a card table and he slumped on his backside next to the first fisherman. The two left standing were still wondering what was going on, when Les kicked the one on the left in the knee. The bloke screamed, tottered for a second then dropped to the floor, clutching his leg. This left the last member of the Narooma Big Rock Fishing Club groggily holding onto the bar with one hand trying to stay on his feet. Les palm-heeled him under the jaw and the fisherman went flying across the chairs and tables, knocking drinks everywhere, finishing up sprawled out on his back in front of the jukebox.

The whole thing didn't take a minute. But it was long enough for any women in the place to start screaming blue murder. Les took a quick look at the four blokes lying all over the floor, oozing blood everywhere, and figured it was time for a bit of travelling music. He put his head down and hurried out the same way he came in. When Les got to the bottle shop he started to run. Then he stopped and cursed out loud.

'Ohh shit! My fuckin back.'

Walking briskly, Les got to the house as fast as he could. He couldn't see anybody following him, so he opened the front door and switched on the light. He shut the door behind him then walked down to the loungeroom and moved gingerly around. He hadn't thrown his back out again. But he'd aggravated it. Bugger it, thought Les angrily. Just what I need. Les circled the loungeroom a few times, rubbed at his back then took his beer soaked T-shirt off and tossed it in the shower. He cleaned himself up, put on a dark blue T-shirt then got a bottle of beer from the fridge and went back to the loungeroom. He had a swallow and turned on the stereo. The radio station was playing The Eagles' — 'Peaceful Easy Feeling'. Yeah. That'd be right, thought Les. Rubbing at his back again, he took his beer out onto the verandah.

Les had another swallow and stared balefully at the harbour lights then up at the stars. I've deadset got a pumpkin for a head, he told himself. I could have walked away and copped it sweet. Or at worst, just given that old mug a backhander. But no. I had to flatten him. And everybody else. Now, as well as stuffing up my back, you can bet the cops'll be looking for me. Shit! Les drank some more beer. Maybe I ought to piss off while I'm in front. Les stared into the night and thought about it for a moment. No, fuck it, he told himself. I'm here now. And this house is too good. And after the trouble Clover went to, she'd think I was a nice idiot. He had another, thoughtful sip of beer. No. I'll just keep my head down and stay away from that one pub. Then blend in with the crowd when it gets here on the weekend. If anyone does say anything, I'll just say it wasn't me. Les looked into his bottle. Sounds all right in theory. Norton finished his beer and belched. Anyway, bugger it! I'm going to see the battle of the bands. He turned for the loungeroom, winced and shook his head. Serves me right for being a mug, he told himself as he stepped inside. Les put his cap on, pulled it down over his eyes, then got his camera and headed out the door.

Going right at the bottom of Browning Street it didn't take long to climb the hill to the golf course and Les felt the walk was doing his back good. He was convinced the worst thing he could do would be to lie down and let it stiffen up. When he got to the top and went past the clubhouse, Les was surprised at the crowd. There were thousands. Mostly parents with kids or young people between twelve and eighteen. The event was being held in a reserve alongside the golf course. Les walked through a parking area then followed a dirt drive that separated the reserve from the trees, and blended in with the crowd. Next thing a band started up.

Across from the trees on the other side of the crowd was an outdoor stage. On it, four young girls in hipsters and T-shirts were belting out some kind of grunge rock. The words were totally indecipherable and they possibly knew three chords between them; the drummer sounded like she'd just got her drum kit that afternoon. But they were up there going for it, and what they lacked in talent, they more then made up for with enthusiasm. Les took his camera out and eased his way through the crowd. When he got closer to the stage, Les aimed his camera and took a couple of photos.

The band stopped and took a bow then began to move off stage. From somewhere an announcer said that was Murdering Mary's last song, give them a big hand and next up was Frenergetic; to be followed by the fireworks. Les moved back from the stage and watched as four skinny young blokes all in black got up, gave their guitars a quick tune then attacked some song they'd written, racing each other like crazy to see who could finish first. Les took a photo and gave the race to the bass player with blue hair. Frenergetic galloped their way through another song and that was it. Apparently because of a heavy lineup and the fireworks display, each band was only allowed two songs. From what Les had heard so far, that was plenty. He moved to the back of the crowd and was lucky enough to find a milk crate near the trees. He sat down, rubbed the sore spot in his back and watched some kids running around like wild things, waving luminous, plastic tubes in the air. Les was wishing he'd brought a few beers with him when the announcer said it was time for the fireworks. The technicians were positioned between the reserve and the clubhouse and, as soon as the announcer stopped, a star shell exploded over the trees with a loud, whistling bang and a huge shower of pink and green.

For a small country town, Les was surprised at the fireworks display. It was quite spectacular and seemed to last forever. Great bursts of red star clusters and showers of gold and blue exploded into the night then rained down from the sky. Les had a great view and sat back and was enjoying it immensely. He tried for a couple of photos and smiled to himself as he watched a trail of bursting silver climb into the night. I know what would go well now, he thought. Some of Woz's pot. Wouldn't that put some colour into the fireworks? Finally, the fireworks finished with one last spectacular explosion that brought a great roar of approval and applause from the crowd. The announcer said that was it and now it was back to the battle of the bands. Next up was Cybertronical Biped. I think that might be enough for me, thought Les, as another band got up and blasted away into the night. He left his milk crate and drifted off with some of the crowd who'd also seen enough.

Les walked back to the road going past the clubhouse and paused. To the right was home, bed and safety. But Norton was still stubbornly determined to have a draught beer. There was a street to the left and if Les wasn't mistaken it was the one that took him into town earlier. Les followed it down then up and, sure enough, just ahead was the main drag and the old wooden hotel on the corner.

The hotel had a restaurant at the back and Les noticed several punters through the windows before he turned the corner. There was an entrance round the corner off the main road, windows faced the street, and at the end another door led into a gaming area. The usual beer ads covered the blue, timber front of the hotel and above was an enclosed verandah and a sign in white: LAWSON'S HOTEL. The old pub seemed to have a nice feel about it, so Les pushed open the door and walked in.

Part of the bar angled round to the restaurant, the rest faced the windows and ran down to a makeshift stage at the end. Lights and fans hung from the ceiling and the wood-panelled walls were covered in old photos and framed newspaper clippings. Two attractive girls were working the bar; one wore a white top and had black hair with a flower in it, the other wore a mauve floral top and had brown hair. Behind them, two older men in white shirts and plain trousers were looking at the till. A duo between songs was standing in front of two microphones and a pair of speakers at the far end of the bar. A brown-haired bloke in a red check shirt and holding a guitar was on the left, next to a dark-haired bloke in all black on the right. About a dozen casually dressed people were seated or standing around the bar drinking and laughing. The smoke wasn't too punishing and Les couldn't see anybody looking for a fight, so he took a stool near the corner of the bar, facing down to the duo. He put his camera on the placemat and ordered a middy of Tooheys from the barmaid with the flower in her hair. The beer was cold and delicious and just what Les had been looking for. Then the guitar player hit a few notes, the drum machine kicked in and the singer in black started warbling 'Teddy Bear'. And the duo wasn't real bad.

Les sipped his beer and ran his eyes around the bar. He was still a bit edgy, but no one paid him any mind. Two blokes wearing polo shirts walked in and Les stiffened as they looked at him. But it was no more than a cursory glance before they went to the bar and got into a shout. Les finished his middy about the same time as the duo finished 'Teddy Bear' and started into 'It's Not Unusual'. Les ordered another middy, with a Jack Daniels and ice on the side for a buzz, and found himself tapping his foot to the music. The duo played 'Eagle Rock' and a few punters got up and started dancing; including one of the men who'd been standing at the till and the barmaid in the mauve top. Les got his camera, walked down and took a few photos. He sat down again and ordered another beer and a JD and ice.

Les was about to take a photo of the barmaid with the flower in her hair when he noticed a woman standing next to him. She had a lean, attractive face with no makeup, inquisitive, hazel eyes and long brown hair parted in the middle. A thick, beige shirt hung over a blue T-shirt getting pushed out by a healthy bust, and the T-shirt hung out over a denim dress, with splits in the side tied by leather laces. Handpainted across her T-shirt were little orange and yellow birds. Les put her age at no more than thirty and figured she was some kind of hippy. He quietly sipped his beer and avoided eye contact.

'Did you get any good photos?' she asked.

'Yeah. I think so,' replied Les, a little indifferently.

'Am I in them?'

'Possibly,' Les gave her a sideways glance. 'Were you up dancing?'

'Yes,' nodded the woman.

'Then I could have got one of you.'

'I'd like a copy. If that's all right?'

Les shrugged. 'Well, I haven't finished the roll of film yet.'

'Are you from around here?' asked the woman.

Les shook his head. 'Canberra. I just got here.'

'Oh? Where are you staying?'

Les started getting suspicious. 'At that big motel near the post office.'

'The Islander.'

'That's it,' nodded Les.

'Are you down for the Blues Festival?' Les nodded. 'Maybe you could leave it at the desk for me?'

'Sure,' said Les.

The woman smiled. 'I'm Grace.'

'George,' replied Les, politely but not over friendly.

Grace stood there a moment. 'Okay George. I might see you again before the night's over.'

'Yeah. Okay.'

Les went back to his beer and watched Grace walk off to join some people near the other end of the bar. She had a shapely behind and her hair bobbed silk-like across her shoulders when she walked. What a bummer, thought Les. Grace isn't a bad sort. If I was a little more friendly, I might have been half a chance there. But after what happened tonight, I don't know. A little town like this, she could be a friend of a friend or something and saw the fight. She might even be a cop. Who knows?

The band finished a fair version of 'I Saw Her Standing There' and took a break. Les ordered another beer and a JD and was starting to get a bit of a glow on. He still didn't drop his guard and kept an eye on the door. But the night was turning out to be all right. Even his back felt better. He took a sip of JD and looked up as a lean, wiry bloke, with a lived-in face, and untidy black hair going a little grey at the sides, walked in the door on his own. He was wearing a black T-shirt with Blondie on the front, a pair of grease-stained, black jeans and scruffy, black gym boots. The bloke nodded to Grace and her friends and the two girls behind the bar then walked round and took a stool near Les. The barmaid with the floral top came over and the bloke exchanged a smile and a few words with her, before ordering a can of VB. He took a long, enjoyable pull on his can of beer when it arrived, then belched into his hand and turned absently to Les. The bloke turned away and looked curiously at his beer for a moment then turned back and stared at Les with an odd, half smile on his face. Les picked up the vibe. It was a look of knowing admiration. The exact look a punter would give some stranger he'd just seen flatten four blokes. Fuck it, Les cursed to himself. I've been sprung.

Les ignored the bloke in the Blondie T-shirt, but he could feel his eyes on him. Finally the bloke leant over.

'Hey mate,' he said. 'I know your face.'

Les shook his head. 'I doubt it, me old,' he answered quietly.' I'm not from round this way. And I only just got here.'

'Yeah, fair enough,' the bloke nodded slowly, continuing to stare at Les. 'You're from Sydney but, aren't you?'

'Why? What makes you say that?' shrugged Les.

'I'm a chef,' answered the bloke. 'A couple of years ago I was working in a restaurant in Paddington called Forty Four. One of the waitresses didn't turn up so I had to help on the tables. You were there with another bloke and two real good sorts. And you left a five hundred dollar tip.'

Les thought for a moment then remembered the night. He was with a notorious drug dealer known as Mullets. Mullets had run out of money one night at the Kelly Club and Les had loaned him a couple of hundred dollars. Which Mullets managed to turn into fifty thousand. Mullets repaid the loan: plus. Then lined up two glamours and shouted Les to dinner at Fourty Four. One reason Les had left the five hundred dollar tip was because Mullets was trying to act low key so he gave Les the cash to pay for the night out. The second reason was that the waitress was absolutely hopeless. She tried her heart out to please them. However, the harder she tried, the more she stuffed things up. But in a crazy, bumbling way. It was like something out of a movie and she had them in stitches all night. So Les left five hundred extra of Mullets' ill-gotten gains on the table. The girl thought he'd made a mistake and chased them up the street. When

Les told her no, that was all right, he was just so impressed with her service, the poor girl burst into tears.

Les looked at the bloke and shook his head. 'Well, that proves it definitely wasn't me, mate. Because I wouldn't leave a five hundred dollar tip, if it was to save my life.'

The bloke smiled and nodded his head. 'All right. But I know I've seen the other bloke's face somewhere.'

You're not wrong there pal, thought Les. Mullets got banged up over a huge shipment and was still on remand in Long Bay. It had been all over the news. Nevertheless, the bloke seemed friendly enough and he hadn't lamped Les from the fight at the hotel. Plus he was spot on with his assumptions.

'So you're a chef are you, mate?' enquired Les.

'That's right,' said the bloke, getting into his beer. 'I work at the other pub down the road. McBride's. I just knocked off.'

'Oh?' said Les. 'I've never been in there. What's it like?'

'All right. I help run the bistro. The food's really good. And I'm not just saying that because I work there.'

Les nodded and had a mouthful of beer. 'Fair enough. I'll have to come down and put my head in.'

'Do that,' said the bloke. 'I'll look after you.' He swallowed some beer and laughed to himself. 'It's a good thing you didn't put your head in tonight though.'

'Oh?' replied Les. 'Why's that?'

'There was an unbelievable fight in the bar.'

'A blue? In a quiet town like this,' Les raised his eyebrows. 'What happened?'

'Four fisherman picked a fight with some bloke and he absolutely creamed them. I came round just after it happened and had to help clean up the blood. It was everywhere.'

'Fair dinkum?' Les looked shocked. 'Who was the bloke? A local?'

The chef shook his head. 'One of the barmaids saw him. Said he was tall and skinny. With brown hair and tattoos.'

'That sounds like a pretty good description,' said Les. 'And did the police come?'

The chef laughed out loud. 'Not for those blokes. It was probably a cop that done it.'

'Yeah?' Norton's eyes lit up. 'What makes you say that?'

'One of the blokes that got belted was Mick Scully. He's a real old thug. Him and his nephew Morgan just about run the place. They even bashed some cops down at Bermagui. Everybody knows it was them. But no one could ever prove it.'

'Fair dinkum?' said Les. 'He sounds like a nasty piece of goods this bloke — what did you say his name was?'

'Scully. Mick Scully.' The chef looked pensive for a moment. 'It would have been a different story though, if Morgan had of been there.'

'Yeah? Why's that?' enquired Les.

The chef made a dismissive gesture. 'When it comes to fighting, Morgan'd beat anyone. He's unbelievable. Him and his uncle have got half the south coast terrorised. Actually, we were all having a bit of a laugh when Mick copped it.'

'Go on,' smiled Les.

The bloke finished his can of VB. 'I wouldn't like to be the bloke though, if Morgan gets hold of him.'

Les shrugged. 'How's he going to find him?' he asked.

The chef shook his head. 'I doubt he will. If the bloke knows what's good for him, he'll have pissed off out of town by now.'

Les looked serious. 'From what you just told me, mate,' he said, 'I can't say I blame him.'

'No,' agreed the bloke.

A warm glow started to spread though Norton, and it wasn't from the Jack Daniels. Suddenly, wonderfully, a whole new vibe had come over the night. There was no heat from the local police. And instead of belting a bunch of drunken fisherman, Les had been right all the time. That bloke in the hotel had mug and bully written all over him. Norton had galloped into town on his white horse, and done a Clint Eastwood. Bad luck about his back. But he preferred that to an assault charge. As for this nephew Morgan, he'd be running around looking for some skinny bloke with tattoos. Norton had done it again.

'So what's your name, anyway, mate?' asked Les.

'Olney.'

'I'm Les, Olney.' Les shook the chef's hand. 'And I've got a confession to make.'

'Yeah? What's that Les?' asked the chef.

'That was me in the restaurant that night, left the five hundred dollars on the table.'

Olney's face lit up. 'I thought it was.'

'It's just that the bloke I was with that night...'

Olney nodded. 'I know. I saw him on TV.'

'Yeah, well, I'm not in the same caper. I help run a small security business in the eastern suburbs.'

'Fair enough Les,' said the chef.

Les patted the chef on the shoulder. 'Anyway Olney, since you caught me out telling porkies, how about letting me buy you a drink. What do you want? Anything.'

Olney looked at his empty can then at Les. 'One of these. With a bourbon chaser?'

'A man after my own heart. And we'll make the bourbon a double.' Les looked seriously at the chef. 'Are you driving?'

Olney shook his head. 'No. I only live up the road.'

'Well, let's make it a triple.'

Les bought the drinks and he and Olney toasted food in general, then Les explained how he was down for the Blues Festival. Olney came from Narooma. But he went to Sydney when work got scarce. He didn't mind working in the city and he managed to save some money. Now he was working at the hotel and hoping to open a place of his own one day. Les noticed Grace checking them out, laughing and having a good time. Les caught her eye, smiled and beckoned her over. She picked her drink up from the bar and came round.

'Grace,' said Les. 'This is my friend Olney.'

'We know each other,' said Olney. 'How's it going Amazing?'

'Amazing?' said Les.

'That's what they call me, George,' said Grace.

Les smiled at her. 'Grace. I have to be honest. When you came over before I was bullshitting you a bit. My name's not George. It's Les.'

'Oh?' said Grace.

'And I don't come from Canberra. I come from Sydney.'

'I had an idea you weren't quite telling the truth,' said Grace.

'Yeah,' confessed Les. 'It's just that I used to take this girl out in Sydney. And you reminded me of one of her friends. We had a bit of a messy breakup. And I thought you'd come over to punish me about it. I'm sorry.'

'That's all right,' said Grace. 'I can be a little forward at times.'

Les looked at the little birds getting pushed out by Grace's ample breasts. But he decided against being smart. 'Also, I'm not staying at the motel. I'm just down the road in Browning Street.'

'Seaview flats?' said Grace.

'No, the big house on the corner.'

Grace raised her eyebrows. 'The Merrigan house?'

'That's the one,' nodded Les.

'Are you staying at the Merrigan house?' said Olney.

'That's right,' said Les. 'The old white joint. It's the grouse.'

'Who are you staying there with?' asked Grace.

'I'm on my own at the moment,' replied Les. 'But my flatmate's joining me tomorrow. His girlfriend's parents own it.'

'And you're on your own there at the moment?' said Grace.

'Till tomorrow. He's going back on Monday. And I'm there till Wednesday.'

'Lucky you,' said Olney.

'Yeah.' Les looked up at Grace. 'Have you ever been inside the house.'

Grace shook her head. 'No. But I'd love to.'

'Okay,' smiled Les. 'Maybe when the hotel closes you can walk me home. Have a cup of coffee or something,' he suggested 'You live far away?'

'Central Tilba.'

'Where's that?'

'About twenty minutes south of here,' replied Grace. 'But I'm staying just over the bridge tonight. Near Bar Beach.'

'Ohh yeah,' said Les. 'I know where Bar Beach is. I walked round there this afternoon.'

'I won't come tonight,' said Grace. 'I'm going home with Julie.' She nodded to the barmaid in the floral top. 'But will you be home tomorrow?'

'Sure,' nodded Les.

'How about I come round in the morning?'

'Okay,' said Les. 'Why don't you make it about nine or so? I'll do my Denise Austin workout early. Then we might have breakfast somewhere.'

'If you're gonna have breakfast,' said Olney, 'go to Carey's.'

'Where's that?' asked Les.

'Just over the road. The red and yellow place.'

'I know it,' said Les. 'I drove past this arvo. That sound all right to you, Grace?'

'Yes,' replied Grace. 'That would be lovely. Thank you.'

'Righto. That's breakfast organised.' Les had a mouthful of beer and picked up his camera. 'Now. How about another a photo? Grace, hop in there next to Olney. Olney, give us your best smile.'

Les took a couple of photos, then got the barmaid with the flower in her hair to take a photo of the three of them. After that the night went swimmingly. Grace was drinking vodka, lime and soda. Les pointed to the money on the bar and said the drinks were on him. The duo got up and slipped into 'Big Girls Don't Cry' and soon had the small crowd dancing and singing. Grace even got a reluctant Les up for a dance. Grace was a bit of a hoofer with a few vodkas under her belt. She shook her boobs and shimmied and showed what the Good Lord gave her. Les with his back, however, shuffled around pretty much as Warren had described him. Like Marriane Faithfull with an axe handle stuck in her date. Olney was a surprise packet. The duo bopped into 'Roll Over Beethoven' and when he got up with the blonde barmaid Olney jived like a hep cat in an old Bill Haley movie. Before long the night was over. The duo finished with 'CC Rider'. Les got another photo taken as they finished their drinks and it was time to go. Les was a shot bird anyway.

'Okay Grace,' he slurred. 'I'll see you tomorrow morning.'

'All right Les. See you then,' she smiled. 'And don't forget your camera.'

'Yeah, right,' Les retrieved it from the bar. 'Olney, I'll see you next time I'm looking at you, mate,' he said.

'See you then, Les,' answered Olney. 'Thanks for the drinks.'

'No worries. G'night.' Les stepped out the door and swung into the street.

After the warmth of the hotel it was quite cool outside and a light breeze coming off the sea hit Les in the face. There were no cars and nobody about. He pulled his cap down, jammed his hands in his pockets and headed down the hill. Les started moving along to keep warm and could feel a painful twinge in his back. Shit, he thought, I wish I hadn't let Grace drag me up on the dancefloor. And why did they have to play 'Let's Twist Again'? Les was still contemplating this as he turned the old brass key in the front door a few minutes later.

The first thing Les did was hit the bathroom, then the kitchen for a tall glass of mineral water. He poured another one and walked into the lounge room. I should watch TV for a while, he smiled. But they didn't have TV at the turn of the century, did they. He decided against putting some music on and took his glass out onto the verandah.

Les drank some more water and felt his head spinning. Bloody hell! Didn't I get myself nice and pissed, he told himself. Thank Christ the pub closed at twelve. But why wouldn't you? What a great result. Everything's sweet. And breakfast with that girl tomorrow. Les stared happily up at the stars and noticed the difference after the air around Sydney. They were everywhere. He'd just started enjoying their brilliance, when one zipped across the night sky. As well as being clear, however, the night was cool; especially in a T-shirt and shorts. Les yawned and looked at his watch. Well, if I'm getting up for a walk and breakfast by nine, I suppose I'd better hit the sack. He finished his mineral water and went inside.

After cleaning his teeth, Les changed into a clean T-shirt and climbed into bed. He turned off the dressing table lamp and scrunched his head into the pillows. The old double bed was roomy, he had plenty of blankets and through the window Les could hear the sea. The big Queenslander was literally as snug as a bug. He was almost asleep and vaguely thinking about Warren and Clover arriving when suddenly it was as if the room had turned into a freezer. A dense, clammy cold settled over the bed and Les felt an icy chill run up his back that made the hairs on his neck stand on end. Holy shit, he thought, pulling the blankets tighter around him. I expected the south coast to be a bit colder than Sydney. But not like fuckin Antarctica. Les rolled himself into a ball and pulled the blankets around him even tighter. But there was no way he could get warm. Ohh bugger this, Les grumbled to himself.

With his teeth chattering like castanets, Les turned on the bed lamp then got up and banged the window closed. Shivering and puffing clouds of steam through the half-lit room, he put on his tracksuit and a pair of socks, then got another blanket out of the wardrobe and spread it over the bed. Trying to rub some warmth into his arms, Les got back under the covers and turned off the light. After a couple of minutes he settled down and started to warm up. Ahh yes, he sighed, contentedly. That's a bit more like it.

With the window closed the room was silent now. Les was almost asleep, when from far away he heard Ricky Martin singing 'Livin' La Vida Loca'. Les half-opened one eye. What the fuck? Ricky Martin kept singing in the distance. It's that fuckin bear, cursed Les silently. I thought I switched the bloody thing off when I put it on the piano. Ricky Martin stopped. Then he started up again. Stupid prick of a thing. I knew there was something wrong with it when I bought it. Les pulled the blankets around him. I'm buggered if I'm getting out of bed though. It's too fuckin cold. But tomorrow, the batteries are coming out. Ricky Martin stopped and Les dozed off.

Les was only asleep for a short while when another noise woke him. This time someone was playing the piano. Not a tune. Just inane clunking like Les had done earlier, only softer. Les half woke up and listened for a moment. The piano stopped. Then it started up again. Les shook his head and shoved it into the pillows. It's all the piss I drank. I'm hearing things. But I couldn't really give a shit if Jerry Lee Lewis was out there playing 'Great Balls of Fire'. There's no way I'm getting up. The piano playing stopped. If it started again Les couldn't tell. He fell straight into a deep, drunken, snoring sleep.

Les woke up the next morning feeling seedy. A knot of pain in his back told him where he was and why he was hungover. He yawned and scratched, then got into a pair of shorts and opened the bedroom window. Outside, it didn't look like too bad a day. He plodded into the bathroom, freshened up, then walked across to the kitchen.

'What the fuck?'

Something had been in there during the night. Lying under the table was a packet of wheatmeal biscuits, the loaf of bread, tea-bags, and a few other things out of the cupboard, along with some cutlery and a broken cup.

Les put his hands on his hips. 'Hello. Looks like the Merrigan house has got rats.'

Les walked across to the pantry. Sitting on a shelf amongst the other odds and ends were two old wooden rat-traps. I thought so, nodded Les, picking one up. Well, I'll be setting you tonight. Something suddenly jogged Norton's memory. That's what was running around on the bloody piano last night. Jerry Lee Rat. Okay Jerry Lee, smiled Les. See how you like tickling the ivories with a broken neck. And when you're lying there all bruised and broken rat, don't, I say don't, expect uncle Les to give you any mouse to mouse resuscitation...

Les replaced the rat-trap then switched on the jug and dropped two slices of bread in the toaster. While he was waiting Les cleaned up the mess. He noticed the rat hadn't broken open the packet of biscuits. So you don't like Shredded Wheatmeal, Jerry. See if you like sinking your teeth into a nice piece of tasty cheese — tied to the trap with cotton. Les made a mug of tea, buttered the toast and walked out to the loungeroom. The bear was sitting on the piano facing the wall. Les placed his mug on the piano and turned the bear round the way he'd left it.

'Go on. Start singing now, you fat bastard,' he said.

Nothing happened. Les pushed the bear in the stomach then lifted up its leg.

It was switched off. Les switched it on and immediately the bear went into action; head nodding, arms waving, singing Ricky Martin.

Les shook his head. 'You've got a mind of your own, haven't you. You little shit.'

Les switched the bear off and left it on the piano. He changed his mind about removing the batteries and took his tea and toast out onto the verandah.

Despite a light southerly blowing, it looked like being a delightful spring day. A band of clouds stretched across the horizon and the sun was sparkling on the harbour. The tide was rapidly pushing in through the channel and a charter boat with a half-dozen people on board was backing out from the jetty. People were fishing and a couple of kids were paddling around on skis. That's what I'd like to be doing right now, thought Les. Having a paddle on that big, blue lagoon. He gingerly bent down and tried to touch his toes. Yeah. Bad luck about that. Les finished his tea and toast and looked at his watch. Well, I suppose I'd better make a move if I'm going for breakfast. The breeze was flicking at the trees above the hill. Les decided to walk up to the golf links and follow the cliffs. He got into his training gear, pulled an old cap down over his sunglasses and set off, locking the front door behind him.

The clubhouse looked bigger in the daytime, when Les reached the top of the hill and golfers were teeing off on the fairways or whizzing around the greens in golf buggies. Watching out for golf balls, Les strode off across the greens in the cool fresh air. The grass felt soft beneath his feet, and the morning dew seeped into his trainers. Les would have loved to have ripped into a good, hard run. But he strode steadily along telling himself how much good the walk was doing his back. He found a path behind the trees and followed it along the cliffs. Out to sea Les noticed a long, flat, rocky island with a lighthouse on it. That must be Montague he surmised. I may as well take a trip out while I'm down here and do a bit of snorkel sucking. I imagine the water'd be clear and there's supposed to be a big seal colony out there. Les followed the cliffs as far as Narooma Beach and stopped.

The view up and down the coast was spectacular. The morning sun sparkled on the water as tiny clouds drifted across the sky, and solitary seabirds hovered lazily above the ocean, taking advantage of the on-shore breeze ruffling the surface. Below the cliffs, fishermen were scattered along the water's edge or around clusters of tall rocks thrusting out of the sand like huge stone fingers. Les saw a flash of silver as one fisherman pulled in what could have been a nice tailor, watched him carry his wriggling catch up to a bucket then headed home. When he got back to the house, an old, box-shaped, maroon Jackaroo, with a Wilderness Not Woodchips sticker on the rear window, was parked behind his Berlina. Grace was bent over in the yard examining an aloe vera plant, and in a pair of tight jeans and a short-sleeved purple shirt, the view from behind was even better than the one from the golf links. Les waited a moment or two before he called out.

'You looking for something, mate?'

Grace stood up carrying a camera in one hand and turned around. 'Hullo Les,' she smiled. 'How are you this morning?'

Les returned her smile. 'A bit seedy from last night. But I'm getting there.'

'Have you been for a jog?'

Les shook his head. 'A walk. I went around the golf links.'

'Isn't it a lovely view from up there?'

'Yeah, fantastic.' Les took his sunglasses off and wiped some sweat from his eyes. 'You been here long?'

'Not long,' replied Grace. 'I've been looking around the yard. All right if I take a few pieces of aloe vera?'

'Help yourself.' Les took the key from his pocket and motioned to the door. 'Come inside and have a look at the house.' He opened the door and ushered Grace through.

Grace entered the old house, then stopped in the hallway and gazed around. 'Oh yes,' she said. 'This is even better than I imagined.'

'It's something else, isn't it,' agreed Les, shutting the door. 'Anyway, why don't you take a look around while I have a shower. There's coffee and that in the kitchen.'

'Okay.' Grace held up her camera. 'All right if I take a few photos?'

'Go for your life,' answered Les.

Les left Grace with her camera and got under the shower. He rinsed his training gear and the beer-sodden T-shirt, towelled off then put on his shorts and a green polo shirt with a denim collar. He got a bottle of mineral water from the fridge, then took his washing out onto the verandah and hung it on the line. Grace was round the other side. She heard Les and came around.

'This view,' said Grace. 'It is absolutely beautiful.'

'It's tops, isn't it,' said Les, taking a drink of water.

'In fact this whole house is fantastic,' said Grace. 'I just love the old piano in the corner and the library. Did you know some of those books are a hundred years old?'

'Yeah?' said Les. 'I hadn't noticed.'

'I got some great photos.' Grace smiled at Les. 'What about the bear? Where did that come from?'

'I bought it at the second-hand shop in the arcade. Have a look at this.'

Les took Grace into the loungeroom and switched the bear on. Grace started laughing as it went into action and took a photo.

'That thing is so cute,' she said.

'Yes,' agreed Les. 'He's certainly got a style all of his own.'

Les switched the bear off and they went back out on the verandah. Grace leant against the railing watching Les and gave him an angled, once up and down.

'So how did you sleep last night, Les?' she asked.

'Sleep?' replied Norton. 'If you'll excuse the expression Grace, I was that drunk last night, I would have slept under a horse pissing.'

'Okay,' said Grace.

'But Christ, it sure gets cold night down here at night.'

'Cold?' said Grace. 'How do you mean — cold?'

'I mean, bloody cold,' answered Les. 'Like Siberia. I had to get up and put my tracksuit on, and throw another blanket on the bed. I was freezing.'

'Where was it cold?' asked Grace.

'In the bedroom,' said Les. 'I closed the window and it was okay.'

'And you slept all right after that?'

'Like a top,' said Les, thinking it best not to tell Grace about the rat. 'Until I woke up this morning. Me and my hangover.'

'Okay.' Grace smiled and continued to watch as Les drank his mineral water. 'Do you know anything about this house, Les?' she asked.

Les shook his head. 'No. Only that it belong's to Clover's parents.'

'It used to be the old government surveyor's hut.'

'This was a surveyor's hut?' said Les. 'Not a bad hut.'

'What I really meant was,' said Grace, 'the government surveyor, Edward Ruddle. His original slab hut used to stand here. In those days there wasn't much down here but rainforest. Then the Merrigans built the house.'

'They sure picked a good spot,' said Les. He turned from the view to Grace. 'So who were the Merrigans? What happened to them?'

'Lander Merrigan owned a sawmill. He and his wife Hildreth drowned when their sulky got swept away during a flood.'

'They got drowned? Oh. What a bummer.' Les ran his eyes around the verandah. 'I suppose having a house like this, they would have left about twenty little orphaned Merrigans too.'

Grace shook her head. 'No. Only one. A son. Eachan. He lived here on his own — before he went insane, and died in a mental hospital.'

'Christ!' said Les. 'The Merrigans sure had a lot of luck — didn't they?'

Grace looked at Les for a moment. 'Have you ever heard of a place called Mystery Bay, Les?'

Les indicated his 'What's On' still sitting on the table. 'I think I saw it on a map. Is it further down the coast a bit?'

'That's it,' said Grace. 'On the way to where I live. Edward Ruddle disappeared there early in the nineteenth century. Along with three other men.'

'Disappeared?' Les found himself interested. 'What? Nobody knows what happened to them?'

'That's right,' said Grace. 'Their boat was seen drifting off Mutton Bird Point before it got washed into the bay alongside. The authorities left it there till it rotted away. And the place ended up getting named Mystery Bay.'

'They left it there? What sort of boat was it?' asked Les.

'A solid wooden clinker. With a big hole in the bottom where the staves were forced out.'

'Forced out?'

'Yes. That's another part of the mystery. The bottom was stove out. Not in. They found most of the men's things still in the boat. But the men had vanished without trace.'

'Fair dinkum? And how do you know all this, Grace?' asked Les.

'Oh, I sort of dabble in local history,' said Grace. 'It gives me something to do during winter.'

'Right.' Les finished his mineral water and indicated with the empty bottle. 'Well. Between Edward Ruddle and the late Merrigans, you wouldn't actually call this spot Happy Valley — would you?'

'It gets even better, Les. At the time of his disappearance, Edward was about to marry a farmer's daughter from Bodalla, Gwendolyn Monteith. He had a gold ring with tiny opals in it, made specially for the occasion. Which Edward swore to wear on his own finger until their wedding day.'

'And he had it on when he disappeared,' said Les.

'That's right,' replied Grace.

Les stroked his chin. 'So what happened to Gwendolyn. Who did she finish up with?'

'No one,' answered Grace. 'She never married. She moved to Moruya, and died of a broken heart.'

Les looked blankly at Grace for a moment. 'I don't quite know what to say, Grace. Until you turned up this morning, I was having a pretty good time living here. Now I feel like moving into a motel.'

Grace laughed. 'I'm sorry, Les,' she said. 'I didn't mean to be like that. It's just that for such a lovely old house, and such a lovely spot, it's got a very sad past.'

'You can say that again.' Les tapped the empty bottle against the railing. 'The mystery of Mystery Bay, eh. Any theories? You give me the impression you're keeping something up your sleeve.'

Grace shook her head. 'No. No theories. Edward Ruddle didn't have any enemies. None of the men had any money on them at the time. And it wouldn't be worth killing four men for a wedding ring.'

'What about the local abos?' asked Les. 'They'd have to be a walk-up start to get the blame.'

Grace shook her head again. 'No. Edward was good friends with both the Murring and the Pyender tribes. So was Gwendolyn.'

Les shrugged and indicated to the sky. 'Maybe Edward and his mates were beamed up to the mother ship.'

Grace gave a shrug also. 'Maybe they were,' she said. 'Who knows?'

Les looked at Grace looking at him, then looked at his watch. 'Anyway. How about we beam over and have some breakfast. I'm getting a bit peckish.'

'Okay,' said Grace. 'We may as well walk up. It's not far.'

'Suits me.' Les started for the loungeroom door.

'Before we go,' said Grace, 'let me take a photo of you.'

'If you want,' shrugged Les. 'You want me to stand on the verandah with the ocean in the background?'

'No. Lean in the doorway. I'll get the light.'

'Okay.' Les propped in the doorway and Grace took two quick snaps.

'That's good,' said Grace. She followed Les into the loungeroom then stopped and pointed to the ghetto blaster sitting above the fireplace. 'Is that working?' she asked.

'Yeah,' replied Les. 'I got it tuned to some local FM station.'

Grace switched the radio on and fiddled with the dial. Next thing there was a blaze of trumpet-playing as a song ended and a gravelly voice went, 'Zatzoo-zatzoo-zazoo-zah'. Then a smoother voice came on. 'That was Louis Armstrong singing "Ain't Misbehavin'". Now let's hear Helen Forrest and the Artie Shaw band, with "I Have Eyes".' Grace turned up the volume and the house filled with some woman's tinny voice, accompanied by muted trumpets, clarinets and a slow riff from a double bass.

'What's this?' asked Les.

'It's a local station. Season FM. They play nothing but old twenties and thirties music.'

Les listened for a moment and was reminded of the old hotel he stayed in at the Blue Mountains. 'It takes you back in time,' he said.

'Doesn't it,' smiled Grace. They listened for a while longer then Grace turned the ghetto blaster off. 'But what do you think?' she said, waving around the room.

'Yes, I see just what you mean,' replied Les. 'It definitely adds a certain ... ambulance to the house.'

'That's ... the exact word I was looking for. Thanks Les.'

'No worries,' smiled Norton. 'Now let's go and have breakfast. After you, Grace.' Les placed his camera in his overnight bag and ushered Grace out the door.

They turned left where Browning met the divide and followed the side street past a small dive shop, an empty shop, then a bigger dive shop. Grace stayed slightly behind Les, watching him as he walked up the hill. They got to the lights just as they were about to change and Grace jogged across to the other side of the main road. Les followed her as fast as he could and nearly got run over by an elderly woman driving a silver Corolla. The woman bipped her horn at Les and frowned at him like he was an idiot. Grace waited on the footpath till Les caught up.

'You've got something wrong with your back, haven't you,' she said.

Les felt a little embarrassed. 'You noticed,' he answered.

'What happened?'

As they were walking up the hill past the shops and the people, Les told her how he'd slipped a disc. Then he told her his back was just coming good when he got a flat on the way down and strained it changing tyres.

'I had physio and every bloody thing,' said Les. 'Now I've stuffed it up again. Talk about give you the shits.'

Grace smiled at Les. 'I think I can help you,' she said confidently.

'You can?' said Les. 'What? Are you a chiropractor or a physiotherapist?'

Grace shook her head. 'No. I can do a little massage. But there's something else.'

'Not aromatherapy or crystal balancing? I got to admit Grace — you do come across as a bit of a hippy.'

'No,' laughed Grace. 'But you'll have to come out to my place.'

'All right.' Les gave his back a quick rub. 'Shit! I'll try just about anything.'

Grace took Les's arm for a moment. 'Okay. We'll see what we can do.'

The red and yellow restaurant was on the corner opposite the hotel. There were windows all round and a sign above the plastic strips in the door said CAREY'S. Les followed Grace inside. Carey's was roomy with polished wooden floors, and the counter and blackboard menu faced the door with the kitchen behind. Near the counter was a rack full of magazines and a computer linked to the internet. The people in black polo shirts and aprons behind the counter were friendly, and knew Grace. Les ordered scrambled eggs on toast with the works and a flat white. Grace opted for an omelette and a cappuccino. Les paid and instead of a number, you got a small wooden object on a stand. Les got a lemon, Grace got a slice of watermelon. They took their little wooden stands and sat facing each other at a table near the far wall. Les had time to check out a few paintings around the walls and the other diners, when their coffees arrived and they got into a bit of chitchat.

Les told Grace pretty much the truth. His family was in Queensland, he lived at Bondi and worked security for a club in Kings Cross that he had shares in. Single, white, heterosexual male. He owned his own house and car, liked music and was down for the Blues Festival.

'That's about my story,' said Les. 'What's yours, Grace.'

'My story?' replied Grace. 'It's a little different to yours, I suppose.'

The food arrived and over the bacon, eggs and toast Grace opened up. Her family came from Narooma. She'd gone to work for a law firm in Sydney, at Ryde, where the lawyers were cooking the books. Grace saw what was going on so she cooked a bit for herself and got away with it before she left. She stayed in Sydney for a while then returned to Narooma where she bought an old farm on five acres at Central Tilba. She made T-shirts and she also had shares in a company in Sydney. Like Les, she did her best to keep fit and, also like Les, she enjoyed good music. Les ordered another two coffees and was wiping his plate with a piece of toast when Grace told him she had a twelve-year-old daughter, who lived with her grandparents in Wollongong.

Les swallowed his piece of toast and gave Grace a double blink. 'Did you just say you've got a twelve-year-old daughter?'

'That's right,' said Grace. 'Ellie. She's got my eyes. But lighter hair.'

Les stared at Grace a little open-mouthed. 'Well how old are you?'

'How old do you think?'

'Somewhere in your twenties. Thirty at the most.'

'I'm forty-two.'

'Forty-two?' Les gave another double blink. 'Christ! You don't look it.'

'I know,' smiled Grace.

Les couldn't help himself staring at Grace. Apart from a few, tiny laugh lines around her eyes, her face was exceptionally smooth and healthy. Her teeth weren't perfect. But there were no gravity lines at the sides of her mouth and the skin round her neck was unwrinkled as were her hands. Forty-two wasn't all that old. But Les had seen a lot of women in their forties. And after years of drink, smokes, coffee and cream cakes, and lying in the good old Australian sun, they looked every minute of it. Not Grace. However, that was just her face.

'Yes,' conceded Les. 'You've certainly looked after yourself. But I still haven't seen you down the beach.'

'What?' said Grace. 'You haven't seen me down the beach?' She unbuttoned the front of her shirt and threw it open. 'How do you think these would go down the beach?'

Sitting up confidently under her shirt, in an almost invisible wisp of lacy black bra, Grace had breasts like two, big, juicy, honeydew melons. Beneath the two gorgeous big melons was a neat six pack. As quickly as Grace unbuttoned her shirt, she did it up again.

'Well,' she said, easing back in her chair. 'How did they look?'

'How did they look?' blinked Les. 'I don't know, Grace. I think I just hallucinated. Maybe you better show me again to be sure.'

'I think you've seen all you need to,' smiled Grace. She looked up as their second coffees arrived.

Les regained his composure, sugared his coffee and took a sip. 'So, were you ever married?' he asked, politely.

'Two years,' replied Grace. 'Russell sold plumbing supplies. Then lost his job a year after we were married. He tried selling paintings door to door and got run over one night walking back to his car. Leaving me with no insurance, a daughter to raise, and a mortgage on an old house in Botany full of cockroaches.'

'Not a bad place, Botany,' smiled Les.

'Yes, delightful,' replied Grace. 'I stuck it out long enough to sell the house without having to owe the bank any money. Then when I got what I thought was fair from the lawyers, I couldn't get out of Sydney quick enough.'

Les looked across Grace and through the restaurant window at the ocean, blue and sparkling along the coast. 'To live down here. I couldn't blame you.'

'Yes. It might be dullsville at times, Les. But when you walk out to your car in the morning, it's still there and it hasn't got an inch of grime all over it.'

'I know what you mean.'

Grace checked Les out over her coffee. 'When were you born, Les?' she asked. He told her and Grace smiled. 'That makes me old enough to be your aunty.'

'Well, you'd be an unreal aunty,' said Les. 'In fact Grace, you're an amazing woman all round.'

Grace smiled across the table. 'That's what they call me, Les. Amazing Grace.'

The girl came and took away the plates. Les thanked her for the excellent food and had another sip of coffee.

'That Olney the chef's not a bad bloke,' remarked Les.

'Olney? We went to school together. He's a really nice person.' Grace looked at Les for a moment. 'Did you really leave a five hundred dollar tip?'

'Yes,' replied Norton. 'But it wasn't my money.'

Grace had a sip of coffee. 'You'll have to call in to the hotel where he works and have a meal. Olney's a good chef.'

'I intend to,' said Les.

'Did Olney tell you what happened down there last night?' asked Grace.

'He said there was a fight in the bar, or something.'

'Or something?' said Grace. 'It's the talk of Narooma.'

'Really?' said Les.

'And it couldn't have happened to a nicer bunch of blokes either,' said Grace. 'I laughed my head off when I found out who it was got beat up.'

'Yes. Olney said they weren't much good.'

'Old Mick Scully and his cronies. Pity his nephew Morgan never got beat up as well,' said Grace.

'Olney might have mentioned him too,' said Les. 'Who's he?'

Grace's cheeks coloured. 'A local bastard.'

Les picked up the vibe. 'I gather you and this Morgan aren't the best of friends.'

'You could say that,' replied Grace.

'What happened?' asked Les. 'Not that it's any of my business.'

'Nothing happened,' she replied. 'Luckily my parents showed up. But the next day he tried to run my father off the road. He could have killed him.' Grace shook her head. 'He's a nut. But bad as well as mad.'

'He sounds like it,' said Les. 'So do they know who it was give it to the blokes in the hotel?' he asked.

Grace shook her head. 'They think he plays football for Ulladulla.'

Les finished his coffee and thought he might change the subject. 'So what's doing tonight, Grace?'

'Well, I don't know about you, Les,' answered Grace. 'But I'm going to the Blues Festival. Aunty Grace has got a three day pass.'

'Me too,' said Les. 'Who are you going with?'

'No one in particular.'

'Would you like to come with me? Warren and Clover should be here by eight. We can all go together.'

'All right,' said Grace. 'I know the guy who runs it. I'll introduce you to him.'

'Unreal. And if you want to have a few drinks, there's a spare room in the house.'

'No thank you,' said Grace. 'I mean, if I do have a few drinks I'll stay at Belinda's.'

'Fair enough. Well, just call round the house about eight. Unless you want to come earlier and have a bite to eat somewhere.'

'No, that's all right thanks. I have to do a few things at home. In fact what is the time?' Grace looked at Les's watch. 'I'll have to get going.'

'Okey doke,' said Les. 'But before we go — my turn to take a photo.'

'What? In this old thing?' smiled Grace.

'That old thing looks pretty good to me,' said Les.

Les popped two photos of Grace and got her to take one of him, then they headed out the door. On the way back to the house, Les got the paper and checked out the dive shops when they crossed the road. The big brown one looked the busier of the two. But Les liked the smaller white one down from it. There were photos in the front window of diving at Montague Island with the seals and stingrays, and the shop had a regular charter boat that went out there game fishing or diving. They got back to the house and Grace stopped at the door of her car.

'Well, thank you very much for breakfast, Les. It was lovely. And thanks for letting me see inside the house,' she said.

'That's all right,' smiled Les. 'Anytime.'

'And I am serious about your back. I can help you.'

'Hey, you've got me,' assured Les. 'I'm coming round to your place.'

'Make sure you do.' Grace opened the door of her car.

'Before you go. What about your aloe vera?' said Les.

'Oh. I almost forgot.' Grace got a plastic bag from the front seat of her car and walked across to the trees. She broke off three pieces, put them in the bag and placed them in the car. 'Thanks for that,' she said.

'I'll see you tonight,' smiled Les.

Grace blew Les a kiss as she backed down the driveway and Les blew her one back off his fingertips, then she drove away. Les went inside to the bedroom and gave himself a double blink in the mirror. Did I just see what I think I did? What about those with breakfast? What about Grace? And she wants to fix my back. I wonder if that's all she wants to fix? Les laughed and tidied up the bed. Imagine if Grace did throw me up in the air. Forget having a slipped disc, I'd finish up looking like the Hunchback of Notre Dame. Les kicked off his casuals, got the paper and his book about old Narooma then walked out to the table on the verandah and made himself comfortable.

Les finished the paper and started flicking through *Narooma's Glorious Past*. 'Noorooma' meant clear water in the local aboriginal dialect and it was once a gold mining and timber town. White people had first been through there in 1797 and people started settling in the area around 1840. Les looked at photos of sawmills and old steamers. Serious men with full beards in high-collared shirts and stern women in black crinoline dresses with white hats that looked like tea cosies. As Les turned the pages, something Grace said earlier intrigued him. Edward Ruddle had sworn to wear his betrothed's wedding ring until the day they were married. If that was the case, Edward must have had very dainty hands.

Les turned a few more pages and couldn't believe it. There was an old black and white photo of Edward Ruddle standing alongside Gwendolyn Monteith, seated in a high-back, wicker chair. Edward had untidy dark hair and a full beard, tiny glasses, and wore a frock coat, watch chain and striped trousers. Gwendolyn was wearing a heavy, pleated dress and a straw hat with the brim turned up. The photo wasn't the best. But Edward looked like a reasonable style of a bloke. Gwendolyn, however, was an absolute beast. She had a miserable, fat face, pushed into a bony, hog head, with that many double chins she could have shuffled them and done card tricks. Resting in her ample lap, her hands looked like two small bunches of sugar bananas, topped off with a body that made Jabba the Hutt look like Elle MacPherson. Gwendolyn was nineteen. Edward was thirty-seven.

'Oh my God!' said Les. 'What a walrus gumboot.'

Les stared at the photo in disbelief and closed the book. Well that's the mystery of Mystery Bay solved, he told himself. Edward's pulled out a photo of his girl and everyone's jumped out of the boat. Edward's got the shits and kicked a hole in the bottom, no one could swim and they all drowned. And you can see why Edward was able to wear his beloved's little band of gold. If the bloody thing could fit round Gwendolyn's pig's trotter, it'd double as a serviette ring. Les opened the book again. Still, he conceded, there probably weren't many stray women down here in those days. And at thirty-seven, plucking a nineteen-year-old's not a bad effort. But, fair dinkum, to marry something like that Edward must have been absolutely desperate. Or too lazy to pull himself. Les turned to the next page. A few pages on he came to a photo of the Merrigans.

'Hello,' said Les. 'It's Lander and the team.'

The photo was taken standing on the verandah with the ocean in the background. There was no breakwater then and the channel was more a wide, sheltered bay with a long wooden jetty running out from the park on the right. Lander was all done up in a check, three piece suit and had grey hair, combed neatly over a full, happy face. Hildreth wore glasses and had her hair in a bun; she also looked happy, in a simple, floral dress with a shawl over her shoulders. Their skinny son, Eachan, had a cap plonked on his head and a crumpled coat over a pair of crumpled short trousers, and was staring into the lens like he'd never seen a camera before. Les smiled at the photo and pictured exactly where they were standing on the verandah when it was taken. He had a good look then turned the page. Towards the end of Jasmine Cunneen's book, was 'The Mystery of Mystery Bay'.

Apart from an old pencil sketch of the boat, sitting on the beach with a hole in the bottom, there were only the names of the other missing men and all the police and officials investigating the case. There wasn't a great deal more than Grace had told Les already. Police initially thought it was foul play, then said there'd been an accident at sea. Important evidence was never properly examined and prominent people thought the police had botched the investigation. The Select Committee of the Legislative Assembly investigating the incident concluded it was murder. The police, the police magistrate and the mining warden said it was an accident. A lot of theories were put forward over the years. But the mystery of Mystery Bay remains unsolved to this day.

Les ran his eyes over the page again, then closed the book. Unsolved to this day? I just solved the bloody thing. The surveyor did it. Les put Jasmine Cunneen's book on the table then went inside and got *The Perfect Storm*. He made himself comfortable and rejoined the crew of the *Andrea Gail* having a wonderful time battling twenty metre waves and two hundred kilometre winds off Grand Banks.

Les read on into the afternoon. He was that engrossed in his book, he didn't notice Narooma coming to life. Cars were arriving down the side street or up Browning and stopping in front of the surrounding holiday flats and houses. Car boots and garage doors were opening and closing, bags and suitcases were getting dumped on footpaths, keys were rattling and getting pushed into locks. Shades were being pulled up and down, taps were being run. The sun began to to go down and lights started coming on. Bottles clinked, cans fizzed open and voices drifted over from the surrounding balconies. Les heard music and looked up. Canned Heat. Coming from a flat on the corner. Other balconies followed suit. John Lee Hooker, John Mayall, Dave Hole. From a house below, Les heard Buddy Guy and Junior Wells, chugging out 'This Old Fool'. From another balcony, Johnny Johnson started tinkling 'Drink of Tanqueray'. Hello, thought Les. Looks like the bloody tourists have hit town for the Blues Festival. And I'm caught in the battle of the ghetto blasters. Trapped in a rock 'n' roll no man's land. He put his book aside, stretched his legs and looked around. Well, if I don't want to finish up missing in action, I'd better start fighting back.

Les walked into the loungeroom and switched on his ghetto blaster. It was still tuned to Season FM. A smooth voice said, 'That was "Thanks for the Boogie Ride", with Anita O'Day. Now let's hear the dulcet tones of Kay Starr and "Secretary to the Sultan".'

'Yes. Let's not,' said Les. He switched the radio off, got a tape and took the ghetto blaster out onto the verandah. He put it on the table facing the jetty and found the power point. 'Instead, why don't we hear Katie Webster, from her CD *Two-Fisted Mama*! And "The Katie Lee".' Les hit the play button and Katie Webster's honky tonk piano joined the other music. 'Fire one for effect,' smiled Les, then went inside and got a bottle of beer.

Les had an enjoyable late afternoon, sitting with his feet up on the verandah, drinking beer, listening to music and watching the world go by. Around in the park someone did a sound check which thumped out across the channel. Les changed tapes and kept drinking beer. Before he knew it, it was well and truly dark and he was getting drunk. He looked at his watch. Shit! I'd better take it easy. Grace'll be here before long and I don't want to open the door with my wobble boot on talking in Icelandic. Les finished his beer and got under the shower.

He had a shave and mulled over what he should do about dinner. Going down to the pub or the RSL might still be a bit risky. There was chicken and salad in the fridge and tins of salmon in the cupboard. Les made some sandwiches and read the paper again over a mug of tea. He cleaned up, then changed into a pair of jeans and a white T-shirt with a hang out denim shirt, and dabbed a little Calvin Klein on his face. Satisfied everything was in order, he went to the kitchen and made a delicious: JD and mineral water with a slice of lime. Les was glancing at some maps in his 'What's On', when there was a knock on the door. Les opened it and Grace was standing on the step wearing a pair of red jeans and a short-sleeved maroon shirt, over a mauve T-shirt with tiny yellow parrots on the front. She had her hair in a ponytail and pinned to her shirt was a little wooden lorikeet with mother-of-pearl eyes.

'Hello Grace,' said Les, cheerfully. 'How are you?'

'Good. How's yourself?' she replied.

'Terrific. Come on in.' Les glanced along the driveway. 'Where's your car?'

'I left it at Belinda's and got a lift over.'

Les closed the door and ushered Grace into the kitchen. He gave her another once up and down and noticed the neat cut of her shirt and the tiny green emblem near the pocket.

'That's a nice shirt,' said Les. 'Where did you get that?'

'I buy them at the hemp shop in Central Tilba,' she replied.

'It looks good over that T-shirt,' remarked Les.

'Thanks.' Grace fingered the emblem. 'Yes, they look good. They feel good, and they last forever.'

'Don't let Warren see it when he gets here. He'll try and smoke it.'

Grace shook her head. 'He could smoke ten tonne of these and it wouldn't do him any good.'

'I know,' said Les. 'I was only joking. But I'll buy a couple of those before I go home. They look all right.' Les rubbed his hands together. 'Can I get you a caarrktail?'

Grace pointed to Norton's glass on the table. 'What are you drinking?'

'Jack Daniels and soda. Or there's beer and Bacardi.'

'How about a Bacardi?'

Grace placed her bag on the table and looked around the kitchen while Les made a Bacardi and orange. He handed it to her and clinked glasses.

'Cheers Grace.'

'Yes. Cheers Les.'

'Would you like to go out on the verandah?' suggested Les.

'All right. After you.'

On the verandah it was quite mild. The sky was full of stars and the moon shone brightly on the channel. The surrounding balconies were down to only a couple of ghetto blasters. But coming from the park was a blur of music and the solid thump of a bass.

'Sounds like the show's started,' said Les.

'Yes. The first band was at seven-thirty. But there's no hurry.' Grace sipped her rum. 'So what did you do this afternoon?'

'Read a book. But you should have heard it out here earlier. It was like the battle of the bands.' Les pointed to his ghetto blaster on the table and told Grace how he was reading when all the people arrived and things started happening. So he put his book down and joined in over a few beers.

'What were you reading?' asked Grace.

'*The Perfect Storm* by Sebastian Junger. Before that, however, I was reading *Narooma's Glorious Past* by Jasmine — someone-or-other?'

'Cunneen,' answered Grace.

'That's her.' Les had a sip of bourbon and looked pensively at Grace. 'You didn't tell me what a ravishing beauty Gwendolyn was, Grace.'

Grace pursed her lips. 'You saw the photo, Les.'

'Saw it? I'll probably have nightmares.'

'Yes,' agreed Grace. 'Young Gwendoline was something else. Wasn't she?'

'Yeah. A sumo wrestler in drag.'

Grace looked out over the railing. 'Just think, Les. Edward and Gwendolyn probably held hands and made love on this very land.'

'How truly romantic,' said Les. 'Lucky Edward.'

Grace turned to Les. 'You have to wonder what he used to stop her from rolling down the hill. Logs, rope, giant tent pegs ...?' Grace put her hands over her mouth and looked around. 'Ooh. I shouldn't have said that.'

'No, you shouldn't,' chuckled Les, having to look away. 'I also found a photo of the Merrigans. They looked fairly normal.'

'Yes,' agreed Grace. 'About your average, eighteen fifties nuclear family. Except young Eachan looks like he's just entered the twilight zone.'

Les raised his glass. 'You haven't got a bad turn of phrase, Grace.' Grace was about to say something when Les noticed headlights pulling up in the driveway. They stayed on for a moment, then they were switched off. 'Hello,' said Les. 'I've got an idea who this might be.'

'Your friends?'

'Something like that.' A minute or so later there was a loud banging on the front door. Les placed his drink on the table. 'I won't be a minute.'

Les walked through the house and opened the front door. Warren was standing one step below wearing a black tracksuit and cap, with a bag in each hand. He looked like he was ready to kill someone.

'Yes,' said Norton. 'Can I help you at all, mate?'

'Ohh get fucked will you,' Warren exploded. 'Why don't you park your car right outside the front fuckin door, and take up the whole fuckin driveway. You dopey-looking cunt.'

'I thought I had.' Les moved aside to let Warren in. 'So how was the drive down? They say the south coast is beautiful this time of the year.'

Warren glared at Les. 'How was the drive down … How do you think the fuckin drive down was? Fuckin hell! I didn't think I was ever going to fuckin get here. And if I have to listen to another one of Clover's fuckin Bob Dylan CDs I'll smash the fuckin thing over her head.'

Les closed the door. 'Where is Clover?'

'I dropped her off at her place. Fuck! That was another shitfight. Getting from fuckin Dalmeny back to here at night. You should have …' Warren stopped and looked around. 'Hey. So this is the old house. Fuck me.'

'Haven't you been in here before?' said Les.

'No. Shit! What about all these old photos and paintings?' Warren had a look in the kitchen and bathroom. 'Hey this joint's fuckin unreal.'

'I'm in that bedroom. There's one across the hall and another off the loungeroom.'

Warren had a look at the bedroom in the hall, then followed Les into the loungeroom. 'I'll take that one.' Warren threw his bag on the double bed and came back out. 'Fuck! What about all the grouse old furniture? Check the old fuckin piano.' Then Warren noticed something missing. 'Hey, wait a minute,' he said. 'There's no fuckin

TV. Where's the fuckin TV? You've taken it into your room, haven't you? You big cunt.'

Les placed a soothing hand on Warren's shoulder. 'Warren. They didn't have TV during the First World War. Anyway, come out onto the verandah.'

Warren followed Les and stopped dead when he saw Grace standing next to the table. 'Shit! How long have you been there?'

Grace raised her glass. 'This is my first drink.'

'Grace, this is Warren. Warren, this is Grace.'

'Hello Grace,' said Warren. 'How are you?'

'I'm fine thank you, Warren. Les told me about you. Where's Clover?'

'She's ... she's at her parent's place. She'll be here later.' Warren stared at Grace, then turned to Les.

'Would you like a drink, Woz?' asked Les.

'Yeah. I wouldn't mind.'

'There's Jackies and ice in the kitchen. Help yourself.'

'Okay.' Warren had another look at Clover, then headed for the kitchen.

Grace smiled at Les. 'So that's Warren.'

Les smiled back and picked up his drink. 'That's him. AKA, the boarder.'

It didn't take Warren long to knock up a double, triple Jack Daniels and return to the verandah. 'Well, cheers everyone,' he said.

Les raised his glass. Grace spoke. 'So how was the drive down, Warren?'

Warren winced as the bourbon bit in. 'Oh, it was ... nice. The south coast's quite lovely this time of the year.'

'Yes it is,' nodded Grace.

'Are you from down here?'

'Central Tilba.'

Warren had another hit on his drink. 'So where do you know gorilla-head from?'

'You mean Les? We met last night. I'm going to help fix his back.'

'He's not still putting on the bad back act is he?' said Warren. 'There's nothing wrong with it, you know.'

'Is this true, Les?' asked Grace. 'You told me you were in agony.'

Les shook his head and held up his empty glass. 'How about we have a refill.'

Grace handed Les her glass. He went out to the kitchen and made two fresh drinks. When he got back to the verandah, Warren and Grace were talking and laughing away. Les handed Grace another Bacardi and orange.

Grace thanked Les and put her drink on the table. 'I might go to the loo,' she said.

Warren waited till Grace was halfway down the hall and turned to Les. 'Fuck! Where did you find her?'

Les gave a casual shrug. 'You know how it is, Woz. They find me.'

'She's not a bad sort,' said Warren, sucking lustily on his JD. 'What about her set?'

'You noticed, Woz.'

'Christ! How could you miss it.'

Les took a sip of JD also. 'So what's doing with Clover? How long before she'll be here?'

'I don't know,' answered Warren. 'About an hour or so.'

Les looked at his watch. 'Well instead of waiting around, we might meet you down there.'

'Please yourself,' said Warren. 'I want to have a shower and unpack my gear anyway.'

'Okay,' said Les. 'I've been to the supermarket. There's coffee and tea and all that in the kitchen, as well as booze.'

'Good on you.'

Warren offered Les some money. Les told him not to worry about it. Then Grace returned. She got her drink from the table and smiled at the boys.

'Warren doesn't know for sure how long Clover's going to be,' said Les. 'So I suggested we meet them down there.'

'She might be a while,' added Warren. 'And I still have to get cleaned up.'

'Suits me,' nodded Grace. 'Little Charlie and the Nightcats are on in about half an hour.'

'Did you say Little Charlie and the Nightcats?' chorused Les and Warren.

'Yes. Haven't you got a program.'

Les shook his head. 'I got a brochure with the tickets. But no program.'

'They never sent you a program?' queried Grace.

'Haven't you told Grace how you got the tickets?' said Warren.

'Didn't you buy them like everybody else?' asked Grace.

'Not really,' said Les. He explained to Grace how he managed to get the tickets. 'So in a way Grace, if I hadn't bumped into The Zap, we probably wouldn't be here.'

'That's not a bad bartering system you have in Bondi,' said Grace.

'It's another world up there. Believe me,' said Les.

Warren gave Les a punch on the arm, 'Where he's known as Lucky Les.'

'I wish.' Norton raised his empty glass. 'Well, what do you reckon Grace? We make a move?'

'That might be a good idea,' agreed Grace. She turned to Warren. 'There's a souvenir stall inside where they sell T-shirts and CDs. How about we meet you and Clover there after Little Charlie?'

'No problem,' said Warren. 'We'll find it and wait for you.'

They proceeded inside. Grace got her bag from the kitchen. Warren made himself another drink. Les got his camera and gave Warren the key, telling him to leave it under the mat. They said goodbye and Warren started to unpack.

Les and Grace walked down the hill and around the jetty and joined the crowd. It was a different scene to the evening before when Les had the place almost to himself. Now there were people everywhere, heading for the festival. Music was coming from inside the park and just past the local pool was an entry for the performers and their trucks with security people in black standing on either side. They rounded the corner and joined a queue at the entrance next to the tourist centre. Les handed over his ticket and was given a plastic tag to put round his wrist that he was assured would stay on for the three days, then Grace had her bag politely searched and they went inside.

There were people everywhere, but the park was long and wide so there was no shortage of room. The souvenir stall selling T-shirts and

CDs was on the left next to some other stalls and opposite was a big red and blue tent with a stage and seating. Further on to the right was a much larger red and yellow tent and round to the left was a smaller green one. Between the largest tent and the entry backstage, a striped booze tent was doing a roaring business. Overlooking everything were two huge trailers full of Portaloos.

Les glanced at his watch. 'Why don't we have a quick look around before Little Charlie comes on,' said Les.

'Okay,' said Grace.

With Grace by his side Les checked out the rest of the park. At the far end were food and drink stalls selling everything from chilli-dogs to authentic bush tucker, from fresh fruit juice to Turkish cuisine and Thai noodles. Other stalls sold alien masks and new age clothing, bottles of oil, jewellery, all sorts of things; and doing a brisk business. Grace went to get two orange juices while Les cast an eye over the punters.

There were plenty of young people. But definitely no ravers with bottles of mineral water. Most of the crowd were in their late thirties and on and some people had brought their kids with them. The dress code was very casual. Plenty of leather and denim, baseball caps and Akubras. Vests and cowboy boots and T-shirts saying what the owner drank or where they came from. The men were all shapes and sizes with a sprinkling of Willie Nelson and ZZ Top look-alikes. The women were either fit with big breasts and long hair, and squeezed into faded jeans, or had their hair shorter and their clothes looser and appeared more into taking life easy. In general, the crowd was pretty much Aussie working class. All enjoying the music and the food, definitely enjoying a drink; and everybody with a smile on their face. Grace came back with two fresh squeezed orange juices and handed one to Les.

'Hey this could be all right,' said Les, picking up a good vibe in the air.

'It always is,' replied Grace. 'And the weather's good this time of year too.'

'It's definitely not cold tonight.'

'Why don't we head over to the tent and find a seat? The band will be on in a few minutes.'

'I'll follow you.'

They weaved their way through the crowd across to the big tent and fluked two seats on the side about ten back from the stage. The stage was all set up and they weren't there long before a huge man, with dark hair and a long face and wearing jeans and a Blues Festival T-shirt, came out on stage. He towered over the microphone and adjusted it to suit him.

'Christ! Check the size of this bloke,' said Les.

'That's the guy that runs the festival,' said Grace. 'Norman Dadd. Everybody calls him Daddy.'

'I wouldn't like to call him names,' said Les. 'He's a big boy.'

'I'll introduce you later. I've known Norm and his wife for years.'

Daddy tapped the microphone and started talking. He had a booming voice and didn't like to waste words.

'Righto,' he said. 'I want to welcome youse all to the South Coast Blues Festival. I know youse are gonna have a good time. And it's good to see youse all again. Now I want youse to give a big South Coast welcome to one of the stars of the show. All the way from the west coast of America. Come on. Put your hands together for … Little Charlie and the Nightcats!'

Three men, an Afro-American and two whites, walked out on stage led by Ric Estrin, wearing dark glasses, an oyster grey suit, a white shirt with a hand-painted silk tie and two-tone shoes. He looked immaculate and confidently took hold of the mike.

'Alllriiiggght,' he said, as the band got behind their instruments. 'I just want to say how great it is to be here in Narooma.' Ric took out his harp, nodded one, two, three four to the band, and then they slipped straight into 'Dump That Chump'. Seconds later the whole tent was rocking.

'Hey, how good's this?' said Les, bopping around in his seat.

'Open your orange juice,' said Grace.

Les took the lid off and Grace tilted a hip flask into it. 'What's this?' asked Les.

'Stolly.'

'Well done, Grace.' Les took a sip, gasped and kept on bopping.

Little Charlie and the Nightcats ripped into everything from 'Don't Do It' to 'Gerontology'. And brought the house down. Between bopping and drinking vodka, Les and Grace managed to get some good photos. The band did one encore, 'I'm Just Lucky That Way'. Then walked off to a standing ovation. Les had a glow from the vodka and so did Grace.

'Weren't they good,' said Grace.

'Were they what!' agreed Les. He looked at his watch. 'I suppose we'd better find Warren and Clover.'

'Yes. We don't want him getting all excited again,' said Grace.

They got up with the rest of the crowd leaving the tent and walked over to the souvenir stall where Les immediately started to drool at the stacks of CDs on sale. He made a mental note to come back with his Visa card and fill his overnight bag. Les felt Grace tap him on the shoulder and turned around as Warren and Clover walked up. Warren was wearing designer jeans, a shiny, grey shirt and a black leather jacket. Clover had on a powder blue top an inch above her navel, a denim mini with a white belt six inches below her navel and red, white and blue cowboy boots.

'Hello Clover,' said Les. 'How are you sweetheart?'

'Good Les,' smiled Clover. 'The house all right?'

'All right? It's sensational. Clover, this is Grace.'

'Hello Grace.'

'Hi Clover.'

Clover looked at Grace for a moment. 'I think I know you. Do you work at a craft shop in Central Tilba?'

'Sometimes,' said Grace. 'My friend Elysia owns it. I sell T-shirts there.'

'Grace Holt originals.' Clover pointed to Grace's T-shirt. 'You're wearing one now.'

'That's right.'

'They're beautiful.'

'Thank you,' smiled Grace.

Les gestured. 'Well, there you go. We're all friends.'

'We just caught the last of Little Charlie and the Nightcats,' said Warren. 'Can he play a harp or what?'

'He doesn't dress too bad either,' said Les.

At that moment, Ric Estrin came over to the souvenir tent to sign autographs and CDs. Considering he'd just performed a scorching gig, he still looked immaculate; not a hair out of place, not a crease in his suit. Coming through the crowd behind him was Norm Dadd. It looked like a tree moving across the park.

He got near and Grace called out 'Daddy'.

Norm looked around. 'Amazing,' he boomed. 'How are you? Everything okay? You got your ticket? You got in all right?'

'Yes thanks,' she answered, reaching up to give the big man a kiss on the cheek. 'Daddy, I want you to meet some friends of mine.' She introduced the three of them, then Daddy looked at Les.

'Les Norton. You work at the Kelly Club with George Brennan.'

'That's . . . right,' hesitated Les.

'George and I are old mates. When I lived at Balmain, we knocked around together.'

'Go on.' Les recollected Norm waiting in a car outside the Kelly Club one night to give George a lift home.

Daddy nodded slowly. 'He told me a bit about you.' Les discreetly placed his index finger in front of his mouth. Daddy understood. 'About when you played football,' he said.

'Yeah. I played for Easts,' said Les. 'But I didn't last long.'

'When did you get here?' asked Daddy.

'In Narooma?' said Les. 'I arrived here late Thursday night.'

'Late?' said Daddy.

Les picked up a certain tone in Daddy's voice and a twinkle in his eye. 'Yeah. I saw the end of the battle of the bands up at the golf links. Then I had a drink at Lawson's hotel. That's where I met Grace.'

'You'll have to come down the other pub and have a drink,' said Daddy. 'McBride's.'

'I intend to,' replied Les. 'I met Olney the chef last night.'

'Olney's a good chef,' said Norm. 'So where are you staying down here, Les?'

'Clover's parent's own a big house in Browning Street. Warren and I are staying there.'

'The old Merrigan house?'

'That's the one. You know, Norm,' said Les, 'there's something I've always wanted to know about George.'

'Oh. What's that Les?'

Les winked at Grace. 'Excuse me a second.' He pulled Daddy aside. 'Are you on to me about what happened in the hotel last night, Norm?' Les said quietly in his ear.

Daddy nodded. 'I was in the bottle shop, and I thought I saw you running out of the hotel. I wasn't sure if it was you. But when I saw what had happened inside, I knew who it was.'

'You haven't told anybody?'

Norm shook his head. 'No. There's half-a-dozen descriptions of you getting around. But one of them's right on the money. So be careful. One of the blokes you flattened has got a real nutty nephew. And he runs with a bad team.'

'So I heard.'

'Any trouble, come and see me. I'll see what I can do.'

'Thanks Norm.' Les slapped Daddy on the shoulder and laughed. 'So that was George.'

'Yeah. That was him all right,' said Norm. He was about to say something else, when a solid bloke with fair hair, wearing a Blues Festival T-shirt and an urgent look on his face came over. 'What's up Spike?' asked Norm.

'One of the women's toilets is playing up, Daddy,' said Spike.

'Ohh shit!' cursed Norm.

'That's part of the problem,' said Spike.

'I have to go,' said Daddy. 'I'll see youse all later. See you, Les.'

'Yeah. Nice to meet you, Norm,' he replied.

The others said goodbye then Warren turned to Les. 'What was that all about?' he asked.

'Oh, George got barred from a hotel in Balmain for fighting,' said Les. 'But he'd never admit it.'

'Knowing George,' said Warren, 'he'd never admit to anything.'

Grace had been to the souvenir tent. She handed Warren and Les a program each. 'There you are,' she said. 'Now you know what's going on.'

'Thanks Grace,' said Les.

'So what are we doing now?' asked Clover.

'Blue Katz are on in fifteen minutes,' said Grace. 'In the middle tent.'

'Blue Katz,' said Les. 'They'll do me.'

'I got time to get some cool ones,' said Warren.

Les looked at Warren, who seemed to be a little on the nod. 'Did you have a few more cool ones after we left?' asked Les.

Warren nodded. 'And a hot one.'

'He's half wasted,' said Clover.

'I'll give you a hand with the drinks,' said Les.

Les and Warren left the girls and walked over to the drink tent. Warren bought four tickets and went to the bar. While Les was waiting for Warren to get served, he didn't notice he was getting a very deliberate once up and down from a beefy bloke with lank black hair, wearing a Jim Beam T-shirt and an earring. The bloke was also waiting for a mate at the bar, who was wearing a red T-shirt. When the bloke in the red T-shirt came back with four drinks, the bloke with the earring pointed Les out. They both gave Norton a very heavy perusal before taking the drinks over to the two denim-clad women they were with. Warren got the drinks, Les took two and they walked back to the souvenir tent. Les handed Grace a Bacardi and took a sip of JD.

'We'd better see if we can find a seat,' suggested Grace.

'Yeah,' yawned Warren. 'I'm knackered. And my back's that stiff from the drive down.'

'Ohh shit, Warren,' said Les. 'Not your back.'

They found four seats on the aisle behind each other. Warren and Clover took the front two, Les and Grace sat behind. They weren't there long when a dark-haired bloke in a Blues Festival T-shirt walked out on stage and took hold of the mike. He had a husky voice and was even more succinct than Daddy.

'Ladies and gentlemen. All the way from South Australia, will you please welcome Blue Katz!'

To generous applause from the people seated, or standing around the tent, the three-piece band came on stage. They were all dressed fairly neatly. But the leader in a dark blue suit and hand-painted tie could have almost given Ric Estrin a run for his money. Without any further to do, Blue Katz slipped into 'Beef Bong Boogie'. Soon the tent was rocking, people were clapping, others were up in front of the stage dancing. Les told Grace he'd have to put any dancing on hold for the time being; Grace understood. Warren was too tired for any dancing and Clover was content to sit and get into the music.

Blue Katz cruised through 'Katman', 'Louise Louise' and 'Red Hot'. More tracks from their CDs, and for their encore did 'Rock Big Daddy Rock'. Then they left the stage to thunderous applause and much whistling. Norton's hands were sore from clapping, but he got some good photos over Warren's head. Grace took some in front of the band. The four of them waited for the tent to empty a little.

'Well, that's one of the best nights of boogie I've had in a while,' said Les.

'Yes. They were unreal,' said Clover. 'What did you think Warren?'

'Yeah. Great,' said Warren, stifling a yawn.

'I took some photos of the dancers,' said Grace. 'And I got one of this guy doing a spin just as his wig came off. I can't wait to get it developed.'

Les had his program out. 'It says on the program, Jacko's Blues Band is on at one o'clock tomorrow. I saw them in Cairns. They're a hoot.'

'If you're coming to see them, I might join you,' said Grace.

'I'll be here for sure,' said Les. 'That bloke in the war bonnet cracks me up.'

Sitting two seats behind, Les and the others hadn't noticed a bloke in a red T-shirt and another in a black Jim Beam T-shirt listening to their every word. The two men nodded to each other then got up with their women and left.

'Are you going back to Central Tilba tonight?' Clover asked Grace.

Grace shook her head. 'No. I'm staying with my girlfriend Belinda in Eastaway Avenue.'

'How are you getting home?' asked Clover.

'With her. She works at Lawson's Hotel. But I'm not sure what time she's finishing because of all the people in town.'

'Mum's picking me up at the house in about thirty minutes. We can give you a lift home if you like.'

'That'd be great, Clover. All right if we call in to the hotel for a second while I tell Belinda?'

'Sure.'

'There you go, Ugly,' smiled Warren. 'Saves you having to drive Grace home.'

'Yeah,' said Les, hoping Grace might have come back for a cool one.

Warren could read the look on Norton's face. 'Lucky Les,' he said. 'You've done it again.'

'Well, I suppose we'd better make a move,' said Clover. 'I don't want to keep mother waiting.'

'Yes. Come on Les,' smiled Grace. 'I'll help you up the hill. You poor old thing.'

'Thanks, Amazing,' he replied.

Part of the crowd were hanging back to see a Creole band still playing in the smaller tent. Les and the others joined the people leaving the park. It was only a short walk to the house and they discussed the bands they'd just seen, and cracked a few jokes. Warren yawned a few times while Les had one quick whinge about his back, then they were standing in front of the driveway.

'Do you want to wait inside?' asked Les.

'No thank you,' replied Grace.

'No. Me either,' said Clover.

'I don't know how you can just piss off and leave me like this,' sniffed Warren.

'It's … relatively easy Warren,' replied Clover. 'I simply say goodnight. And go home to mother.' She put her arms around Warren. 'But I'll be around for breakfast tomorrow darling, pet, dove.'

'Do you want to have breakfast again, Grace?' asked Les.

'Yes. That would be nice. Same place, same time?'

'Yeah. Carey's. Nine o'clock. You going to join us Clover? We had breakfast there this morning. It's pretty good.' Les winked at Grace. 'The view's not bad either.'

'I know Carey's,' replied Clover. 'But why don't we make it about ten. Have a bit of a sleep in.'

'Good idea,' said Warren.

'Okay then,' said Les. 'Ten o'clock it is.'

A metallic blue Holden station wagon with a woman behind the wheel pulled up out the front. The woman gave the horn a quick beep.

'Here's mum now,' said Clover.

Warren walked across to the car with Clover. Grace smiled and put her arms around Norton's neck.

'I had a lovely time tonight,' she said. 'Thanks Les.'

Les put his arms around Grace's waist. 'I didn't do much,' he shrugged.

'You didn't have to. You were just nice company.'

Les smiled. 'You weren't bad yourself.'

Grace returned Les's smile then kissed him full on the mouth. Her lips were warm and firm and Les returned the kiss avidly. He felt a tiny snap of Grace's hot, sweet tongue and was just getting into the swing of things when she stopped. Les opened his eyes and looked into Grace's.

'I'll see you in the morning, handsome,' she said.

'Okay,' said Les. 'See you then.'

'And when the band's finished ... we might take a look at your back.'

'Righto.'

Grace gave Les a quick kiss, untangled herself then walked across to the station wagon and got in the back seat next to Clover.

'See you, Clover,' Les called out.

Clover waved through the window. 'Bye Les.'

They drove off and Warren walked back. 'I left the key under the mat,' he said.

'Well, why don't you get it and open the door,' said Les.

'You're closest,' replied Warren. 'You open it. If you can get your fat arse round your car.'

Les shook his head, got the key and opened the door. He closed it behind them and turned the light on in the kitchen. 'You want a cup of tea or something.'

'No,' Warren called out from the bathroom. 'I'm fucked. I'm going to bed.'

'Yeah. Me too,' said Les. He left the electric jug and had a drink of water.

Warren propped in the doorway and yawned. 'I'll see you in the morning, dude. If you get up early, try not to wake me will you.'

'I'll be like a little mouse. See you in the morning, Woz.'

Warren dragged himself off to his bedroom. Les went to the bathroom, cleaned his teeth then started climbing out of his clothes and into his tracksuit. He looked at the bedroom window and decided to leave it open. If it got cold again he had plenty of blankets this time. He yawned, closed the bedroom door then switched off the light and got under the covers. Les thought about Clover for a while and mulled over what Daddy had told him. Before long, however, he was snoring. What sounded like thunder woke Les during the night and he noticed it was chilly again. But he went straight back to sleep.

Les had a dry mouth and a sore back when he got out of bed the next morning. But no hangover. Outside it looked like being another nice day. He stretched, got into a pair of shorts and went to open the bedroom door. It was jammed.

'What in the fuck!'

Les pulled and wrenched the solid old door, but it wouldn't budge. Something was jammed underneath. A piece of rusty metal. Les picked up a shoe and belted whatever it was back out, then opened the door. The piece of rusty metal was a horseshoe. Les picked it up, looked at it for a moment then placed it on the kitchen table and walked into the bathroom. Their shaving gear was scattered all around the floor, along with the towels, and there was water all over the toilet seat.

'What the ...?'

Les stared at the mess. Not the rat again, surely? Then a humourless smile appeared on his face. Warren. He'd stumbled into the bathroom during the night, pissed everywhere then thrown a wobbly looking for his headache tablets. Same as he did at home when he was out of it. The goose. Les cleaned up the mess, got himself together then walked into the kitchen. While he was waiting for the kettle to boil, the reason for the horseshoe sitting on the kitchen table dawned on him as well. Warren again. He would have had a good look around the house when he unpacked, gone downstairs half-tanked on bourbon with a torch, and spotted those old horseshoes. Would Warren go to all that trouble? Ohh shit yeah. Anything to annoy the landlord. That's why he kept calling him Lucky Les all night. And locking Lucky Les in his room with a horseshoe would be hilarious. Hah-hah-hah! But just to rain on Warren's parade, the landlord wasn't going to bite. Les picked up the horseshoe, opened the front door and threw the thing right up under the trees. It never happened. Les dusted his hands and shook his head. If you ask me, Woz has been in that advertising agency too long.

Les made a mug of tea and a couple of slices of toast and went out into the hallway. The door to the loungeroom was closed; Les opened it and stepped inside. The bear was on the piano facing the wall and Les could hear snoring coming from Warren's room. Les had half a mind to turn the bear on and push it inside Warren's door. Instead, he took his tea and toast out onto the verandah.

There were more clouds around than the day before and the southerly was up a little. But people were fishing or strolling around the jetty and the activity on the lagoon had increased. Les stared across the channel as he sipped his tea and ate his toast. He did a few light stretches and decided to walk around the golf links again. He rinsed his mug, changed into his training gear and set off.

With the southerly in his face, Les found the walk the same as the day before. Enjoyable, but again he would have loved to burst into a run. However, Les kept going, crisscrossing the greens, and before long he started to get a sweat up. He stopped at the beach and noted there were more fishermen than yesterday and the waves were bigger. Les touched at his toes a few times and attempted some sit-ups and crunches but was forced to give the idea a miss. So he headed home. Warren was still in bed. Les had a shower, got into a green Nautica T-shirt and cargos and walked up to get the paper. The two dive shops were open. Les called into the smaller one on the way back.

The counter was on the left with a doorway at the rear leading to a filling station. The wall behind the counter was arranged with certificates and the wall opposite was shelved with snorkelling gear and spear guns. The front of the shop was stacked with scuba tanks and racks of wetsuits, and on the wall near the front window were blown-up photos, as well as maps and posters. A fair-haired bloke, wearing a white T-shirt with Wagonga Dive Shop on the front was behind the counter, fiddling with a spear gun trigger mechanism. As Les approached, the bloke looked up and smiled.

'Yes mate? What can I do for you?' he asked, cheerfully.

'I'd like to take a trip out to Montague Island,' answered Les. 'Have a look around and do a bit of snorkelling.'

'Okay,' said the bloke. 'We're pretty well booked out till next week. But wait till I check.' At that moment the phone rang. 'I won't be a sec.'

The proprietor started talking on the phone and going through his bookings. Les browsed amongst the posters and photos on the wall. Even behind a face mask there was no mistaking the proprietor looking through the porthole of a rusting wreck and another of him stroking a big potato cod. One photo blown up to poster size stood out from the rest. Printed across the top was: 'How We Don't Run A Dive School'. In smaller print in the bottom right hand corner, it said: 'Photo By Ray Bissett'. The photo was taken at Ben Buckler the day Les was there with Ray and the diver drowned. Norton's face lit up. Well I'll be buggered, he thought.

Les stared at the poster-size photo in astonishment. It was like living the moment again in IMAX. He could see the anguish on the instructor's face as he worked on the diver he'd just rescued. Sense the shock and exhaustion amongst the other divers laying or milling around the rocks. You could pick out a woman diver standing apart from the others with her head down being sick. Les was amazed at the clarity and detail of the photo. He could read the brands on the wetsuits, spot a lock of light brown hair poking out from under the woman diver's hood. See the vomit on the face of the rescued diver. Almost count the barnacles on the rocks.

'Hey, you're in luck mate,' said the bloke, hanging up the phone. 'There's been a cancellation. And I can get you out there tomorrow morning.'

'Okay.' Les walked back to the counter. 'Hey mate, where did you get that big photo?'

'The photographer's a mate of mine,' replied the proprietor. 'He sent it to me and I had it blown up.'

'I was there the day that happened,' said Les, excitedly. 'I was with him.'

'You were with Ray? Really?'

Les told the proprietor how he'd arranged to get some tips from Ray on underwater photography, but it was too rough. Then they came across all the drama as they were walking back. 'Looking at that photo,' said Les, 'is just like being there again. It's uncanny.'

'It certainly is,' agreed the bloke.

'Where do you know Ray from?' asked Les.

'Ohh shit. We're old mates. I come from Clovelly. Me and Ray used to dive together all the time.'

'I'm only a snorkel sucker,' said Les. 'But I like underwater photography.'

'Well, you won't find a better bloke to teach you than Ray. He's won over ten awards.' The proprietor laughed. 'He's a funny bastard too.'

The proprietor's name was Ian. He could get Les on a boat called *The Kingfisher*, leaving the jetty at nine the next morning. And seeing Les was a friend of Ray's, he'd give him a ten percent discount. Les thanked him and paid with his Visa card.

'It's funny,' said Les. 'The day that happened, I was walking back along the beach and a surfer committed suicide.'

'That's right,' said Ian. 'I saw it on the news. What a day.'

'It was.' Les shook his head. 'I don't know about surfing, Ian. But you can keep scuba diving. I had one go at it. I'll stick to snorkelling.'

'Yeah. I know what you mean,' said Ian. 'You got to be super careful. Any people we take out, we give them the full-on, silkworm treatment.' Ian glanced over at the photo. 'I'd hate to have something like that on my conscience.' As he spoke, a young Japanese couple walked in. The man was wearing Coke bottle glasses, the woman was about four feet tall and looked like she'd never been in anything deeper than a spa bath. 'Hello,' winked Ian. 'Talking about silkworms ... Mushi, mushi.' The two Japanese smiled and bowed towards the counter.

'I'll leave you to it, Ian,' said Les, waving his receipt. 'Thanks for everything,'

'No problem, Les. Have a good time out there.'

Les pocketed his receipt and walked back to the house. The front door was open, Warren was in the kitchen in a T-shirt and shorts holding a glass of orange juice and Glen Miller was swinging in the loungeroom.

'Hello,' said Les. 'You finally dragged yourself out of bed.'

'Hey, what about this fuckin unreal radio station,' said Warren. 'They've just played Cab Calloway, The Andrew Sisters, Rudy Vallee. If I'd known about this, I would have brought my white dinner jacket.'

'Maybe Brian Ferry'll lend you one of his.' Les tossed the paper on the table, got a glass of water and looked at Warren. 'So how are you this morning, Woz?' he asked.

'All right,' answered Warren, glancing at the headlines. 'But Jesus! Doesn't it get cold down here.'

'Cold?'

'Yeah. That room's like a fuckin deep freeze. I had to get up and put every blanket I could find on the bed. I felt like Omar Sharif in *Doctor Zhivago*.'

'It did get a bit chilly at one stage last night,' admitted Les.

'Oh and one other thing, Les,' said Warren. 'I know you like your little jokes and all that. But did you have to get up in the middle of the night and play the fuckin piano? And set that stupid bloody bear off?'

'*I* was playing the piano last night, Woz?'

'By playing, I mean clunking up and down on it like a moron. I'm in there freezing to death, trying to get to sleep. And you're playing Elton John.' Warren turned back to the headlines. 'But if that's what turns you on, so be it.'

'Warren. I've got some news for you, mate.' Les told Warren about finding the mess in the kitchen the day before then got a rat-trap from the pantry to prove his point. 'So there's rats in here. They get in the kitchen and they like to run up and down on the piano. I meant to set this last night. But I forgot.' Les put the rat-trap back in the pantry. 'As for the bear, there's something wrong with it. It goes off on its own.'

'It wasn't you then?' said Warren.

'No Warren. It wasn't me,' said Les, deliberately. 'I don't do childish fuckin things.'

Warren shrugged. 'If you say so. Actually the bear's a ripper. Clover had it going. She loves the bloody thing. Where did you get it?'

Les told Warren where he got it and how much it cost. 'I might give it to Clover for letting us have the house.' Les looked at his watch. 'They should be here soon.'

'Ohh yeah, for sure. Clover thinks punctuality has to do with flat tyres.'

Les read the paper out on the verandah, then gave it to Warren and tidied up his room. Warren read it then they both sat on the verandah, enjoying the view. A couple of ghetto blasters were playing CDs on the surrounding balconies.

But Warren insisted on listening to Season FM. He was tapping his toes to Andy Kirk and his Twelve Clouds of Joy playing 'Boogie Woogie Cocktail', when there was a knock on the door just before eleven.

'Look at that,' said Warren, holding up his watch. 'Right on time.'

Footsteps sounded along the hallway then Grace and Clover stepped out onto the verandah. Grace was wearing faded jeans and one of her originals in white, with a beige pelican on the front. Clover was wearing hipsters, and a blue Hawaiian shirt four sizes too big for her. There were pecks on the cheek and smiles and greetings all round, then Grace and Clover leant against the railing sizing the boys up. Grace spoke first.

'So how did you sleep last night?' she asked.

'Yes. Did you sleep all right?' said Clover.

'Yeah. It got a bit chilly at one stage,' said Les. 'But I was okay.'

'Forget chilly,' said Warren. 'It was bloody freezing. I've never been so cold in my life.'

Clover looked at Warren over her glasses. 'Freezing cold?'

'Where was it cold?' asked Grace.

'In my bedroom,' said Warren. 'Are there any electric blankets, Clover?'

Clover shook her head. 'Was there anything else besides the cold?'

'Only the rat in the piano,' smirked Warren. 'And the bear going off.'

'Rat in the piano?' said Clover.

'Yeah,' replied Les. He told them about the noise the night before, then waking up to the mess in the kitchen and finding the rat-traps in the pantry. 'Only I forgot to set the trap last night. Jerry Lee Rat'd be in rock 'n' roll heaven right now.'

'What was that about the bear going off, Warren?' asked Grace.

'Les said there's something wrong with it,' shrugged Warren.

'I think it's the batteries,' said Les. 'They're wired wrong.'

'And it went off on its own,' said Grace.

'Yeah. It even dances round in circles,' said Les. 'I told you, it's got a mind and style all of its own.'

'Anything else, Les?' asked Clover.

Les thought for a moment. But he didn't have the heart to tell Clover her boyfriend got up during the night and pissed all over the bathroom. 'No. Nothing else,' he replied.

Grace and Clover exchanged glances. 'A piano-playing rat and a dancing bear,' said Grace.

Clover shook her head. 'What next?'

'I'll tell you what's next,' said Warren. 'How about breakfast.' He glanced at his watch. 'Oh shit! Look at that. Ten o'clock already.'

'We stopped to pick some flowers,' said Clover.

'You could have picked half of Amsterdam.' Warren got to his feet. 'Come on, let's go. Whose car are we taking?'

'Car?' said Grace. 'It's five minutes up the hill.'

'There's a hill?' said Warren.

Les locked the front door, Grace locked her Jackaroo and they set off. Les told them about booking a trip to Montague Island and about the photo in the dive shop. They crossed the road, wended their way through the Saturday morning crowd and were soon at Carey's.

The restaurant was packed; even the tables outside were taken. But they were lucky enough to arrive just as four people were getting up from the same table Les and Grace had the day before. They ordered, Les picked up the tab, then they got their little wooden objects and sat down. This time Les got a banana. Their coffees arrived and they got into a bit of chitchat about the night before, about clothes, the house. Les told Clover about the photo of Lander Merrigan in Jasmine Cunneen's book.

'That was my great, great uncle,' said Clover. 'We've got the original photo at home. Poor old Lander and his wife were drowned.'

'Yeah, Grace told me,' said Les. 'And their son Eachan finished in the rathouse.'

'My hundred-and-forty-eighth cousin removed, or something,' said Clover.

'So how did your parents end up with the house?' asked Les.

'It's been in the family for years. Now dad owns it.'

'It's the most beautiful house,' said Grace.

'How come your parents don't live there?' asked Warren. 'It's a fantastic spot.'

'They're happy at Dalmeny,' said Clover.

'Do you ever rent it out?' asked Les.

'Now and again. But only to people we know.'

'Your hunk of a boyfriend, Warren

 punched him on the shoulder. 'That's

hey had a lovely, long breakfast talking and
Varren ordered more coffees and they
n. When they finished their second coffees
ve. On the way home, Les called into the
s the photo. Ian was on the phone again;
inted the photo out to the others. They were impressed. Grace was still talking about it when they were standing on the verandah back at the house.

'That's hard to imagine,' she said. 'You see one drowning. Then you walk along the beach and see another.'

'Yeah. Poor bloody Edwin,' said Les.

'He was such a nice person,' said Clover. 'Everybody liked him.'

'Bad luck about his girlfriend,' grunted Les.

'Yes,' said Clover. 'You and Serina never quite hit it off, did you?'

'I'd like to hit it off with her. With a size twelve Doc Marten. Right up her thrill-seeking Khyber.'

'Now don't be like that, Les,' smiled Clover.

'I still can't get over the view from here,' said Grace, looking out across the channel. 'It's so beautiful.'

Les snapped his fingers. 'Hey, I just thought of something. I won't be a minute.'

Les got his keys and walked out to the car. He'd completely forgotten that the stabilising binoculars Eddie had given him were still in the boot. He got them out and returned to the verandah.

'Have a look at the view through these, Grace,' he said, taking them out of their case and handing them to her.

Grace held them to her eyes. 'Oh yes. Don't these make a difference!' She had a good look around then handed them to Clover.

'Look at that,' said Clover. 'I can see right up to Dalmeny. These are great, Les. Where did you get them?'

'Off a friend,' said Les. 'I forgot they were in the car.'

They all had a look then realised it was time to make a move if they were going to see Jimbo's Blues Band. They left the house and walked down to the Festival. At the entrance they showed their wrist tags and joined the people inside.

'Does anybody want a cool one?' asked Warren.

'Not on top of all that food,' said Clover.

Les agreed. 'Count me out.'

Grace pointed out the big tent where Jimbo was playing. 'Why don't we find a seat?'

There were plenty of people around, but it wasn't as crowded as the night before. They got four seats, six back from the stage, and weren't there long before Jimbo strolled on stage wearing a red hat and a Hawaiian shirt. The band followed and Jimbo walked up to the mike. He rambled away about having a singalong, then produced a piece of cardboard with the lyrics to 'What A Wonderful World This Would Be' on it.

'So you got it,' he said pointing to the words. 'Don't know much about ... Don't know what a ... Okay. Here we go.'

The crowd got into into it. Les and the others sang along. When the band finished that song, they slipped straight into 'Bye Bye Baby'. And behind all the fooling around, Jimbo and his band were tighter than a vice done up, and he had one of the best blues voices in the business. They scorched it and several other songs. Les and Grace took photos. The band played some more howling rock, then Jimbo stood on his head and sang two songs. He stood up, put on his Indian war bonnet and wore it till they finished the set. They did 'Statesborough Blues' for an encore and finished to a tumultuous applause.

'That guy,' said Clover. 'He is ... what can I say?'

'They can boogie,' said Warren. 'I know that.'

Grace pointed to her program. 'They're on again tomorrow.'

'I'll be here,' said Les.

Warren rose to his feet. 'I got to have a snakes.'

'Okay.' Clover pointed towards the middle of the park. 'See that table and bench seats? We'll wait for you there. You want anything?'

'Yeah. Grab me a fruit juice, will you.'

Warren left for the toilet. The others moved across to the wooden table. Clover and Grace went for the drinks while Les minded their bags, then they stood around waiting for Warren. They finished their fruit juices and after a while Les looked at his watch.

'Where's Warren gone for a leak?' he said. 'The state forest?'

'Yes,' agreed Clover. 'He's certainly taking his time.'

'He might have stopped at the souvenir stall,' suggested Grace.

A minute or two later, Warren appeared walking unsteadily through the crowd. He looked pale and the two men who had been checking Les out the night before were standing on either side of him. One was holding Warren's arm and another man with a thick moustache followed behind. Walking in front as if he owned the park, was a tall, heavy-framed man with thick, tattooed arms, wearing black jeans and a yellow Big Rock Fishing Club polo shirt. He had a mop of unruly black hair pushed back from a wide, bony forehead, and on either side of a flat nose, two beady, dark eyes glared menacingly at everything in sight.

'Oh shit,' said Grace. 'It's Morgan bloody Scully.'

The man holding Warren pushed him towards Les and the others. Warren bumped against the table and Clover took hold of his arm.

The tall man gave Les a heavy once up and down. 'So you're Les Norton.' He had a dull, rasping voice and when he opened his mouth, his teeth looked like a row of charred railway sleepers. 'You're a shitty fuckin waiter. You live in Cox Ave Bondi. And this is your little bumboy, Warren Edwards.'

'I don't know what's going on, Les,' said Warren. 'They grabbed me coming out the toilet and went through my wallet. They found out where we live and I told them you were a waiter.'

'That's okay, Woz,' said Les. 'Are you all right?'

Warren winced and held his stomach. 'Yeah. I'm all right.'

Les turned to the tall man. 'Okay. That's me. I'm a waiter. I work in a restaurant at Bondi. Now what's your problem . . . ?'

'Morgan,' rasped the man in the polo shirt. 'And you're the cunt with the problem. That was my uncle, and his mates, you bashed up in the pub last night.'

Les slowly shook his head. 'I'm not sure ...'

'Ohh don't give me the fuckin shits,' snapped Morgan. 'It was you.'

'All right,' said Les, tightly. 'It was me. So what?'

'So what?' Morgan's eyes blazed. 'So you're pretty good bashing up old blokes when they're drunk. Let's see how you go against someone a bit younger.' Morgan jabbed a thumb in his chest. 'Me.'

'You want to fight me over those four clowns?' said Les. 'You're kidding.'

'No I'm not fuckin kiddin'.' Morgan nodded towards the entrance. 'You and me. Outside.'

Norton's mind started racing. He was seething at what Morgan and his thugs had done to poor Warren and under normal circumstances he would have ripped straight into Morgan on the spot, big and all as he was. But these weren't normal circumstances. Norton's back was buggered. If he went outside he was on a hiding to nothing. And even if could put up half a fight, Morgan had three big mates with him. It was time for Les to do a Brer Rabbit. And Brer Rabbit better be able to tap dance pretty bloody fast. At that moment Norman Dadd loomed up in a bulky T-shirt and jeans with four nervous-looking security people.

'Not in here, Morgan,' he said, loud and clear.

'Ohh don't shit yourself, Daddy,' said Morgan. 'Nothing's gonna happen in here.' He turned and glared at Norton. 'But it will outside.'

Les looked back at Morgan and half smiled. 'Hang on a moment, Morgan,' he said easily. 'You're going about this all the wrong way, baby. You're blowing your cool.'

Morgan glowered at Les. 'I'm what?'

'You're blowing your cool, brother. When you come to a fork in the road, take it. You're walking backwards when you should be putting your best foot forward. There's fire in your eyes, but you got water on the brain. You're surrounded by yes men and stuck in nowheresville. You've got the world on a string and enough rope to hang yourself.'

'What the ...?'

'You're that far down, Morgan,' continued Les, 'rock bottom is three flights up. Someone's pulled the rug from over your eyes. You're a cool swinger, but you can't handle the heat. You've got to roll off your high end and adjust your tone control dude. Opportunity's knocking ...'

Morgan's face coloured and he turned to his team. 'What's this cunt talking about?'

'I don't know,' shrugged the man with the moustache. 'But fuck him anyway.'

'What am I talking about?' said Les. 'What am I saying? What am I trying to tell you? Is that what you're asking me?'

'I'm not asking you anything,' said Morgan. 'I just fuckin want you outside.'

'That's what I'm saying,' said Les. 'Anything and everything. And anything's better than nothing.' Les smiled at Morgan. 'In other words, why don't we do it for money?'

Morgan stared at Les, looked at his mates for a moment then stared back to Les. 'For what?'

'For money,' said Les. 'I'll fight you for five thousand dollars.' Les watched Morgan's eyes knit together and he could hear the boulders slowly rumbling around behind the big man's forehead. Morgan's mates stayed quiet. Standing in front of his security staff, Daddy looked surprised as well as interested. Warren and the others were still mystified.

'Well. What do you say, Morgan?' said Les.

'I'm ...'

'Look at it this way, Morgan,' said Les. 'If we go outside and fight, the cops'll come and break it up. We'll both get pinched and it'll cost you money. I'll leave town still in one piece. And you'll have proved nothing. Right?' Morgan half nodded in agreement. 'There's no way I can beat you,' continued Les. 'But with money riding on the result, at least I'll have a go.' Les gestured to Morgan. 'Well. What do you reckon? You're a big, hard man. Are you game enough to back yourself in a fight?'

'He's got a point there, Morgan,' said Daddy. 'Are you game?'

'Game? Of course I'm fuckin game,' asserted Morgan.

'Have you got five grand?' said Daddy.

'Yeah.'

'Righto,' said Les. 'Then it's on. In here one o'clock Monday afternoon after lunch, when there's no one around. Just the blokes packing up.' Les motioned for Morgan and Daddy to come in closer. 'That all right with you?' he asked Morgan.

'Yeah,' grunted Morgan.

'Will you hold the money, Norm?'

'No worries,' said Norm.

'I'll have my five grand here in half an hour. Can you do that?'

'Yeah,' nodded Morgan.

'And if anybody gets pissed and starts fighting before Monday, he forfeits his money. Right?'

Morgan nodded morosely. 'Right.'

'Good idea,' said Norm.

'Okay,' said Les, stepping back. 'That's the rules. We'll meet here again on Monday.'

Morgan pointed a calloused finger at Les. 'Forget the fuckin rules. You just be here Monday, you big-mouthed prick. Because if you're not, I know where you live. And I'll come looking for you.'

'He's not joking,' said Norm seriously. 'I know these blokes. They'll come after you all right.'

Les held his hands up. 'Fair enough. I'll be here.'

'Make sure you fuckin are.' Morgan gave the nod to his mates and they left.

There was a brittle silence for a moment as Les looked pensively around him, then caught Clover's eye.

'What in God's name was that all about?' she asked.

'How about I explain everything back at the house.' Les turned to Daddy. 'Norm. Okay if I have a word with you on your own?'

'Sure,' replied Daddy. 'Come over to the souvenir tent.'

Les caught Clover's eye again. 'I won't be long.'

Norm dismissed his four, relieved, security people. Les walked with him and the others as far as the souvenir tent, then followed Norm. At the rear of the tent was a caged-off annexe with a wire gate. Norm opened the gate and they stepped into a room full of T-shirts, cartons of CDs, brochures and other merchandise. There was a table and two plastic chairs in the middle. Norm sat down on one chair and Les sat facing him across the table on the other.

'Well Norm,' said Les. 'You saw what happened outside.'

'I sure did,' answered Norm. 'You're not bad on your feet, are you?'

'Norm. I've only got about a grand on me. And my credit cards. Can you spring me the five grand? You know me and who I run with. I'll have it back to you first thing next week.'

'Spring you the five grand?' said Norm. 'Mate, I'm backing you. I'm going to organise the side bets.' Norm grinned and rubbed his big hands together. 'You'll be the underdog. I'll get three to one.' Norm threw back his head and laughed. 'Morgan's bloody good. But he sure ain't you.'

'Norm. Before you get too carried away,' said Les, 'I've got a fucked back.'

'You've what?'

Les told Norm about his back and how he aggravated it in the fight. 'What I was mainly doing out there was buying time. I couldn't knock a sick pygmy off a piss pot at the moment.'

'Oh,' said Norm. 'That could be somewhat of a handicap if you're going to fight Morgan.'

'Yeah,' agreed Les. 'But I'm getting some treatment on my back. I might be all right.' Les looked directly at Norm. 'If not, I'll ring Eddie. He'll be here in four hours.'

Norm put his hands in front of him and looked away. 'I didn't hear that.'

'I know,' said Les. 'That is taking things to extremes. And I'll cop all the heat if the big goose suddenly disappears. But I don't fancy finishing up a cripple either.'

Norm stared at Les. 'So what happened in the pub?'

Les shook his head. 'It was half my fault.' He told Norm how the fight came about. How he lost his temper then simply went into the swing of things. 'In a way I don't blame that bloke for sticking up for his uncle. I did go a bit overboard, I suppose.'

'Hey,' said Norm. 'Don't be too concerned about sorting out old Mick and his mates. They're cunts. And my missus has had to go around Mick's place plenty of times and patch his wife up after Mick's had a few drinks.' There was a rap on the gate. It opened and a woman half the size of Daddy, with long dark hair and glasses walked in, wearing slacks and a Blues Festival T-shirt. 'Hello. Talking about wives,' said Norm. 'Here's the Handbrake now. Les this is Marina. Marina, Les Norton.'

'Hello Les.'

'Hello Marina. Nice to meet you.'

Marina looked at Norm. 'We need some more extra large T-shirts.'

'Okay. I'll bring them out.'

'And some Little Charlie CDs.'

'No worries.' Marina left and Norm turned back to Les. 'All right. I'll put up the five grand. What are you getting done to your back?'

'I don't know. Grace thinks she might be able to help me.'

'Amazing's working on you? Well, you're in good hands.' Norm lumbered to his feet then opened a drawer in the table. 'Before you go. Have this.' He handed Les a length of black cord, with a plastic ticket on a swivel that said: Narooma Blues Festival — GUEST.

'What's this?' asked Les.

'It lets you go backstage and meet the bands. Have a coffee and a bite to eat if you want.'

Les stood up and put the backstage pass in his pocket. 'Thanks Norm. That's unreal.'

'No worries,' said Daddy.

'And thanks, for everything else, Norm. I really appreciate it.'

'That's okay, Les. I'll see you later.'

'Yeah. See you.'

Norm started going through the cartons. Les left him to it and headed for home, instinctively looking around as he walked out the front of the park. But Les felt he was safe for the time being. Nothing would happen before Monday. When he got to the house the door was open and the others were out on the verandah with a pot of tea sitting on the table. The colour had returned to Warren's face, but he wasn't doing any stand-up comedy. They all stared silently at Les. Les gave them a weak smile and a half wave.

'Hi.'

'Yeah hi,' said Warren. He took a sip of tea. 'Shit it's good living with you, Les. Next time, as well as getting kidnapped, I might get knifed. Or shot.'

'Are you all right, mate?' asked Les, genuinely concerned.

'Yeah. One of those clowns punched me in the stomach, that's all.'

'Which one?'

Warren ran a finger across his top lip. 'Groucho Marx.'

'Right.' Les patted Warren on the shoulder. 'And thanks for the bit about the waiter, Woz. You're bloody staunch, mate.' Warren shrugged a non-reply.

Clover gave Norton a very calculated once up and down. 'All right Les,' she said. 'Exactly what is going on?'

Les indicated to the teapot. 'Okay if I have a cup of tea?'

Les poured himself a cup of tea, added milk and sugar and told the others the whole story. 'I suppose I should have told you about the fight. Except I felt like a dill and I honestly thought no one knew it was me. But they must have seen us out together. So they grabbed you, Woz, to get some info on me. Sorry about that mate.'

'So it was you all the time, that beat up Mick Scully and his friends,' said Grace.

'Yes Grace. It was me,' admitted Les.

Grace looked at Les and shook her head. 'You're certainly something else, Les. Aren't you?'

'I have to go to the toilet,' said Warren, getting out of his chair.

Clover put her hand on the pot. 'I'm going to put the kettle on again.'

They left, leaving Grace and an uncomfortable Les on the verandah.

'Yes. You're something else all right,' said Grace, continuing to stare at Les. 'One minute you're George from Canberra. You're staying at the Islander Motel. You had a terrible breakup with your girlfriend — oh, and I look like one of her friends. You hurt your back changing tyres. Then you're asking me about the fight and do they know who it was? Do you ever, sort of, get round to say, going within flying distance of the truth at all, Les?'

Les looked at Grace for a moment. 'Okay,' he said. 'I don't blame you having the shits with me. But I wasn't really lying to you, Grace. I was only trying to cover my arse. That's all.'

'Ohh yeah.'

'Look. What happened in the hotel was just bad luck. And you don't really think I want to fight this gorilla on Monday do you?

Christ! I'll probably get my head kicked in. As well as lose five thousand bucks. Which I just talked Daddy into putting up for me. And if I remember right, Grace, when I did mention the fight, you said "Oh, couldn't have happened to a nicer bunch of blokes. Pity Morgan wasn't there too." Right?'

Grace shook her head. 'Yes. But...'

'No buts. The thing is, Grace, you said you could help me with my back. And now I need your help. Bad. And that's the truth.'

'The truth?' said Grace. 'Hah!'

Clover returned with the jug of hot water and poured some in the teapot. Warren followed her out and sat down. Les looked at Grace who was staring at the ocean.

'So what's the story, Grace? Are you going to help me?'

Grace continued to stare at the ocean, then she looked at Norton. Finally she turned to Clover. 'Clover, have you got a biro in your bag?'

'Sure. Here you are.' Clover handed Grace a biro and a notebook.

Grace placed the notebook on the table and clicked the biro. 'Here's how you get to my place.'

A huge grin spread across Norton's face. 'Grace,' he said, 'you won't ever regret this. I promise.'

'Yeah, yeah.' Grace started writing directions on the piece of paper. 'Your name is Les, isn't it? That is your car out the front?' Grace paused for a second and looked around her. 'This *is* number three Browning Street?'

'Now come on, Grace,' said Les. 'Don't be like that.'

Grace drew a little map with her address and phone number on it and handed it to Les. 'I'll see you about five.'

Les looked at the piece of paper. 'Grace. What can I say?'

Grace picked up her bag. 'How about goodbye as I back down the driveway.'

Grace farewelled the others and said she'd catch up with them later that night. Les walked Grace out to her car and opened the door. He felt like kissing her. Instead, he smiled as she started the engine.

'Five o'clock?'

'Five o'clock,' replied Grace. She looked at Les for a moment, then blew him a kiss. Les blew one back off his fingertips and watched her drive off. Then he walked back out to the verandah where a fresh cup of tea was waiting for him

'Are you fair dinkum going to fight that dopey, big relation of yours on Monday?' said Warren.

'I got to, haven't I, Woz,' said Les, taking a sip of tea. 'Five grand is five grand.'

'What about your back?'

'Don't matter. Grace reckons she can fix it. Besides, I told Daddy you were going to back me up.'

'What?' said Warren. 'I'll be leaving for Sydney straight after breakfast.'

'Not without me you're not,' said Clover. 'I've heard about Morgan Scully. He's all mean and horrible.'

Les shook his head. 'Jesus. You sure know who your friends are, don't you.'

They finished their tea then Warren had to to drive Clover back to Dalmeny. Les didn't know what time he'd be back from Grace's. He'd catch up with them later. Les put everything away then walked back out onto the verandah. It hadn't been the best of days. And the thought of having to either fight Morgan Scully, or bury him somewhere with Eddie, weighed heavily on Norton's mind. What should have been a few days resting and listening to music had turned out to be a giant pain in the arse.

Out in front of the house the water running through the channel looked blue and inviting. And if there was anything to ease a troubled mind, it was an hour or so of snorkelling. While you were floating around looking at the fish or whatever, you switched off. And Les needed to switch off. He climbed into a pair of Speedos and his rubber vest, tossed his disposable camera in with his towel and snorkelling gear and strolled down to the jetty.

People were walking by or fishing near the boats and on the right, a large, white catamaran bobbed peacefully at its mooring. Facing the catamaran was a bench, where two fishermen had finished cleaning a catch of salmon. Beneath the bench a concrete landing sat at the water's edge. Les stood on the landing, rinsed his face mask then pushed out into the channel.

The water was beautiful and clear, running over a white, sandy bottom covered in sea grass. There were fish everywhere: whiting, bream, leather jackets, schools of fat blackfish. It wasn't deep near the jetty and Les drifted along with the current, diving around the boats and under the catamaran. Laying on the sand beneath the catamaran was the skeleton of a huge marlin, picked clean. Spread across the sand, it had a sad beauty about it so Les dived down and took a photo. In barely two metres of water, he came across a school of blackfish feeding on the bottom. Les swam amongst them and they appeared completely oblivious to him, munching away on the seagrass right in front of his face mask. It was amazing. Les floated amongst the blackfish for a while taking photos, then chased a big leather jacket through the piers, watching its tiny fins going a hundred to the dozen, before photographing it framed in front of a mooring rope. Les floated out to the deeper water and got several shots of a big black stingray moving across the bottom, as well as some mullet, before swimming back to the piers. After a while Les looked at his watch. He went on to photograph several big whiting that had joined the blackfish, then got out of the water and walked back to the house.

Les rinsed his gear under the shower and had a shave. He figured Grace would probably be giving him some kind of massage and he'd end up covered in oil, so he wore a pair of dry Speedos, shorts and the T-shirt he had on in the fight. He put a sweatshirt in his overnight bag, then locked the house, leaving the key under the mat for Warren. He fired up the Berlina and took the road out of town.

It didn't take long to leave Narooma behind. Traffic was light and the drive through the countryside in the late afternoon was pleasant. He crossed Coruna Lake and at the top of a rise a sign on the left pointed to Mystery Bay. That's not far at all, thought Les. I'll check it out for sure. Further along a sign on the right said Central Tilba and Tilba Tilba. Les took the road for Central Tilba.

A yellow barn with a sign saying CENTRAL TILBA ENGINEERING appeared amongst the trees on the left, and further on a little wooden church stood on the right. Past the church the countryside opened up into green rolling hills full of granite boulders. Down on the right, opposite a long, wide valley, Les could see the red roofs of Central Tilba snuggled against the surrounding hills. He continued on, then turned right at the war memorial and slowed down as he entered the main street.

It was very pretty. All the old heritage cottages and houses on either side of the road had been colourfully painted and preserved and turned into craft shops and cafes. The post office was on the left and further on the local hotel. Amongst the shops on the right, a big one had a sign in the window: THE HEMP EVOLUTION. That must be where Grace gets her shirts, mused Les. Most of the shops were closed and apart from the hotel, there weren't many people around and few cars. Les drove past a Tibetan Import shop up on the left, more colourful shops, and further on where the road dipped down was the old cheese factory. He checked the map Grace had given him. Two kilometres on the left past the cheese factory.

Les followed a narrow, winding road that climbed through green hills studded with granite boulders, and the odd farm with a few cows nosing amongst the grass. Further on, next to a blue oil drum letterbox, a white gate hung back in a driveway surrounded by trees. A white sign welded on top of the letter box said: GRACELAND.

Les followed the driveway up until it levelled off at a clearing circled by trees. Opposite the trees, Grace's 4WD was parked in front of a yellow picket fence; beyond the fence and in front of the house sat a garden full of flowers. The house was all wood and painted white and green with a yellow roof and looked like one of the old heritage homes in Tilba. Steps led up to a front door set beneath an arch supported by two wooden poles, with windows either side. A narrow verandah ran from the left of the house and around the front. Les took the steps to the front door and stopped. A black female Staffordshire, with a huge head and a bark like a dinosaur, came skidding around the corner of the verandah. Bristling and snarling, it took up a position between Les and the front door.

Les stepped back from the door and held his palms up. 'Good girl,' he said quietly. 'Good girl. You're just doing your job. Good girl.'

The dog continued to snarl at Les when the door opened and Grace came out wearing a blue hemp shirt with her hair combed in two pigtails either side of her head.

'Morticia. What's the matter, baby,' she said, and put her hand inside the dog's collar. The dog settled down a little but continued to growl at Les. 'This is Morticia,' said Grace. 'She's our little baby.'

'She's a little beauty,' said Les. 'And she does her job too.'

'Yes. She looks after us.'

Grace reached over and gave Les a peck on the cheek. Les pecked her back. The dog noticed this and stopped growling. Les knelt down and softly called the dog.

'Morticia. Come here girl. Come on. I'm a friend of Grace's.'

Morticia looked suspiciously at Les, then reluctantly came over. Les patted her on the head, then put his fingers where her spine met her tail. He started scratching and rubbing and Morticia began wiggling her muscly behind and wagging her tail. She rolled her eyes back and looked up at Les.

'How's that, sweetheart?' The little dog continued to wag its tail and smiled up at Les as he kept scratching and rubbing. 'Yes. You're head's not the best, Morticia. But you've got a great little arse.'

Grace was impressed. 'You've got quite a way with women, haven't you Les. I don't think I've ever seen her like that around strangers before. Especially men.'

'It's just a matter of pushing the right buttons.' Les gave Morticia a pat on the head and stood up.

'Anyway. Come inside,' said Grace. 'You found the place all right.'

'Yeah, easy,' said Les. 'And I saw the turnoff to Mystery Bay.'

Inside was a little like the Merrigan house. High ceilings and a long hallway, with the kitchen and bathroom opposite, and two bedrooms either side. The polished timber floor along the hallway led to a large loungeroom and another door opened onto an enclosed verandah. Facing an open fire, a red velvet lounge suite sat on a Persian carpet and against one wall was a TV and stereo. Paintings of birds and old photos of Tilba hung on the walls, tasselled lamps sat in the corners and near the door to the verandah was a large, black, fitness ball.

'This is a really nice old house,' said Les. 'By old I mean like the ones in Tilba. Heritage style.'

'Yes. This was a gold merchant's home,' said Grace. 'It was built in the eighteen hundreds.'

'It's in bloody good nick.'

'Thanks. Can I get you something to drink? There's some beer. Or white wine.'

Les shook his head. 'A mineral water will do thanks.'

Grace went to the kitchen and came back with a bottle of sparkling and handed it to Les. 'So what did you do this afternoon?'

'Went for a snorkel with my disposable camera,' he replied. He told Grace about the fish round the jetty. 'What did you do?'

'Finished a few T-shirts. Cleaned the house.'

Les nodded then looked at Grace over his bottle of water. 'So how are you going to fix my back, Grace?' he asked.

'I'll show you later. But first, come with me.' Grace slipped on a pair of trainers. 'I want to show you something while there's still light.'

Grace put two empty wine bottles and a screwtop jar into an overnight bag, then took Les out through the enclosed verandah to a set of stairs leading down to an open yard. The yard backed onto the surrounding valleys and granite-studded hills and a trail led from the yard through a small patch of trees. Morticia trotted over from the verandah and Les followed Grace up a steep hill as the trail followed a small stream running below on the right. After they'd climbed for a while, Les paused to catch a glimpse of the sun setting on surrounding valleys. He could see a couple of farmhouses below, the roofs of Central Tilba to the right, and the ocean in the distance. Les commented to Grace about the view, then they climbed further up the trail, before Grace stopped at some trees facing a huge mass of granite boulders. There, the stream gushed and bubbled down the hillside from out of the rocks. Morticia had a drink and Grace pointed along the watercourse to a rocky pond edged with small trees, down in the valley below. Alongside the pond was a timber-built pumping station.

'You see that pond down there? That's on the Hillier property. They've got cattle living to twenty-one and still producing calves at eighteen. Twins.'

'Shit!' said Les. 'That's amazing for cattle.'

'Their sheep live to fifteen. Joe Hillier and his wife are both in their eighties and they're as fit as fiddles. She still rides horses.'

Les looked at Grace. 'You're not going to tell me it's the water?'

Grace nodded. 'Exactly. These scientists from the CSIRO heard about the cattle. So they came here and tested the water. It's full of minerals. Especially magnesium bicarbonate.'

'What's that do?'

'Flushes the toxins and carbon dioxide out of your blood.'

'And you've been drinking it?'

'I started just after I bought the property. Believe me Les, Amazing Grace wasn't looking too amazing when she left Sydney. Not after having Ellie and going through all that other drama.'

'So that's your secret,' said Les.

'That. Plus exercise and a fairly healthy lifestyle. But remember I told you I had shares in a company in Sydney. It's a soft drink company. They're bottling the water as Eureka Water. And because it comes through my property they're paying me a percentage on every case.'

'How's it going?' asked Les.

'They've only just started. But they're hoping to get a big spread in the papers and on TV. So it could take off. And if it does...'

'Aunty Grace is laughing.'

'Exactly.'

'Well, good on you,' said Les. 'I hope you sell a million.' He bent down, cupped a hand and took a drink. 'It sure tastes all right.'

Grace flashed Les a sly smile. 'That's just Eureka lite, Les. Follow me.'

With Morticia trotting alongside, Grace took Les further up the hill to the end of the trail. After that, they scrambled up the hillside and over rocks to a clearing, where a tiny spring seeped from a crack in a huge wall of granite and gently overflowed into a small rock pool at the base. The water was crystal clear and shone like silver in the rays from the late afternoon sun. The bottom of the pool was covered in what appeared to be fine, white sand.

Grace placed her bag in front of the rock pool. 'This is the other Eureka water,' she said. 'The high octane stuff.'

'It is?' said Les.

'Yep. I didn't tell the soft drink people about this one. It starts way back under all this granite. I don't know what's in it. But it's anti-inflammatory. Every time Ellie or I get a bruise or a sprain, we drink some. And it heals in no time.'

Les cupped his hand again and took a mouthful. 'It's got a kind of bitter-sweet taste. Not bad actually.'

'You have to stir up all the sediment on the bottom,' said Grace. 'That's where all the goodies are.'

'And you reckon this will fix my back, in time for Monday with Morgan.'

'It should. With a bit of massage.'

Les stared into the little rock pool. 'I'll take your word for it.'

Grace took the screw top jar from her overnight bag and scooped it into the pool, till the sediment on the bottom swirled through the water like snow. She filled the jar and the two wine bottles, sealed the tops then put them in her overnight bag and hoisted it over her shoulder.

'Righto,' she said, indicating down the trail to Les. 'Let's get back while we've still got light.'

The sun had gone when they reached the house. Morticia went round to her kennel at the side and Les followed Grace up the back stairs. As they kicked off their shoes and walked through the enclosed verandah, Les noticed a screen printing set-up near several clotheslines hung with neatly printed T-shirts.

'So this is where the Grace Holt originals originate,' he said.

'Yes. It keeps me out of mischief.'

'You've got a big fan in Clover.' Les watched as Grace put her bag in the loungeroom then followed her out to the kitchen.

Grace's kitchen was nicely set up. A double window above the sink looked out into the valley, a wooden table and chairs sat in the middle, and a rack of copper cooking utensils hung above the stove. Amongst the magnets and things pinned to the fridge was a photo of a pretty, fair-haired girl in denim, holding Morticia.

'Is that your daughter?' asked Les.

'Yes. That's Ellie. Smelly Ellie. She'll be home on Tuesday.'

'She's half a good sort,' smiled Les. 'A bit like her mother.'

'She's going to be good-looking when she grows up,' said Grace. 'That's when I'll buy a shotgun. Are you hungry, Les?'

'I'm always hungry, Grace. And even when I'm not hungry, I can still eat something.'

Grace pointed to the table. 'Have a seat. I baked some eggplant parmigiana.'

Grace took a large container from the fridge, scooped a pile of food onto a plastic dish and placed it in the microwave. When it pinged she served up two platefuls with rice and crispy bread and butter. Les had a mouthful and nearly fainted. The eggplant was cooked to perfection in a beautiful tomato and onion sauce, and over the top was a layer of lightly baked cheese with more bite than an alligator. Les had another mouthful and looked at Grace.

'Grace,' he said. 'This is absolutely sensational. I've never tasted anything like it.'

'Amazing's not a bad cook on her day,' said Grace. 'But it makes a difference if the eggplants are fresh. And I get a special cheese in Tilba.'

'It's delicious,' said Les, stuffing some more into his mouth, along with a lump of bread.

They finished with coffee, Grace placed what was left back in the fridge then put the dishes in the sink and turned to Les.

'Have you had enough to eat?'

Les patted his stomach. 'Plenty.'

'Okay. Come inside, and we'll have a look at your back.'

'You want me to get my gear off?' said Les. 'I got Speedos on.'

'Okay,' replied Grace.

Les followed Grace into the lounge and got down to his blue Speedos. Grace rolled the fitness ball over and told Les to sit on it with his hands resting on the back of the lounge and facing away from her. Les had seen these big rubber balls, but had never used one. He did as he was told and as soon as he sat on it he could feel his spine straighten and his stomach muscles contract.

'Hey, these are all right,' said Les, bouncing lightly up and down.

'Didn't your physiotherapist put you on one of these?' asked

Grace.

'No. All I got was ultrasound.'

Grace ran her eyes over Les. 'You're in pretty good shape, aren't you.'

'I train a lot with a mate who used to be a top middleweight fighter.' said Les.

'What about you, Les. Can you fight?'

'I can handle myself a bit,' shrugged Les.

'So I believe.' Grace smiled at Les and put her hand on his back. 'Are you a gangster, Les?'

Les smiled up at Grace. 'No. But some of my best friends are.'

'Yeah, right. So where is it sore?'

'Just above my kidneys.'

Grace ran her hand along Norton's spine. 'Yes. I can feel the swelling. Does this hurt?' Grace pushed her knuckle into Norton's vertabrae.

'Ow!' winced Les. 'Does it what.'

'Okay.' Grace walked over to a cabinet and came back with a small bottle. 'You know what this is, Les?'

Norton had a look and shook his head. 'No.'

'Hemp seed oil. It's the best massage oil there is.'

'If you say so, Grace,' said Les.

Grace tipped a little on her hand and rubbed it into Les's back. Gently at first then a little firmer. 'How does that feel?' she asked.

'Unreal,' said Les, rocking gently on the rubber ball.

Grace stopped and rubbed some oil on her right knee then got a footrest. She placed her foot on it, put her hands on Les's shoulders and pushed her knee against his spine. 'Okay Les,' she said. 'Start bouncing up and down on the ball. Not too fast. Just nice and steady.'

Les did as Grace instructed. It hurt a little at first, then the pain eased. After a while, Grace's knee in his back began to feel good.

'Ohh yeah,' said Les, closing his eyes. 'That feels unreal.'

'I told you I could help you,' said Grace. 'Your spine's sitting straight, and the sore point's getting massaged at the same time.'

Les kept slowly rocking up and down. 'Whatever it is, it's certainly working.'

'Good. How about we listen to some music?'

Grace walked over to the stereo, put a CD on, then returned to the rubber ball and pushed her knee back into Norton's spine. Les started bouncing up and down again and some good rock 'n' roll drifted over.

'Hey, this is all right,' said Les. 'Who is it?'

'Jools Holland's Big Band Rhythm and Blues. I ordered it from Sydney.'

Grace pulled Les back against her knee as he gently bounced up and down to the music. It was so relaxing, Les kept drifting off; he lost all track of time. Another track finished, Grace took her knee away and pushed her knuckles into Norton's back. She massaged his spine for a while then gave Norton's neck and shoulders a rub before she finally stopped.

'There you go,' said Grace. 'How do you feel now?'

Les opened his eyes, blinked and arched his back. 'That's unreal,' he said. Les turned around on the ball and looked at Grace. 'The sharp pain's nowhere near as bad as it was. I just feel kind of stiff.'

'That's understandable. You've just had a really deep massage.' Grace went to the kitchen and came back with the jar of water. She shook it up, unscrewed the lid and handed it to Les. 'Here. Drink this.'

Les gulped it down easily, sediment and all. 'Thanks,' he said, and handed Grace the empty jar.

'That will get your system used to it. Too much can make you upset in the tummy, if you've never had it before. But the two bottles — I want you to drink one when you get up tomorrow morning, and the other one before you go to bed Sunday night. You got that — George?'

'No worries,' smiled Les.

Grace put the jar back on the coffee table then stood in front of Les and smiled down at him. 'And by Monday afternoon, you should be fighting fit.'

'Are you going to come down and cheer me on?' asked Les.

Grace shook her head. 'No. I'd like to see Morgan Scully get what's coming to him. But I wouldn't like to see you get hurt.'

Les smiled softly up at Grace and leant back against the lounge. 'Grace. Come here,' he said.

Les took Grace's hand and drew her down onto the rubber ball. She spread her legs, sat on Norton's knees and placed her hands on his shoulders. As she did, her skirt rose and Les glimpsed a pair of very lacy, white knickers. He put his hands on Grace's ribs and they started slowly rocking around on the ball.

'What are you doing, Les?' asked Grace.

'Nothing,' answered Les. 'Just seeing if you can straighten two spines at once. That's all.'

'Ohh yeah.'

Les kept rocking away against Grace in time to the music. Whether it was the sudden infusion of minerals, or Grace's sensational melons moving up and down in front of his nose, Les wasn't sure. But suddenly Mr Wobbly had eaten a can of spinach and turned into Popeye the sailor man. Grace felt it as Les kept rocking steadily away.

Grace looked directly into Norton's shining, brown eyes. 'You're a bit of bastard. Aren't you, Les?'

'That's not very nice, Grace.'

'It's true though.'

'No. Not really. It's just that I keep meeting people who bring the bastard out in me.'

'Do they now?' said Grace.

Les looked directly back into Grace's lovely hazel eyes. 'Do they what.'

Les kissed Grace's lips and Grace kissed him back. It wasn't long before the kissing got very passionate as they rocked up and down on the fitness ball. Les felt the tip of Graces's tongue like a whiplash and slipped his hands under her shirt. He ran them gently over her back, then unbuttoned her shirt. A moment later, Grace's magnificent, unfettered melons were out in the open. Mr Wobbly started tossing his head around and thumping his chest.

Grace stopped kissing Les and looked into his eyes. 'Les,' she said quietly.

'Yes Grace,' replied Norton, knowing it was all too good to be true, and he would have to put his toys away.

'Rub some oil into my boobs.' Grace took her shirt off, dropped it on the floor then reached down and got the bottle of hemp seed oil. 'Can you do that, Les?' she smiled, tipping a little into Norton's hand.

'I'll ... manage somehow,' said Norton.

Les rubbed the oil into his hands then placed one on each of Grace's melons. Grace closed her eyes and rocked slowly up and down on Norton's lap as Les started smoothly massaging. Sideways, up and down. Around in circles. Tenderly squeezing her nipples till they firmed and stuck out like big, pink arrowheads. Les massaged away, scarcely able to believe how firm Grace's boobs were for their size. And they were the absolute real deal as well. Mr Wobbly, meanwhile, could believe. He started howling and screaming and trying to rip his way out of Norton's Speedos. Grace arched her back, rubbed herself against Les and sighed. Les watched her pigtails swaying from side to side and leant forward and kissed her. Grace kissed Les back and soon the kissing went from passionate, to steamy delicious.

Grace chewed Norton's bottom lip then slipped her tongue in his ear. Les winced as he felt Grace's hot breath and kissed the tenderness of her neck. He kissed her eyes then ran his hand up and down her spine and over the firmness of her stomach, before slipping his hand between Grace's legs. Grace crushed her mouth onto Norton's as he stroked the beautiful, wet tenderness of her ted. Finally, Les lifted Grace to her feet, stood in front of her and eased her knickers off. He turned her around and sat her back down on the fitness ball facing him. Grace took hold of the lounge behind her as Les spread her legs apart, then he got to his knees and pushed his face into her ted.

Grace moaned and writhed on the fitness ball, gripped the back of the lounge and kicked her legs as Les slid his tongue inside her and sucked tenderly. He squeezed her behind and rolled his head around in unison with the bouncing ball pushing his face hard against her as Grace moaned and licked her lips with delight. Les went for it, flicking his tongue around like a rattlesnake and before too long Grace gave a long squeal of ecstasy and got her rocks off. Les came up for air, picked a few pubic hairs out of his mouth and got into it again.

Naturally, Les was soon filled with lust and yearning desire. But Mr Wobbly had become possessed. The werewolf had completely taken over and he was foaming at the mouth, howling his angry little head off, wanting to play hidings. Les fought the beast as long as he could before his willpower collapsed and he was forced let Mr Wobbly have his evil way.

Les stood up, helped Grace to her feet then got out of his Speedos. He sat back down on the ball and made himself comfortable, then drew Grace towards him. Grace spread her legs as Les held her backside then she laced her hands behind Norton's neck and straddled him.

Les pushed himself in and the warmth and firmness of Grace made him shudder. Grace groaned and came down, then she brought her knees up and it didn't take long to get a steady rhythm going, up and down on the fitness ball. Every so often Les would lean back, Grace would come down, and he'd go in deeper.

'Ohh. You know what that ... feels like, Les,' said Grace.

'No,' panted Les. 'What Grace?'

'Like ... one of those stalls ... at the show. Where you ... hit the stump with a mallet. And see how ... high you can go.'

'How am I goin'?'

'Ohh. Every now and again ... you hit the top. Ohh yeah, like that.

Oh fuck!'

With Grace clinging to him, Les relaxed and bounced away into the evening. The pain in his back was bearable and Grace and the ball were doing all the work; Les felt he could go all night. Grace's pigtails were whirling like the blades on a helicopter, and from the expression on her face it looked like she hoped he would. She hooked her ankles up over Norton's shoulders, Les went in deeper and the ball went faster. Then Les felt the urge engulfing his body; building up inside him like a volcano. Grace started to howl, Les screwed his face up and sweat trickled down his back. Then it was all systems go. Les had ignition, he had lift off. He jammed his eyes shut and blasted off into the galaxy.

'Ohh shit! Ohh Christ! Aarrgghhhh!'

'Oh my God! Oh my God! Oh! Oh! Owwhhhh!'

Finally the ball stopped bouncing and Grace stopped trying to choke Les. Les stopped trying to rip Grace's backside off and Morticia stopped barking at the front door. Les blinked his eyes open and stared at Grace. Grace stared back at Les.

'I have to go to the bathroom.'

Norton's chest was heaving. 'Okay.'

Grace stood up and left. Les got to his feet and climbed unsteadily into his Speedos then flopped on the lounge. The last track on the Jools Holland CD cut out as Grace sat down alongside him wearing a yellow shower robe with a fluffy white towel over her shoulder. In her hands were two bottles of sparkling mineral water. She handed one to Les.

'Just what I need,' said Les. 'Thanks.'

Les gulped down half the bottle, Grace drank some of hers and started wiping Norton's shoulders.

'Your soaking,' she said.

'Yeah,' he replied. 'I hope I haven't messed up your lounge.'

'That's okay. How's your back feel?'

'All right, I think.' Les winked at Grace. 'The rubber ball worked splendidly.'

Grace smiled back at Les over her bottle of water. 'That wasn't quite what I had in mind.'

'No,' said Les. 'Amazing what they can do though.' Les gave Grace's leg a gentle squeeze. 'Any chance of putting that CD on again Grace? I missed the last tracks.'

'I wonder how that happened?'

Grace put the same CD on again and they sat on the lounge with their bottles of mineral water listening to Jools Holland. Grace had a good stereo and Les was thoroughly enjoying it. He settled down and Grace rested her head against his shoulder. Les massaged Grace's scalp and, as she relaxed, one of her oil-glistening melons slipped out from under her robe. Les spotted it about the same time as Mr Wobbly. Next thing, the werewolf took over again and Mr Wobbly started climbing out of Norton's Speedos, angrier than ever.

'Hello,' said Les. 'I think there's some one here wants to see you, Grace.'

Grace looked down at Norton's throbbing boner. 'You just behave yourself, Mr Norton,' she said. 'Or you're going to hurt your back.'

'Not on the magic ball I won't.'

'Maybe. But aunty Grace is a little sore.'

'Oh. Oh well,' said Les. 'It doesn't matter.'

Grace smiled at Les with a strange glint in her eye. 'Doesn't it?'

Grace slipped Norton's dick out of his Speedos, dipped her head and proceeded to give him a spanking blow job. Les didn't know what hit him as Grace sucked and licked and gently squeezed his balls, while she sighed with delight. Before Les knew it, sweat formed on his brow, his face began to twist out of shape and, feeling like he was going to have a heart attack, Les collapsed back onto the lounge; groaning again, he got his rocks off.

Grace had a drink of water and gave Norton a minute or two. 'So how was that, Les?' she asked.

Norton was laying back on the lounge with tears in his eyes. 'Ohh. Ohhh shit!' he mumbled.

'Well, if that's all you've got to say — bugger you.' Grace started hauling Les off the lounge. 'Come on. If we're going to the Blues Festival tonight. You'd better go home and get ready.'

'Okay,' said Les, stumbling back into his shorts. 'So what's doing? Do you want to come with me this time, and I'll drive you home in the morning?'

'No. I'll have a shower. And meet you at the house in about an hour. I'll stay at Belinda's again.'

'Okay.'

Les put his T-shirt on, Grace put the two bottles of mineral water in his overnight bag, gave him the instructions again, then walked him to the door. Les gave her a quick kiss goodbye, patted Morticia on her massive head and walked to his car. It felt a bit nippy out in the hills now, so he put his sweatshirt on before getting behind the wheel. He tooted the horn and drove off.

Apart from a few people in the hotel, it was all over as Les drove through Tilba. He hung a left at the war memorial towards the turnoff. When he got there, Les caught a glimpse of the ocean in the distance and noticed the sky was full of clouds and the southerly had picked up. It didn't appear as if it was going to rain. But the weather had definitely changed. He slipped a tape on then swung left and headed for Narooma. As Red Rivers started thumping out 'Baby Blue Buick', Les started thinking. What started off as a rotten day had turned out gravy. He'd been sucked and fucked. Fed beautiful food. Given a fantastic massage. And with a bit of luck Grace's special mineral water might fix his back.

There was a break in the clouds and the moon appeared for a few moments. Les looked up at the sky and grinned. You like me boss, don't you. Despite all the shit you lay on me. And the pain and suffering you put me through. Underneath, you like me. Come on. Admit it. As he cruised along something else occurred to Les. He felt he'd made a friend in Grace, and he remembered saying to her that if she helped him, he promised her she'd never regret it. Les smiled and stroked his chin. Besides the gigantic mumble on the grumble he gave her, there could be another, even nicer way to return the favour.

There were people and cars around as Les drove through Narooma. When he pulled up at the house, Warren had parked his car against the front door. The key was under the mat; Les opened the door and stepped inside. Ray Anthony and his Orchestra were hitting 'In The Mood' in the loungeroom and Warren and Clover were in the kitchen hitting the sauce. By the smell, they hadn't long finished a hot one.

Warren was wearing black jeans, a blue check shirt and his leather jacket. Clover had on a red cap, a tiger-striped top under a red cardigan that went past her knees, jeans, and cherry red Doc Martens.

They were very cuddly and by the looks on both their faces, Les surmised they'd made good use of the empty house while he was away.

'Righto,' said Les. 'Who owns the bloody yellow Celica out the front? You couldn't park it any closer to the front door could you.'

Clover narrowed her eyes at Norton. 'Don't get too cheeky big fellah,' she said. 'Remember your bad back. I might just jump up and sit you right on your arse.' Clover then had an attack of the giggles and spilt her drink.

Warren raised his JD and soda. 'What she said, dude.'

Les shook his head. 'Jesus Christ. What are you pair into?'

'Just a few cools ones,' said Clover. 'And the odd hot one. You want some.'

'Maybe after I have a shower,' said Les.

'Actually,' said Clover, 'I've got something special for us besides pot. I'm saving it for tomorrow.'

'Clover,' replied Les, sagely. 'If you think I'm going to drop a disco biscuit, and start dancing and talking at a hundred miles an hour and tell Warren I love him, you're playing with yourself.'

Clover shook her head. 'No. Better.'

'Yeah, righto.'

'So how was your day with Grace?' asked Warren. 'Bit of nudge, nudge, wink wink, there Ugly?'

'No,' replied Les. 'We went for a walk in the hills. I had an absolutely fantastic meal. Heard an absolutely fantastic CD. And had a... terrific massage. It was great day all round.'

'What's her house like?' asked Clover. 'She invited me out tomorrow.'

'Nice. But watch out for the dog.'

Les left Warren and Clover to it and got under the shower. He had a shave, dabbed on a little CK then got into his jeans and a blue, Margaritasville T-shirt he'd bought in Florida; he put a hang out denim shirt over the top. He gave himself a detail and walked back to the kitchen. Warren and Clover were drinking away steadily and going over the Blues Festival program.

'Hey. You seen who's on tonight?' said Warren.

'No. Bjork? Celine Dion? Surprise me, Woz.' Les got a tall glass and made himself a super, monster delicious.

'Dave Hole. Holy Dave. And that other band you saw in Cairns, that you're always on about. Rock Solid Steve and the Scorchers.'

'You're kidding,' said Les. 'Rock Solid and the boys. I might even have a hot one.'

'Are they any good?' asked Clover.

'Only if you like rock and a roll,' smiled Les.

'Well, I like rock and a roll, Les,' mimmicked Clover. 'In fact you and I might get up for a dance big guy.'

'Okay. But only if the masseur says so.'

'So what did Grace do to you?' asked Warren.

Les told them how Grace massaged him with her knee on the fitness ball. He said nothing about the porking and polishing. And he kept quiet about Grace's secret spring. But he told them about the other one and what was in it and how Grace was hoping to make some money through the soft drink company.

'So that was my day kiddies,' said Les, making himself another delicious. 'But Grace should be here soon. She'll tell you anything else you wish to know. I imagine.'

'If she's forty two,' said Warren. 'I'm going to buy a forty-four gallon drum of that Eureka Water. She is absolutely amazing.'

'Evidently that's what they call her,' said Les. 'A . . .' There was a soft rap on the door. 'Hello. I'd say this is the person in question now.'

Les put his drink on the table then walked across and opened the door. It was Grace, looking very foxy in a brown, suede Mao jacket, beige jeans and a light green T-shirt, with a goanna on the front. She had her hair down and two mother-of-pearl seahorses dangled from her ears. A brown leather bag that matched her boots hung loosely over one shoulder. Les stood at the door, staring down at her.

'Well. Are you going to let me in?' smiled Grace.

'I'm sorry,' said Les, moving aside. 'But I was just thinking. They have to bring in a law against women like you looking so beautiful.'

'And there should be a law against men like you being such dropkicks.' Grace stepped inside and gave Les a kiss as he closed the door. 'How are you?'

'Terrific,' said Les. 'My back feels that good, I'm thinking of getting up later and showing the locals some new dance steps.'

'I'd advise against it after the massage,' said Grace. 'Give your back time to settle down.'

'Okay. You're the doctor,' said Les.

Grace entered the kitchen to warm greetings from Clover and

Warren. Clover gushed a little over Grace's clothes. Warren just stared at her. Les made her a Bacardi and orange. Grace took a sip and noticed Norton's T-shirt.

'Margaritasville,' she said, pointing with her drink. 'You're not a parrot head, are you Les?'

'Warren and I have been known to have a few Jimmy Buffett CDs amongst our collection,' admitted Les.

'So have I,' said Grace. 'My favourite's "Fruit Cakes".'

'Mine too,' said Clover, quickly. 'Hey Grace. You know anybody in Miami can gimme a passssssport real quick?'

Grace sat down and they all got into a tipsy, light conversation. Grace had been to Florida and saw Jimmy Buffett in Miami. Les had also been to Florida and they'd all been to Hawaii. Clover arranged to give Grace a lift home again and as they were talking Clover rolled a couple of joints. She put them aside and turned to Grace.

'Have you ever tried mushrooms, Grace?' she said.

'You mean Tiger Stripes? Not for a while.'

'Tiger stripes?' said Les.

'They're the local variety,' said Grace. 'Somewhere between Victorian Blue Meanies and Queensland Gold Tops.'

'I bumped into a friend from school,' said Clover. 'She gave me some.'

Clover walked over to the fridge and came back with a brown paper bag. She opened it and inside were half-a-dozen mushrooms with brown and orange stripes on top.

'That's them,' said Grace.

'I'm going to make some coffee tomorrow night,' said Clover. 'Care to join in?'

'Sure. Why not,' shrugged Grace. 'It'll certainly put some colour into the last blast of the festival.' She smiled at Norton. 'You ever tried these, Les?'

Les shook his head. 'No.'

'What about you, Warren?'

Warren shook his head also. 'No.'

'They're fairly mild,' said Grace. 'They only last about six hours.'

'And you get a flashback, a couple of days later,' said Clover.

'A flashback?' said Les.

'Yes,' smiled Grace. 'But only for a little while.'

Clover turned to Warren. 'You still keen, Warren?'

'Yeah, why not.'

'What about you, Les?'

'Yeah I suppose so. Though I hate bowing to peer pressure.'

'Hey unreal,' said Clover. 'Sunday night at the Blues Festival, off our trolleys.'

'I can't wait,' said Les.

Grace looked at the two joints sitting on the table and the bag of dacca. She opened the bag and squeezed one of the heads. 'These look all right,' she said. 'Where's this from?'

Les pointed to Warren. 'The boarder's. He grows it in the backyard.'

'Really?' said Grace. 'I put a few plants on the property next door, now and again.'

'Do you get helicopters and sniffer dogs down here?' asked Warren.

'Yes. The pains in the arse,' said Grace.

'It's a pain in the arse all right,' said Warren. 'Fair dinkum. If they carried on about people importing heroin and cocaine as much as they carried on about people smoking pot, there wouldn't be a drug problem.'

'Yes. But you have to understand,' said Clover. 'The government gets votes out of busting people for having a bit of pot. And it makes the cops look like they're doing something about the drug problem.'

'Yeah. While they're selling heroin and cocaine,' said Warren. 'It gives me the shits. You have a smoke after work, and they jump all over you. Shoot up after robbing an old lady and they give you a safe house.'

Les gave the others a frosty look. 'I don't know how you can say that about the NSW government and the police,' he said seriously. 'I happen to have friends in the police force.'

'Ohh wonderful,' scoffed Warren. 'And your boss wouldn't have ever bribed any of them either. Would he?'

'Price? Never.'

'Never stopped, you mean.'

Les pointed a finger at Warren. 'Warren. I will not have you bad mouthing the integrity of Mr Galese and the Kelly Club. We run a very respectable business up there. Next thing, you'll being accusing us of money laundering and organising murders.'

'Sorry Les. I forgot. Eddie only does the cleaning.'

'And very efficiently too.' Suddenly Norton's eyes narrowed. 'Hang on a minute. What's this?' Les reached over and undid a couple of buttons on Warren's shirt. He patted him down, then pulled Warren's hip flask out of his leather jacket and shook it. 'You rotten little bastard, Warren. You're wearing a wire. It's you that's been ratting us out. Jesus Christ! When Eddie finds out about this. You'll have more holes in you than a gas ring.'

'You really are a gangster. Aren't you, Les,' said Grace.

Warren laughed derisively and snatched his hip flask back from Norton. 'No. But some of his best friends are.'

'Hey, talking about holes,' said Clover. 'We'd better make a move if we're going to see Dave Hole and Rock Solid.'

'Yeah, you're right,' said Les. 'Bloody women. You'd talk all night.' Clover and Grace looked at Les like he was a dud TV commercial they were watching for the two hundredth time. 'Sorry about that ladies,' smiled Les. 'Just making sure I hadn't lost my touch.'

'Hey. What about de ganja, mon,' said Warren. 'Are we goin' to smoke de spleefs?'

'I think so,' answered Clover. She put the mushrooms back in the fridge, fired up a fat joint and it started going the rounds. 'Hey, I just thought of something,' she said. 'What if Morgan Scully and his gang are down there?'

'Yeah. That's a worry,' agreed Warren.

Les shook his head and blew out a great cloud of smoke. 'I can't see any problem if he shows up.'

'I hope you're right,' said Grace. 'But I'd keep away from him. He is a bit mad you know.' She took a toke and handed the joint to Warren.

'I hope you're right, too,' said Warren, disappearing behind a cloud of smoke. 'Because if anything starts, I'm saving the women.'

They finished the joint and Les felt it definitely put a spin on the night. Even the old music coming from the loungeroom sounded better. They decided not to bother about the other joint. Les turned the ghetto blaster off in the loungeroom, then they picked up their bags, cameras, hip flasks and whatever and headed for the door.

'Hey just a minute,' said Les. He went to his room and came back with the GUEST pass Norm had given him round his neck. 'What do you reckon gang?'

'Where did you get that?' said Warren.

'Daddy gave it to me,' replied Les breezily. 'In case I want to go backstage and mingle with the other stars. I might even get up and do a gig man.'

The others looked at each other. 'You don't have to be seen with us, if you don't want to,' said Grace.

'Yeah. And don't worry about doing a gig, Les,' said Warren. 'You are a gig. Now open the door, you big goose.'

Les shook his head. 'The good old tall poppy syndrome. You couldn't wait to cut my legs off. Could you.'

The walk down seemed to take longer this time. But it was a lot more fun. They got to the jetty and the music coming from the festival seemed to be everywhere. Grace had hold of Norton's arm as they threaded their way through the people and Clover had hold of Warren. They arrived at the entrance to find Norm standing there checking some receipts. He saw them and smiled.

'Hello Grace,' he boomed. 'Les. How is everybody?'

'Good thanks, Daddy.'

'Morgan's in there.'

'Really?' said Les. 'I must make sure I say hello before the night's over.'

Norm pulled Les aside. 'I put him in the picture. He won't start anything tonight. But shit, he's mad keen for Monday.'

'Fair enough,' nodded Les.

'Listen. He's put his five grand up. And I can get three to one about you. How's your back?'

'A little better,' said Les. 'Don't say anything though. We might get fives.'

'Sweet.'

Les rejoined the others; the security gave their bags a quick flick, and they went through.

'Oh my God!' said Clover. 'Did you hear that. Morgan Scully's inside.'

'Shit! I don't like it,' said Warren.

'Ohh for Christ's sake,' asserted Les. 'You're just being paranoid. Nothing's going to happen. Trust me.'

'I'm not paranoid, Les,' said Grace, taking hold of Norton's arm. 'But don't go away. There's a lot of people here that are. And they're all out to get me.'

'Why don't we buy some drinks. Then find a seat,' suggested Les. 'Do you think you can make it to the bar and back with me, Woz?'

Warren looked around. 'Christ! I hope so,' he replied.

The queue wasn't too long and Les and Warren came back with a tray of drinks. They walked over to the middle tent and managed to get four seats together about a dozen rows from the front, then settled down amongst the crowd. Warren and Grace pulled out their hip flasks and topped up all their drinks then after a quick 'cheers' they had a mouthful each. The band hadn't come on stage yet and some good music was coming quietly through the speakers. Les was nicely out of it and would have been content to sit there all night and listen to what was playing.

'Hey, how good's this?' said Clover. 'We're right in the middle of the speakers.'

'I don't know what this music is,' said Warren. 'But it's unreal.'

Les sipped his drink and checked out the other punters. They were a happy-looking crowd, a few heads were bopping around here and there and Les surmised he and the others weren't the only ones who had been partaking in illegal drug activities that night. His eyes wandered back towards the stage, then Les gave a double blink. Sitting five rows in front of them was a huge, unmistakable man's head wearing a black cowboy hat over a black T-shirt. The man in the cowboy hat was with two ordinary-looking blondes in denim and leather and another big man in a check shirt and a black baseball cap.

Les turned to the others. 'Hey. Look who's sitting right in front of us.'

The others stared then Clover gasped and put a hand over her mouth.

'Oh my God! It's him.'

'Oh shit! It is too,' said Warren.

The others held their drinks and sank back in their seats. Les sipped his bourbon and stared at Morgan's tree stump neck sitting beneath his hat. That was the only thing Les didn't like about smoking pot. It brought out the Bugs Bunny in him. He sipped some more bourbon and looked around the grass near his feet. Lying under the seat in front of him was a thick, juicy apple core, that someone had left from the previous concert.

'Grace,' said Les. 'Would you hold my drink for a second please?'

'Sure,' replied Grace, taking Norton's bourbon.

Les picked up the apple core and got to his feet. He aimed carefully then flung the apple core at Morgan as hard as he could, splattering it all over the big man's neck and his mate sitting next to him.

'Hey Boofhead! Yeah, you in the hat,' Les yelled out. 'Take the bloody thing off. You're blocking our view.'

Grace's jaw dropped, Warren went grey and Clover buried her face in her hands. The people around them thought it must be some kind of joke. Morgan lumbered to his feet and spun around hyperventilating with rage. He saw Les standing there with a silly look on his face and started to shake.

'Well. You heard me possum eyes,' said Les. 'What, are you deaf as well as stupid ... Get the bloody thing off. Or do you want me to come down there, rip it off your head and shove it up your blurter. You inbred moron.'

Morgan's mate stood up alongside him; it was the bloke with the thick moustache who had punched Warren. Before they got a chance to do anything, a tall bloke in a Blues Festival T-shirt appeared on stage and took hold of the mike.

'Ladies and gentlemen. Will you please give a big welcome on stage. To ... Rock Solid Steve and the Scorcherrrsssss.'

The audience erupted into wild applause as Morgan stared daggers at Les. Les gave him a friendly little wave and sat down. Still shaking with rage and his face absolutely purple with anger, Morgan turned and sat down too. So did his mate. The band got behind their instruments and did a quick sound check.

Warren stared at Les, his eyes like dinner plates. 'Are you fucking insane?'

Clover stared into her drink. 'We're dead. I know it.'

'Les,' said Grace, urgently. 'If you're like this after one joint, I would seriously reconsider the mushrooms tomorrow.'

Les had been keeping his eyes on Morgan. He turned to the others. 'I told you nothing would happen.' Les smiled and pointed towards Morgan. 'Look.'

The others followed Norton's finger. Morgan had removed his hat and placed it on his knees.

'My God,' said Clover. 'He's taken his hat off.'

'I don't believe it,' said Grace.

'Well why wouldn't he?' replied Les. 'Shit! I asked him politely enough.'

The band was just like Les remembered them in Cairns. The happy-faced bloke with the goatee beard and the Hawaiian shirt on bass, the lead singer in the horn-rimmed glasses with the rigger's belt full of harmonicas and the guitarist with the Elvis hairstyle hunched over his Fender. Behind them, their long haired drummer was poised ready to start hammering the tubs. The lead singer said something Les didn't quite catch, then the band ripped into 'Love So Much' and the tent erupted.

'Oh yeah,' said Grace.

'Rock and a roll,' squealed Clover, banging her head from side to side and almost losing her glasses.

'I told you they were good,' smiled Les.

People started dancing in front of the stage and by the time the band had scorched through 'Burn Rubber Burn' and 'Queensland Moon', Grace and the others were down the front as well; Clover and Grace were dancing and taking photos at the same time. Les couldn't join in the dancing. But he went down and took photos. He noticed Morgan and his friends giving him filthy looks, so he smiled back at them and took their photo as well.

Les sat down and after a while the others joined him, then they topped their drinks and rocked happily away till the Scorchers finished with 'Skinny Skinny Skinny'. The band waved to the audience then left. When the applause died down, Les and the others went into a huddle about the band and finished what drinks they had left.

'I got some great photos of you dancing,' said Les.

'I got a great photo of you taking photos,' said Grace.

Clover glanced towards the stage as the tent emptied. 'Hey look. Morgan's gone.'

'Thank God for that,' said Warren. He looked at Les. 'Why don't we get some more drinks, and find a seat before Dave Hole comes on.'

Everybody agreed so they got up and walked to the front of the tent. Waiting outside was Morgan, his mate, and the two women, all looking like they'd all just bitten into a plate of bad oysters. Clover saw them first.

'Oh my God!' she said, and hid behind Les with the others.

Les was still very much in Bugs Bunny mode. 'Great band, Morgan,' he said cheerfully. 'If you're into that sort of music. Or are you more a techno-house, dance club, kind of guy?'

Morgan stepped in front of Les and pointed to his hat. 'You see this hat?' he rasped.

'Is that what it is,' replied Les. 'I thought you'd brought your washing with you.'

'It's only an old one. But when I'm finished with you on Monday, I'm going to shove it right up your arse.'

'Fair enough,' said Les. 'But make sure you take it off first won't you.' He turned to the others. 'Come on. Let's go and get a drink.'

Les ignored Morgan and led the others to the booze tent. The queue wasn't long and soon Les and Warren returned with a tray of drinks. They all toasted each other and took a sip.

'I have to give it to you, Les,' said Grace. 'The spinnaker's on the wrong end of your yacht. But you're bloody cool. I was shitting myself back there.'

'So was I,' said Clover. 'I still am.'

'I told you before. Nothing's going to happen tonight.' Les smiled and raised his drink. 'It's all sweet.'

'Don't count your luck,' said Grace. 'We're not home yet.'

Les put his arm around Grace. 'Why shouldn't I count my luck? I've got you with me. Amazing Grace.'

'I like you, Les,' smiled Grace.

'I like you too, Grace.' Les gave Grace one on the cheek and they walked over to the main tent.

This time they had to sit apart. Les and Grace got two seats on the side. Warren and Clover found another two further down from them in the middle. There was no sign of Morgan and his friends. Les swallowed some bourbon, then Daddy lumbered out on stage and took hold of the mike.

'Orrrright. Here he is. Come on, give a big welcome. Dave Hole. Come on!'

The crowd started clapping and cheering as Dave Hole led his band on stage wearing a vest and a baseball cap. He plugged his guitar in, nodded to the band, and they tore straight into 'New Way To Live'. From that it was 'Every Girl I See' followed by 'More Love Less Attitude'. And the crowd loved every note. Dave scissor-kicked and duck-walked across the stage. He worked the slide on his guitar till it screamed and sparks were flying off the frets. Les and Grace took photos, bounced up and down in their seats and listened in awe as Dave racked up more blistering solos, through 'Cold Women With Warm Hearts' and 'Take A Swing'. The band did a swag more songs off all their albums, then came back for an encore with 'Bullfrog Blues', before finally walking off to a standing, cheering ovation.

'Well Grace,' said Les, 'I don't think we can complain. It hasn't been a bad night of rock 'n' roll.'

Grace shook her head. 'Wow! I don't think I could take any more after that.'

The crowd started to leave. Clover and Warren came over. Les and Grace put their cameras in their bags and stood up.

'What did you think?' asked Les,

'Unreal,' said Warren. 'Especially when he finished with "Bullfrog Blues".'

'I like "Crazy Kind Of Woman",' said Clover. She turned to Grace. 'I suppose we'd better start walking up to the house. Mum will be here soon.'

'Any sign of — you know who,' said Warren, running his eyes over the crowd.

'No,' answered Les. 'But I wish there was. I'd like to put the hard word on his girl. She wasn't a bad sort.'

'Yes,' agreed Clover. 'If you fancy Harpo Marx in drag.'

They joined the crowd exiting the tent and kept going. Les had his arm around Grace as they went by the jetty and Warren was arm in arm with Clover. Although the pot had worn off, they were still laughing and joking as they strolled along. Nevertheless, Warren was avoiding any shadowy areas and looked very relieved when they reached the front yard.

'So what's the story tomorrow?' asked Les. 'I'm going to Montague Island at nine o'clock.' He glanced up at the cloudy sky. 'Don't look like being much of a day for it though.'

Grace turned to Clover. 'I told Alysia I'd help her in the shop till one. Why don't you call over after then and we'll have lunch?'

'Okay.'

Warren yawned. 'I'm having a sleep in.'

Clover took hold of Warren. 'Then why don't we all do our own thing tomorrow. And meet back here at six. For a double shot, decaf-mushroom latte.'

'Sounds good to me,' said Warren, leaning against Clover.

Les shook his head. 'Like I said, Clover, I can't wait.'

The station wagon pulled up out the front. Warren waved to Clover's mother without bothering to walk across to the car. Les hadn't met her. But he gave her a wave also, then put his arms around Grace. Grace slipped her arms around Les and he kissed her.

'Thanks for everything today, Grace,' he said. 'I'll see you tomorrow night.'

'I'll see you then.' Grace shook her finger at Les. 'Now don't forget to drink your water in the morning. Every last drop.'

'No I won't. Goodnight Grace.'

'Goodnight Les.'

Les said goodnight to Clover, then she and Grace piled into the station wagon and it drove off.

Warren let go another huge yawn. 'Shit I'm tired,' he said.

The yawn was infectious. 'You're not Robinson Crusoe,' said Les. He got the key from under the mat, opened the door and they stepped inside. Les locked the door and walked into the kitchen.

'You feel like anything, Woz?' he asked, getting a bottle of water from the fridge.

'Yes. About ten hours sleep,' said Warren. 'I'm rooted.' Warren went to the bathroom then came back and propped in the kitchen doorway. 'I couldn't believe it, when you hit that big goose with the apple core,' he laughed. 'You're fuckin insane.'

'I know what I'd like to hit him with,' said Les.

'Yeah,' agreed Warren. He let go another yawn. 'Shit! I hope that bloody rat doesn't wake me again tonight.'

'Hey. Thanks for reminding me, Woz.' Les put the bottle of water back in the fridge, took out a packet of cheese then got a rat-trap from the pantry. 'See how Jerry Lee Rodent likes this.'

Les broke off a piece of cheese and tied it to the trap with a thread of cotton from a tea towel. Warren watched absently as Les baited the trap, when the temperature in the kitchen suddenly plunged to what felt like below zero.

'Shit!' said Warren, as clouds of steam formed in front of his face. 'How fuckin cold is it.'

'There must be a bloody draught in here.' Les put the trap down and rubbed the goose bumps on his arms while his breath also turned to steam. 'It's probably coming from under the house.'

'Coming from fuckin Siberia'd be more like it,' shivered Warren. 'Ohh fuck this. I'm going to bed. It's freezing. See you in the morning, Les.'

'Yeah, see you then.'

Warren moved off into the hallway leaving a cloud of steam behind him in the kitchen. 'Hey, what *is* under the house?' he called out from the hallway.

'What was that?' Les yelled back.

'Doesn't matter. I'll see you in the morning.' The loungeroom door closed followed by the door to Warren's bedroom.

Les knitted his eyebrows for a moment then shook his head. He sprung the trap and left it on the floor under the table then turned out the kitchen light. After going to the bathroom, Les took off his clothes and climbed into his tracksuit. He got under the blankets and switched off the bedlamp. It didn't seem as cold in the bedroom and before long Les had warmed up and was almost asleep. Warren was right, he smiled. The look on Morgan's face when he turned around in the tent was a hoot. But one way or the other, there wouldn't be much laughing on Monday. In the quiet darkness of the old room, Les let his mind drift off to more pleasant things and soon he was sound asleep.

When Les woke up around seven the next morning he felt pretty good. He'd slept well, he had no sign of a hangover and although his back was still stiff from Grace's massage, the pain in his spine had eased. A quick peek out the window said it didn't look like being much of a day however. He went to the bathroom, then changed straight into his training gear and walked into the kitchen. Rubbing his hands together, Les had a look under the table. The trap wasn't there, or anywhere else in the kitchen. Mystified, Les picked at his chin for a moment, then smiled. I've got him. He's wounded and dragged the trap somewhere. All I have to do now is find Jerry's mangled corpse before he stinks the place up. Les pointed. Probably in that side room. But first, a cup of tea and toast. With just a little grated cheese. Les put the kettle on, popped two slices of bread in the toaster, then opened the fridge and reached inside.

'WHACK!!!'

'Shit a fuckin brick!' Les flew back as the rat-trap slammed down a centimetre from his thumb.

Norton stared at the rat-trap sitting next to the tomatoes and milk with the piece of cheese still attached. Gingerly he took the trap out and placed it on the table. Fuckin hell, he scowled. That could have broken my bloody finger. Norton's eyes narrowed towards the front bedroom. Fuckin Warren. He's getting sillier by the minute. No, Les shook his head. Not even Warren's that stupid. You know what, I reckon the poor, silly bastard's walking in his sleep? I think I'd better have a word with the boarder. Before he does somebody an injury. Particularly me.

Les removed the piece of cheese and placed the trap back in the pantry. He made his tea and toast then walked down the hallway and opened the door to the loungeroom. The bear was on the piano facing away from the wall and snoring was coming from Warren's room. Les stepped out onto the verandah and leant against the railing.

There was still no sign of rain. But the sky was grey and it was cool with a southerly blowing. Not much of a day for a boat trip out to Montague Island. Les watched the people round the jetty and listened to some music coming from the nearest balcony while he worked out his game plan. He'd walk to the pier again and check out Bar Beach. Les finished his tea and toast, put his cap on and set off.

Whether it was the festival atmosphere or he just had a good vibe about him, Les wasn't sure. But almost everybody he passed on his walk either smiled or said hello. Even some old ladies picking up rubbish by the side of the bridge stopped for a moment and smiled when Les strode past. Les smiled back at everyone as he ambled steadily along and in what seemed like no time at all he was standing on the breakwater. There was a decent wave running and a group of surfers were getting some hot barrels off Bar Beach, while some fairly solid swells were pushing into the Bar. Les couldn't tell how rough it was out to sea. But it looked very bumpy and, beneath a grey sky, the water was dark and uninviting. He did a few light squats and watched the surfers for a while then headed for home.

Les kept the two bottles of mineral water Grace had given him in his room and it wasn't hard to gulp one down after the walk; the bitter-sweet taste was quite good. He had a shower and put on his tracksuit, then walked up and got the paper and some more film. He didn't notice Ian in the dive shop on the way and Warren was still in bed when he got back. Les made a couple of toasted sandwiches and washed them down with some fresh tea while he read the news. After that, he checked his cameras and got his diving gear and everything else together. He couldn't see himself getting in the water on the day. But part of the island might be sheltered. Making sure he had his ticket, Les shouldered his bag and walked down to the jetty.

The Kingfisher was moored between the catamaran and the other boats. It was all white with a red cabin at the front, wide beamed and ten metres long. Aerials and fishing rod holders poked up in the air, a flag dangled off the stern and a radar dish sat on top of the cabin. There were no steps; you climbed straight in from the jetty. Standing at the rail holding a clipboard was a beefy, bearded, red-haired bloke wearing sunglasses, shorts and a white T-shirt with Kingfisher Cruises across the front.

'Are you the skipper?' asked Les.

'That's me, mate. Neville. Everyone calls me Nev.'

'Okay Nev,' Les handed Nev his ticket. 'I'm Les. Ian sent me.'

'Good on you, Les. Climb aboard. We got two more to come and we'll shove off.'

'Righto.'

Les piled on board. There was a seat running along the stern and two other seats below the cabin. A set of steps went up to the cabin on the right and another set in the middle went down to the galley. Above the steps in the middle was a storage space full of orange life jackets. A young couple in warm clothes were standing near the stern and an older bloke and his wife wearing shorts were seated next to the steps beneath the cabin. The young couple were your average Australians. The older bloke had glasses, thin hair and ears like frying pans; his wife was dumpy with a worried look on her face. Les gave them a half-smile and took the seat opposite on the other side of the storage space. He placed his bag between his legs, took out a bottle of water and had a sip while they waited for the others to arrive. Les was looking around, avoiding eye contact, when two young girls wearing blue tracksuits and sunglasses — one girl much heavier than the other — climbed on board. They had jet black hair and very olive skin and Norton guessed by their complexions and mannerisms they were European or Middle Eastern. They sat down on the seat along the stern and Nev put his clipboard down.

'Okay folks,' said Nev. 'This is *The Kingfisher*. I'm Neville. Welcome aboard.' Neville then went into his tourist spiel for the thousandth time.

Montague Island was nine kilometres south east of Narooma, around eighty-two hectares in area and pinched in the middle. After Lord Howe it was the second largest island off the NSW coast. The trip out and back, going around the island, plus snorkelling would take the best part of four hours. Neville went on about other things of interest. But Les was only half listening. Big Ears thought he was being funny and kept interrupting all the time making stupid remarks. Finally Neville pointed to the life jackets and informed them it was deadly imperative everybody wore one when they were crossing The Bar. The Bar was deadly and dangerous. Ships had sunk there. People had drowned. Great sea monsters lurked beneath The Bar. Neville made crossing The Bar sound like going around Cape Horn in the *Cutty Sark*. Oh. And if anyone was interested, the sunglasses he was wearing were special polaroids. A snap at twenty bucks each.

'Okay folks,' said Neville finally. 'Let's put our life jackets on and we'll get going.'

They all took a life jacket from the storage space and while they were strapping them on, Les got into a little polite conversation with the two girls and the young couple. The young couple were from Penrith and down for the Blues Festival so they'd decided to take a trip to Montague Island while they were in Narooma. The two girls were Iranian and came from Yagoona. They too were down for the festival and the thinner one was, like Les, going to Montague to go snorkelling; particularly to dive amongst the seals. Les ignored Big Ears. He took a photo of everyone putting on their life jackets and when Big Ears saw Norton's camera, he offered to take his photo. To keep him happy, Les handed Big Ears the camera, then watched as he looked at it like it was the control panel on the space shuttle and went on to stuff up two photos. Les took his camera back as the skipper checked them all out.

'Okay,' said Neville, satisfied everybody was secure. 'Let's get going.'

Neville cast off then climbed up to his cabin and started the motor. Les and the others either found a seat or somewhere safe to stand as the skipper carefully manoeuvred *The Kingfisher* away from the jetty. Soon, they were motoring slowly up the channel.

They got to The Bar as four decent swells came through and the boat started dipping up and down and rocking from side to side. Les held on to a pipe above his head and realised what Neville had meant about having a life jacket on when crossing The Bar. As well as being quite narrow, the water wasn't all that deep at the mouth; if any sort of a sea was running it would be extremely dangerous. They hit another couple of swells as they cleared the entrance, then Neville veered right and gunned the motor.

The Kingfisher was noisy and vibrated like a floor sander. Out to sea, the ocean was rougher than Les had anticipated and sheets of spray came splashing over either side of the boat as it pitched up and down in the swells. Nevertheless, Neville yelled down from his cabin that it was safe to take their life jackets off if they wanted to. As soon as they did, Big Ears got up on his seat and poked his head around the corner of the cabin, straight into a huge blast of water that immediately soaked him to the skin. Everybody tried not to laugh and Les took a photo as Big Ears sat down and tried to appear nonchalant while his dumpy wife looked more worried than ever. They bumped and rolled through the troughs and Les remembered Neville saying they'd probably see dolphins on the way out. They might even see whales. The others were looking out to sea and Les was watching the landward side of the boat when he gave a double blink. Swimming slowly along the surface a hundred metres from the boat was a huge shark. There was no mistaking its triangular black fin and the black tip of its tail flicking through the chop. Les poked his head up the stairs.

'Hey Nev!' he yelled out. 'Did you see that?'

Neville turned around from the wheel. 'See what, Les?'

'That bloody big shark out there,' pointed Les.

Neville shook his head. 'Nah. No sharks out here. It was probably a dolphin.'

Les stared at the skipper for a moment. 'Yeah righto,' he said, and returned to his seat.

Les knew a shark when he saw one. He'd seen them up close and personal. He'd seen them eating people. And that was a bloody shark. A big one. Les gazed at the deck and gave his head a slow, thoughtful shake then sat back with his bottle of mineral water as they bumped and rolled their way out to Montague island. Eventually they got there and Nev slowed down on the leeward side. Les stood up with the others to check it out.

There wasn't much to see. A long, low, uneven island of lumpy, grey rock with a small lighthouse on top near some old houses. Sitting in a small cove down from the lighthouse, was a landing with a crane and a lifeboat next to a rail leading up to a white shed with a red roof. There were no trees and little colour. The only vegetation was brittle scrub and patches of green and brown kikuyu grass. The place reminded Les of documentaries he'd seen about bleak, windswept islands off Scotland and Northern England. Maybe if the sun was out it might have looked all right. But on a cloudy day with a southerly blowing — VFO. Les took a few photos and returned to his seat. Nev left the engine idling and came down from the cabin.

'Well, this is it,' he said, warmly. 'Montague Island. Only land mass between Australia and South America.'

With Big Ears butting in again, trying to be funny, Nev went on with his spiel about the island. The tuna industry. When Zane Grey starting big game fishing off the island. Penguins, whales, giant squid. How an entire tribe of aborigines paddled their canoes out over a hundred years ago then got caught in a storm going back and they all perished. Les, however, wasn't the slightest bit interested. He was wishing he was somewhere else, instead of bobbing up and down on a boat out in the middle of nowhere on a lousy day, having to put up with Big Ears. Les stayed in his seat and did his best impersonation of a Trappist monk, till Neville said they'd check out the rest of the island, along with the seal colony, and they got going again.

Les took his binoculars out and scanned the island. It looked even worse. Then Neville informed them the seal colony was coming up and went in closer to the rocks. There were two seals: an old, brown bull and his mate.

The only sign of any other seals were patches of white seal shit splashed all over the rocks, as if a team of gyprockers had just emptied their work buckets. Nev yelled down that the seal colony must be out chasing fish. Les couldn't really have given a toss and went back to searching around with his binoculars hoping he might see a whale or something.

They got to the south side of the island, with Les focusing out to sea, when charging up the coast came a fleet of over thirty yachts under full sail, taking advantage of the southerly. They were all shapes, colours and sizes and made a great sight, ploughing through the white-capped swells about half a kilometre out from the island. Les saw them before the others and yelled up the stairs.

'Hey Nev! What are all the yachts in aid of?'

Nev peered out to sea. 'Ohh yeah. That's a special Bermagui to Ulladulla and back yacht race they organised for the long weekend. I forgot all about it.'

'They look good,' said Les.

'Yes, they do,' agreed Neville.

Les went back to peering through his binoculars, as the others crossed over for a better view.

The yachts were tacking and straining, their sails billowing in the wind, and as they drew closer Les could make out some of the names. *Trumpeter. Witchy Woman. Wind Dancer. Emily. Barbarella. Kerouac.* Hey, that's a good name for a yacht, thought Les. I've read *On the Road* twice. I'll check it out and see if its spinnaker's at the right end.

Les zeroed in on *Kerouac*. It was a wide-beamed, blue and white, ten metre ocean-going job with a sizeable cabin and the name along the side in red. A black rubber ducky was lashed securely across the bow, and an Australian flag flew off the stern. There was a man at the helm and two other men and a woman sitting up on the far rail. The yacht was tilted towards him and Les hit the stabilising button. The crew were all wearing sunglasses and dark sailing outfits with laced up hoods. Les could make out thick moustaches on the men and a strand of bright hair wisping across the woman's sunglasses. He zeroed in on the woman when the yacht tacked and the crew all ran across to the opposite rail and sat with their backs to him as the yacht angled in towards the rest of the fleet. Les watched the yachts move up the coast before they disappeared, as Neville brought *The Kingfisher* back around to the leeward side of the island.

They stopped in the same sheltered place as before. Neville cut the engines then came down and went into a bit of a spiel about the seals. While he was talking, he picked up a bucket and started tossing pieces of fish over the side of the boat. There was a swirl of shiny black in the water as several seals came in and took the pieces of fish.

'There you go,' said Nev. 'I knew they were here somewhere.'

'Oh look at that.' The thinner of the two girls turned to her friend. 'Quick Massoameh. Get the camera.'

By now Grace's mineral water, along with the other water he'd been drinking, had flushed through Norton's system and he was bursting for a pee. He got up and went downstairs to use the toilet. Like all fishing boats, the galley stank of rotten bait and diesel, and when he opened the door, the toilet was jammed. Les looked around for something to piddle in. But there was nothing, and the smell downstairs, along with the pitching boat, was making him sick. Les went back upstairs to find Big Ears and the thinner of the two girls had stripped down to their costumes to go snorkelling with the seals. The girl noticed Les watching them as Neville handed out the diving gear.

'Come on,' she said. 'Before they swim away.'

Les turned to Neville. 'What about sharks?'

Neville ignored the worried look on Norton's face. 'Nah. No sharks out here,' he replied, breezily.

Les peered over the side of the boat. They were in around fifteen metres of water next to a ledge that dropped into bottomless, cobalt blue. Running beneath the water towards the island he could make out some huge, white rocks edged with grey and black. It was overcast, the water was deep and gloomy and full of fish pieces, and seals were a shark's favourite food. Especially White Pointers. And Les had already seen a possible Great White on the way out. Les turned to watch as the young girl and Big Ears got into their face masks and flippers while Neville kept tossing more bloody pieces of fish to the circling seals. By the time Big Ears and the girl had geared up, the boat had drifted well away from the seals. Nevertheless, Big Ears and the girl pushed off the back and swam blissfully out to them. Les watched in horror. But he was absolutely busting for a pee. He also felt like a big blouse still standing by the side of the boat with his snorkelling gear in his bag.

'In you go mate,' said Neville.

Les stared across at Big Ears and the girl swimming around out in the middle of nowhere circled by half a dozen seals chewing on pieces of fish.

'Oh,' squealed the girl. 'One just swam between my legs.'

'Go on,' her friend said to Les, holding up her camera. 'I'll take a photo of the three of you.'

Les looked at everyone watching him. 'Yeah righto,' he said.

Les got into his rubber vest, slipped into his flippers then shuffled to the landing bay at the back of the boat and rinsed his face mask and snorkel. He put them on, saw Neville give him the thumbs up, then took a deep breath and pushed off the landing bay.

The water was deep and dark and cold, and edged in gloomy blue-black, with huge, shadowy, boulders tumbled across the bottom. No seaweed and no movement except for a few clusters of small school fish. Exactly as Les had seen in other documentaries about White Pointers in The Great Australian Bight. All that was missing was the shark cage and a six metre, Great White, with its teeth bared, either coming in out of the gloom or up off the bottom. Without letting go of the landing bay, Les strained and pissed as hard and as fast as he could, feeling blessed relief and the water warming up around him. As soon as he finished, Les gave Mr Wobbly a quick shake, then hopped back on the boat and took his face mask off.

'Yeah,' he said, brightly. 'It was good. Didn't see any seals though.'

Ignoring the others, Les pulled his vest off then wrapped a towel around his waist and got his camera. If Big Ears and the girl were going to get taken he may as well get a photo. Nothing happened, however. The seals swam off, Big Ears and the girl snorkelled in and got back on the boat safe and sound. Les put his camera away, got dressed, then went back into Trappist monk mode, as Neville started the engine and they headed for Narooma.

With the wind behind them going home, it wasn't long before they were approaching The Bar and it was time to put their life jackets on again. They crossed The Bar without incident and Les was the first one off the boat when they tied up at the jetty. He thanked Neville for a wonderful day, said goodbye to the others and walked up to the house glad to be back on dry land.

Warren's car wasn't outside, the key was under the mat and there was no sign of Warren when Les let himself inside. He made a cup of coffee then had a shower and rinsed his snorkelling gear. By now Les was getting hungry. He put on a blue T-shirt, cap and cargos, got his overnight bag and Visa cards and headed for the festival.

The venue was fairly crowded with people getting the most from the last day of the concert. Les showed his wristband and walked straight across to the foodstalls at the back of the park. The Turkish stall smelled enticing and the owner in his braided vest had a swarthy friendliness about him. Les got a plate of beans, lamb, rice and vegetables and other things that looked tasty, then found a seat at the table where they'd had the drama the day before, and washed everything down with a freshly made pineapple and orange juice. While he was eating Les checked out the punters and listened to some music drifting across from the tents. It sounded like Jimbo's Blues Band. Les finished his meal then got a takeaway coffee and found a seat in the red tent and sat back to watch Jimbo and his band do their thing. They were just as tight as the day before and had the crowd rocking. Jimbo finished in his Indian headdress, Les applauded loudly with the rest of the crowd, then left the tent and walked over to the souvenir stall.

There were that many CDs Les didn't know where to start. So first off he bought a stack of T-shirts and caps for Billy, himself and anyone else he could think of, including Roxy in South Australia. Then he started on the CDs. He just pointed to the ones with covers he liked and finished up with everything from Ronnie Dawson to Pete Cornelius and the DeVilles to Blue Katz. And a stack of compilation records. *Big City Blues* to *Blues Road Trip* featuring everybody from The Johnny Nocturne Band to James Harman to Pat Boyack and the Prowlers. Most of the musicians and bands Les had never heard of. After leaving both his Visa cards quivering wrecks, Les crammed as much as he could into his overnight bag and carried everything back to the house.

There was still no one home. Les got a beer and packed all his purchases into two cardboard cartons. He was drooling at some of the music but decided to wait till he got back to Chez Norton then get into it with the help of Warren's prohibited substances. Les tidied his room and sorted out a few other things and later, when he was sitting in the kitchen reading the paper, a car pulled up in the driveway. Warren walked in wearing a T-shirt and jeans, designer sunglasses and driving gloves.

'Woz,' said Les. 'What's happening baby?'

'I found a nice, winding road in Bodalla State Forest. So I thought I'd see what the Celica could do.'

'The westie finally come out in you, eh.'

'You bet. I was chucking donuts and burnouts. It was megaramic.'

'That's good, Woz. I like to see you enjoy yourself.'

Warren got a glass of water from the fridge. 'So how was Montague Island?'

'In a word Woz, up to shit.'

They exchanged pleasantries about their day. Les told Warren about the trip out to the island, seeing a shark and shitting himself when he went in the water. The only thing of interest was the yachts. Warren had a sleep in then breakfast on his own at Carey's. He read the paper at the house and listened to the radio then went for a burn along the backroads. He didn't have a bad day. Les showed Warren what he'd bought, then Warren made two mugs of coffee, tuned the ghetto blaster to Season FM and Les followed him out onto the verandah. They sat facing the ocean. Despite the overcast sky, it was still pleasant watching the boats bobbing up and down at their moorings and the people walking around the jetty. Les held up his mug.

'I wonder what your crazy girlfriend's coffee's going to be like tonight?'

'Yes. I wonder,' replied Warren.

'What if we trip out and never come back.'

'Yeah. We might finish up living in Nimbin or somewhere. Just another couple of hippies with our brains fried.'

'I think yours are fried now.' Les was about to mention Warren's sleepwalking, but he thought he'd wait until Clover and Grace arrived so Warren would have to face up to it in front of the others.

'At least you don't have to worry, Ugly,' said Warren. 'You ain't got any brains to fry.'

'If I take too much lip like that from you, I'm sure I ain't.'

'So how's your back now, anyway?' asked Warren. 'Grace going to give you another massage?'

Les looked into his coffee. 'I'll let you in on a little secret, Woz.' Les told Warren about his romp on the rubber ball with Grace and how she topped him off afterwards. 'You know me, Woz. I never say too much. But it was some of the best porking I've ever had. You ought to get one of those rubber balls and give it a run with Clover.'

'And she just handed you the bottle of oil, and said rub it into that giant monster set of hers.'

Les shrugged. 'I could only do what she asked, Woz.'

'Fuck! What are they like? Are they as good as those photos of Tara Moss in *Black + White* magazine?'

'Are you kidding, Woz? They make Tara Moss's tits look like a couple of old football socks.'

Warren drained his coffee and raised the cup to Les. 'You are truly the chosen one, Les. You have been blessed.'

'They don't call me Lucky Les for nothing,' winked Les.

Warren looked at his watch. 'Well it's not getting any earlier. I might have an Eiffel Tower and get my shit together.'

'Okey doke.'

They rinsed their cups and Warren got in the shower. Les lay on his bed and read some more of his book then had a shave when Warren finished. He dabbed a bit of CK on his craggy face then got into his jeans, And 1s and a blue and white polo shirt with a light blue collar. When he walked into the kitchen, Warren was wearing black jeans, a brown shirt with black stripes and his black leather jacket. He'd just made them a monstrous delicious each.

'Cheers Woz.' Les took a mouthful and blinked. 'Christ Warren. How much bourbon did you put in this?'

'I'm not sure,' replied Warren. 'But there wasn't much room for the ice, the slice and the soda water.'

Lionel Hampton and his Octet were wailing 'Jack the Fox Boogie' on Season FM in the loungeroom while Les and Warren were hitting the trail to deliciousville in the kitchen, and it wasn't long before they had a glow up. It was Norton's turn to make the drinks when there was a knock on the door. Les walked out and opened it. Clover was standing on the bottom step in a pair of white hipster jeans, a collarless white shirt and a blue T-shirt with yellow parrots on the front that she'd obviously got from Grace.

'Yes young lady? Can I help you?' he asked.

'You're the one that'll need help if you don't get out of the road,' said Clover. 'Where's that man of mine?'

'You must mean Mr Edwards. Do come in.'

Clover walked into the kitchen and threw her arms around Warren as Les closed the door.

'My God,' she said, smelling Warren's breath. 'How long have you two been on the turps?'

'Not long,' said Warren. 'Would you like one?'

'Yes. I wouldn't mind.'

Warren snapped his fingers and nodded to the fridge. 'Another delicious, Riff Raff. Plenty of ice.'

'Yes master,' bowed and scraped Les. 'Coming right up.' Les just about had the drinks made, when there was another knock on the door. 'Ohh shit!' he groaned. 'Who the bloody hell's this?' Les opened the door again and it was Grace. Her brown hair was down and shining like silk and she was wearing tight blue jeans, a Wrangler jacket and a black T-shirt with magpies on the front. A pair of black coral earrings caught the light as they dangled from her ears, and over her shoulder was a smart, black denim bag.

Les looked down at her. 'I suppose you want to come in too.'

Grace shrugged. 'It doesn't worry me that much. I can go over the RSL and have a drink if you like.' She stepped inside and gave Les one on the lips. 'How are you, George?'

'Good,' smiled Les, closing the door. 'Clover's inside. She beat you by about two minutes.'

They walked into the kitchen and the old house seemed to light up with the arrival of Clover and Grace. Les got all the drinks together then they sat back and talked about their day.

'So your trip out to Montague Island wasn't so good, Les,' said Grace.

'On a nice day, it'd probably be all right,' replied Les. 'But today...' He shook his head. 'And I was certain Big Ears and that girl were going to get eaten.'

'What did you do when you came back from Grace's?' Warren asked Clover.

'Helped mum round the house then read a book,' Clover replied.

'What are you reading?' asked Les.

'*Fetish*. By Tara Moss,' answered Clover.

Warren caught Norton's eye. 'We were only talking about that earlier.'

'You were?' said Clover.

'Yeah. It didn't get a bad write up in the paper.'

'She's a really good writer,' declared Clover. 'I'm quite enjoying it.'

'Cool,' replied Les. 'If it's all right, I'll borrow it off you when you've finished.'

They talked away and ripped into the delicious while Season FM pumped out the hits and memories from the flapper era. Before long everyone was starting to feel no pain.

'So what's doing with these mushrooms?' asked Warren.

'Yes. I think it's about time I made the coffee,' replied Clover.

Clover put the kettle on then got the Tiger Stripes from the fridge, emptied them out onto a chopping board and started dicing them up while the water boiled. She tipped the mushrooms into a jug, added instant coffee, plus a little evaporated milk and honey, gave it a stir then poured out four mugs and handed them around. It looked like a cross between greasy dishwater that had run out of detergent and lumpy mushroom soup.

'Well. Here we go.' Clover raised her coffee and took a mouthful.

Les took a mouthful of his and nearly gagged. 'Ohh yuk!' he said. 'It definitely isn't Moccona.'

Warren screwed up his face. 'Christ! It tastes like someone eating curried rat just shit in my mouth.' He blinked and swallowed some bourbon.

'You get used to it,' said Grace, sipping away on hers.

'Yeah. I'll bet you do. Ohh bugger this,' said Les, and drained his mug, washing away the taste with delicious.

'I think that's the best idea,' said Warren, doing the same thing.

The girls finished theirs and there was a collective silence.

'So what happens now?' said Les.

'Give it time,' said Clover. 'Be cool.'

'Yes. Be cool Les,' said Grace.

Les settled back, took a sip of his delicious, then turned to Warren. 'Okay Woz, old mate,' he said. 'Now that everybody's here. Do you know you're walking in your sleep?'

Warren screwed his face up at Les. 'I'm what? Ohh piss off.'

'I'm fair dinkum, Woz. Remember when I set that rat-trap last night? And I left it under the kitchen table?'

'Yeah,' nodded Warren.

'I got up this morning and it was in the fridge.'

'There was a rat-trap in the fridge?' said Clover. 'What? Still set?'

'Yeah,' nodded Les. 'I went to get some milk and it nearly took my bloody finger off.'

'Well, I didn't put the bloody thing in there,' declared Warren.

'But that's not all,' continued Les. 'When I got up on Saturday morning, our shaving gear was scattered all over the bathroom floor. And someone had pissed all over the seat. No prizes for guessing who.'

'Your shaving gear was all over the bathroom?' said Clover.

'Everywhere,' said Les. 'I cleaned it up and didn't say anything. But before that, I had to force my way out of my room.' Les turned to Warren. 'Because someone had jammed a bloody old horseshoe under my door.'

'You had a horseshoe jammed under your door?' said Grace.

'Yeah. I nearly had to break the door down to get out.'

'And you reckon I did it?' Warren looked at Les, quite put off.

'Well, of course you did. That's why you've been calling me Lucky Les all the time. I know your warped sense of humour, Woz.'

Warren looked directly at Norton. 'Les. Apart from the rat and the bear waking me, I've been sleeping like a log. I haven't moved. And where would I find a bloody horseshoe? And if did, I can think of a better place to stick it than under your door.'

'Woz. Get fair dinkum. You got it from under the house. Mate. I know it was only a joke,' smiled Les. 'And that's cool. But sleepwalking can be a worry.'

Warren stared at Les. 'I got a horseshoe from under the house? You moron. Remember last night in the kitchen? When it turned freezing cold?'

'The kitchen got cold?' said Clover.

'Yeah. Like a bloody morgue. So Einstein here said, "There must be a draught coming from under the house".' Warren turned to Les. 'And when I was walking to my room, I asked you, you goose — "What is under the house?" Because I haven't bothered to look.'

Les thought for a moment. 'Shit! You did too.'

'Hello,' said Warren. 'We've made contact with the lost tribe.'

'Well if that's the case' said Les, 'who …?' Suddenly a strange, tingle ran up Norton's spine. He sat back in his seat, a surprised look on his face. 'Shit! What was that?'

Grace caught Clover's eye, then smiled serenely at Les. 'Why don't we leave it till tomorrow?'

'Yes,' agreed Clover. 'Why don't we talk about it in the morning, boys?'

Les blinked at the girls as if he was now looking at them through a shop window. 'Yeah,' he nodded. 'Why don't we.'

Warren was staring at something on the table. 'Yeah, good idea. Why don't we.'

Les looked around and the room had changed shape. There were no straight lines or sharp edges. Everything had been rounded off. The table, the fridge, the kitchen cabinets. It all looked as if it was moulded out of plasticine.

'Are you all right, Les?' asked Grace.

'Yeah,' nodded Les, staring at his drink. The ice cubes had lights in them and it was glowing in his hand. 'Yeah. I'm good,' he said, slowly.

'How are you Warren?' asked Clover.

'How am I?' replied Warren, looking around. 'I'm not sure. Did Tinkerbell just fly through here sprinkling stardust everywhere?' He looked at his hand. 'Hey. It's all over my fingers.' Warren blew on his fingers and started to laugh. 'Shit! Look at that,' he said.

'Why don't we take our drinks out onto the verandah, and have a look at the night,' suggested Grace.

'Sounds good to me,' said Les. 'Do you know the way from here?'

Grace smiled across at Clover, then back to Les. 'Follow us Les. It's not far.'

'Hey. Don't leave without me,' said Warren.

Les got up and followed the others down the hallway to find it had turned into a green, glowing tunnel. The ceiling had heightened and the floor was narrower, while the doors on either side looked like the entrances into an igloo. Around him the air seemed denser, almost like water, and Les felt as if he was wading as much he was walking. They stepped into the plasticine loungeroom and there were colours going everywhere. His ghetto blaster had grown legs and was singing to him, the piano looked like a whale and the bear standing on the whale's head seemed the same size as Les, with a big, friendly smile spread across its face. They walked out onto the verandah and Les leant against the railing with his drink and gazed up at the sky.

It was still cloudy. But in the clear patches the stars were buzzing round like fireflies. The rolling clouds looked like herds of cattle charging across the sky, then they turned into endless hectares of gigantic, pink, grey mushrooms. The water in the harbour had changed to blue, molten lava and the ocean looked like a huge indigo blanket covered with tiny, silver feathers and someone was shaking it. He turned to the surrounding buildings and they'd turned into funny, colourful drawings, swept by convections of more colour. It was beautiful. And it was all beautifully drawn. Les turned to the others.

'Hey. You know what it's like?' he said. 'It's like I've landed in Toon Town.'

The others had disappeared. Instead, Warren had turned into Mickey Mouse, complete with a huge pair of white gloves. Clover was Minnie Mouse in a pair of Doc Martens with her hair punked up. And Grace's Wrangler jacket was now a black leather Brando jacket and she looked like a cross between Barbarella and the Terminator.

Les started laughing. 'Holy Shit!' he said.

'What's the matter, Les?' asked Grace.

'You're not going to believe this.' Les told them what he was seeing.

'That's okay, Les,' said Grace. 'You know what you look like to me? Foghorn Leghorn. Wearing a Blues Brothers outfit.'

'I reckon Yogi Bear,' said Clover. 'In a tuxedo.'

'No, no. You're both wrong,' said Warren. 'It's Yosemite Sam in a white Elvis jump-suit.'

Les gave Warren a crazy look. 'Whooh! You make me so mad, you long-eared little varmint. I ought's to blast the hide clean offen' your fur bearin' carcass.'

Suddenly they all fell about laughing like they were going to piddle themselves. After a while they settled down and Les turned to the sky again. Now it was all pink and blue with chunky little yellow and white clouds edged with Mayan writing. He looked at the top of the railing running along the verandah and it had turned into a bright green railway line, with tubes of toothpaste for sleepers. Someone had left a white cup sitting on the railing. While everything round it was turning into all sorts of things and all kinds of colours, Les concentrated on the white cup, telling himself it was a white cup. Nothing else. And it stayed a white cup. Okay, Les told himself, as well as expanding your mind, the mushrooms work on your subconscious. But it's only a trip. You go along with it and have some fun. But just be cool and remember you can come back to reality. It's only your imagination. He left the cup and turned to the others, and for a moment they looked normal. Then they went back into cartoon form. Les looked across the street at a telephone pole and it turned into a gigantic, blue cactus. Then the cactus got up and walked away, crouched forward like Groucho Marx. Les could hear its footsteps sounding like someone beating on a bass drum as they faded into the distance. Les shook his head. At least I think it's my imagination.

'How are you handling things, Les?' asked Grace.

Les turned around and Grace was still Barbarella. 'Not too bad,' he replied. 'I just watched a telegraph pole turn into a cactus and walk away.'

'The boats on the jetty changed into storks a little while ago,' said Clover. 'And flew out to sea holding baby orang-utans in their beaks.'

'How are you going, Woz?' asked Les.

Warren had his eye on a moth circling the light on the verandah. 'I'm just watching this fighter jet. It's firing golden arrows all over the place. And they're exploding into showers of hundreds and thousands. It's unreal.'

'What about you, Grace?' asked Les.

'I'm into the Mandelbrot Set,' said Grace.

'The what?' said Les.

Grace pointed to the sky. 'Can you see an odd-looking black hole up there?'

Les stared up at the sky. 'Yeah. I think I can,' he said.

'Keep watching it,' said Grace.

Les stared intently at the black hole. At first it looked a silhouette of the bear. Then it turned into a fat little Buddha shape with a pointy cap. From out of the black hole flowed countless paisley patterns of every colour and design imaginable: they were continuously forming and re-forming as they spread across the sky into space. Million and billions of them. It was like watching an epiphany of never-ending, ethereal, coloured patterns pouring from a huge kaleidoscope. It was spiritual, metaphysical and the strangest, most surrealistically beautiful thing Les had ever seen.

'Holy smoke!' he said. 'Look at that.' Les turned to Grace. 'Is that the eye of God?'

'Sort of,' answered Grace. 'It's the Mandelbrot Set. Have a few Tiger Stripes and you don't need a computer to click into fractal geometry.'

'Whatever,' said Les, totally incredulous.

After staring at the amazing colours, Les turned to the house. The windows had changed into eyes and the door was now a mouth. One of the eyes winked at him and a huge, Rolling Stones tongue flicked out of the mouth. Four rats dressed in jockey colours came sliding off the tongue pulling a pumpkin coach with a boardrack full of surfboards. The coach flew off over the railing and disappeared towards the golf course which had turned into a Jurassic Park full of pink and green dinosaurs; they were strolling arm in arm across the links carrying paper umbrellas. Les watched them for a moment then looked at his watch. Although it had melted like in a Salvador Dali painting, Les could still tell the time and he was amazed how fast it had gone. Unlike smoking pot where time often slowed to a crawl — mushrooms sped things up.

'Shit! If we're going to the concert,' he said, holding up his watch, 'we'd better make a move. Look at the time.'

'Hey, you're right,' said Grace. She turned to the others. 'Will we get going?'

Warren was aghast. 'That concert and all those people. It's going to be a complete freak-out.'

Clover smiled and put her arm around him. 'It'll be fun. You wait and see.'

'What if you know who's in there,' said Les, ominously. 'He'll look like Godzilla.'

'Oh God!' wailed Warren. 'Don't say that.'

'It's all right,' said Grace, holding up a biro. 'I've got my disintegrator, death ray gun with me.'

They went inside and somehow Les was able to turn off the radio, find his guest pass, get the rest of his stuff together and turn the lights off except for the one above the front step. When the others got their things together they all rallied out the front before walking down the hill to the jetty.

Walking down the hill was like going down a ski slope. They all leaned to one side as they turned left at the bottom and slid past the boats at the jetty. It was a full-on Toon Town trip now. Everything was a drawing by Harry Crumb and everybody they saw was a cartoon character in strange, colourful clothes. Even the people's eyes poked half-a-metre out of their heads. They showed their passes and the security staff in black all looked like Darth Vader. Inside was pandemonium. There seemed to be cartoon characters running everywhere, honking horns and banging on drums. Music was coming from one of the tents and Les could see notes and cleft tones spinning high above the crowd. The weather was changing and amongst the patches of spinning stars the clouds were flying across the sky as in time-lapse photography.

'We have to remember this night,' said Les.

He handed his camera to a cartoon character in a blue zoot suit with a huge yellow fedora who was walking past and asked if they would take a photo. The character in the zoot suit was most obliging. Les gathered the others around and the character took two photos. Each time the flash went off it was like a phosphorous bomb exploding. Les thanked the character, retrieved his camera and turned to the others.

'What about drinks?' he asked.

'Yes. Good idea,' said Warren. 'I mean no. I mean yes. I mean ...'

'Ohh shut up, Warren,' said Les. 'Come and give me a hand.'

'I can't,' said Warren. 'I can't.'

'Yes you can. You stupid hippy. Come on.'

Les dragged Warren over to the drinks tent and got four delicious. Paying for the drinks was a trip in itself. The fifty dollar bill had turned into an Indian blanket and his change looked like playing cards and gambling chips. All the drinks were full of glow worms wearing snorkelling gear. With not much help from Warren, Les handed the drinks around then they followed Grace across to the blue tent. Somehow they got four seats together and managed to arrive just as Pete Cornelius and the DeVilles came out on stage.

'This guy's really good,' said Grace. 'He's only eighteen.'

'I don't know if I've heard of him,' replied Les.

'He's from Tasmania.'

Les looked up at the stage and it was a mess of lights going everywhere. Comets and shooting stars whirled above the band, then an Egyptian Pharaoh in a chariot drawn by four black horses galloped above the stage, before heading out through the top of the tent. Les tried to concentrate on the band. The lead singer was wearing a plain, dark blue shirt and black trousers. The bearded drummer had on a black T-shirt and jeans and the other guitarist was wearing a cap and a Levi's jacket. Next thing the lead singer turned into Zeke Wolf with this huge, bushy tail and the two others in the band turned into Heckle and Jeckle. Bloody hell, thought Les, and settled back in his seat as the band went straight into 'If You Be My Baby'.

The music didn't sound quite as deep and smooth as being stoned. But it was still great and the light show was fantastic. Zeke Wolf and Heckle and Jeckle were boogeying away on stage while a small crowd of cartoon characters bounced up and down in front of the band as the rest of the cartoon characters in the audience got into the music. Norton's delicious tasted like he was drinking liquid fire and he sipped away as the band did 'All My Heroes Are Dead', 'After School Blues', the old Johnny O'Keefe classic, 'She's My Baby'. Heaps of others and a sensational version of 'Riders On The Storm'. Then it was over. Les looked at his watch and again couldn't believe how fast the time was going. He turned to Barbarella, Micky and Minnie.

'What did you think?' he asked.

'Unreal,' answered Clover.

'I still don't know where I am,' said Warren.

'Yeah. Come to think of it. How did we finish up in here?' Les asked Grace.

Grace shrugged. 'We just did. Next up is Jo Jo Zep and The Falcons. They're the last act of the night. But I don't like our chances of getting a seat.'

'It doesn't matter,' said Clover.

'Yeah. I don't mind standing up,' said Les. 'In fact I don't care what happens one way or the other tonight. I'm having a ball.'

'That's good,' smiled Grace. 'But we'd better make a move. They're on in fifteen minutes.'

They left their seats and shuffled through the Toonies over to the booze tent. Les and Warren got another round of drinks and they joined the crowd standing outside the big tent. Les got Grace to hold his drink while he took his camera out and started taking photos of the crowd. They were still all Toonies in Toon Town clothing. But every now and again, one would slip back into almost human form and Les was convinced he was getting photos of their auras. One woman with long black hair had a blue, green and silver aura around her, radiating a metre from her body.

There was a great roar then the musicians came out on stage. Over the heads of the crowd Jo Jo Zep and The Falcons looked like the cast of Cirque du Soleil and Munchkins on steroids. Then they blasted off with 'Honey Dripper' and the Toonies all went mad.

Les was rocking and laughing along with the others when he looked away and noticed a skyscraper had broken off from Toon

Town and was walking towards them. The skyscraper stopped in front of Norton, a big gap opened near the top floors and a voice boomed out.

'Hey Les! Can you do me a favour?'

Les squinted up at the skyscraper and it partly took on human form. 'Ohh yeah,' he answered. 'What is it, Norm?'

Norm handed Les a video recorder. 'You know how to work one of these?'

'Sure,' replied Les. Billy had one and he'd lent it to Les for a week. Les was thinking of buying one.

'I'm flat out. The Handbrake's hurt her ankle. Can you come backstage and video Jo Jo and Wilbur Wilde for me?'

'Righto,' said Les.

Norm turned to the others staring blankly up at him. 'I'll send someone over with some seats for you. Okay Les. This way mate.'

Les followed the skyscraper through the backstage entry, past several tents and offices and a guests' tent full of chairs and tables. There were staff standing around doing whatever it was they were doing, looking like shiny, black robots with mirrors for eyes and old FJ Holden radiator grills for mouths. Pounding music was thumping from above Norton's head. He followed Norm up a set of steps onto the back of the stage and stopped dead in his tracks.

On the left, surrounded by more robots in black, were all the mixing panels, glowing and blinking like the control room on a space ship. On the right Cirque du Soleil was blasting away loud enough to raise the dead, and in the middle was the crowd, swarms of frantic Toonies, twisting and turning and bouncing into and tumbling over each other. Then half the Toonies dissolved into snapping, carnivorous plants, wrapping themselves around the poles and spiralling up the sides of the tent. The plants in front of the stage changed back to Toonies with gorilla heads, wearing straw boaters and blazers. They all looked up at Les and started yammering, and hopping from one foot to the other beating their chests. Next thing, Les picked up the energy emanating from the crowd. It came at him in convections of shimmering light, almost knocking him off his feet. The skyscraper smiled over at Les.

'Okay Les,' it boomed over the crowd. 'Away you go. Start filming.'

Les looked at the video camera and it had changed into a Stinger surface to air missile launcher. 'Righto.' Les raised the camera to his eye, and pressed the button. A rocket fired out and exploded in a burst of flowers above the band as they slipped into 'The Shape I'm In'. After that, Les just winged it.

The band thumped out one song after another and the crowd kept changing into one shape after another; meanwhile, anti-aircraft fire exploded above their heads showering them with fruit salad shrapnel, as lights and rockets flew over the band and whirled round the tent. Through the viewfinder, Wilbur Wilde looked five metres tall and Joe Camilleri looked five metres wide. The rest of the band had turned into penguins wearing top hats, waddling around with their instruments on a skating rink made of rainbow-coloured ice edged with luminous coconut trees and gingerbread guard towers. A technician hit the smoke machine, the stage fogged up and the band all turned into a bunch of Jack the Rippers, wearing long capes, tartan top hats, mini-dresses and fishnet stockings. Les wandered around filming and doing his best to keep out of the band's way. He looked over and the skyscraper gave him the thumbs up. Les panned the camera over the crowd and seated near the side of the tent he could see Barbarella, Mickey and Minnie. They saw Les and waved and Les waved back.

What songs the band played Les wasn't sure. It was just loud, hot and smoky on stage and Les roamed around thinking he'd beamed down onto an alien planet. The band played 'Chained To The Wheel' and walked off past him. The skyscraper ambled over to the microphone, strangled it to death and told the Toonies to put their hands together for Jo Jo Zep and The Falcons. The Toonies did what they were told and Circus Soleil came back and did 'Rock Me Baby All Night Long' for an encore, and that was it. Everything seemed to be all over before it even started. Les filmed the band leaving the stage then walked across and handed the skyscraper back his video camera.

'Thanks for that, Les,' said Norm. 'How did you like it backstage?'

'It was great,' replied Les. 'Unreal.'

The skyscraper edged in a little closer. 'How's your back now?'

'My back?'

'Yeah.'

'Oh my back. It's good. It's still there behind me I think.'

Norm stared at Norton. 'Are you all right, Les?'

'Yeah,' nodded Les. 'As a bean. We had a smoke earlier. That's all.'

Norm winked. 'Don't turn up stoned tomorrow.'

'No. I'll be cool. Anyway, I'd better get back to Barbarella, Mickey and Minnie.'

'Who?'

'The Toonies I came with. I'll see you tomorrow, Norm,' smiled Les.

'Yeah . . . right.'

Les left Norm and worked his way back through the crowd to the others. They were still sitting at the side of the tent staring into space.

'Hey. How's things?' Les asked them.

They looked up at Les and Grace spoke. 'How did you finish up on stage?' she asked.

'Norm asked me to video the band,' replied Les. 'It was a madhouse. Were they any good?'

'They were great,' said Warren. 'And it was mad down here too.'

'How are you feeling now, Les?' asked Clover.

'All right,' replied Les. 'I'm starting to straighten out a bit.' He looked at his watch and shook his head. 'Shit! I can't believe how fast the night's gone.'

'Yes,' agreed Grace. 'Time certainly flies when it's all over the place. And you're in another dimension having fun.'

'Does it what,' agreed Les. 'And you're right about time. It seems to bend.'

'What are we doing now?' asked Warren.

'We'd best head for home,' said Clover. 'Mum will be along soon.'

'Righto,' agreed Les. 'Let's make tracks.' He helped Grace to her feet and they all started to make their way to the entrance.

No one said much on the way home. They were all starting to come down and everyone was in their own little world. Arm in arm they made it to the front of the house and stood around looking at each other.

'So what's doing tomorrow?' asked Les.

'I don't know,' said Warren. 'What's tomorrow?'

'Monday,' said Clover. 'We're going home. Remember?'

'Ohh yeah, that's right,' nodded Warren.

'Why don't we all have breakfast together before you leave?' suggested Grace.

'Yes. I'd like that,' said Clover.

'Good idea,' agreed Les. 'There's something I want to talk to you about too.'

'We'll talk over breakfast.' Grace snuggled up to Les and put her arms around him.

'Hey. Here's mum now,' said Clover.

The station wagon arrived out the front in a blaze of light with Clover's mother behind the wheel in her dressing gown. Clover said goodbye to Les, then kissed Warren goodnight and walked over to the car. Les smiled down at Grace.

'Well. I don't think I'll forget tonight in a hurry, Grace,' he said.

'No. Me either,' replied Grace.

'What time do you want to have breakfast?'

'About nine or so?'

'Sounds good to me,' said Les. 'I'll see you then.'

'Goodnight Les.'

Les gave Grace a tender kiss goodnight, then she walked across to join Clover. As she got to the car she called out, 'Don't forget to drink your water.'

'I won't,' Les assured her.

The boys waved them off, Les opened the door, then they walked inside to the kitchen and Warren turned on the light.

'Fuck! What a night,' blinked Les. 'I'm still seeing things.'

Warren looked a little drawn and pale. 'I don't think I'm in any hurry to do that again. It was all right. But at times there, I was just seeing too much weird shit.'

'You should have seen it up on that stage,' said Les. 'It was insane.'

Warren yawned and rubbed a hand across his neck. 'Mate. I'm going to have a snakes and hit the sack. I'm rooted.'

'I won't be far behind you, Woz.'

Norton went to his room and sat on the bed, still seeing coloured lights and stars similar to when you get a knock on the head or let out a violent sneeze. He changed into his tracksuit and heard Warren shuffling down the hallway.

'What time are we having breakfast?' Warren called out.

'Grace said around nine,' Les called back.

'See you then, Les.'

'Righto.'

Les went to the bathroom, then got the last bottle of mineral water, took it out to the kitchen and opened it. He didn't feel all that thirsty and it wasn't easy drinking a large bottle of mineral water in the middle of the night. But Les kept glugging and yawning away till it was all gone. Suddenly the temperature in the kitchen dropped down to below freezing. Shit, cursed Les, rubbing his arms as his breath immediately turned to steam. Here we go again. Back to bloody Siberia. This joint's fucked. Les was about to get up and go to bed when he glanced across the kitchen. A peculiar green glow was coming from under the front door and reflecting along the hallway. Les watched the strange light and shook his head. Fuckin hell, when do these bloody mushrooms wear off? he asked himself. Next thing, he heard a noise coming from around the cars. Feeling suspicious, he got up and opened the front door.

Les stared into the yard and all he could see at first was the same green glow. Then he noticed a slightly built, not very tall man standing near Warren's Celica. He was wearing a straw hat with a black ribbon around it, a crumpled, grey frock coat, matching trousers and lace-up boots. An untidy beard covered his face and perched on his nose were a pair of John Lennon glasses. Les wasn't sure in the light, but he looked to have blood on the sleeve of his coat and his left hand appeared to be missing. Whoever it was, he didn't say anything. He just stared silently at Les with an expression of sad anger in his eyes.

'Yeah, what do you want mate?' said Les.

The man with the beard continued to stare at Les without answering.

'What's up?' said Les. 'Do you want something? What are you hanging around the cars for? What do you want?'

Without saying anything, the man with the beard slowly raised his right arm and pointed away from the house towards the ocean.

Les screwed his face up. 'What . . . ?'

The man still kept his silence and simply stood in the green glow pointing south. Les figured he must be drunk and had been in a fight or something.

'Listen mate,' said Les bluntly. 'If you don't want anything, piss off. And get away from the cars. Go on. Fuck off.'

The man kept staring at Les then lowered his arm and started to walk away, still staring at Les over his shoulder. Finally, he disappeared into the darkness taking the green glow with him. Les waited for a moment, then shut the door, turned the light off in the kitchen and went to his bedroom.

Bloody hell! That's all I need, thought Les, after he switched off the bedlamp and climbed under the blankets — some drunken yobbo trying to steal one of the cars. Anyway, he'd better not come back. Unless he wants that empty bottle right between the eyes. Les gathered the blankets round his neck and shivered. Shit, it's fuckin cold in here. Les stayed still and started to warm up. Norton watched the last coloured lights exploding in his mind's eye and before long he had put the intruder behind him and was snoring peacefully.

L es blinked his eyes open before seven the next morning absolutely bursting for a piss. He rolled out of bed, hurried to the bathroom and hosed away like a draught horse. God! I didn't think that was ever going to finish, he thought, as he flushed the toilet. There must have been a gallon. Les splashed some water over his face and stared at himself in the mirror. Anyway, I'm up now. He cleaned his teeth then changed into his training gear and walked into the kitchen. While the kettle was boiling and the toast was browning, he stared at the floor and mulled over the previous night. His mind was still a bit gluggy. But slowly the cogs and wheels started turning and Les smiled round the kitchen. It had certainly been a night with a difference. He made a mug of tea, buttered his toast and walked down the hallway into the loungeroom. Everything looked normal and steady snoring was coming from Warren's bedroom. Les stepped out onto the verandah and took up his usual position, leaning against the railing.

The weather had cleared up. It was fairly warm, the southerly had turned light nor'-east and apart from a few clouds the sky was bright blue. A lovely day to be fishing off the jetty, walking around or having a surf. Not much of a day to be fighting some gorilla in a park, mused Les. He placed his mug of tea on the railing and touched his toes. He touched them again, swung his arms from side to side, and his brow furrowed. Something was wrong. Les did some squats then stretched his legs on the railing. He laced his hands behind his head, twisted his torso and did some side bends. Something was wrong all right. The pain and stiffness had completely vanished from his back.

'The bloody mineral water,' Les said, out loud. 'Grace. You doll.'

Les got down on his behind and did some crunches then rolled over and snapped off thirty press-ups, before jumping to his feet and running up and down on the spot. Not only had the pain in his back gone, all the other kinks in his body had disappeared too. From football, fighting, getting shot: even the sinus in his broken nose had cleared up.

'Shit! I can't remember ever feeling this good,' said Les. Ecstatically, he grinned up at the sky. 'Boss. What can I say? Thanks mate. And give that girl a medal.' Les quickly finished his tea and toast, put his cap and sunglasses on and tore off out the front door towards the golf links.

Les walked down Browning Street, stopped at the bottom and looked at the hill going up to the golf course. He took a breath then sprinted to the top like Sylvester Stallone taking the steps in *Rocky*. When he got there, he was barely puffing. Les felt he could run all day. He was about to take off again, then stopped. No. I'll put the run on hold for the time being. I've got a big day in front of me. And you never know who's around. Norton straightened his cap and set off across the golf links at a fast walk.

Les was moving that freely he felt his feet were hardly touching the ground and, before he knew it, he was overlooking Narooma Beach. He stopped to watch the people fishing near the rocks for a second, then started crisscrossing the golf links, stopping to do sets of push-ups and crunches or shadow box around the low-hanging branches under the trees. After a while Les checked his watch and decided to head back home. On the way, he found a metre of fence paling laying near a tree. He jammed one end in the ground, pushed the other against the tree then, taking a quick look around to make sure no one was watching, smashed a short right into the length of paling, snapping it in half. Les propped one of the shorter pieces of paling against the tree and whacked it with a short left. It only cracked. But there was plenty of power in his fist. Norton looked at the two pieces of wood for a moment then continued thoughtfully on his way.

The way Les felt, he knew he could kick Morgan Scully's arse to the Queensland border. And he couldn't wait to do it. But there was betting involved now, and most of the money would be on Morgan. If Les did too quick a demolition job on him, the punters might think he'd pulled a scam. Daddy was holding the prize money and running the show. But Les was still one out in a country town. If the locals got the shits at the result, anything could happen. This meant he'd have to carry Morgan for a while and make it look convincing without getting hurt. Which wouldn't be easy with an angry, big mug like Morgan. By the time Les got back to Browning Street, however, he had an idea.

Les still couldn't believe how good he felt as he walked in the driveway, when he stopped abruptly and took off his sunglasses. The rear window of Warren's car was smashed. Pieces of broken glass were scattered over the bonnet and sitting amongst the pieces on the back seat was a horseshoe. When he bolted out of the house earlier Les hadn't noticed. Les checked to make sure his car was all right, then walked over to the trees. He had a look around before taking another look at a Warren's car, then went inside and had a shower.

Les washed his training gear, hung it out on the verandah, changed into his blue cargos and a grey Hahn T-shirt then walked up to the newsagency. The idea he had earlier was just inside the door; a metal stand stacked with packets of cheap toys for kids. Amongst the Floating Eyeball, the Fly in an Ice Cube and Fart Powder, were packets labelled Vampire Blood Capsules: Scare Your Friends. Each packet contained four capsules of fake blood. Les bought two packets and the paper then walked back to the house. Warren was still in bed. Les poured himself a glass of water then went and banged on Warren's door.

'Hey Warren! Get out of bed.' Les banged on the door again. 'Warren. Are you awake?'

'Mmmrrgghhburrnngh,' came a horrible, strangled reply. 'Fuck! I am now.'

'Good. Get your arse out here. I want you to see something.'

There was more grumbling before Warren opened the door wearing his tracksuit and blinking at the light. 'What the fuck's up? What time is it?'

'Go and have a look at your car, Woz,' said Les.

'What?'

Warren shuffled off down the hallway and Les went out onto the verandah with his glass of water. He'd barely had two mouthfuls when a string of expletives echoed round the side of the house. Next thing, Warren came cursing up the hall way and out onto the verandah.

'Have you seen my fuckin car?' he howled.

'What do you think I got you out of bed for?' said Les.

'Who the fuckin hell did that?'

'I don't know,' answered Les. 'But there was a bloke hanging round out the front last night.' Les told Warren about chasing off the man with the beard before going to bed. 'It might have been him.'

'What a cunt,' said Warren.

'At least it's not your windscreen,' offered Les.

'Ohh yeah, great. You know how much a rear window is for a fuckin Celica.'

'No. The same as one for a piecost, I suppose.'

'A piecost?' said Warren. 'What's a fuckin piecost?'

'About two dollars fifty with sauce.'

'Ohh what's the fuckin use?' groaned Warren.

'Woz,' said Les. 'Why don't you go and have a shower and get ready. Grace and Clover will be here soon.'

'Yeah righto.'

Warren shuffled back to his bedroom then had a shower while Les read the paper in the kitchen. Les had just finished when a car pulled up in the driveway. He heard voices and a few moments later Grace and Clover walked in the front door. Clover had her bags with her. She left them in the hallway, then they both stepped into the kitchen, each wearing T-shirts and jeans.

'What happened to Warren's car?' asked Clover

'I'm not sure,' said Les. 'Warren's inside. Maybe you should ask him?'

Clover walked off to the front bedroom leaving Grace in the kitchen. Les folded the paper and smiled up at her. 'Good morning Grace,' he said.

'Hi,' replied Grace. She gave Les a quick once up and down. 'So how are you this morning?'

'Come here,' Les indicated with his head.

'What?'

'Come here.' Grace came over and Les pulled her down onto his knee then kissed her all over her neck.

'Goodness,' flustered Grace. 'What was that for?'

Grace took a chair and Les told her about the pain in his back disappearing and how good he felt all round.

'You're a genius, Grace,' said Les. 'I don't know what to say.'

Grace was all smiles. 'That's great,' she said. 'I knew it would work.'

'Work? It's nothing short of a miracle.'

'And you sprinted up the hill?'

'I flew. My shadow was flat out keeping up with me.' Les rubbed his hands together. 'Poor bloody Morgan. He won't know what's hit him.'

Grace looked sagely at Les. 'Don't be too sure, Les. He's a big man. And I've seen what he can do to people.'

Les was about to say something when Clover and Warren walked into the kitchen. Warren was still wearing his tracksuit. But he looked much better after a shower.

'Warren tells me you had an intruder last night,' said Clover.

Grace turned to Les. 'An intruder?'

'Yeah. In the front yard.' Les pushed out a chair. 'Okay Clover. Grab a seat. I'd like to have a word with you. You too Grace.' Les waited for Clover and Warren to get comfortable then he zeroed in on Warren's girlfriend. 'Righto Clover, what's going on?'

'Going on?' replied Clover. 'How do you mean, Les?'

'How do I mean? All right,' said Les evenly. 'This house, both your little ears prick up when me and Warren mention things that keep happening. Like the bear, and the rat in the piano. And the cold. And you're always asking us how we slept.'

'So?' shrugged Clover.

'So,' repeated Les. 'Our stuff laying around the bathroom and the rat-trap in the fridge. And the horsehoe under my door. I thought that was Warren. But it wasn't.' Warren smiled, vindicated as Les pointed his finger at Clover. 'Anyway, forget all the other shit for the moment. But that horseshoe sitting on the back seat of Warren's car. It's the same one that was under my door. I threw it under the trees out the front. Now, if Warren didn't stick it under my door, who did?' Les narrowed his eyes at Clover. 'You? Grace? Elves?'

Clover glanced at Grace then looked directly at Norton. 'Okay Les,' she said. 'I'll give it to you straight. The place is haunted.'

Warren sat up in his chair. 'Haunted?'

'Yes. There's a presence in the house,' said Clover.

'That's right,' added Grace. 'The Merrigan house has a poltergeist. It's the town's best kept secret.'

'Well, I'll be buggered,' said Les. 'How bloody slow am I?'

The girls looked at Norton without saying anything.

'So what happened?' asked Les. 'Did someone get murdered in here?'

'No,' answered Grace. 'We think it's Edward Ruddle.'

'The surveyor?' Les stared at Grace for a moment. 'Hey wait a minute,' he said. Les hurried out to the table on the verandah and came back with Jasmine Cunneen's book. He sat down and flicked through the pages till he came to the photo of Edward Ruddle and Gwendolyn Monteith. 'That's him,' said Les, stabbing his finger on the page. 'That's the bloke I saw out the front last night. Only he was wearing a straw hat.'

'Edward actually appeared last night?' said Grace.

'Yeah,' answered Les. 'In this green cloud. I thought I was still tripping.'

'Oh my God!' said Clover. 'That was the ectoplasmic aura. You saw the real deal, Les.'

'Christ! A bloody ghost,' said Warren.

'What exactly was he doing out the front, Les?' asked Grace.

'Nothing really. He was just standing near the cars staring at me.' Les thought for a second. 'Then he held his hand up and pointed. Like he was trying to tell me something.'

'So what did you do?' asked Grace.

'I told him to piss off.'

'And did he?'

'Yeah. He just vanished into the night.'

'Then came back later,' said Clover.

'But why would he want to break my window?' asked Warren. 'I've never done anything to him.'

'This is the fifth day people have been in the house,' said Clover. 'That's when the presence starts to get violent. After the fourth day.'

'Terrific,' said Les.

'Now you know why we never rent the place,' said Clover. 'We can't rent it. We can't sell it. We can't do anything with it. We're stuck with it.'

'That's what happened to Eachen,' said Grace. 'Edward drove him insane.'

'Well, why didn't you tell us what was going on?' asked Warren.

'Yeah. You could have warned us,' agreed Les.

'Oh, you both would have laughed at me,' said Clover. 'Besides that,' she smiled, 'I wanted to know what went on in here.'

'Thanks Clover.' Les turned to Grace. 'Naturally you were in on this too?'

'Well, I'd heard so much about the place, Les,' answered Grace.

'So when it turned freezing cold in here at night,' said Warren, 'that was Edward cruising around.'

'Yes. That was the ectoplasm, sweetheart,' smiled Clover. 'Edward's cool vibe from the spirit world.'

'Shit!'

There was silence for a moment, then Les looked around the table. 'So what do we do now? Call Ghostbusters?'

'No,' said Clover, rising to her feet. 'We go and have breakfast. Grace has got something she wants to show you.'

'Yes. Let's have breakfast,' said Grace, also rising from her chair.

'Yeah, suits me,' said Les. 'Ghost or no ghost. I'm that hungry, I'd eat the arse out of a dead werewolf.'

They got their things and walked up to the restaurant. The girls were chatting away, quite pleased that thanks to Les they could now verify who the spirit was. Warren was glad he was getting out.

Carey's wasn't crowded and they were able to get a table near the window. They ordered breakfast, Les paid and they got their little wooden objects again. Les couldn't help but laugh when Warren got a pineapple. They sat down, the first coffees arrived, then they started talking about the night before and the mushrooms. Grace reminded them that they'd have a flashback sometime tomorrow.

The waitress brought the food over and the conversation swung back to the house. Clover told them how the presence never made itself felt before midnight. Why? She didn't know. The house had never been broken into or vandalised. The locals gave it a wide berth. Some kids from Sydney got in there once. One fell over the balcony and broke his leg. Another had his fingers crushed when a door slammed on them. A medium from Sydney stayed there two nights. Although she never identified the spirit, she said it was seeking something. But it was trapped around the house. And until it got what it sought, it would remain in the house and the violence would continue. Clover's parents avoided any publicity and apart from one small story in the local paper, they'd managed to keep everything away from the mainstream media. All up, it was a lovely old house.

But it was also a giant pain in the arse — thanks to Edward. Their second coffees arrived and Les turned to Grace.

'Clover said you had something you wanted to show me?' he asked her.

'Yes.' Grace opened her bag and took out a small folder of photos. 'I only got these this morning. But remember when I came round the house and took some photos?'

'Last Friday?' said Les.

'That's right. And I took a couple of you standing in the doorway out on the verandah. Take a look.' Grace slid the photos over.

Les looked at the photos. They were good, happy snaps. He was facing the sun with a smile on his face and he looked fit and relaxed without posing.

'That's definitely me,' said Les. 'Handsome devil that I am.'

'Arguably,' said Grace. 'But have a look at the doorway off the lounge. Up on the right.'

Les peered at the photos. It was a little dark inside the house. Then he saw it, sticking out of the door jamb. A shadowy hand and wrist.

'Bloody hell!' exclaimed Les. 'Look at that. It's a hand.'

'Give me a look.' Warren picked the photos up from the table. 'Shit! It is too.'

'You can bet that's Edward's hand,' said Clover.

'Just letting us know he was around,' said Grace.

'Is it in any of the other photos?' asked Les.

Grace shook her head. 'No. Only those ones.'

Les continued to stare at the photos. 'That's one of the weirdest things I've ever seen.'

'Yes. Kind of spooky, isn't it,' said Grace.

Warren handed the photos back to Grace and turned to Les. 'Brrrhh,' he shuddered. 'I'm glad you're staying there Ugly, and not me.'

'Yeah. Not for much longer,' replied Les. 'I'm booking into a motel. Before Edward starts leaving funnel web spiders round the house or something.'

'I don't blame you.' Warren looked at his watch and turned to Clover. 'Well, Clover dearest,' he said. 'We'd better make a move. We've got a long drive home.'

'Yes,' she agreed. 'And it's going to be a breeze too.'

'Yeah,' nodded Warren. 'Thanks to Casper, the not so friendly, bloody ghost.'

'Hey Warren, how much money have you got on you?' asked Les.

'Money? About three hundred bucks.'

'Can you get any more on your Visa card?'

'Yeah. Another four hundred. Why?'

'You got any money on you, Clover?' asked Les.

'A couple of hundred,' she replied.

'Can you get some more from the ATM?'

'About the same as Warren. Four hundred.'

'Okay,' said Les. 'Can you give it to me? I'll give it straight back to you as soon as I get home.'

'What's with all the money?' asked Warren.

Les winked at Grace. 'I'm feeling pretty good. And I want to back myself this afternoon.'

'That's right,' said Warren. 'You've got to fight that relation of yours from Queensland. I forgot all about it.'

'And you want to ... back yourself?' said Clover.

'Yeah,' answered Les. 'I reckon I'm a chance to beat him.'

Clover shook her head. 'I've heard you're pretty good, Les. But Morgan Scully? Christ! He eats crowbars and shits barbwire.'

'You haven't been into those mushrooms again, have you Les?' asked Warren.

'No. But thanks for all your support,' said Les. 'A hanged man would get the same from a length of rope.'

'Sorry mate,' smiled Warren. 'It's just that I've seen the opposition.'

'So can I get the money?'

'Yeah, come on,' said Clover. 'There's a bank opposite the paper shop.'

They all rose from the table, then walked down to the lights and crossed the road to the ATM. With what Les came up with, they were able to raise two thousand five hundred dollars between them. Clover would call into Dalmeny on the way home and get some travelling money from her mother. Les counted the money in front of everybody, then they walked back to the house.

While Clover helped Warren pack his gear, Les got a whisk broom from the boot of his car, took the horseshoe from Warren's, placed it near the steps and brushed away the broken glass. Grace got a dustpan and broom from the kitchen and helped. Before long Warren's car was tidied up, his bags were in the boot with Clover's and everyone was standing in the driveway.

'Well Les,' said Warren. 'What can I say? Good luck with that big goose this afternoon.'

'Thanks Woz,' replied Les. 'I'll tell you all about it when I get home.'

'See you then, Ugly.'

Les gave Warren a pat on the shoulder, Clover gave Les a goodbye kiss on the cheek and kissed Grace goodbye, promising to keep in touch. Clover got in the car and Warren started backing down the driveway. He tooted the horn and they disappeared towards the highway.

Les turned to Grace. 'So what did you think of the boarder?'

'He's lovely,' she replied. 'They both are.'

'Yeah. They're all right, aren't they.'

Grace smiled at Les. 'So you're moving out of the house?'

'Yeah,' nodded Les. 'I'll book into a motel this afternoon. I'm not scared or anything, I'm absolutely terrified ... What if Edward turns out to be a raving poof?'

'If you're a good boy,' said Grace, pulling gently at Norton's belt buckle. 'I might let you stay in the spare room at Graceland tonight.'

Norton's eyes lit up. 'Fair dinkum?'

'Yes. But only tonight. I'll have to kick you out first thing tomorrow. Ellie gets here in the morning. And I want to spend the day with her.'

'Unreal,' said Les. 'I'll bring something with me.'

'Okay. That would be good.' Grace looked up at Norton for a moment. 'Les. If anything should go wrong this afternoon, ring me, and I'll be straight over.'

Les smiled back at her. 'Nothing should go wrong, Grace. But I'll ring you anyway.'

Grace let go of Les and opened her bag. She found her purse and handed Les a fifty dollar bill.

'What's this?' asked Les.

'That's my last fifty dollars till Ellie's grandmother gets here tomorrow,' replied Grace. 'I want to place a bet on you.'

'You want to back me with your last fifty dollars?'

'Why not? It's my money.'

Les looked at Grace for a moment then pocketed the fifty. 'I'll make sure you get extra good odds.'

'Thanks.' Grace fumbled for her keys. 'I have to go.' She ran her hand across Norton's cheek and kissed him goodbye then got in the Jackaroo. As she backed down the driveway, Grace poked her head out the window. 'Les. Be careful this afternoon.'

Les smiled and gave Grace a wave as he watched her drive off, then picked up the horseshoe and went inside.

Les placed Grace's fifty on his dressing table, shook his head, then put the horseshoe in the pantry and walked out onto the verandah. He watched the ocean for a while then looked at his watch and went back to the bedroom to change. Amongst his T-shirts was a plain white one with a small pocket on the front. Les wore that out over his training shorts, slipped on his thongs, packed his camera and a towel in his bag, then removed the capsules of fake blood from their packets. He placed four in the pocket of his T-shirt and the rest in his shorts, along with the twenty five hundred dollars. After a glass of water in the kitchen and a quick trip to the bathroom, Les put his Bugs Bunny cap and sunglasses on, picked up his bag and walked out the door, closing it softly behind him.

Les took the way to the park along the jetty. As he passed the baths, he noticed the hessian was still up but the tents had all been pulled down. Two men were standing at the side entry and there appeared to be quite a commotion inside. Les walked round the front to find a small queue at the entrance. Above the entrance a plastic sign said: GALA SPORTING EVENT. FIVE DOLLARS DONATION FOR THE LIONS CLUB. LUCKY DOOR PRIZE. Two women in jeans and jackets were standing behind a table taking donations and handing out tickets. Les joined the queue and waited his turn.

'What's the story, ladies?' he asked.

'The Lions Club is having a boxing match,' said one lady with dark hair. 'It's five dollars in and there's a lucky door prize.'

'Yeah. What's the lucky door prize?' asked Les.

'A special meat tray from the Lions Club.'

'Unreal. So who's fighting?'

'A man from Sydney and a local boy. They're both heavyweights. And it's a grudge match.'

'Sounds good,' said Les.

He fished a fifty from his pocket and handed it to the woman with dark hair. She gave him a ticket and counted his change into his hand.

'Thank you,' said the woman. 'And have a nice day.'

'I'm sure I will. Thanks.' Les pocketed his change and walked inside.

Along with the big tents, the food stalls had gone from the end of the park and in their place a large crowd had formed out from the fence. To the right was a small caravan with a table in front of it and standing next to a whiteboard, you couldn't miss Norm's bulk in a Blues Festival T-shirt. As Les approached he noticed Norm's wife and another woman, both wearing Blues Festival T-shirts, seated at the table taking bets and putting the money in a metal strongbox. Les strolled over and caught Norm's eye.

'Les, how are you mate?' he called out. 'Come over here.'

Les said hello to Marina and stepped behind the table. 'How are you, Norm?'

'Good mate. So who are you here with?'

'No one. I just paid my five dollars. Got my lucky door prize ticket, and joined the happy crowd.'

'You paid to get in?'

'Yeah. You're not bad, Norm. I'll want to get my money's worth.'

'Shit! Sorry about that, Les. Anyway, come over here.' Norm took Les behind the whiteboard. 'There's been a change in the rules.'

'Oh?'

'Yeah. It's going to be three five minute rounds with a minute in between. We had to open up the betting.'

'Open up the betting?' said Les.

'Yeah. Morgan's been backed into the red. This way they can bet which round it'll finish. Or if it'll go the distance. If it does go the distance, you get two minute's break. Then you fight to the finish.'

'Does Boofhead know what's going on?'

'Yeah.'

'And what are the odds?'

'Morgan's two to one on. You're fives.'

'Beautiful.' Les took out his money and handed it to Norm. 'There's twenty-five hundred there, Norm. Less the five dollars I had to pay to get in. Put the lot on me at five to one.'

'Righto. And I'll fix up the five bucks.'

'And Norm. No matter what happens. Don't stop the fight, unless I quit or I get knocked out. Okay?'

'Okay,' said Norm. 'And you needn't worry about getting a fair go. None of Morgan's mates'll try to step in. If they do, I got plenty of willing boys here that'll sort 'em out.'

'That's good,' said Les.

'So how are you feeling anyway?' asked Norm. 'Is your back any better? You must be pretty confident putting two and half grand on yourself.'

'Just call it incentive, Norm,' he replied. 'And yes. My back is a little better. But we'll just have to see what happens.'

'Morgan's keen. I know that,' said Norm.

'Where is the prick anyway?' said Les. 'It's past starting time.'

Norm stared over the crowd. 'Here he comes now.'

Les turned around to see Morgan storming through the crowd wearing a black tracksuit and Blundstones. He was with four mates and beneath his old, black, cowboy hat his face looked meaner and uglier than ever. As soon as he saw Les his eyes brimmed over with hatred.

'You're late, you big goose,' said Les, pointing to his watch. 'Where have you been? Pulling yourself in the shithouse?'

Morgan started to hyperventilate. 'I'm fuckin here now,' he rasped.

'I see you're still wearing that silly fuckin hat too,' said Les. 'Or have you been stealing tonneau covers off old utes?'

A cruel smile formed on Morgan's face. 'Oh, I made sure I wore my hat.'

Morgan's mates were looking at Les as if he was a dead man walking. Les noticed a hub-bub going through the crowd with the arrival of Morgan and there was a last minute surge at the betting table.

'Now, you know the rules, Morgan,' said Norm.

'Fuckin rules,' spat Morgan. 'I'd like to get into it right here and now.'

'No. You go over to other side of the ring where that chair is.' Norm pointed across the grass. 'That's your corner. You wait there. Okay?'

Morgan turned around and saw an outdoor chair sitting in front of the crowd. He gave Les one last filthy look then turned to his mates. 'Come on,' he grunted.

'And you take that one there, Les.' Norm pointed to another plastic chair on the opposite side of the ring. 'And seeing as you're on your own, Spike'll be your second.'

Les turned to a solid fair-haired bloke in a pair of shorts and a Blues Festival T-shirt standing behind him. It was the bloke that came up to see Norm about the blocked toilet on Friday night.

'Hello Spike,' said Les.

'G'day Les,' replied Spike. 'How are you?'

'Not bad,' smiled Les.

'Well. I suppose we may as well get into it,' said Norm.

'Yes,' agreed Les. 'Too late to get out of it.'

Les walked over to the his chair, placed his bag under it and sat down. He kicked off his thongs and took his cap and sunglasses off, then gave his arms a stretch and casually slipped a couple of blood capsules out of his shorts into his mouth. The crowd had surged forward and while he was getting his camera out of his bag, Les looked across the ring at Morgan's corner. Morgan had taken his jacket off and over his pants he was wearing a black, Jack Daniels T-shirt with the sleeves hacked off. He still had his Blundstones on and he'd handed his hat to the solid bloke with the moustache.

Les handed his camera to Spike. 'You know how to work one of these, Spike?'

'Yeah easy,' replied Spike. 'Me missus has got one.'

'Okay. Just take a few in the first round. Then take plenty in the second.'

'What about the third?'

'Spike. Something tells me there ain't gonna be a third.'

Marina had closed off the betting and the crowd had now formed an orderly ring. However, it was starting to get restless. Norm, the consummate showman, sensed this and strode into the middle of the ring carrying a bell. Seated in his outdoor chair, Les scanned the punters and was surprised to see a lot of elderly women. Standing behind Morgan were the four fishermen Les had belted in the hotel; all heavily bandaged and either wearing splints or carrying walking sticks. Les smiled across the ring and gave them a little wave. They declined to wave back. Norm rang the bell above his head and the crowd settled down.

'Okay,' boomed Norm. 'Youse all know why youse are here. And what it's all about. To help the local Lions Club. We're havin' a no holds barred, grudge match. Between local boy — Morgan Scully ...' Norm waited as a ripple of applause and several cheers from

Morgan's sycophants ran through the crowd '… and a tourist down from Sydney. Les Norton.'

Another ripple of applause ran through the crowd, accompanied by booing and several shouts of 'Poofter. Fairy. G'arn, get back to Sydney — you red headed-poofter'.

'All right, settle down,' boomed Norm. 'Anyway. We wish both contestants well. And don't forget, after the fight we've got the lucky door prize. Thirty T-bone steaks and two scotch fillets. Donated by the Lions Club. Righto. Would the two contestants please come to centre ring.'

Les got up and walked across to Norm. So did Morgan. Standing in his bare feet Les was a good six inches shorter than Morgan and nowhere near as heavy. But he was just as wide across the shoulders. Morgan glared down at Les as Norm spoke.

'Righto boys. You both know the rules.'

'Apart from this goin' three rounds, there ain't no fuckin rules,' said Morgan.

'Them's the rules,' said Norm.

'Do we shake hands first?' asked Les.

'Get fucked,' said Morgan.

'What about a kiss?'

'Ring the fuckin bell, Daddy,' snarled Morgan, 'before I kill this cunt.'

'Righto boys,' said Norm. 'Back to your corners. And come out at the bell.'

Morgan stormed over and stood next to his mates. Les went back to his corner and sat down. Spike gave his shoulders a rub.

'How do you feel, Les?' he asked.

'Good as gold, Spike,' answered Les. 'Who'd you put your money on?'

'No one. Even though I don't like your chances. If I won any money backing that big arsehole, I'd be dirty on myself.'

'Spike,' smiled Les, 'I couldn't ask for a better man in my corner.'

Norm stood in the middle of the ring and pointed to Les and Morgan. 'Are you both ready?' Morgan and Les nodded. 'Okay. Let's get into it.' Norm rang the bell and stood back.

Les got up and moved to centre ring with his fists up. Morgan came charging out of his corner hissing and snarling and throwing monstrous haymakers. Each punch had immense power behind it and would have taken your head off. But they were that telegraphed, Les easily got under most of them and caught the rest on his arms. As Morgan threw another flurry of bombs, Les shuffled to the side and poked out a couple of soft left jabs that caught Morgan in the face and then a short right to his ribs that wouldn't have crushed a SAO biscuit.

Morgan brought his hands down and grinned fiendishly at Les. 'You got fuckin nothing.'

'I know,' said Les. 'But I'm doing my best. Give me a break.'

Morgan threw another flurry of bombs and let go a kick to Norton's stomach that would have crushed his sternum. Les slipped the kick and poked another two feeble lefts into Morgan's face.

'Go on. Smash him, Morgan,' came a voice from the crowd.

'Give it to the cunt, Morgan.'

'Stick it up him, Morgan. The poofter.'

Hello, thought Les, as he shuffled around Morgan. The crowd's getting restless. I think it's time I gave them what they came for. He moved towards Morgan as the big man fired a up a John Wayne special and a huge straight right came barrelling towards Les. Les rode the punch with his forehead, bit on the capsule then spun around and fell to the grass, spitting the crushed capsule out of his mouth in a huge spray of blood.

'Yeah. That's the way, Morgan,' screamed a voice from the crowd. 'Smash him.'

Down on his hands and knees, Les smeared vampire blood across his face as Morgan aimed a huge kick at his head. Les rolled with it and bit down on another capsule, spurting up blood like a fountain.

'Yeah. Kill him Morgan.'

'Atta boy Morgan. Kick his fuckin head in.'

Les spread some blood over his T-shirt, while slipping another two capsules from his pocket at the same time. He palmed them into his mouth then rose shakily to his feet and faced Morgan. Morgan charged in throwing punches like a mad man. Les blocked or ducked most of them, rode a big right with his forehead, then bit on another capsule and fell to the grass coughing up blood. Amazed at how much the capsules contained, Les smeared blood over his face, in his eyes and into his hair. He rubbed some more on his T-shirt, then lurched to his feet and defiantly shaped up to Morgan.

Morgan turned and smiled at the crowd then charged into Les again. Les poked out another two ineffective left jabs as Morgan let go with another huge right, a haymaker. Les rode it, bit the other capsule and teetered back, spraying blood from one end of the ring to the other.

By now Les was covered in blood from head to foot; it was an awful sight. Morgan loved it and his piggy eyes were glowing. He ran in and threw another flurry of punches just as Norm rang the bell to end the first round. Morgan threw another punch after the bell. Les ducked it and staggered across to his corner.

'Shit Les. Are you all right?' said Spike, as Les flopped down in his chair.

'Yeah. He hasn't laid a glove on me,' replied Norton.

'Hasn't laid a glove on you? Have you seen your face?'

'Couple of grass burns, that's all,' said Les, palming another two blood capsules into his mouth.

Norm came over with a worried look on his face. 'Les, I know you told me not to stop the fight. But mate, you're a mess. You could end up getting badly hurt.'

Les spat out a gob of false blood. 'Turn it up. He's as weak as piss. I can take him anytime I want.'

Spike looked up at Norm. 'What do you want to do, Daddy.'

'We'll go another round. But if he takes much more punishment I'll stop it. I'm not going to stand around and watch someone get killed.'

'Hey Spike,' said Les. 'How many photos did you take?'

'About six.'

'Okay. Go for your life during the next round.'

Norm took another worried look at Les, then went back to centre ring and rang the bell for the start of round two. Keen for action, the crowd surged forward.

Les rose wearily from his seat and shuffled towards centre ring. Morgan strode confidently out of his corner and Les shaped up just in time to walk into another one of Morgan's John Wayne specials.

Riding it easily, Les bit on another capsule then fell to the ground spurting out more fake blood. He clambered to his feet before Morgan could boot him in the ribs and poked out another couple of ineffective jabs, as Morgan charged in throwing more, huge bombs. Les rode them or caught them on his arms and went down again. Soaked in blood, Norton dragged himself to his feet and stood groggily in front of Morgan like an exhausted bull waiting for the Matador's coup de grace. By now a change had come over the crowd. They all expected Morgan to win, but the fight was turning into a slaughter.

'Stop the fight,' came a voice from the crowd.

'Come on. He's had enough.'

'Yeah, somebody stop it.'

One woman shielded her eyes. 'Oh God! This is making me sick.'

Morgan looked at Les all battered and bloodied, then smiled and turned to his mates. 'Hey Rossy,' he called out. 'Give me my hat.'

The man with the moustache stepped across, and handed Morgan his black Akubra. Morgan put it on then stared into Les's blood filled eyes and tapped the brim.

'You know where this is going smartarse, don't you?' said Morgan.

Morgan stepped up to Les and brought a massive fist back to finish him off, when unexpectedly Les moved into Morgan and slammed his right knee into the big man's groin. Morgan went white and howled with pain. Les kneed him again then stepped back and, like a cobra striking, hammered two murderous left hooks into Morgan's face. Just as quickly, Les went underneath and thumped a left and right rip into Morgan's mid-section. Suddenly an audible gasp of disbelief rippled through the crowd. With his fists still at the ready, Les stopped for a brief moment to study Morgan. He looked beaten already. His mouth was shredded and all his front teeth were smashed in; he was out on his feet, trying feebly to hold his throbbing balls and his fractured ribs at the same time. Smiling to himself, Les dropped his right knee, and with all his weight behind it, banged a right uppercut onto the point of Morgan's chin. The punch sent his hat flying and shattered his jaw like a tea cup. Morgan's eyes rolled back, he made a grab at thin air, then his legs went from under him and he pitched forward onto the grass slightly bumping into Les on the way. Les went down with him, then rolled aside at the last second as Norm rang the bell and the crowd started cheering. Ignoring the cheers, Les staggered to his feet wiping fake blood from his eyes and squinted blindly at the faces around him

'What's going on?' he said. 'I can't see. Who won?'

With real blood pouring from him, Morgan lay crumpled on the grass at Norton's feet unconscious. Even though a lot of the crowd had lost their money, they kept clapping and cheering at Norton's heroic effort. Morgan's dumbfounded mates came in to pick him up and Les caught the eye of the bloke with the moustache.

'Hey Rossy,' said Les. 'You got a minute?'

Morgan's mate stopped, and walked up to Les. 'What do you want?'

'Nothing really,' answered Les.

Without saying another word, Les hit Rossy in the mouth with a quick, straight right and followed it up with a bone crunching left hook. His mouth a mess and his cheekbone fractured, Rossy started to totter, when Les buried his left foot into his sternum. As he fell forward, Les brought his right knee up and spread Rossy's nose across his face like a handful of mince.

'Actually, that was for Warren,' smiled Les. He left Morgan's mate bleeding on the grass then walked across to his corner.

'Fair dinkum, Les. That's the gutsiest thing I've ever seen in my life,' said Spike. 'And you flattened Rossy too.'

'The last one was personal,' said Les, putting his watch and thongs back on. 'Did you get plenty of photos?'

'Yeah. I almost finished the roll.'

'Good on you.' Les took his camera from Spike and put it in his bag as Norm came over.

'Les,' he said, incredulously. 'You are un-fuckin-believable. I was ready to stop the fight and call an ambulance.'

'I told you I could take that big goose whenever I wanted to,' replied Les.

'Fuck me. Listen. Do you want us to get you a doctor?'

'A doctor?' said Les.

'Yeah. For your face. You're going to need a heap of stitches. You've probably lost some teeth too. I know Morgan has. So's poor fuckin Rossy.'

Les spat out a gob of vampire blood. 'Don't worry about it. I got some band aids back at the house.' He picked up his bag and put his sunglasses on. 'Where's the back way out of here, Norm? I want to piss off.'

'Over this way. I'll show you.' Norm turned to Spike. 'Spike. Keep an eye on the Handbrake and Louise will you. They got all the money.'

'Righto Daddy. Hey, I'll see you later, Les.'

'Yeah, see you Spike. And thanks for everything.'

Les skirted the crowd behind Norm and followed him out past several tents and caravans to the side entrance. The two blokes standing on either side saw Les covered in blood and stepped back horrified.

'Are you sure you don't want to see a doctor, Les?' asked a puzzled Norm.

'I'm positive,' said Les. 'But I will want to see you about my money.'

'Sure,' said Norm. 'I got to sort things out first. Can you come back later?'

Les thought for a second. 'How about I meet you up at the pub on Tuesday night about nine? McBride's. I'll get it then.'

'Okay Les. That'd be good. We'll have a beer.'

'In the meantime, can you give me a hundred bucks, Norm? That was all the money I had earlier.'

'Yeah. No worries.' Norm pulled out two fifties and handed them to Les.

'Thanks mate.' Les pocketed the hundred then whipped off his blood spattered T-shirt and put it in his bag. 'I'll see you tomorrow night.' Norton turned and double-timed it back to the house.

Les let himself in the door and dropped his bag in the hallway then stripped off and got under the shower. Bloody hell, he chuckled, as he watched all the fake blood swirling down the plughole. This is like the shower scene from *Psycho*. He washed all the fake blood out of his hair and everywhere else, then towelled off and checked himself out in the bathroom mirror. There were bruises on his arms and a couple on his forehead, plus a small mouse near his left eye. He'd skinned his knuckles on Morgan's teeth and there were minor grass burns on his elbows and knees. Too easy, smiled Les. Much better than Morgan. Getting belted'd be bad enough. But losing five grand as well. Shit! that would hurt. Les wrapped the towel around him and poured some bourbon over his knuckles in the kitchen sink, then changed into a clean pair of cargos and a dark blue, Cooktown Resort T-shirt. A beer would have gone down well. But Les thought he'd wait and ring Grace first with the news. He put his cap and sunglasses back on and walked down to the hotel.

McBride's was fairly crowded with people having a drink and a post-mortem after the fight. There was no one in the bottle shop and Les didn't expect anyone would recognise him. They'd all be expecting someone who looked like he'd just crawled out of a car wreck. There was a phone just inside the door. Les dropped some coins in and dialled Grace's number. It was engaged. He tried twice more and gave up. Then he stepped over to a blonde girl in a black uniform behind the counter and bought a bottle of Turkey Flat Butcher's Block Mataro Shiraz and a bottle of Rosevear's Tasmania Riesling. He paid cash, then took the wine back to the house and put both bottles in the fridge. He had a glass of water then walked up to the butcher shop and bought a dozen, beautiful lamb cutlets, bacon and a few brisket bones. There was a phone box just up from the butcher's; Les dropped some coins in and this time Grace answered.

'Hello?'

'Grace. It's Les. How are you?'

There was a pause for moment. 'How am I? How are you?'

'Good as gold,' replied Les.

'What? You're all right?'

'Yeah. Never felt better in my life.'

'But ... I. Julie was at the fight. She said you won. But you took a terrible beating. There was blood everywhere. An ambulance came and everything. God, I was just on my way over.'

Les laughed. 'Are you sure she was at the same fight?'

'Les, don't fool around. Are you all right or not?'

'Yes Grace. I'm all right. Truly.'

'Okay,' answered Grace. 'If you say so.'

'So what time do you want me to call over?'

'Well. You may as well come over at six. And I'll finish what I was doing.'

'Righto.'

'Les, you're such a bastard. I don't know what to believe.'

'Ohh, that's nice isn't it,' said Les. 'You've just won a heap of money. I busted my poor arse to make sure you did. And you call me a bastard. Fair dinkum Grace, are all the women down here your age as horrible as you?'

'Les ...'

'Don't bother saying it Grace. I'll see you at six.' Les blew Grace a quick kiss over the phone and hung up. I wonder what I am going to tell Grace when I see her, he chuckled, as he headed home. The truth I suppose. It would make a nice change.

Back at the house, Les put the meat in the fridge and opened a bottle of beer. He took it out on the verandah, sat down and after a couple of mouthfuls, belched, looked around and shook his head. For a bloke that gets around a bit, he told himself, Christ, you're dumb at times.

That first night in the house: the piano playing in the middle of the night and things all over the kitchen the next morning, and I convince myself it's a rat. And the wiring's rooted in the bear. Everybody I meet, as soon as I mention the Merrigan house, they look at me like I got a face full of boils. Even the two old girls in the op-shop. I thought they were just a couple of old biddies the way they were going on. Then Grace and Clover. No wonder they wouldn't come inside after midnight. Everybody was in on the act bar me. And when I finally see Edward's ghost, I think it's a burglar and tell him to piss off. Les shook his head. I wonder what he's got the shits about though? Probably the bloody cold. Les raised his bottle to the house. Anyway Edward, you can shove the place up your freezing cold arse after tonight. I won't be here.

Les switched his thinking to more pleasant things. Like the fight. I wonder if Norm videoed it? I hope he did, he chuckled. I'll definitely get a copy to show Billy and the rest of them. They'll crack up. Les started thinking about Grace and her magic mineral water and the astonishing effect it had on him. It was liquid gold. He might ask her for a little more to take home with him. Les finished his beer and watched a couple of kids paddling a kayak across the clear, blue water in the lagoon. He had plenty of time before driving out to Grace's. Time for a little snorkelling.

Les was tossing up whether to have another beer first, when there was a brisk knock on the door. Hello, thought Les. I wonder who this is? He'd left the front door open and when he walked down the hallway an uneasy feeling settled in the pit of Norton's stomach. Standing on the steps were two tall men with grainy faces and brown hair, wearing white shirts, ties and dark trousers. One had his hair parted and wore a moustache. The other had a buzz cut. They weren't wearing guns. But Les knew they hadn't knocked on the door to sell him an insurance policy. As he approached, the two men looked at him suspiciously.

'G'day fellahs,' said Les, as pleasantly as he could. 'What can I do for you?'

'Les Norton?' said the one with the moustache.

'Yes. That's me,' replied Les.

'I'm Detective Bischof. And this is Detective Stenlake.'

Les shook his head and resigned himself once more to the inevitable. 'Okay. What have I done?'

'You haven't done anything,' said Detective Bischof.

'I haven't?' said Les.

'Well, you have done something,' said Detective Stenlake.

'Yeah. You did us a favour,' said his partner.

Les was a little puzzled. 'A favour?'

'Giving it to that prick Morgan Scully.'

'Oh.' Les brightened up. 'Well in that case ... Do you want to come inside? There's a cold one in the fridge.'

'No. That's okay,' said Detective Bischof. 'Actually, Daddy sent us round to see if you were okay. He was worried.'

'No, I'm okay,' said Les. 'Couldn't be creamier.' He looked at both detectives. 'So I gather you're not all that rapt in Morgan either.'

'Mate. We've been trying to nail that big lump of shit for years,' said Detective Bischof. 'And to see him get stitched up like that. It was music to our eyes.'

'And his mate Mick Ross,' added Detective Stenlake.

'So we just called in to see you're okay, and to shake your hand,' said Detective Bischof.

'My pleasure,' said Les, shaking both detectives' hands.

'We backed you too,' said Detective Stenlake.

'You did?'

'Yeah. We thought we'd done our dough too,' said Detective Bischof. 'Christ! You were taking an awful battering there at one stage.'

'Then I came good,' said Les.

'You sure bloody did,' agreed Detective Stenlake. He looked at Norton for a moment. 'Les. I have to be honest. A while ago, you looked like you'd been dragged under a train. Now you haven't got a mark on you? What...?'

Les smiled at the two detectives. 'Let's just say I'm a quick healer.'

The two detectives shook their heads. 'All right. We'll leave it at that,' said Detective Bischof.

'Hey before you go,' said Les. 'What's Scully's caper? If you don't mind me asking?'

'Anything he can get his big, hairy hands into,' said Detective Bischof. 'But mainly cars.'

'Cars?' said Les. 'As in, driving them without the owner's permission?'

'Well put, Les,' smiled Detective Stenlake. 'Scully and his mates drive up to Sydney, or down to Melbourne, nick a couple of cars on the way and flog them at the other end.'

'They know exactly what they're doing,' said Detective Bischof. 'And they know we can't follow them around all the time.'

'Can't you put a bit of pressure on some of his team?' asked Les. 'There must be witnesses or someone dirty on him.'

Detective Stenlake shook his head. 'No one's game to say a word. Everyone's shit scared of him.'

'In the meantime,' smiled Detective Stenlake, 'at least we got something to laugh about when we see him.'

'He'll love that,' said Les.

'So when are you going back to Sydney, Les?' asked Detective Bischof.

'Wednesday,' answered Les. 'Probably early.'

'Well if you get a chance before you leave, call in and have a coffee or something.' Detective Bischof pointed. 'The cop shop's just over there.'

'Okay,' said Les. 'But I'll be down here again. I like Narooma. Next time I'm in town you can shout me a beer.'

'You're on,' said Detective Stenlake.

Les said goodbye to the two detectives and watched them get inside a white Holden Commodore. He gave them a wave as they drove off then went back to his seat on the verandah

Shit! What about that, thought Les. A visit from the wallopers. At least it was a friendly one for a change. Les gazed out over the water and tried to relax. But being a fringe dweller when it came to the law and dealing with the police, an uneasy feeling still lingered in the pit of Norton's stomach. He was about to have another beer and changed his mind. No, he told himself. I'm going snorkel sucking. That's the best way for a dude to chill out. He changed into his old shorts and rubber vest, got his gear together and walked down to the jetty.

The water was just as clear as Saturday and there were even more fish around. Les chased four, fat leather jackets around the piers with his camera and out in the channel he saw another two big stingrays. The blackfish were back munching on the weed and Les joined them for lunch. One came right up to his face mask and he actually pushed it aside with his hand. Les snorkelled around, having fun using up what film was left in the disposable camera, then got out and walked back to the house.

Les had a shave and a shower, rinsed his gear and, figuring it could be a bit brisk sleeping out at Grace's, changed into his dark blue tracksuit which could double as pyjamas. The sun was just starting to go down, but there was still plenty of time, so he got another beer and took it out on the verandah.

It was a beautiful, late afternoon and Les was in a good mood as he sat and enjoyed the view. Getting out of the house for the night and having dinner at Grace's was perfect. She'd probably turn the TV on after, or they might even watch a video. Les hadn't watched TV since he left Sydney and he wasn't missing it all that much. But sitting back after a meal and watching a video, with maybe a little hanky panky thrown in, would be absolutely delightful. He'd even offer to give Grace a back rub if she wanted.

Les was contentedly sipping his beer when he noticed that a yacht had come through The Bar with its sails furled and was motoring slowly up the channel towing a rubber ducky. The water in the channel was like glass and the sun setting behind the surrounding hills gave the surface a golden sheen, making it all a lovely picture as the yacht moved effortlessly through the water. The yacht had turned side-on to the house where the channel curved round in front of the jetty and Les was thinking of taking a photo, when he thought the yacht looked familiar. Instead of getting his camera from inside, Les got his binoculars and checked it out. It was the *Kerouac*. One of the yachts he'd seen going past Montague Island the day before.

'Hello. It's the *Kerouac*,' he smiled. 'Anyone seen Jack? He's probably on the road.'

Les continued to watch the yacht moving up the channel. There were two dark-haired men on deck wearing black tracksuits and trainers. Les could pick out their watches and moustaches, even the expressions on their faces. They weren't talking and appeared serious. But they were fit and looked as if they spent a lot of time in the sun. Les was gazing away when the same woman he'd seen before came up from the galley wearing a dark blue tracksuit; the hood was down and this time she wasn't wearing sunglasses. Les watched her step out onto the deck, stared into the binoculars, and gave a double blink. He fine-tuned the viewers and pressed the stabiliser button. There was no mistaking the haughty features and the swirl of bright, orange hair. It was Serina: the late Edwin's grieving ex-girlfriend. Well I'll be buggered, Les said to himself. You know it's funny, but just for a moment, I thought that was her yesterday. I wonder what she's doing down here? The bloody yacht race of course. She's obviously getting her thrill-seeking rocks off again. Pity she didn't fall overboard on top of that big shark I saw.

Les watched Serina walk over to one of the men near the stern, wrap her arms round his neck and kiss him on the lips. Nice to see her broken heart's starting to mend too, he mused. Les zeroed in on Serina just as she turned towards the house and for a few moments it was like looking right into her cool, green eyes. The yacht motored towards the bridge and Les put the binoculars down. Well, that's enough to turn you off your day, seeing her down here, he frowned. I just hope I don't bump into the moll. Because if she has another go at me now that Edwin's not around, I'll tell her to get well and truly fucked. Les looked at his watch. Anyway. I got better things to do than worry about that hump. He finished his beer and went inside.

Les put the meat, the wine and a few other things in his overnight bag, along with the white T-shirt covered in false blood bundled inside a plastic bag. He picked up the key and had a last look around the house.

'Okay Edward,' said Les. 'The place is all yours. Try not to wreck too much if you can help it.'

Les locked the front door then got in his car and drove off. He was smiling about something as he drove past the turn-off to Mystery Bay, and still thinking as he drove through the deserted streets of Central Tilba. In no time at all he was parked outside Grace's and walking up the front steps. Right on cue, Morticia came skidding around the corner barking and howling like an Andrewsarchus out of the ABC show *Walking with Beasts*.

'All right. Don't shit yourself, Morticia,' said Les. 'It's only me.' The dog settled down a little as it picked up Norton's familiar voice. But it still watched Les carefully as he took something out of his bag. 'There you go, you little shit.'

Les handed Morticia a juicy piece of brisket bone. The dog took it neatly and, with its tail stuck straight up in the air, trotted back round to its kennel. Les was about to knock on the door when Grace opened it wearing a pair of cut down Wranglers that clung to her backside like a coat of paint and a grey T-shirt with two cute little sugar gliders on the front. Her hair was shining and parted to one side and she wasn't wearing makeup. She stared at Les.

'Good evening, young lady,' said Les. 'Is your mother in?'

Grace continued to stare at Les. 'Come in,' she said.

Grace closed the door and Les followed her down to the kitchen. He placed his overnight bag on the kitchen table and smiled at Grace as she turned around.

'All right. What's going on?' said Grace.

'What do you mean?' asked Les.

'You know what I mean.'

'I'm not sure if I do,' said Les. 'But while I'm here Grace, have you got a washing machine?'

'Of course. Out in the laundry.'

'Good.' Les took the white T-shirt out of the plastic bag and threw it to Grace. 'Wash that for me will you.'

'Oh my God!' Grace recoiled, and let the blood spattered T-shirt fall to the floor. 'Take it away. Please.'

Les picked up the T-shirt and held it up in front of Grace. 'It's only vampire blood,' he laughed.

'It's what?'

'I'll tell you in a minute.' Les put the T-shirt back in the plastic bag and took out the two bottles of wine. 'Does that look any better?'

Grace seemed to recuperate. 'Oh yes. Very nice.'

'Good,' said Les. 'But first. Do I get a kiss? I mean. No slipping the tongue in or anything. Just one of those kisses … women sort of give blokes when they're happy to see them.'

'Who says I'm happy to see you?'

'Yeah, fair enough. But could you pretend? Cause I'm happy to see you.'

Grace put her hands on Norton's hips and gave him the sweetest little kiss on the lips imaginable. Les opened his eyes and smiled.

'See that wasn't hard, was it.'

'Don't bet on it.' Grace let go of Les. 'I'll open the wine.'

'I brought some other goodies too.' Les took the meat from his bag and put it on the kitchen table.

'Goodness,' said Grace. 'You even brought bones for Morticia.'

'Grace. When Les Norton eats, everybody eats.'

Grace opened the Riesling, poured two glasses and handed one to Les. 'Cheers Big Ears,' she said.

'Yeah. Here's looking up your old address.'

The wine was very good: dry, delicate, with a tiny taste of citrus.

'Not too bad,' said Les.

'It's lovely.' Grace took another sip of wine and gave Les a once up and down. 'Okay George. I give up. Julie said you were an absolute mess. But apart from a little bruise near your eye, you haven't got a mark on you. And did you punch up a guy called Mick Ross too?'

Les nodded. 'Yeah. That'd be Rossy. The bloke that hit Warren.'

'God. He's almost as bad as Morgan Scully.'

'He sure wasn't looking too good, last time I saw him.'

'So what did happen? Unless that mineral water of mine's got some other, unknown, healing properties.'

Les had a mouthful of wine and grinned. 'It was fake blood.'

Les told Grace about buying the vampire capsules and putting them in his pocket then gave her a blow by blow description of the fight. He even told her about the police calling around. He didn't tell her about seeing Serina on the yacht. But when he'd finished, the bottle of wine was almost gone and Grace was holding her sides.

'Les Norton. You are an absolute bastard,' she said.

'Yes. I do have my moments of absolute bastardry,' agreed Les.

'And you went easy with him. Bloody Morgan Scully.' Grace shook her head. 'I can't believe that.'

'I was just feeling that good,' said Les. 'But for all his size and everything, he's slower than the Russian national anthem.'

'Then you knocked out Mick Ross too. God! You're not bad.'

'Yeah. Well I king hit him,' admitted Les.

Grace wrapped her arms around Les and kissed him again: a little longer this time. 'Come on tiger. Get your bag and I'll show you your room.'

The spare room was on the right past the bathroom. There was a single bed with a blue duvet and matching sheets and a window faced out onto the valley. Near the bed was a small dressing table, a few photos of old Central Tilba hung on the walls, and stacked against the walls on the yellow carpet were boxes of plain T-shirts.

'You'll be as snug as a little bug in a rug in here,' said Grace.

'Unreal,' said Les, dropping his bag on the bed. 'And I don't have to worry about bloody Edward. Thanks Grace.'

'You're welcome handsome. Now let's work out what to do with those lamb cutlets. They look good enough to eat.'

Grace basted the cutlets with chilli and coconut sauce and put them under the griller, then made some mashed kumera and a rocket salad with balsamic, honey dressing and shaved almonds. While everything was cooking, they talked about this and that and had a few cool ones. Les let Grace drink most of the red wine while he had a couple of cans of VB she had in the fridge. The meal was sensational and while they were eating Les told Grace he'd pick up her winnings at the hotel on Tuesday night.

'When are you going back to Sydney?' she asked.

'Wednesday,' replied Les. 'I'd like to stay a bit longer. But after all the drama, it might be best if I got going. I'll drop your money in first though.'

'That's all right,' said Grace. 'What time do you think you'll be leaving?'

'Around lunch time.'

'I'd like you to meet Ellie before you go.'

Les glanced across at the photo on the fridge. 'I'd like to meet her too. She looks like a real little sweetheart.'

'She is. Especially when she gets her own way.'

It didn't take long to wash and dry the dishes and put the leftovers in the fridge with glad-wrap. Grace was impressed at how domesticated Les was. Les said it came from living with Warren and they didn't make a bad casserole either when it came to a pinch.

'What do you feel like doing now?' asked Grace.

'I don't care Grace,' replied Les. 'You're the boss.'

'Would you like to watch a video?'

'Yeah righto,' said Les. 'What is it?'

'*Blow* with Johnny Depp. Julie loaned it to me.'

'Unreal. I missed it when it was on at the movies.'

'I want to see it again,' said Grace. 'Everybody should see it. If this movie wouldn't turn you off getting into cocaine, nothing would.'

'Yes,' agreed Les. 'You're guaranteed to finish up one of three ways getting into coke. Dead, broke or in gaol.'

'Right on.' Grace raised the last of her wine. 'Shall we have a joint first?'

'The "erb",' smiled Les. 'Why not "oman"?'

Grace already had a hot one rolled which they smoked in the kitchen before they went inside. It wasn't bad pot either; almost as good as Warren's. Les mellowed out on the lounge while Grace got the video together, then she sat down next to him.

'I've fast forwarded all the other stuff,' said Grace. 'So the movie will come straight on.'

'All right.'

Grace had a nice TV and it was tuned in through a good stereo. Les was laid back on the lounge feeling no pain when the movie came on. There was absolute silence for a few moments. Next thing, the Keith Richard riff from 'Can't You Hear Me Knocking', whacked out of the speakers and Les nearly fell off the lounge.

'Holy shit!' he yelled.

'Isn't that unreal?' laughed Grace.

'Christ!' said Les. 'I thought my bloody head was going to come off.' The movie began and Les started to laugh. 'I know why you wanted me to watch this,' he said. 'The bloke's called George.'

'Shh! Watch the movie,' said Grace.

By the time George and Tuna moved to California and started selling pot, Grace and Les were snuggling up to each other. When George's horrible mother shelved him to the wallopers, Les was massaging Grace's scalp and neck. Just after George met Pablo Escobar, Grace was sitting on a cushion in front of Les, and Les was rubbing her shoulders, sinking his thumbs into her rotator-cuffs while she was crooning. When George got shelved by his mates and copped thirty years for trafficking cocaine, Grace had her T-shirt off and Les was rubbing her back with hemp oil. By the time the video ended, they were both looking forward to bed.

'Would you like to tuck me in now, Aunty Grace?' asked Les. 'George has had a big day and he's tired.'

'All right snookums,' said Grace. 'Would you like your teddy bear too?'

'No. That's all right,' smiled Les. 'Just ted will do.'

Les followed Grace to the spare room where they got down to the naughty, naked nude, and climbed under the duvet. Les figured they'd had ample foreplay on the lounge. But he still wanted to give Grace's lovely ted a bit of a detail. He kissed her for a while, then ran his tongue down her neck, around her nipples, over her stomach and in between her legs; and then went for it. Grace kicked and squealed and got her rocks off before Les finally surfaced. Grace took hold of Mr Wobbly to give him a quick polish. But reluctantly, Les had to drag Grace away. If Grace's sweet lips had gone within cooee of Mr Wobbly it would have been a disaster. Instead, Les spread Grace's legs and slipped the angry little fellow into his favourite hiding place. On the rubber ball it was good. But in a nice firm bed with his back healed, Les was able to put the big ones in. Grace sighed and moaned. Les kissed her neck and lips while he worked steadily away. It was the sweetest lovemaking and Les wished he could go all night. But eventually it just got too good. Les arched his back, lifted Grace's legs and with Grace yelling encouragement, poured himself into her.

After a while Norton's chest stopped heaving and the stars spinning in front of his eyes faded away. He had his arm around Grace: Grace was snuggled up to his chest with her eyes closed.

Les half-opened one eye and looked at Grace. 'Shit! How good was that.'

Grace nodded. 'There's definitely nothing wrong with your back now. That's for sure.'

'I'm just going to close my eyes for a minute,' said Les.

'Okay,' said Grace.

Norton's snoring woke him up and it was pitch black. He groped around the bed to find Grace had gone and he was on his own. Isn't that lovely, he thought. I bring her two bottles of wine, lamb cutlets and back a winner for her. And she leaves me to sleep in the wet spot. Thank Christ I didn't waste my money on flowers. Les quietly used the bathroom, put his tracksuit on and climbed back into bed. It was lovely and warm under the duvet. Les pulled it up under his chin, smiled into the darkness and in no time the big Queenslander was snoring like a baby.

Les woke up the next morning to the smell of bacon cooking and Fleetwood Mac singing 'You Make Lovin' Fun', coming from the kitchen. He went to the bathroom, freshened up and walked into the kitchen. Grace was at the stove with her back to him. She'd just had a shower and put on a light blue tracksuit. Les sneaked up behind her and tickled her under the ribs. Grace tensed for a second and turned around.

'Hello George,' she smiled. 'How are you this morning?'

'Terrific.' Les slipped his arms around Grace and gave her a peck on the forehead. 'How's yourself. You look very sparkle-arkley.'

'I'm good. I was just about to call you. Did you sleep all right?'

'Yeah. Like a baby. That little bed was unreal.'

'Would you like a glass of ruby red grapefruit juice. I just squeezed some.'

'Reckon,' said Les. 'I love the stuff.'

From the fridge Grace got a pitcher of juice she'd sweetened with a little honey and poured two glasses. Les commented on how nice it was then sat down at the kitchen table and stretched.

'Ahh yes. Nothing like a nice leisurely breakfast,' he winked.

'Be as leisurely as you like, Les,' said Grace, turning off the griller. 'Just as long as you've got all this food shoved down your throat and your arse out the door in half an hour.'

'That's what I like about you, Grace,' smiled Les, taking another sip of juice. 'You're so romantic.'

Grace served Les a huge plate of scrambled eggs and bacon, along with fresh brewed coffee and toast, then joined him. The food was delicious and Les got into it, knowing Grace wanted to have everything out of the way by the time her daughter arrived. They had time to joke about last night and discuss the movie, before Les finally wiped his plate with a piece of toast, washed it down with a second cup of coffee and burped quietly into his hand.

'Grace, that was sensational,' he said. 'Thanks a lot.'

'That's quite all right,' replied Grace. 'I'm glad you enjoyed it.'

'I'm full. I know that.' Les rose from the table. 'Do you want a hand or anything?'

'No. That's all right.'

'Okay. I'll grab my bag and get going.'

By the time Les got his bag from the bedroom, Grace already had the dishes stacked in the sink and was running the hot water. She stopped what she was doing, smiled at Les and walked him to the door. Morticia was sprawled stomach down on the verandah. She looked up at Les, rolled her eyes back and gave her tail the slightest suggestion of a wag.

'I hate kicking you out like this, Les,' said Grace. 'But ...'

'Hey. No problems,' said Les. 'I understand. I'm just rapt you let me stay here for the night.' He put his arms around Grace and they had a quick kiss. 'I'll ring you. And I'll call in tomorrow with your winnings.'

Grace let go of Norton's hand. 'Okay. We might have lunch before you go back. The three of us.'

'Righto. See you then.' Les started off down the steps. 'See you, Morticia. You little shit.' The dog wagged its tail a fraction more and Les walked across to his car. He started the engine and bipped the horn as Grace waved him off. A few minutes later Les was driving through the quiet streets of Central Tilba towards the highway.

It was a beautiful spring day: warm and sunny, with a light breeze stirring the leaves in the surrounding trees and a scattering of fluffy, grey clouds moving across the sky. Les was patting his stomach and feeling good as he turned left onto the highway back towards Narooma. What a top day, he smiled. And how good was that breakfast? Christ! She gave me enough. Les put his foot down and overtook an old, blue Kombi wagon blowing smoke. So what have I got to do today, he thought, easing back on the accelerator. Oh yeah. Move into a motel. That's going to be a nice drag just for one night. And what about all that food we got left? Bugger Edward and his tantrums. Les cruised along thinking he might book into the motel he told Grace he was staying at when he first met her. He was smiling at the irony of this when he came to the Mystery Bay turn-off. Ohh yeah, thought Les. I'm not in any hurry. Why don't I check it out? Les hung a right and followed the road down past several small farms. The paddocks soon became trees and Les was driving into Mystery Bay before he knew it.

On the left, a narrow dirt road led into a small, deserted camping area, with a wooden pole placed across the entrance, near a council sign that read: CAMPING AREA CLOSED TILL FURTHER NOTICE. KEEP OUT. Les followed the bitumen up past a cluster of houses on the right to a low headland and a sign saying CAPE DROMEDARY NATIONAL PARK, did a U-turn then drove back into an empty parking area where another sign said MYSTERY BAY. He pulled up facing the ocean and had a look around.

Two beaches, split by a spit of sand and rock, formed a wide, sheltered bay edged with trees. Stony outcrops pushed away from the sand and all through the bay clumps of rock stuck out of the water to form small islands. The bay finished on the right, at the flat headland next to the national park, and on the left, finished down at a long ridge of jagged rock running out from the sand near an old, concrete boat ramp with a crack in the centre. The ridge of jagged rock formed a safe inlet between it and the low cliffs further around from the camping area, where a large cave at the water's edge opened up towards the bay. The tide was out and the water in the bay was crystal clear over the sand and the reefs running into deeper water; in the distance was Montague Island.

So this is Mystery Bay, mused Les. The place where Edward and his mates ate the pie. Les shook his head. Stuffed if I know how, he thought. It looks as safe as a bank out there. Les stared at the sun sparkling on the clear, blue water. One thing I do know — I feel terrific and this is a snorkel sucker's paradise. I'm going straight home to get my gear. Les reversed the car around and headed for Narooma.

Now that the long weekend was over and the Blues Festival had ended, Narooma was back to its sleepy, peaceful self. Les stopped to get the paper and some milk, before pulling up in the driveway at Browning Street. He got his bag, opened the front door and walked into the kitchen.

'Oh shit!'

Edward had been during the night and things were laying everywhere. Cutlery, plates, pots, pans, even the tea towels and pot scourers were scattered around the floor. However, there was no food. Trepidatiously, Les opened the fridge and the cupboards, but couldn't see any loaded rat-traps or knives poking out. Les put the milk away and looked in the pantry. The rat-traps were there. But the horseshoe was missing. Les walked down to the lounge room. His cassettes were scattered across the carpet and the bear was facing the wall. The horseshoe was jammed under the bedroom door.

'Ha-ha-hah! Fooled you, Edward. You fuckin goose,' said Les. 'Warren's gone home.'

Les pulled the horseshoe out from under the door, dropped it on the lounge and walked into his bedroom. All his clothes were tossed around the floor, along with the pillows and blankets and his new CDs. Les looked at the mess and shook his fist.

'Not happy — Edward.'

It was the same in the bathroom. His shaving kit was spread across the floor along with his towel and the roll of toilet paper. Les left it and went back back to the kitchen. Shit! Where do I start? Bugger it. I'll sort my tapes out first. Les walked down to the loungeroom and started replacing his cassettes into their numbered containers.

'Edward,' he muttered. 'You're a pain in the fuckin arse. You know that? And your girlfriend wears army boots.'

Les put the last cassette away and looked out the door at the sun shining on the lagoon. Ohh stuff this, he thought. It's too good a day. I'll clean the rest up later. Wasting no time, Les put his Speedos on under his shorts, got his gear and shoved it in his bag then locked the house and climbed into his car. Seconds later he reversed out into Browning Street and headed for the highway to Mystery Bay.

There was nobody around and this time Les chose the car park closer to the camping area. He got his bag, locked the car and started walking along the beach towards the old boat ramp. Half way up the beach was a big, grey log. Les thought he might leave his gear there. He walked up, dropped his bag on the sand then sat down on the log and figured out his game plan. It wasn't hard. Just snorkel around all those little islands, and maybe swim round the ridge sticking out from the beach, into the inlet where the cave was. I can't see any sharks hanging around here, he hoped. And if I do spot one, I can jump straight out onto one of those little islands. Les was about to gear up when he felt several drops of cold sweat form on his brow. Next thing, a tingle like an ice cube getting dropped down his back ran along his spine, the sunlight got brighter and the clouds started whizzing across the sky like they were being driven along by a cyclone.

'Hello,' said Les. 'I think this is that flashback Grace was talking about. Shit!'

Oh well. Nothing much I can do about it, he thought. Les sat down with his back against the log and made himself comfortable. Just kick back and take the merry-go-round, through Toon Town again. I wonder how long it'll go for?

This time, however, it wasn't like before. Instead of plasticine shapes and Toonies, everything started to spiral crazily, as if Mystery Bay was getting sucked into a vortex of raging colours, somewhere above the horizon. Next thing, there was flash of blinding white light, like a nuclear explosion, forcing Les to close his eyes and turn away from the speeding vortex. But even with his eyes shut the light was still blinding. After a while the light faded. Les blinked his eyes open and looked around

The houses on the hill were gone, the roads were gone, the car parks had disappeared; so had the camping area and the old, concrete boat ramp, along with the log he'd been resting against. Now it was all trees. Huge trees towering up to the sky with trunks as wide as houses. Cedar, ash, red gum, blue gum, ghost gum, ironbark. Around the bottom of the trees, crystal clear streams trickled around moss-covered logs, shaded by huge, spreading ferns. Les was sitting on a beach at the edge of an ancient rainforest. From out of the rainforest, flocks of parrots and other birds screeched and dived through the air. Sulphur-crested cockatoos, rosellas, rainbow lorikeets, king parrots, turquoise parrots, corellas, bulbuls, kingfishers, kookaburras, magpies, orioles ... All in countless numbers. Bush turkeys and lyrebirds moved around the streams, the sky above the ocean was alive with sea birds. A mob of red and grey kangaroos came bounding along the beach, straight through a mob of wallabies being chased into the rainforest by a pack of dingoes. All the little islands in the bay were coated in white and crammed with barking seals: big, fat brown ones, some with pups. Others were swimming between the islands or lying on the sand. A school of playful dolphins swam into the bay, had a quick look around then swam straight out again. The tide was high and the water in the bay was teeming with schools of fish, while the bottom was covered in black stingrays foraging through the sand. Montague Island was green in the distance and the ocean between the island and the mainland swarmed with whales, breeching and blowing water as they swam past.

Shit! What the fuck's going on, wondered Les? A movement behind him made Les turn around. Two wiry aboriginal men dressed in loincloths and carrying spears and small wooden shields appeared at the edge of the rainforest. Both had beards and tribal markings across their chests, and their hair was pushed back and bound tightly on top of their heads. Each man's teeth were sparkling white and their skin was as black and shiny as onyx. One pushed his spear in the ground and rested his right foot against his left knee, while the other pointed to something on the beach. He said something to the other man in their tribal dialect, then they turned around and disappeared back into the rainforest.

Les watched the two men leave and noticed movement in the branches of some nearby gum trees. They were crawling with koala bears. He turned back to the beautiful, blue ocean and the pristine landscape. Behind the ridge at the end of the beach was the cave. Now I know what's going on, Les told himself. Somehow those mushrooms have sent me back in time.

Everything was crystal clear and razor sharp, and Les gazed around in wonder, taking in the unique setting of beauty and tranquillity. It was nature at is gentlest and loveliest and Les hoped he was going to be there for hours. Suddenly, a sinister movement in the water over to his right made him sit up. From out of nowhere, six massive killer whales came charging into the bay. They were as big as locomotives and with their fearsome teeth and sleek, black bodies reflecting the sun, they made an awesome display of beauty and power as they slashed ominously through the water. And the pod knew exactly what it was doing. To cut off any escape, two whales swam towards the ridge jutting out from the sand, two moved behind the islands while the last two charged straight into the terrified seals. The herd immediately went into a barking, yelping panic. Some seals managed to clamber up onto the islands, others made it to the beach with their pups. Those that didn't, got ripped to pieces or were simply gulped straight down as the killer whales went into a feeding frenzy, turning the water into a churning, red boil of blood, guts and lumps of seal meat.

The killer whales gorged themselves on any seals they could find, except for one. It was too big and fat to clamber up onto the rocks and its escape to the beach was blocked by the killer whales. All it could do was bark and flounder around in the gore. The pod watched the terrified seal, before the biggest one swam up alongside it, and with one mighty flick of its tail, sent the seal spinning up in the air like a football. It tumbled around, end over end then splashed down in front of the other killer whales. The seal bobbed to the surface and another killer whale swam over, flicked its tail and belted the seal back across to the first killer whale. The seal splashed down again and the first killer whale flicked it back to the others. Singing to each other, the killer whales spread out, formed a circle, and started belting the hapless seal back and forth between them in a macabre game of shuttlecock. This was a side of nature Les had seen on TV, but forgotten about. Nature at its most savage. Les watched the callous display in fascinated horror when another movement made him spin around to the left.

Coming from the cliffs behind the inlet, a boat suddenly appeared on the scene. It was a wide-beamed, wooden clinker, with two men rowing in the middle, another seated in the bow with his back turned taking notes, and another man standing at the tiller. The three men in the front were all wearing plain calico shirts and pants, and straw hats with turned up brims and black bows dangling at the back. The man at the tiller had a beard and funny little glasses, and was wearing the same kind of straw hat over a grey frock coat with matching trousers. The two men in the middle kept rowing unawares towards the killer whales, while the man in the bow concentrated on his notes. The man at the stern noticed all the blood in the water, then saw the killer whales and started yelling and pointing. The man in front stood up and turned around and the two men in the middle stopped rowing. The boat's momentum, however, took it into the pod just as the biggest killer whale gave a powerful kick of its tail and sent the seal sailing high into the air. The huge, fat seal spun lazily above the water, then came down right in the middle of the boat like a bomb landing.

The wooden boat rocked crazily as the seal smashed straight through the bottom staves, sending the man in front head first over the bow and the two men rowing straight into the blood-stained water, along with their oars. The man with the beard gripped the tiller, but was somersaulted backwards over the stern. Wondering where their plaything had gone, the killer whales looked up and saw the men struggling in the water around their crippled boat. Les had read about killer whales in Eden helping whalers herd whales, even saving the men from drowning at times. However, this pod must have been the bad boys on the block. They simply looked at the four men in the water as fresh food items and charged straight in.

The first to get eaten were the men in calico. They hardly had time to scream before they were either torn to bits or swallowed whole. For his size, the man on the tiller could swim a little and was stroking furiously across the inlet towards the cave. He was going all right when the biggest killer whale loomed up behind him and took him all in one bite. All except for his left hand which was left floating on the surface. The killer whale turned around, still swallowing the man with the beard, and with a lazy flick of its tail inadvertently sent the hand sailing across the inlet towards the cave. There was a ring on one of the fingers and Les watched it glinting in the sun as the hand turned lazily through the air before landing in the right side of the cave. A few seconds later, the battered and bloodied seal floated to the surface behind the boat. Another killer whale saw it and charged in giving the seal a flick with its tail to get the game going again. The killer whale's aim was a bit out and this time the seal crashed into the cliff face above the cave, dislodging several rocks and some of the ceiling, before it tumbled lifeless onto the rocks at the entrance. The biggest killer whale, the leader of the pod, was tired of playing; it swam over and threw itself onto the dead seal, dragging it back into the water in its huge jaws, where it gobbled it down like a cat swallowing a goldfish. The leader then swam back to the others, clicked and sang something while leisurely blowing clouds of vapour into the air; the rest then all followed the biggest killer whale towards Montague Island to see who they could terrorise out there. Behind them, the mother seals that had survived the slaughter were barking across the bay trying to find their pups, while the sea birds and school fish swarmed at any scraps in the blood-stained water. The clinker, its staves smashed outwards and the men's belongings still inside, was left drifting near the islands with its gunwales poking out above the water.

Les watched the empty boat moving slowly with the current, when the rushing vortex appeared out of nowhere and started spiralling above the horizon again, and everything around him began to evaporate. The rainforest and all the wildlife disappeared, to be replaced by materialising roads, car parks and houses. The whales out to sea vanished as the camping area reappeared behind him, along with the boat ramp and the old log on the beach. Before Les knew it, everything was back the way it was. He blinked at the sunlight as a family in a station wagon pulled into the parking area, then he wriggled across the sand and sat with his back against the log again.

Although it had all been no more than a shocking, psychedelic illusion in his mind, Norton's sense of shock was tinged with sadness. It was awful to see the seals and the men getting torn apart so brutally. But it was sad to think what had happened to the rainforest and all the wonderful wildlife. For just a short time, Les felt he'd caught a glimpse of paradise. Well I'll be buggered, thought Les. I didn't think the flashback would be like that. Shit that was real — too real, if you ask me. Several thoughts flashed through Norton's mind and his face turned quite serious. Something strange is going on here, he told himself. I'm picking up this weird vibe. Fuck it. There's something I have to do.

Les got up and walked down near the old boat ramp. It was a fair swim around the ledge to the inlet. But the tide was out, and an exposed shelf of rock on the other side of the ridge jutting out from the beach ran beneath the cliffs and finished above the water not far from the cave. Les went back to the log and changed into a pair of old shorts and a T-shirt. He slipped on his rubber booties, and with a small clasp knife in his pocket set off along the beach.

The shelf running round to the cave turned out to be jagged folds of slippery rock, poking up between pools of tangled seaweed and it was difficult to get a foothold. Somehow Les managed to clamber unsteadily over the rocks without twisting his ankle, to where the ledge ended. There he found another smaller cave, filled with smooth boulders and pebbles washed around by the waves, and on this side of the big one. Between the two, they formed a lovely, blue grotto and a boat would have fitted in there easily, especially at high tide. Pity the boat crew couldn't have rowed in here and got in the cave, he mused. They would have been as safe as a bank. Les jumped off the rock shelf into waist deep water and waded across to the big cave, then scrambled up onto a ledge at the mouth and stepped inside.

The cave was big and gloomy with a small entrance at the other end and Les could make out the coloured, volcanic strata around the walls and ceiling; it looked like marble cake. The floor was rough under his feet and strewn with jagged rocks, and on the left side of the cave a wide rock ledge covered in pebbles and stones stuck out from the wall. Les stepped over to the right side of the cave and smiled. Apparently there'd been a big sea recently and most of the pebbles and stones had been washed away, leaving a trench running along the bottom of the wall. How lucky's that, thought Les. Even if it does turn out I'm wasting my time, I don't have to dig that far to waste it. Les got down on his knees and started scooping away the pebbles from the bottom of the trench.

It wasn't easy going with his bare hands and the pebbles kept rolling back into the trench. What Les really needed was a garden spade. But at least the stones were smooth and he didn't get any nicks or cuts. Les got down into the trench and kept digging away to the gentle sound of pebbles clicking against each other and waves lapping against the rocks outside. He scooped and dug until his legs got cramps, finding nothing but more and more pebbles. Les stopped to wipe a little sweat from his brow. So much for my psychedelic archeological dig, he smiled to himself. I should have known it'd be a waste of time. Oh well. Doesn't matter.

The tide was turning, and a wave hit the rocks out front with a noisy slap that echoed round the cave. Les was thinking of throwing in the towel when his fingers touched something under the pebbles. It felt like small pieces of driftwood. Carefully Les scooped away the pebbles and his eyes lit up. It was the skeleton of a hand, the bones discoloured with age. Not a big hand. But definitely a hand and still very much intact. Les picked it up and got out of the trench.

'Holy shit! I don't believe it.'

Les looked at the bony hand, feeling like he'd just won Lotto. I got to put it down somewhere and have a good look. He looked around the cave, thought maybe over on that ledge near the wall ... Bubbling inside, Les started pulling his T-shirt off and walked over to the ledge. He laid his T-shirt across the rocks on top and placed the hand on it, then stared at the hand in amazement. Still sitting on the third finger was a ring. Well raise my rent, thought Les. I knew I picked up some weird vibe after that flashback. Wait till I tell Grace.

Les went to rest his foot on the ledge and it slipped off. He put his foot back and it slipped off again. Norton's brow creased. The sole of his booty was wet. But for solid rock, the ledge was awfully soft. Les left the hand and brushed away some rocks and pebbles. It wasn't a ledge. Underneath all the stones was a black tarpaulin that had been been daubed with brown, white, ochre and yellow to match the walls of the cave.

The tarpaulin was covering a mound roughly six metres by three and waist high. Les stepped over to the right side of the mound, kicked away the rocks and pebbles at the bottom then squatted down and lifted up the edge of the tarpaulin. Underneath were rows of neatly piled green sacks. Les took out his clasp knife and cut one open. Inside the sack were ten, clear, thick, plastic bags full of white powder. Les didn't know that much about powder drugs. But it was too white to be heroin and too fine to be speed. He let the tarpaulin down, stood up and shook his head in astonishment.

'Fuckin cocaine. I don't believe it.'

Les looked along the tarpaulin. How many sacks there were was hard to estimate. But each plastic bag would have been a kilogram, and at ten bags to a sack there would have to be at least a thousand bags under the tarpaulin. Probably two. Another chill ran up Norton's spine; and it wasn't from the mushies. For that amount of coke and the money involved, if the people behind the shipment found out you knew about it, they'd murder you as quick as look at you. Les replaced the rocks he'd kicked away, carefully wrapped the hand in his T-shirt, then walked across to the front of the cave and stepped back into the water. Holding the hand above his head, he waded over to the shelf, and with the help of an incoming swell hoisted himself up and made his way back along the rocks to the beach.

As calmly as he could, Les ambled back to the log, collected his gear and walked across to his car. He took his wet shorts off and with a few butterflies kicking around in his stomach, placed his things inside and started the engine. As he reversed slowly around and started to drive off, Les had a good look over the camping area and up the dirt road into the trees, then proceeded steadily along the road leading to the highway.

Minutes later he was speeding back to Narooma. Les didn't notice any cars following him so he slowed down. Before long he'd reached town safely and was pulling up in the driveway of the house. He picked up the T-shirt, got his bag from the back seat and went inside, closing the door behind him. He placed the hand on his dressing table, then got a beer from the fridge: half went down in one huge gulp. Les took the rest out onto the verandah and sat down.

Well that was certainly a day with a difference, he told himself. Thanks to Clover's mushrooms, it looks like I've solved the mystery of Mystery Bay. But what about all that fuckin cocaine. Shit! Where did that come from? Thank Christ no one saw me, or I doubt if I'd be sitting here now. Les took a grateful sip of beer and winked up at the sky. Anyway, forget about the okey. They can shove it up their arse for all I care. Finding that hand's all I'm interested in. That was absolutely unbelievable. Extremely pleased with himself, Les finished his beer and had a quick shower.

After changing into a clean T-shirt and his blue cargos, Les placed the T-shirt with the hand on the bed and carefully unwrapped it. He looked at the hand from all angles before slipping the ring from the third finger. The ring was covered in grime after laying in the cave for all those years. But Les could see it was gold with jewels inlaid around the band and an inscription inside. Les took the ring into the bathroom, ran some hot water and washed it with soap. He dried it off then brushed it several times with toothpaste. After a while the ring came up almost like new. Les dried it off, got another bottle of beer and took the ring out to where he'd been sitting on the verandah.

It was stamped twenty four carat gold and inlaid with six tiny hearts made from black opal. The inscription inside read: *To Gwendolyn. All my love. Now and Forever. Edward.* As well as hardly being able to believe what he'd found, Les was also moved. Shit! That's really lovely, he smiled. And it's such a beautiful ring. Thoughtfully sipping his beer, Les turned the ring over in his fingers letting it catch the sun. You know, I've been bagging poor Edward, because, according to that photo, his fiance was a dog. But they say love is blind. And Edward must have really loved her. Les raised his beer to the house and took a sip. Good on him. Bad luck they never got to walk down the aisle together. Les slipped the ring onto the top of his little finger and shook his head in admiration as he watched the fire in the opals. An antique like this, he mused — solid gold and inlaid with black opal — it'd be worth a motza too. Smiling happily, Les finished his beer, then took the ring inside and placed it back on the finger he'd got it off. He wrapped the hand up in a white T-shirt that had been lying on the floor and put it back on the dressing table. Les left the mess in his room and walked out to the mess in the kitchen. Now all I have to do is clean up Edward's shit after him. Les couldn't help himself and called out to his bedroom.

'Hey Edward! Any chance of a hand?'

Les started with the cutlery. While he was putting it away, he decided against moving into a motel. It was too much trouble just for one night and he'd stay in the house. As for Edward? He'd just have to sort it out when he arrived. Les mulled over a couple of other things. But before long he started thinking about the huge pile of cocaine.

It had more than likely been brought in on a yacht, then transferred to the cave in a rubber ducky, he surmised. And whoever the team were they were pretty bloody smart and knew the area. That cave was ideal. Easy to get into by boat. But quite difficult otherwise. And if anybody did put their head in the cave, it was that dark, and the dope that well concealed, you wouldn't know it was there. It probably wouldn't be there long anyway. Les dropped some more spoons into a drawer. It's funny, he laughed to himself. But the team did me a favour. If they hadn't dug up all those rocks and pebbles to cover the tarpaulin, I probably wouldn't have found the hand. So I got that to thank them for. Les dropped the last fork into the drawer. And I thought the trench was caused by a big sea. Hey. Why woudn't I? Les stared at the floor for a moment and started on the cups and saucers. Their timing was spot on too. The Blues Festival in town. The yacht race. You can bet they used those for cover. The camping area closed. He'd had a good look around as he was leaving. You could get a truck in there and lower a rope with a pulley over the cave easy. You'd have all the toot out and loaded up in no time. Not a soul around and the nearest house up the hill on the other side of the beach. Yes, conceded Les. Whoever they are, they're smart bastards all right. They covered their arse from just about every angle imaginable. If coke dealers weren't my particular cup of tea, and they would have shot me if they saw me, I'd almost say good luck to them. Almost. Les put the last plate in the top of the cabinet and caught his reflection in the small glass door. Suddenly the Wile E. Coyote, light bulb above his head blinked on.

'Ooohh! What's that you say, Shintaro?' exclaimed Les.

Smart bastards on a yacht? With a rubber ducky? That know the area? Les's eyes narrowed. Did I see someone answering that description only just the other day? I sure did. Fuckin Serina. Orange hair and all. Les shut the cabinet door and sat down at the kitchen table.

Bloody Serina, thought Les. She'd got nicked over a shipment of coke in WA. She comes from Narooma. She'd know about that cave and everything else. She walked last time. Why not have another go? What's to stop her from driving down here, picking up that yacht in Bermagui, then helping to unload the coke after the race on Sunday night or something? There's yachts going everywhere. They just cruise into Narooma the next day, then move the coke out when it suits them. Les felt the hairs on his neck tingle. One shouldn't cast aspersions. But I reckon you could lay odds Serina's in that pile of coke up to her tits. Les folded his arms and frowned towards the hallway. Okay. I know it's personal between me and her. But I've always had my doubts about that low moll. Especially after what happened to Edwin. So has Eddie. Les shook his head glumly. Weird isn't it? One day I'm walking along Bondi and there's poor bloody Edwin dead on the sand. Next thing I'm watching teary-eyed Serina, down the beach with all Edwin's friends seeing him off. A few days after that, there she is. Coming up the channel in Narooma all over some other bloke. And sailing past Montague Island in a yacht race the day before. Les reflected on seeing the wisp of orange hair under her hood before the yacht tacked. Funny how I thought it was her too. Next thing, the light bulb started blinking above Norton's head again and he rose up from the table.

'The day Edwin ate the pie,' said Les, staring around the kitchen. 'What was my smart arse remark? Two drownings for the price of one?'

Les strode out of the house without closing the door, and hurried straight up to the Wagonga Dive Shop. Ian was behind the counter reading *Underwater* magazine. He looked up when Norton walked in and smiled.

'G'day Les,' he said cheerfully. 'How are you?'

'I'm good Ian,' replied Les. 'How's yourself?'

'All right. Bad luck about the other day, mate. The weather turned sour.'

'Yeah. It wasn't the best,' agreed Les.

Ian half-smiled. 'Neville said you weren't in the water long.'

'No. I never quite got to see the seals. Ian. Have you got a magnifying glass?'

'Yeah. There's one under the counter. I use it to go over maps.' Ian reached around under the counter and came up with an oblong-shaped magnifying glass with a little circle in the corner for closer scrutiny. 'Here you are.' Just a little curious, Ian handed the magnifying glass to Les.

'Thanks,' said Les. 'I won't be long.'

'Go for your life,' shrugged Ian.

Les walked across to Ray Bissett's photo and ran the magnifying glass over it. Big and all as the photo was, the extra magnification really brought it up; and if Les thought he saw anguish and despair on the divers' faces before, now he could almost read their minds. He moved the magnifying glass to the woman diver being sick. She had twin tanks on her back and was holding her mask and flippers in one hand. But the woman diver wasn't bent over being sick. She had her head down, walking away from the other divers towards the stairs leading up to the parking area on the point. And through the little circle in the magnifying glass, the lock of hair poking out from under the hood of her wetsuit wasn't light brown. It was orange. Les had another look to make sure, then walked over to the counter and handed Ian back his magnifying glass.

'Find what you were looking for?' asked Ian.

'Yeah,' nodded Les. 'Yeah. I did. Thanks Ian.' Les turned and left Ian to his magazine.

Les started thoughtfully back towards the house. The two beers had made him a little hungry. There was a cake shop just back from the hotel. Les walked down to buy a couple of depth charges.

The front window of the Seaview Bakery was stacked with wedding cakes, ham and cheese buns and other goodies. A bell rang over the flyscreen door as Les walked inside. Under the counter were racks of delightful-looking cakes, and the Seaview special — their famous banana muffins. A tall brunette in a white dress smiled at Les from behind the counter.

'Yes. What would you like?' she asked, politely.

Les pointed to the blackboard menu above the pie warmer behind the counter. 'Two steak and onion pies, please.'

'Rightoh.'

The woman put the two pies in two white paper bags, Les paid her and walked back to the house. He made a cup of tea, squirted some tomato sauce into the two pies and took everything out onto the verandah. The pies were very good. Les washed one bite down with a mouthful of tea, had another, and started thinking poignantly about Serina.

The low, rotten moll. That was her in Ray's photo. I reckon she's necked Edwin. And you don't need to be Sherlock Holmes with a magnifying glass to work out how.

She's swum across from Ben Buckler while Edwin was out surfing, timed it right, then just swum up and grabbed him. She'd know Edwin's distinctive surfboard. She'd know his movements on the day. She probably kissed him goodbye before she went and put her Scuba gear on. And a superfit woman like Serina wearing twin tanks would get across Bondi Bay and back easy. Impossible? Me and Eddie did the same thing in Port Stephens. It took us a minute. Yes, concluded Les. I reckon that's how she did it. She might have even known that dive school would be there in the morning and used them for cover. But if that's how, why? Les started on his second pie, and chewed thoughtfully.

Knowing Edwin, I'd say he was the weakest link. Apart from smoking pot and maybe having a toot now and again, Edwin wasn't a dealer. But somehow he's got involved in the shipment. Being so close to Serina, he'd have to know what was going on. Maybe the team put pressure on him because he had an import business? Help wash the money or something? But the thought of risking twenty years in the puzzle hasn't appealed to a party boy like Edwin. So he's politely said include me out. Except coke dealers, as well as being mad raving paranoid, are completely ruthless. So rather than have a loose cannon running around, they've decided to off him. I don't care what anyone says, there's no way Edwin committed suicide. He was too popular and had too much going for him. No. Bottom line, Edward's shit himself so the team's said he had to go. And Serina was the girl who knew the best way to do it. So she did. *Exeunt* Edwin.

Les finished his second pie and washed it down with the last of his tea, pleased with the way he'd worked things out. And he was pretty sure he was right. However, there was a downside to this. The thought of Serina killing Edwin and getting away with a multi-million dollar drug shipment began to burn Norton's arse something awful. So what should I do now, he asked himself? Les absently tapped his empty mug on the table. Well, I figure I've got three options.

One. I can be a concerned citizen and ring the police. Les shook his head vehemently. No. No fuckin way. There's a chance they'll tape my voice or something. And friendly or not, I've just had a visit from the wallopers. They know I've been down here. If the team get nicked, and I've been seen in the vicinity, I'm going to get involved somehow. And I've been seen in Serina's company a heap of times. Christ! We all had our photos in the local rag once sitting outside the Toriyoshi. Guilt by association? Conspiracy? What if the team finds out it was me that tipped off the cops? They might. What if the cops say no, I wasn't involved, but I'm called in to give evidence. No. No matter what, if I ring the cops, it's going to come back on me. I just know it. So that's out.

Two. I could burn it? Yeah. Swim out with a big pile of wood, some newspaper and box of matches. Or take some petrol. I'd need gallons. Plus all the flames and fumes in the cave. If I didn't get burnt to death, I'd suffocate. No. Too dangerous. Plus all the flames and smoke coming out of the cave. By the time I got back to my car, some concerned citizen would see me driving away and take my number plate. So that's out. Three. I could swim out with my trusty little clasp knife and cut open all the bags? That'd only take me a week, while I'm covered in coke from head to foot. I'd end up with a huge noseful or a lung full. And that definitely ain't no good for one's health. Not to mention the team coming back and finding me in there. Les shook his head dejectedly. Apart from dynamiting the cave, there was nothing he could do. No. If it is you Serina, you've won. You've pulled off a big one. I only hope you choke on it. You orange-headed dropkick.

Les stood up and walked across to the railing. He leant against it, put everything out of his mind and stared out at the ocean and up the coast. This bloody Narooma certainly is a good spot, he thought. You could buy a weekender or a house down here for the right price too. A bit cold in the winter. But summer'd be fantastic. Only a few hours from Sydney and Aunty Grace just up the road. It's a thought. Les watched another fishing boat coming up the channel then peered down into the backyards of the houses below. One had a small fountain in it; in the form of a cherub, with little wings and bow and arrow, continuously piddling. That reminds me, thought Les. I've still got to clean the fountain out in my backyard. My back was too crook before. I'll do it as soon as soon as I get home. Fuck! The last time I did it, I nearly burnt the bloody house down. And everything else. Shit! Wasn't that a lot of fun?

Just like now, the solar pump had stopped working. And through Norton's negligence, the little pool round the fountain had got full of slime and turned into a breeding ground for mozzies. So Les had gone to a pool shop and bought a five litre container of Ozone Accelerator; enough to clean out an Olympic pool. He tipped a bit in the little pool round the fountain and put the container on the grass just as the phone rang. Les didn't bother to put the cap back on, and as he went to pick up the phone, knocked the container over without noticing. It was his mother on the phone ringing up from Dirranbandi to see how he was getting on in the big smoke. Les settled down for a cosy chat and before long he and the old girl got a bit of a roll on. Les was wandering around with the remote when he noticed clouds of steam and smoke coming from the backyard. He hung up on his dear, sweet mother and raced out to see what was going on. Half the container had poured into the soil and a crater had formed, billowing out smoke and steam like a small volcano. The acrid fumes and the heat being generated were unbelievable. To make matters worse, the whole, burning, seething mess was heading towards the shed and the pile of wood under which Les had buried all his ill gotten gains.

Les had grabbed a hose and started pouring water into the crater. But that only seemed to make it worse. So he grabbed a shovel and started digging like a madman. Les almost dug up half the backyard before he finally got it under control. Even then, the crater kept steaming and giving off heat for hours. But it was a close thing. If the heat had got to the shed, full of paint, thinners and other inflammable items, it could have been a disaster. After that, Les just used a little chlorine in the fountain. The Ozone Accelerator that was left, along with the container, got tossed into a dump bin on a building site.

Les reflected as he gazed down at the cherub piddling away in the backyard below, and glanced at his watch. He took his mug to the kitchen then got his money and credit cards and walked up the road again. On the other side of the traffic lights, past the Wagonga Dive Shop, was a large hardware store and pool shop. It wasn't quite closing time. But the fair-haired bloke wearing a white shirt and standing behind the counter, looked as if he wished it was. He gave Les a tired smile as Les walked in.

'Yeah mate? How can I help you?' asked the bloke.

'Have you got ten litres of Ozone Accelerator?' asked Les.

'Should have. Wait'll I have a look out the back.'

Les waited patiently and looked at a couple of drills while the bloke in the white shirt, went to a room at the rear of the store. He came back carrying two large, white containers with blue labels and placed them on the counter. It was the same brand Les had used when he almost burnt down Chez Norton.

'There you go mate,' said the bloke. 'Last two left. Otherwise you'd've had to've gone to Ulladulla.'

'Unreal, me old,' smiled Les. 'What's the damage?'

The bloke looked the price up in the book. Les paid with his credit card then took the two containers back to the house and left them in the bathtub.

Norton spent the rest of the afternoon cleaning up the house and packing his things while he mulled over his game plan. He'd be leaving early in the morning, so unfortunately he wouldn't be having lunch with Grace and her daughter. He'd call in with her winnings and maybe have a quick cup of coffee. But that would be all. However, there would be another time, Les assured himself. You could back it in. Les also decided against having dinner at the hotel. Olney had promised to cook him a good meal. But after the fight there on Thursday night and one thing and another, Les felt the less time spent in the hotel the better. Pick up his winnings, have a beer and come home. Then await the arrival of Edward, with his spiritual, irritable bowel syndrome. If things got out of hand, he'd drive down the road and sleep in his car. By the time Les had everything packed and cleaned up, it was dark and he was hungry again. There was enough eggs, ham, tomato, cheese and other things to make an omelette. Les cooked a monster over two beers and washed it all down with tea and toast. After cleaning up and packing the rest of the food into cartons, he dumped anything over in the bin then locked the front door and walked up to the phone box to ring Grace. He dropped the coins in the slot and got straight through.

'Hello?'

'Grace. It's Les. How are you.'

'Les. What's happening dude? How's things?'

'Terrific. You sound like you're in a good mood. Did Ellie arrive okay?'

'She sure did. Not long after you left.'

'That's good,' smiled Les. 'So what are you doing now?'

'Nothing,' replied Grace. 'Sitting in the kitchen reading a magazine. Why?'

'All right,' said Les. 'I'll get straight to the point. Grace. Did you have a flashback today?'

'Ohh shit yeah,' answered Grace. 'Lucky Ellie was down the road on her bike, with Morticia.'

'What happened?'

'What happened? Let's just say Les, the hills were alive … with the sound of UFOs landing.'

Les laughed out loud. 'Grace. You're not going to believe this,' he said. 'But I got taken back in time.'

'You what?'

Les told Grace what he saw and about digging the hand up in the cave. He didn't mention the cocaine. But told Grace a big sea must have washed the rocks away under the wall of the cave and he didn't have to dig far. There was an audible silence at the other end of the line when he finished.

'So, what do you think of that Grace?' asked Les.

'Les … that is the most fantastic thing I've ever heard,' answered Grace. 'You're psychic.'

'I don't know what I am. But the hand's sitting in my bedroom wrapped in a T-shirt with the ring on the third finger. And that's what was inscribed on the ring. I'll admit, I was touched when I read it.'

'Why wouldn't you be?' said Grace. 'That's beautiful.'

'Yeah, it is,' agreed Les.

'So what are you going to do with the hand? And the ring?'

Les thought for a moment. 'I'll let you know tomorrow.'

'Okay,' said Grace.

'And Grace,' said Les, 'I got a bit of bad news.'

'Bad news?'

'Yeah. I'll be heading back early tomorrow. I just rang home and something's come up at the club. So I won't be able to have lunch with you and Ellie.'

'Oh. That's a shame,' said Grace. 'I was looking forward to it.'

'Yeah. So was I,' said Les. 'But you know how it is when you're a gangster. These things happen.'

'Well, I don't know how it is Les, to be honest,' said Grace. 'I'm not a gangster. Am I a gangster's moll?'

'How about a gangster's friend,' said, Les. 'I didn't move into a motel either.'

'Are you still in the house?'

'Yeah,' laughed Les. 'It could be a fun night.'

'Shit! Be careful,' advised Grace.

'I'll be okay,' said Les. 'So what time will you be up tomorrow?'

'Around seven. A bit earlier maybe.'

'Okay. I'll be out then. And Grace, do me a favour will you.'

'Sure. What is it?'

'Keep what I just told you between the two of us for the time being.'

'All right. No problems. I think that might be best anyway.'

'Good on you, Grace,' said Les. 'Okay. I got to go up the pub and get our money. Wish me luck with Edward tonight.'

'I will. And Les. If Edward does turn out to be a raving poof...'

'Yeah?'

'Try and sleep with your back to the wall.'

'Thanks Grace. I'll see you tomorrow morning.'

'Bye.'

Les hung up and headed for home. Sleep with my back to the wall, he said to himself, shaking his head. Jesus, they're good aren't they.

Back at the house, Les checked everything again. The place was clean, he was sure he hadn't forgotten anything. His tapes were in order. Les snapped his fingers. Shit! That's what I forgot to bloody do. Get a photo of the hand. I don't think I got any film left. And everything's bloody closed now. He got his camera out of his bag, checked the window at the back and smiled. There were five shots left. Les took the hand out to the loungeroom, unwrapped it and sat it on the dressing table right under the light. He took three photos from different angles, a close up of the ring, and left one shot in the camera for luck. Les put the ring back on the bony finger, wrapped the hand in the T-shirt and left it sitting on the coffee table. He put the camera back in his bag and sorted out a few more things then, locking the door behind him, walked down to the hotel.

Les was running a bit late when he walked in the side door. The hotel was fairly crowded and you couldn't miss Norm standing at the corner of the bar with Spike and a couple of other blokes, all wearing jeans and T-shirts. A little further down was Morgan's uncle and a beefy bloke with a mullet, both in yellow, Big Rock Fishing Club, polo shirts. The bloke with the mullet was drinking a schooner. Morgan's uncle was drinking spirits through a straw. They saw Les walk in the door and blanched. Norm and Spike looked as if they'd had a few and gave Les a double, triple blink as he stepped up to them.

'G'day Norm. Hello Spike,' said Les, breezily. 'How's things?'

'Les?' said Norm. 'How are you?'

'Les?' Spike shook his head. 'It is you, isn't it?'

'Of course it's me,' said Les. 'Who were you expecting? Russell Crowe?'

Spike shook his head again. 'No. It's just that …'

Norm butted in. 'Les. The last time I saw you, you looked like they just pulled you out of tank full of piranhas. Now you haven't got a mark on you. What the fuck's going on?'

'I'm a quick healer,' shrugged Les. 'I take lots of kelp tablets.'

'Yeah, all right,' said Norm, exchanging glances with Spike.

'Well,' said Les, rubbing his hands together 'Are you going to stand there like a stale bottle of piss Norm? Or are you going to buy me a beer?'

'Yeah, right,' replied Norm, downing the last of his schooner. 'What'll you have?'

'A schooner of New would be just fine thanks Norm.'

'Coming right up.'

Norm turned to the bar and got a round of drinks. Spike kept staring at Les. Les noticed he was getting some mystified looks from the other punters as well. Morgan's uncle and his mate were eyeballing him like he was the devil incarnate.

'So how are you, Spike?' said Les. 'Thanks for the other day.'

'No worries,' said Spike. 'Les. Like Norm said, something weird's going on here.'

Les patted Spike on the shoulder. 'Spike. Don't tell anyone. But I'm in league with the devil. Whooohhh.'

'I wouldn't bloody be surprised,' replied Spike.

Norm turned around with the drinks and handed Les his schooner. Les thanked him and raised his glass.

'Well. Here's to Narooma,' said Les. 'You blokes don't know how lucky you are living down here. It's the grouse.'

'Cheers Les.'

The beer was cold, fresh and delicious. Les took a good pull and licked his lips.

'So have you got my money, Norm?' asked Les.

Norm patted his jeans. 'I sure have.'

'Okay,' nodded Les. 'We'll get to that in a minute. The important thing is, who won the lucky door prize? I kept my ticket.'

Norm shielded his eyes and exchanged glances with Spike. 'Les,' said Norm, shaking his head. 'Please don't ask.'

'Why? What's up?'

Norm nodded to his left. 'You see who's down the other end of the bar?'

'Yeah,' replied Les. 'Morgan's uncle. The reason all that shit happened in the first place.'

'You see the bloke with him. That's Ambrose Migner. One of Morgan's mates.'

'Ohh yeah,' said Les, turning to the two men. 'I thought I recognised him. He was with Morgan the day they grabbed Warren.'

'He won it,' said Norm.

'Oh shit,' said Les, smiling into his beer. 'Which means...?'

'That's right,' said Norm. 'Morgan's jaw's wired up. His uncle's jaw's wired up. Mick Ross, the other bloke you flattened, he's got no front teeth and his jaw's wired up too. They're all eating and drinking through a straw. And Ambrose has got a fridge full of choice steak waiting to go on the barbecue.'

'And he's not game to light the fuckin thing up,' grinned Spike.

Les shook his head, looked sage and raised his glass. 'You know, when I hear things like that, I truly believe there is something out there.'

'I'll drink to that,' said Norm, downing half his schooner.

Les smiled at Mick and Spike. 'Would you excuse me for a sec?'

With his beer in his hand, Les walked down to Mick and Ambrose.

'G'day,' smiled Les.

They both looked at Les and barely nodded their heads.

'Fair enough,' acknowledged Les. 'You can't cop me any more than I can cop you. But I just want to tell you something.' Les moved in a little closer and looked right into Mick Scully's eyes. 'Okay. I went a bit overboard with you and your mates in here on Thursday night. I should have just given you a backhander and left it at that. But you've got a fuckin big mouth bloke. And from what I can gather, you got what you deserved.'

Mick didn't say anything. But he got the picture. Les turned to Ambrose.

'So you're Ambrose. And you won the lucky door prize. Good luck to you Ambrose. Get into those steaks. Because after what you did to my mate, you're lucky you still got your fuckin teeth too.' Ambrose gulped into his beer. 'But I've had my fun,' said Les. 'I'll let it go at that. I just want you to give your big, boofheaded mate Morgan a message for me. Okay?'

'Yeah,' nodded Ambrose.

'Good,' said Les. 'Now listen. I'm not a fuckin waiter. I'm a horrible cunt. And if you. Or Morgan. Or any of your mates are thinking about a square up with me. Be very careful. Because if I even think you are, I'll be back here, with some cunts even more horrible than me. We won't fuck around. You won't even know we're here, until you're looking up, and we're shovelling dirt on you. You got that?'

'Yeah all right,' nodded Ambrose.

'Lovely,' said Les. 'And if you don't believe me, ask Daddy.' Les smiled at the two men. 'Have a nice evening. And enjoy all that grouse steak.'

'What was that all about?' asked Norm, when Les returned.

'I just gave Ambrose and Mick a message for Morgan,' said Les.

'I think I get the picture,' said Norm.

'I think they did too,' said Les. 'And if they don't believe me, I told them to ask you. Now what's happening? I think it's my shout.'

They laughed and joked about this and that. Norm said he hoped Les didn't mind him sending the cops round to the house. But he was worried. He thought Les was concussed and the ambulance was full. Les said that was okay; the two detectives were both good blokes. Norm and Spike still couldn't get over Norton's miraculous recovery. Les steered the subject around to Norm doing all right on the day because all the money was on Morgan. Finally, Les steered the subject around to his money.

'Well I may as well pick up my whack, Norm,' said Les.

'Okay. Here it is, right here.' Norm pulled a large, thick envelope from inside his jeans and handed it to Les.

'How much did you make it, Norm?' asked Les, weighing the money in his hand.

'Twenty five grand,' replied Norm.

'That's ... a bit more than I made it, Norm,' said Les.

'Let's just say, your arithmetic's a bit better than mine, Les.'

'Thanks Norm.' Les shook the big man's hand then finished his beer. 'Well, those two beers were delicious. And I'd love to stay. But I'm expecting someone.'

'No worries,' said Norm. 'When do you reckon you'll be in Narooma again?'

'Before the next blues festival. That's for sure,' smiled Les. Les shook hands with Spike and shook hands with Norm again. 'Thanks for all your help, Norm. I owe you one. And I'll say hello to George Brennan for you. See you mate. See you Spike.' Les turned to go when Norm called out.

'Hey Les! What did you say you took again? Kelp tablets?'

Les nodded. 'Them. And apricot oil. It works for me.' Les exited the hotel and walked back to the house.

Well that was good of Norm, thought Les, placing the money in his overnight bag. An extra five grand. He sure must have cleaned up. Les went to the bathroom then changed into his tracksuit and put on an extra pair of socks. He checked the front door was locked then left the light on in the loungeroom, kitchen and hallway. There was some soda water left in the fridge. Les made a delicious, had a sip then took it into his room. He switched on the bed lamp then lay back on the bed with *The Perfect Storm* and opened it to the page he'd marked.

'Into the Abyss. *The Lord bowed the heavens and came down, thick darkness under his feet. The channels of the sea were seen, and the foundations of the world were laid bare. Samuel. 22.*'

Shit! I think I could have done without that. Les sipped some more bourbon, started reading and waited.

It was zero visibility. The pilot had issued a mayday on the Air National Guard frequency that he was going to ditch the helicopter when Norton's bed lamp started flickering on and off. Les looked up as the other lights started doing the same thing. He closed his book and sat up. A rapid vibration rattled the house and Norton's bed began to shake. In an instant, the temperature in the bedroom dropped to freezing; this was a damper, much clammier cold than before, and it sunk right into Norton's bones.

'Hello,' said Les, flippantly. 'Heee's baaacckk.'

Leaving great clouds of steam in his wake, Les stepped out into the hallway where it was even colder again. He rubbed his arms briskly, spreading more clouds of steam along the hallway through his chattering teeth, and watched the flickering lights. Next thing, an awful, anguished moan lowered through the house, accompanied by ghoulish laughter that seemed to come from everywhere. Les turned around and the doorway was suddenly framed by streams of fluorescent green light pouring through the sides and underneath. Les stared as the light coming from round the door intensified into a foggy, green glow in the hallway. In the centre of the glow, an eerie figure began to take shape. It was the coal-black outline of a man.

'G'day Edward,' said Les. 'Nice of you to drop in.'

Les was immediately answered by a powerful force hitting him in the chest like a crash tackle, knocking the wind out of him. Arms and legs flailing, Norton skidded backwards towards the loungeroom where he crashed heavily into the door frame, before falling face down in the hallway.

'Ohh shit!' grunted Les. 'That bloody hurt.'

Les rose to his knees and was straightaway grabbed by the scruff of the neck, dragged along the hallway and flung head first into the front door. He just had time to throw his arms out in front of him or his skull would have been split open against the heavy wooden frame. Les spun around, seeing stars, and landed on his rump with his back against the door.

'Shit!' spluttered Les, trying to shake the cobwebs from his brain. 'What are you fuckin trying to do, Edward. Kill me?'

Les felt himself being dragged to his feet by the front of his tracksuit before getting flung forward along the hallway. He hit the floor in a clumsy somersault, rolling over on his back wondering what day it was. He brought his head up as a massive weight fell across his body, pinning him to the floor. It was like all those bags of cocaine had been stacked on top of him, slowly crushing him, and he was powerless to move. Les tried to breathe, his chest heaving in short, choking gasps as if he was having a violent asthma attack. The weight got heavier, pressing Les against the floor, crushing the very life out of him. Les choked off a cry of pain and felt himself blacking out.

'Jesus Christ!' screamed Les, with what little air he had. 'Get off me Edward. You're killing me you cunt. I can't fuckin breathe.' The weight crushed Les further into the floor and his eyes started to swim. 'Edward,' gasped Les. 'Edward listen to me. I've got something for you. The ring. Edward … the ring. With the little black opals. "To Gwendolyn … All my love. Now … and Forever … Edward. Now … and Forever …" Edward. Ohh shit!' begged Les. 'Edward. Get off me. Please.'

The lights flickered crazily. The howling and moaning got louder along with the fiendish laughter. Then it stopped and the weight eased. His chest heaving up from the floor, Les groaned with relief and sucked in all the life-giving air he could.

'Ohh Jesus!' garbled Les, as the freezing cold air filled his lungs. 'Thank God!' Les was starting to get his breath back, when he was dragged bodily to his feet again and shoved against the wall. 'Okay, okay Edward,' panted Les. 'I've got it. It's all right. Just follow me.'

Clutching his midriff, Les staggered into the loungeroom. He picked up the T-shirt with the hand inside, turned around and lurched down the hallway to the front door, leaving clouds of steam hanging in the frigid, green glow behind him. He opened the door to find the green glow all round his car. Les put the T-shirt on the roof and unwrapped the bony hand. The hand immediately took on a glow of its own, the gold ring beginning to shine while the fire danced in the tiny opals. Les stood back from the car and pointed.

'Edward look!' he cried. 'There's your ring. Still on your finger where you kept it for Gwendolyn. The ring Edward. There it is. Look.'

Les drew back from the green glow swirling around his car as the same black shape that was inside appeared by the passenger side door. The eerie, green light swirled in the darkness and the shape became a little man with a beard, wearing a frock coat and trousers. Norton left him and backed inside the front door, slamming it shut behind him. With the green glow still radiating into the hallway from outside, he leant his back against the door and slowly got his breath back.

Les could never remember being so terrified. The invisible weight that had lain all over his body had almost crushed the life out of him. Another minute and Les knew he would have stopped breathing. And the supernatural strength he'd been up against was incredible. Les was a big, strong man. But the poltergeist had tossed him around the hallway like he was a rag doll. After a while Les settled down and noticed the green glow had stopped. He pushed himself away from the front door, got the bourbon from his room and gulped it down in the kitchen, then stared into the sink, grateful that what had happened appeared to be over. Les had played Edward and the supernatural a little lightly and almost paid the price. He turned off the lights in the house then went back to his room and flopped down on the bed exhausted. His chest hurt, so did his neck, and Les knew he'd have bruises all over him tomorrow. But at least he was alive. With the bed lamp still on, Les lay on his bed in the cold before finally dragging the blankets over him.

Suddenly, the cold went away and the room returned to normal. Not only that. A beautiful feeling of peace and tranquillity washed over Les leaving him warm and relaxed. Any pain or anxiety had vanished and his mind filled with beautiful thoughts and colours. It was sensational. Even the house around him seemed like a big, cosy old friend taking care of him. It was just a beautiful, beautiful feeling, like nothing Les had ever experienced. Instead of lying on the bed, Les felt as if he was floating above it. It was absolutely marvellous. Les reached over and switched off the light then closed his eyes and let his head sink into the wonderfully soft pillows. In no time, Norton fell into the deepest, most refreshing sleep imaginable.

Les blinked his eyes open the next morning to the delightful sound of magpies whistling in the trees alongside the verandah. He felt great after an exceptionally good night's sleep and was pleasantly surprised to find he had no bruises or aches and pains of any description. Les stared up at the ceiling and reflected on the previous night, but soon put the unnerving events out of his mind. He rolled out of bed and went to the bathroom. After flushing the toilet, he stepped across to clean his teeth and abruptly stopped in front of the sink. Someone had taken the soap and written something across the mirror in beautiful, old script. It was just one word.

Thankyou.

'That's all right, Edward,' said Les. 'Thanks for not killing me.'

There was one photo left in his camera. Les got it from the bedroom, angled it across the mirror so the flash wouldn't mask the writing and took the last shot. The camera started to wind back and Les reached for his toothbrush. After freshening up, he went back to the bedroom and changed into his blue cargos and the same T-shirt he had on the night before, then walked into the kitchen where another surprise was waiting for him. Sitting on the kitchen table was the horseshoe with the bear standing in the middle. Les smiled again and pushed the little bear in its fat stomach. Straight away it started singing 'Livin' La Vida Loca' and waving its arms around. Les waited till the bear finished then switched it off and sorted out some tea and toast. While he was waiting, he opened the front door and walked out to his car. His T-shirt was folded up on the roof of his car and the hand was gone. Les picked up his T-shirt and took it inside.

'Well Edward. I think you finally got what you were after,' smiled Les, closing the door behind him. 'Say hello to Gwendolyn for me.' He put the T-shirt into his room and went back to the kitchen.

Les got his tea and toast together and walked out onto the verandah. Unfortunately, the day didn't match his good mood. The sky had clouded over, it was cooler, and the southerly was blowing again. Not much of a day for the beach, figured Les, as he sipped his tea and watched two boats pass each other in the channel. He strolled along the verandah nibbling on a piece of toast, checking things out for the last time. I'm going to miss this old house, he thought. I hope Clover's parents don't sell it now that Edward's gone. I'd like to stay here again. Actually, they don't even know he's gone. I should keep quiet about it and make them an offer. Les laughed to himself. Knowing my luck though, another ghost would move in and take over from Edward. Les finished his tea and toast and rinsed his mug in the kitchen.

After checking everything was packed and ready to go, Les got his diving gear together and put it it the car with his overnight bag. He then took the two containers of Ozone Accelerator out of the bathtub and stowed them carefully in the boot. After locking the house, he put his cap and sunglasses on, climbed in the car and headed south, past the turn-off to Mystery Bay and on to Tilba. Apart from one or two people outside the garage, there was no one around and not much happening in Tilba. A few minutes later, Les pulled up in front of Grace's house and got out of the car with his overnight bag.

A pretty young girl was seated across the top of the front steps wearing a white, Stussy sweat shirt over a pair of yellow tracksuit pants and trainers. Her hair was long and lighter than Grace's and her face a little pointier. But she had her mother's eyes. Morticia was standing next to her rolling out a low, menacing growl, as if to say 'Yes. I know who you are and all that. Just don't try anything with the kid.' Les walked almost to the top of the stairs and stopped.

'Hello Morticia, you little dag,' he said, then turned to the girl. 'Hello. You must be Ellie.'

'That's right,' replied the girl. 'Are you George?'

'Yeah. That's me,' answered Les. 'Gorgeous George.'

Les offered Ellie his hand. She gave it the softest shake and giggled.

'You're even bigger than mummy said you were.'

'Big and ugly,' smiled Les. 'But I like dogs and I'm environmentally friendly.'

The girl looked evenly at Les. 'Mummy said you're from Sydney.'

'That's right. I live in Bondi,' said Les. 'Have you ever been there?'

'Once. When I was really little. Where do you know Mummy from?'

'Where? Oh, your mummy knows some friends of mine in Sydney. They like your mummy's T-shirts. We were down for the long weekend and we all had lunch together. I'm on my way back to Sydney now, and I just called in to say goodbye.'

'Are you going to stay for breakfast?'

Les shook his head. 'No. I'd like to. But I won't have time.'

Ellie put her arms around the dog's neck. 'Do you like Morticia?'

'I sure do,' said Les. He reached across and patted Morticia on the head. 'She's beautiful. Aren't you Morticia?' The dog half-closed its eyes and lolled its tongue around.

'I think she is,' said Ellie. The young girl stood up and smiled at Les. 'We're going round the back to play.'

'Okay,' said Les. 'Nice talking to you Smelly. I mean Ellie.'

The girl giggled again. 'You're funny. Come on Morticia.'

Les watched them run off around the verandah then looked across as the door opened and Grace stepped out wearing a tracksuit and her hair in a ponytail.

'All right, George,' she said. 'What lies have you been filling my poor, innocent, young daughter's head with?'

'None really,' replied Les. 'Just covering my arse as usual. And mum's. Actually she's a bit of a sweetheart.'

'I know.' Grace gave Les a quick kiss on the lips. 'Come inside.'

Les followed Grace down to the kitchen and placed his bag on the table.

'Would you like a cup of coffee?' she asked.

'I just had a mug of tea,' answered Les.

'Okay. How about a smoothie?'

'All right. Thanks.'

Grace took a jug from the fridge and poured Les what looked like a pink milkshake. 'Try that.'

Les took a mouthful and raised his eyebrows. 'Holy smoke! How good's this? What is it?'

'Custard apple and strawberry. I have to make them for the blonde or she starts whingeing. Good, aren't they?'

'Reckon!' Les swallowed some more and smacked his lips.

'So sit down,' said Grace. 'Tell me about yesterday. Surely you're not in that big a hurry.'

'Forget about yesterday,' said Les. 'Wait till I tell you about last night. I'm lucky to bloody be here.'

Les sat down at the table. Grace got her coffee and sat opposite while Les gave her the lowdown on everything, except finding all the cocaine in the cave. Grace had one sip of coffee and sat gobsmacked. When Les was finished, Grace's coffee was cold and she was shaking her head with a blank look on her face.

'Yeah,' said Les. 'I left the hand on the car. And there was the thank you on the bathroom mirror. I took a photo with the last shot left in the camera. As soon as I get them all developed, I'll send you some copies.'

'My God!' exclaimed Grace. 'What you told me yesterday was fantastic enough. But this on top of it.' Grace shook her head again. 'I don't know what to say.'

'Yeah. It's totally bizarre all right,' said Les. 'But I think I did the right thing. I'm sure that's all Edward wanted.' Les pointed above. 'Now he and Gwendolyn are out there somewhere on their honeymoon.'

'Yes. They probably are,' agreed Grace. 'Unbelievable.'

'Exactly,' nodded Les. 'That's why I think we should keep it between us for the time being. I'll tell Clover when I get home. And Warren. And that's it. Maybe one day, we'll sell the story to a magazine.' Les laughed into his glass. 'But I doubt if even a magazine'd believe me.'

'You know, Les,' said Grace. 'Even though it's a weird, crazy thing, it's also quite beautiful. The love between Edward and Gwendolyn. Don't you think?'

'I agree,' nodded Les. 'But there was no need for him to bring her around last night and let her sit on me.'

Grace threw back her head and laughed. 'God you're a bastard.' Grace settled and looked evenly at Les. 'So what's happening now, George? You're off back to Sydney, leaving me and Ellie behind like a couple of chattels?'

'Chattels? Jesus you're good,' protested Les.

'Doesn't matter,' said Grace. 'But I got you something to take back with you.'

'You have? Oh.'

Grace stood up and went to the loungeroom. She returned holding a white paper carry bag with Tilba Fashions printed on the side and handed it to Les.

'There you go, George,' she said.

Les opened the bag and took out a dark blue T-shirt. There were two parrots cuddling up on the front and a smaller one on the back with its wings spread. They had beautiful, soft blue faces, a hint of red on their green and blue wings and striking, gold breasts. Grace had captured their colours perfectly.

'Ohh Grace,' said Les. 'That's unreal. They're the same parrots I saw when I was tripping out yesterday too.'

'Turquoise parrots,' said Grace. 'Neophema pulchella. You don't see many around these days. Check out the one on the back.'

Les turned the T-shirt back over and peered at the open wings. Very, very subtly, Grace had printed his name along the feathers in blue and gold.

'Fair dinkum,' blushed Les. 'I don't know what to say. That's the nicest present anyone's ever given me. Thanks Grace.' Les reached over the table and planted a kiss on Grace's lips.

'That's all right,' she smiled.

Les looked at the T-shirt and shook his head. 'Honestly Grace. What did I do to deserve this?'

'I don't know,' said Grace. 'Because you're an absolute bastard.'

'I am too,' agreed Les. He carefully folded the T-shirt up and put it back in the bag. 'Anyway. I got something for you too. It ain't much. Just your winnings.' Les opened his overnight bag, took out an envelope and handed it to Grace. 'There you go, mate,' he smiled. 'Don't spend it all at once.'

'Thank you. This will come in very handy too. Believe you me.' Grace took the envelope, felt it and frowned. 'What...?' She opened the envelope and her jaw dropped. 'My God! How much is here?'

'Twenty grand,' answered Les.

'Twenty thousand dollars!' Grace stared at Les. 'What? Are trying to tell me, you were... four hundred to one?'

Les nodded. 'I told you I'd get you the best odds.'

'Bullshit! No.' Grace shook her head and pushed the envelope back across the table. 'I can't take this.'

'All right. Don't,' shrugged Les. 'And you can take your T-shirt and stick it in your arse too.'

They both looked up as Ellie came running into the kitchen.

'Mummy. Mrs Hillier's outside on Apples.'

'Okay,' flustered Grace. 'Tell her ... tell her I'll be out in minute.'

'All right.' Ellie ran out the same way she ran in.

'Mrs Hillier?' asked Les. 'Is that ...?'

'Yes. The old girl from next door,' said Grace. 'She's ridden up to see Ellie.'

'Well, that could be my cue to get going.' Les stood up and placed the T-shirt in his overnight bag. 'Now if you'll walk me to the door. I'll take my beautiful T-shirt and be on my way.'

Grace looked at the envelope full of money sitting on the table then turned to Les. 'You are a bastard, Les. I hope you know that.'

'Grace. I told you before,' smiled Les. 'I'm not really. I just keep meeting people who bring the bastard out in me. You just happened to bring out a bit extra.'

Les followed Grace down the hallway and she stopped just inside the flyscreen door. Les imagined she wanted to give him a goodbye kiss. But not in front of Ellie or the neighbours. Les definitely wanted to give her one. And a good one at that. He dropped his bag on the floor as Grace put her arms around his waist and looked up into his eyes.

'So when are you fixin' on riding into town again, stranger?' she said.

Les put his arms around Grace and looked at her wistfully. 'Don't rightly know little lady,' he answered. 'But I reckon, between your eggplant parmigiana, your mineral water, your custard apple smoothies. All the this, that, and the other, not to mention you saving my neck ... I reckon I'll be a hankerin' to ride through here again real soon maam.'

'Do that stranger.'

Grace gave Les a long, lingering sweet kiss. Les Held Grace tight and if her kiss had lingered a second longer, Les would have had trouble getting away. Finally, he reluctantly let Grace go and picked up his bag.

'I'll ring you tonight,' he said. 'After I get home.'

Les followed Grace out onto the verandah. His car was parked on the left, and over to the right Ellie and a woman in sunglasses were standing next to an old pinto mare with a sway back. The woman was as straight as a gun barrel and suited the denim shirt, old jeans and brown RM Williams she was wearing. A thick head of long, grey hair tumbled down from beneath a big straw hat. The horse had its head down nuzzling at Morticia who was playing with it.

'So that's your next door neighbour,' said Les. 'I wish I had some film in my camera. They'd make a great photo they way they're all standing there.'

'She's not bad for eighty-two, eh,' said Grace.

'No,' agreed Les. 'I love her old horse.' He held out his hand. 'Well, goodbye Amazing Grace,' he said formally. 'Thank you for everything.'

'Yes. You too, George,' replied Grace, shaking Norton's hand. 'Thank you for everything.'

Les pointed his finger at her. 'I'll ring you tonight.' He turned and walked across to his car.

Les caught the woman's eye and smiled at her as he waved to Ellie. The woman smiled back. Ellie smiled and waved back, Morticia barked and the horse whinnied. Les got in his car, tooted the horn and drove off. In the rear-vision mirror Grace was waving from he verandah. Minutes later, Les was driving under a leaden sky through empty Tilba, past the Hemp shop.

That's what I meant to get too, he regretted. Some hemp shirts. Grace looked great in hers. Impassively, Les turned left towards the highway. Grace looked good in anything, he thought. And I should be having lunch with her and Ellie. But no. Not me. I have to be a complete fuckin idiot. And then I have to get out of town because I can't mind my own fuckin business. Fair dinkum. When God was giving out heads, I think I was at the end of the queue and he gave me a pumpkin. Les turned left at the highway and in what felt like too short a time, pulled up in the car park near the camping area at Mystery Bay and cut the engine.

Compared to when it had been calm and clear before, today the water looked murky and the southerly had stirred up the ocean. The tide was higher also and choppy swells were breaking against the rocks and around the little islands. The only sign of life was an old bloke fishing at the other end of the bay and a woman walking a small, grey dog. Les shook his head at his own foolhardiness and got out of the car.

As soon as he opened the back door and started taking his clothes off, the butterflies started kicking around in his stomach again. He looked up into the camping area and couldn't see anybody. Les climbed into his rubber vest and his old shorts, put a hanky and his clasp knife in his pocket then opened the boot. He tied the necks of two containers together with a short piece of rope, then closed the boot and buried the car keys behind the front right tyre. Carrying his diving gear in one hand and the two containers of Ozone Accelerator in the other, Les set off along the beach with the southerly whipping at his ears, towards the ridge of jagged rock sticking out from the sand.

The shelf on the other side was covered over by the tide and waves were pushing into the inlet and up against the mouth of the cave. Les clambered over a narrow pinch in the ridge and rinsed the facemask in a small rock pool. He had another look around while he got into his diving gear, but apart from the two people at the opposite end of the bay he couldn't see anybody. Les picked up the two containers and shuffled to the water's edge, took a breath, then bit on his snorkel and plunged in.

The water was gloomy and the swells had stirred up the bottom. Huge beds of seaweed growing amongst the rocks swirled in the white water and visibility was down to barely a couple of metres. Clutching the two containers to his chest, Les kicked furiously towards the cave, waiting for a killer whale or something to appear from behind the seaweed rolling around in the white water and grab him. But apart from the odd kale swimming amongst the seaweed and a few rock cod moving around their caves, there were no other fish, let alone any sharks or killer whales. He bumped against some rocks just below the surface and got a snorkel full of water as a swell washed over him. Les swooshed it out, then the rocky, sandy bottom turned to pebbles washing against each other in the undercurrent and he was at the front of the cave. He saw a swell coming, went with it, swam straight up the rocks into the mouth and got to his feet.

Les hurried inside the cave, whipped off his mask and flippers, then carried the two containers over to the mound. He untied them and started brushing rocks from the tarpaulin. Once he'd removed enough, Les dragged the tarpaulin back to one end and the amount of cocaine sitting in the cave momentarily took his breath away. He took his hanky from his pocket, wrung it out and tied it around his face, then climbed up in the middle of the mound and made a hole amongst the sacks of cocaine. When it was big enough, he opened his clasp knife and started quickly slashing open the surrounding sacks and plastic bags. Soon cocaine was going everywhere, coating him in a thin, white crust. Les slashed open some sacks along the side of the mound and watched the fine, white powder tumble to the floor of the cave like flour. Satisfied he'd slashed open enough sacks, Les picked up the two containers, unscrewed the tops and started pouring Ozone Accelerator into the hole in the mound. The pool cleaner reacted to the cocaine in a flash, immediately turning the hole into a boiling, bubbling crater just like the one in his backyard. In seconds, clouds of smoking cocaine were rising up from the intense heat into the cave. Les climbed down and slashed open the sides of both containers then dumped them in the middle of the mound, letting the liquid pour out into the cocaine. He watched in astonishment as the two containers buckled and melted before his eyes. He folded up his clasp knife then grabbed the tarpaulin, running it back over the pile of sacks to keep the heat in, and tossing some heavy stones back on top for good measure.

It wasn't long before smoke started spewing up from under the edges of the tarpaulin and Les could see the mound moving and boiling underneath. Suddenly the ghastly, acidic fumes started seeping through Norton's wet hanky. Shit! Time I was out of here, he told himself. Les whipped off the hanky, held his breath while he hurried into his snorkelling gear, then flip-flopped over to the mouth of the cave and plunged straight into the water; he broke all records swimming back across the inlet to where he'd jumped in. Puffing a little, Les pulled himself up onto the rocks then took off his face mask and looked back to see clouds of steam rising from the mouth of the cave before they disappeared into the wind. Well, I reckon that'd have to be the world's biggest crack pipe, he smiled.

Les took off his flippers, walked back to the car and retrieved his keys. He was too excited to worry about the butterflies in his stomach as he took off his wet shorts and vest and wrapped a towel around his waist. But there was no one around and this time Les smiled at his good fortune. He put his T-shirt on, got behind the wheel and before long he was on his way back to Narooma.

Lee Kernaghan was twanging 'Texas QLD 4385' when Les pulled up in the driveway. Well that's that, he chuckled. Bad luck I won't be around when Serina and her gang put their heads in the cave. Try chopping that up on a mirror and shoving it up your hooter. That's if it is Serina, of course. But, too fuckin bad if it's not. Les turned off the engine and grabbed his gear. Now. Let's get the fuck out of Dodge.

Without wasting any time, Les had a quick shower, changed into the same clothes he had on and started packing everything into the car. What do I need for a souvenir, he thought? The horseshoe. That'll do. I've already got the bear and about half a million photos ready to get developed. Les put the horseshoe in the bag with his diving gear and put it in the boot along with everything else. He placed his overnight bag on the seat next to him and his tapes, then went inside and had a last look around the house. Yeah, I'm going to miss this old house, he told himself again as he walked along the verandah. Even allowing for Edward nearly killing me. It was fun. And what about that view? Les closed the door to the verandah and walked into the bathroom. He looked at the message on the mirror and decided to leave it. I'll tell Clover what happened when I get home and her parents can come round and take a photo in case my one doesn't turn out. Les had a last look in the kitchen, made sure all the lights and everything were turned off, then stepped outside and locked the front door. Now, all I have to do is take the key back to the op-shop. What were those two old girls' names again? Edith and Joyce. That's right. Jiggling the solid brass key in his hand, Les walked down to the op-shop.

The only other car in the side street, was a white, dual cabin truck with ropes in the back, parked outside the cake shop. The op-shop was open for business. Les stepped inside. Edith was standing with her back to the door, wearing a pair of grey, woollen slacks and a black cardigan, and dusting some bricabrac when Les walked in. She didn't hear him, so Les called out cheerfully.

'Good morning! Is that you, Edith?'

Edith turned around and peered at Les through her red-framed glasses. 'Oh good morning, Mr Norton,' she smiled. 'How are you?'

'Good thanks,' replied Les. 'Where's Joyce?'

'She'll be in later.'

'Fair enough,' said Les. 'Anyway, I just called in to return the key. I'm on my way back to Sydney.' Les handed Edith the key. 'There you are.'

'Oh, thank you, Mr Norton.' Edith put the duster down, pocketed the key and straightened an imaginary knot in her grey hair. 'So did you enjoy your stay in the Merrigan house?' she asked, smiling congenially.

'Yeah, it was a blast,' replied Les, happily. 'I've never had such a good time in my life. Especially listening to that radio station that plays all the old songs.'

'Season FM,' said Edith.

'That's the one,' nodded Les. 'I can never get enough of Fred Upstairs and Ginger Rogers.'

'Yes. I like them too,' beamed Edith. 'And tell me, Mr Norton. Did you sleep all right at night in the house? Were the beds comfortable?'

'Comfortable? Edith, my bed was that comfortable, I was asleep the minute my head hit the pillow. I slept like a baby.'

'Oh isn't that nice,' said Edith.

'It was funny though,' said Les. 'One of the old tenants called in and stayed with me a couple of nights.'

'One of the old tenants, Mr Norton?' enquired Edith.

'Yeah. He used to live there. Nice bloke too. Edward Ruddle.'

'Edward Ruddle?' gasped Edith.

'Yeah. Not a very big bloke,' said Les. 'Wore a beard and funny little glasses. Said he was a surveyor.'

'Edward Ruddle the surveyor?' Edith put a hand over her mouth.

'That's him,' nodded Les. 'He said he'd been working down at Mystery Bay. He's getting married next week out at Bodalla to a girl named Gwendolyn Monteith. He showed me a photo of her. Big woman. A little plain. But nice.'

'Oh dear.'

'He invited me to the wedding too,' said Les. 'If didn't have to go home, I'd be out there with bells on. I love a bush wedding.'

'Mr Norton, I might have to sit down for a moment.' Edith plonked herself down in a cane chair near a rack of clothes.

'Anyway. I'd better get going,' said Les. 'Goodbye Edith. I'll see you next time I'm in Narooma.'

'Goodbye, Mr Norton.'

Les smiled and left the shop. As he did he noticed a white porcelain teapot near the door, with Narooma written on the side and a sketch of the jetty. He didn't really need it. But it was only three dollars and it'd make another good souvenir. The bell had just rang above the door to the cake shop and Les was standing on the footpath going through his pockets to see if had the right change. He didn't notice a group of people standing outside the cake shop until he heard a familiar voice.

'Well, well, well … If it isn't Bondi playboy and big shot underworld figure, Les Norton.'

Les looked up in the direction of the cake shop and didn't blink an eye. 'Oh, hello Serina,' he smiled.

'Hello, Les,' she said, deliberately.

Serina had stepped out of the cake shop followed by three swarthy, unsmiling men with unkempt black hair and thick moustaches. Like

Serina, they were all wearing dark tracksuits and gym boots and carrying white paper bags and boxes from the cake shop. With her mane of orange hair, Serina stood out like a beacon.

'So what brings you to Narooma, Serina?' asked Les. 'Family?'

Serina exchanged glances with the three men. 'We're down here for a yacht race,' she replied.

'Oh, of course. The one from Bermagui to Ulladulla,' nodded Les. 'You're right into that sort of thing, aren't you.'

Two of the men said something to Serina and got into the white truck, leaving one man standing next to Serina.

'So what are you doing down here, Les?' asked Serina.

'I came down for the Blues Festival,' he answered.

'The Blues Festival?' Serina twisted her face up. 'That was over days ago.'

'Yeah, I know,' answered Les.

'So what's a big, swinging, city boy like you doing still hanging round a dump like Narooma?'

'I dunno, Serina,' answered Les. 'It's got me beat. But I was just on my way home when you saw me.'

Serina nodded to the op-shop. 'And did I just see you coming out of an op-shop counting your money?'

'Yes Serina,' Les nodded slowly. 'You did.'

Serina turned to the man next to her then gave Les a caustic once up and down. 'Well, we all know you're tight with a dollar, Les. But what's a guy who owns a home in Bondi, and works at the Kelly Club helping old Price Galese wash piles of money, doing in fucking op-shops?'

Les thought for a moment. 'I'm fucked if I know Serina, to be honest,' he replied. 'It's a dead set fuckin mystery to me.' Les gave her an oily smile. 'Anyway. If you'll excuse me. It's a long drive back to Sydney. And I have to get on the road. See you, Serina. Nice talking to you as always.' Les nodded to her friend. 'See you, mate.' Without waiting for a reply, Les turned and walked back to his car.

Les started the car, drove up the side street, then did a U-turn at the lights and stopped at the garage opposite the hotel. He got out and proceeded to fill the tank. Fuck it, Les cursed to himself as he stared at the numbers going round on the bowser. They've sprung me. Well, that's fucked that, hasn't it. And that's them behind the coke all right. The truck and the rope proves that. But fuck it. How's my bloody luck. Les kept looking at the bowser and out the side of one eye watched the white truck go past. Serina and her friends never gave him a second look. He followed the truck as it disappeared down the hill towards the park and unexpectedly the sun appeared from behind the clouds. On the other hand, thought Les, why has it fucked things? They don't know that I know about their coke. And I doubt if they picked up on my little innuendos outside the op-shop. I'm just a goose as far as Serina's concerned. And when they do find all their coke looking like a giant pile of steaming seal shit, what are they going to do? They're not going to race into the hardware store asking if somebody just bought ten litres of pool cleaner. They won't have a clue what happened. They'll just cut their losses and get to the shithouse out of Narooma. They could even think it's another drug syndicate trying to put them out of business.

The meter stopped running when Norton's tank filled and he replaced the nozzle on the bowser. In fact, smiled Les, I'm glad I bumped into Serina and her friends. I reckon they've just done me another favour. Les screwed his petrol cap back on and walked across to the office.

While the young bloke in the blue denim shirt was swiping his Visa card, Les searched his pockets again for change. He signed the receipt and pointed to a yellow pay phone near the door.

'Is that phone working all right, mate?' asked Les?'

'Yeah. No problems,' replied the young bloke, handing Les his receipt.

'Thanks.'

Les walked over to the phone, dropped some coins in the slot and dialled. It didn't take long to get through.

'Hello?'

'Grace. It's Les. How are you?'

'Les? What ...?'

'Grace. You're not going to believe this. But I just rang home. And everything's sorted itself out at the club. Do you and the other chattel still want to have lunch?'

THE END

Available now

LEAVING BONDI

Robert G. Barrett

Les figured by tossing $50,000 into the Gull's movie he'd become the next Sam Goldwyn. Only someone put a bomb on the film set. And who gets the blame? Now Norton's a fugitive from the law, desperate to prove his innocence.

Satanists, drug dealers, nutty poets, blabbermouth disc jockeys — everybody between Sydney, the Blue Mountains and South Australia wants a piece of Les Norton, movie magnate. Alias Forrest McNamara, book publisher. And Norman Bates's mother. The only person who found the real Les Norton was the May Queen — with a little help from the Avis navigator.

So what are Norton's chances of clearing his name and coming up smelling of roses? VFO. But rely on Les to come up smelling of something.

ISBN: 0 7322 6870 2

Available now

MUD CRAB BOOGIE

Robert G. Barrett

Les caught the DJ's eye. 'Hey mate,' he said. 'If I give you ten bucks, will you play two songs for me?'

'Mate,' replied the DJ. 'For ten bucks, I'll play you Tiny Tim singing *A Pub With No Beer* in Vietnamese.'

Look out Wagga Wagga, Les Norton's in town and he feels like dancing.

Extreme Polo. The wildest game on water. That's what it said on TV. All Les had to do was drive down to Wagga Wagga for an old mate who owed him a favour, Neville (Nizegy) Nixon, and pick up the Murrumbidgee Mud Crabs. Then keep them at Coogee till they played the Sydney Sea Snakes in the grand final at Homebush Aquatic Centre. And naturally there would be a giant earn in it for him. Why not? thought Les, he had the week off from work.

Next thing, Norton was on his way to the Riverina to meet the locals, the lovelies and oogie, oogie, oogie — do the Mud Crab Boogie.

ISBN: 0 7322 5843 X

Available now

GOODOO GOODOO

Robert G. Barrett

Wolfman Les — Rock 'n' Roll DJ.

Another good idea down the gurgler...

What should have been a quick gig on a radio station followed by a whitewater rafting holiday in Cairns finishes up a mud-soaked four-wheel drive trip to Cooktown with Norton looking for two missing scuba divers! The army, the air force and half the Queensland water police couldn't find the two missing divers. So what chance does Les have?

Along the way Les meets a kooky little space cadet who spends her time chasing UFOs and predicting the future; man-eating crocodiles; heat and humidity; and strangers everywhere out for his blood. Then, in a place of indescribable beauty, he uncovers unimaginable terror...

From FM radio to FN Queensland, *Goodoo Goodoo* is a roller-coaster ride of thrills and spills and shows once again why Robert G. Barrett is one of Australia's most popular contemporary authors.

ISBN: 0 7322 6737 4

Available now

THE WIND AND THE MONKEY

Robert G. Barrett

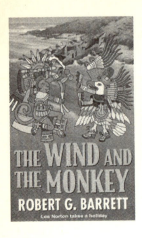

A week's holiday in Shoal Bay, courtesy of Price Galese. All Les had to do was help Eddie Salita get rid of a crooked cop. Why not? Les always wanted to visit Port Stephens. And nobody liked Fishcake Fishbyrne that much anyway.

The first night in town, Les gets arrested by the federal police then collared by a drug-crazed, feminist author. The hit turned out to be a complete nightmare. Next thing, it's a night drive into Newcastle with Eddie to sort out a team of local heavies.

Somehow in the middle of all this Les meets Digger. Sweet Christian girl from The Church of the Peaceful Sea. Digger was a fiery little enigma wrapped in a burning secret. Digger found God. Les found Elvis. Together they journeyed to Virgin Island, discovered love and solved a mystery.

ISBN: 0 7322 6707 2

Available now

SO WHAT DO YOU RECKON?

Robert G. Barrett

There was a time when Robert G. Barrett was 'in his forties, out of gaol, out of work, had three books published, but was stone motherless broke'. Political correctness had him confused and he had no desire to be more literary, even if he was the author of books that had been described as 'the scatological nadir of the pile' and 'insidiously revolting ... pray God they don't get published overseas'.

Then, through a twist of fate and good fortune, along came *People* magazine, who signed Barrett to produce a weekly column focusing on Australian life and its heroes and villains. *So What Do You Reckon?* is a collection of the best of these columns. Many are outrageous and all are written in Barrett's highly popular and immediately recognisable style. Together they represent an often funny, always entertaining and uniquely telling assessment of modern-day Australia.

ISBN: 0 7322 5961 4

Available now

THE ULTIMATE APHRODISIAC

Robert G. Barrett

Aussie Vietnam veteran Ron Milne was on a good thing growing Indian hemp on the tiny Micronesian island of Lan Laroi. Besides being President, the natives treated him as a god. To the American DEA he was a dangerous criminal. President of the United States Clifford J. Clooney decides to invade.

Onto this island of sun, surf, beautiful women and mysterious ruins arrives Bondi surf journalist Brian Bradshaw. Brian came to find a story, then return home to write it. He didn't expect to get involved in something almost impossible to comprehend, fall in love and get taken literally for the ride of his life.

All Lan Laroi wanted to do was sit peacefully in the sun away from everybody. The little island had absolutely no intention of starting a third world war. But if Lan Laroi had to fight a world war, the little island had no intention of losing.

Robert G. Barrett's *The Ultimate Aphrodisiac* moves away from Les Norton. However, it still has all the action and humour you would expect from the king of popular Australian fiction. Plus much more. A blockbuster with a twist, told at a cracking pace, we believe it to be his best yet.

ISBN: 0732271681